Chasing the Moon

A MODERN-DAY RETELLING OF THE GREEK MYTH OF SELENE AND ENDYMION

S.M. SOTO

Chasing the Moon

Cover by Najla Qamber Designs
Photography by Regina Wamba
Editing by Paige Smith, Jenny Sims, and Rebecca Barney
Formatting by Stacey Blake

A modern-day retelling of the Greek Myth of Selene and Endymion.

He was the sun, and she was the moon. A love like theirs was never destined to last.

Selene Drake has always been the girl that blends into the background.
The wallflower.
Quiet.
Unnoticed.
Sweet as can be.
It never bothered her, she preferred slinking into the shadows.

When she first laid eyes on Endymion Black, she fell irrevocably in love with him.
The bad boy.
Cold.
Distant.
Handsome as ever.
For years, she pined after the unattainable boy who had somehow burrowed his way into her heart.

Until everything changed.

One unforgettable night bridled with passion and forbidden lust destroyed her naïve heart and reshaped her innocent soul. It sent her fleeing from the only town she'd ever truly known.

Six years later, Selene is back in Dunsmuir and the boy she spent years loving in silence, has now turned into a man. A man with his sights set on her. Somehow, the tables have turned, and this time around, he's the one doing the chasing, determined to claim her heart as his. Only, he doesn't realize, she has a secret of her own.

One with the potential to change their lives forever.

Chasing the Moon is a full-length second chance standalone with a guaranteed HEA.

Happy Reading!
XO, S.M. Soto

More books by
S.M. SOTO

THE CHAOS SERIES

Deception and Chaos

Blood and Chaos

Love and Chaos

THE SAN DIEGAN SERIES

Scoring the Quarterback

Damaged Heart

THE TWIN LIES DUET

Kiss Me with Lies

Bury Me with Lies

STANDALOnes

Hate Thy Neighbor: An Enemies-to-Lovers Romance

Ache: A Second Chance Romance

A Cruel Love

COMING SOON

The Seasons of Callan Reed

Jake Wilder

The Consequence of Hating You

Redemption and Chaos

Corruption and Chaos

Muerte and Chaos

Playlist

Lucid—QUIN ft. Infinity

All Of The Stars—Ed Sheeran

Magic Hour—Jhene Aiko

Love In The Dark—Jessie Reyes

The Real Her—Drake ft. Andre 300, Lil Wayne

Wrong Direction—Hailee Steinfeld

Moon River—Frank Ocean

Us—James Bay

Ocean—Martin Garrix ft. Khalid

Rewrite the Stars—James Arthur & Anne-Marie

Playing With Fire—Thomas Rhett ft. Jordan Sparks

Somebody—The Chainsmokers, Drew Love

Try Me—The Weeknd

You Are The Reason—Calum Scott

Landslide—The Chicks

Before You Go—Lewis Capaldi

Dancing With Your Ghost—Sasha Sloan

Paradise—Anderson Rocio

Selenophile: (n) a lover of the moon; someone who finds joy and peace of mind from the moon.

For the moon lovers.
The old souls.
And every Daddy's girl.

Chasing the Moon

"In ancient times, it was said that the goddess Selene drove the moon across the sky. Each night, she followed Helios, the sun, to catch his fiery rays and reflect the light back to earth. One night on her journey, she looked down and saw Endymion sleeping in the hills. She fell in love with the beautiful shepherd. Night after night, she looked down on his gentle beauty and loved him more until one evening, she left the moon between the sun and the earth and went down to the grassy fields to lie beside him.

For three nights, she stayed with him, and the moon, unable to catch the sun's rays, remained dark. People feared the dark moon. They said it brought death and freed evil forces to roam the black night. Zeus, king of the gods, was angered by the darkness and punished Selene by giving Endymion eternal sleep. Selene returned to the moon and drove it across the night sky, but her love was too strong. She hid Endymion in a cave, and now, for three nights each lunar month, she leaves the moon to visit her sleeping lover and cover him with silver kisses. In his sleep, Endymion dreams he holds the moon."

Prologue

Selene

JULY 2007

I FELL IN LOVE WHEN I WAS JUST ELEVEN YEARS OLD. ALL IT TOOK WAS ONE glance, three unsteady breaths, and five measly seconds to turn me to putty. There was a foreign swarm of butterflies so powerful it made me nauseous. My heartbeats were irregular, and since then, nothing in my life has been the same.

The first time I laid eyes on Endymion Black, I fell irrevocably in love with him. He was an enigma in our town—the stranger everyone wanted a piece of. On his fifteenth birthday, he moved to Dunsmuir, a small town in California, and he turned the quiet, familiar place upside down.

I remember that first day like it was yesterday. The moment has ingrained itself in the deepest depths of my mind, playing on a constant loop. Even now, just thinking about it lights a fire in my soul.

My dad and I were at the grocery store picking out a dessert for my birthday. Each year, my dad would drive me to the local Grab-N-Go, and I'd head to the bakery section to find the best-looking cake. And each year, it was always the same. A triple chocolate cake with my name written in pink icing. That was another thing I'd later realize would connect me to Endymion. Among a handful of other things, we shared the same birthday—July twenty-second.

As always, Mom and Dad were fighting, so when he took me to the grocery store, it was really just an excuse to get away from my mother. I don't remember a time in my life when my parents weren't at each other's throats. They pretty much hated each other's guts. They were always shouting, always arguing about bills and money, and to make matters worse, they didn't even sleep in the same room at night. Surprisingly, they never laid a hand on each other, but sometimes, when I went to bed, I wondered what would happen if I wasn't there. Would they even be together anymore?

Did I even want them to be together anymore?

I think there's a point in every child's life when they want their parents to stay together forever, even if the discussion of separation or divorce is on the table. I was past that point. I just wanted the fighting to stop and wanted them to be happy, even if that meant separately. I wanted a normal childhood instead of this farce of one I'd been given. Just one peaceful night when I didn't have to listen to my iPod on full blast to block out their arguing. I didn't want to take sides. I didn't want any part of it.

Dad split up with me at the grocery store, opting to get a pack of beer and letting me head toward the bakery. The glass display cases were in sight when I spotted him. With broad shoulders and muscles in his back that my dad didn't even have anymore, I paused in the middle of the aisle and stared at the stranger in an odd state of shock. It rolled through my body in waves, paralyzing me. I was positive he was the most handsome boy I'd ever seen, just from what I saw looking at the back of him.

He had light brown hair, long and messy at the top. It was styled in the I-just-showered-and-I'm-too-cool-for-school look. He was dressed casually in a plain white T-shirt and jeans. With a mind of their own, my feet inched closer and closer until I was standing in front of the packaged danishes. Using the shelf and packaged goods display as a hiding spot, I peered around, stealing glances at him. He was browsing the cakes inside the glass.

Just like I was supposed to be doing.

Even Mrs. Cahill, as she pushed through the doors from the back kitchen, stopped short at the handsome teen before her. I didn't know what his face looked like yet, but that tug deep in my gut, coiling and tingling, told me he was handsome. And when he spoke for the first time? My heart's normal pitter-patter turned irregular. I don't think it's ever beaten the same again—not since that day. He had a voice you could feel roll through your body in an exhilarating, otherworldly sensation. My eleven-year-old brain short-circuited, and all my attention was focused on the guy standing right in front of me. I willed him to turn and feel my presence. Anything to get a look at his face without feeling like a creeper.

I grasped onto the crescent moon around my neck for courage. When I was nervous or needed an extra push, the necklace always gave me that extra something. It was a gift from my parents almost two years ago. For as long as I could remember, I'd been obsessed with the moon, and my parents? Well, it was no secret they indulged me in my obsession. The necklace was silver and dainty, a crescent moon hanging from a 3D moon with real meteorite dust inside. Strangely, since the first time I put the necklace on, it'd given me strength when I normally had none. A talisman of sorts.

I'd always been the painstakingly shy and quiet wallflower who blended into the shadows, unseen and thoroughly unnoticed. I had a hard time speaking up for myself and an even tougher time separating my need to be liked by everyone.

"Selene, sweetie, what are you doing over there?" Mrs. Cahill asked loudly, finally taking notice of me. Her attention caused *him* to turn, and a ragged gasp ripped from my chest when I got a full look at him. He was quite literally the most beautiful guy I'd ever seen. I didn't think any boys my age were cute. There were a few celebrities I had crushes on, but no one, and I mean no one, compared to him.

I opened my mouth to speak, but the words got stuck in the back of my throat. He had defined cheekbones and a strong jaw that clenched as he took me in. He seemed angry or irritated to be standing there in the bakery section. As if this was the last place he wanted to be. But what catapulted him beyond any good-looking guy I'd ever seen before were his light green eyes flecked with white, or maybe gray. Bright, like the color of summertime moss. I had never seen such a color in someone's eyes before. They were a kaleidoscope of greens.

I could feel the heat of his gaze on my skin, and when his eyes clashed with mine, I forced a swallow that felt so overworked, I feared I might've swallowed my own tongue. There was a hardness in the depths of his eyes that softened when he saw me standing there. Shaking my head slightly, I hoped it would clear my thoughts as though I was seeing things. It wasn't possible that this guy was *this* handsome. Surely, he'd be famous if that was the case. He'd have his own spread in *Seventeen* or *J-14*. I blinked rapidly when his plump lips twisted into a soft smile as he regarded me.

"Hey, kid."

Two words were all he spoke, but they crushed me, nonetheless. The dart of his words was poisonous, burning as it spread. I didn't want to be a kid. I didn't want him to see me as a child. I wanted him to think I was as beautiful as I thought he was. Because that was exactly what I thought of this boy standing before me. He was damn beautiful.

I swallowed down the lump in my throat and risked a couple of steps toward him and Janet at the glass display. She was staring at me oddly, eyeing me with narrowed and scrutinizing eyes. This was the first of many here in Dunsmuir who would start catching onto my crush.

Not wanting to look like a weirdo anymore, I inhaled a deep, stabilizing breath and closed the distance, coaching myself on how to act naturally as I stood beside this handsome guy, trying not to fidget.

"Where's your dad, Selene? Are you guys out shopping for your birthday treat?" She smiled, already knowing our routine.

Janet had been the baker here since this place opened. Each year, she rang us up and made sure the cake I chose always had my name and a moon drawn with pink frosting. I was, without a shadow of a doubt, the moonchild here in Dunsmuir.

I glanced at the guy out of the corner of my eye and ducked my head when I felt my cheeks heat. "Uh, yeah. He's getting beer and after dinner snacks, I think."

"Well, what are you having? The usual? And what can I get you, hon? Are we still doing the birthday cake, too?" She directed the last portion of her question at him. A smile lit up her face as she pointed back and forth between us. "Happy Birthday to you both."

I felt his gaze lingering at the side of my head, so I turned to look at him. He stared down at me with an odd expression on his face, before turning back around. "Yeah, let's do the cake, and"—he paused, glancing down at me—"Happy Birthday, kid."

"Happy Birthday…" I trailed off, waiting for him to tell me his name. As he dug into his back pocket, pulling out some cash from his weathered leather wallet to pay, he finally gave me what I wanted.

"You can call me End."

Without another word or even a glance back, he left, taking all the air from my lungs with him.

That was when I first knew Endymion and I would never work. He was otherworldly, and I was…me. Too plain, too young, too quirky to ever capture his attention. That didn't mean I'd ever stop trying.

Over the course of the years, while Endymion and his family got settled here in Dunsmuir from Lake Tahoe, my crush on him only grew, to the point I was sure everyone in town knew about it except him. He always called me kid, and he never looked at me twice. It was like I was insignificant.

I wasn't smart enough.

Interesting enough.

Pretty enough.

Or maybe I was just too young, and therefore, off his radar.

For the first few weeks they were settling in, I did everything I could to run into him again. It wasn't easy. I was still in middle school, and he was heading to high school. We didn't exactly hang out in the same crowds. Fortunately, I did see him every once in a blue moon at the grocery store and at the mall, but each time, he never looked twice.

Not that I expected anything different. I wasn't the kind of girl you looked twice at. I was the girl who would go most of her life unnoticed, and I had come to terms with it.

I took to writing his name in my journals and wondering if one day he'd notice me. Little did I know, the competition would make that feat nearly impossible. In a small town like ours, when a hot guy moved in, the girls, and even the women, flocked toward him. They tried to covet and steal what I laid eyes on first.

Endymion got the most male attention I'd ever seen in my entire life. It was probably his looks, his unique name, and the mystery surrounding him. Whatever it was, I wasn't the only one in town fighting for his attention. And the likelihood was, I never would be. Endymion and I would never work out. We were destined for failure, that was all I was sure of.

Chapter One

Selene

AUGUST 2008-PAST

On my way home from school, I heave a deep sigh when I glance around at the groups of kids. Everyone who walks home has their own cliques. Everyone but me. It's usually just me and my best friend, Julia. We walk to and from school every day, except when it rains or snows. That's where our parents draw the line. But today, Julia missed school because she's "sick," leaving me to my lonesome. I don't have very many friends besides Julia, and the ones I do have are more acquaintances than anything else. Which is precisely why I'm walking home all alone.

I let out a surprised squeak and clutch the thick book to my chest when a few of the high schoolers run past me, hooting and hollering. One of them clips me in the arm, nearly making me drop my pride and joy. A few years ago, my dad bought me this thick book filled with legends from Greek mythology. Those faraway tales speak to me on a different level than regular fiction, which is why I don't enjoy reading anything else.

Right when I think their horseplay is good and over, another one of the jerks bumps into me as he runs by, and, this time, instead of my book almost tumbling to the ground, it's me. I lose my footing, causing my knees to skid along the concrete. I let out a hiss of pain, my eyes slamming shut against the burning of my flesh. My knee-caps may be battered, but at least my book is safe.

"Hey! Watch it!"

My breath leaves me in a sharp gasp, and my body tenses at the sound of the voice I'd know anywhere. I feel someone crouch beside me, and when I glance up through the curtain of hair that's shielding most of my face from view, my breath lodges in my throat.

Endymion Black.

He's kneeling in front of me, peering through my dark strands, as those bright green eyes study me. "You all right?"

Forcing a thick swallow, I'm afraid my violently pounding heart is so loud he can hear it. Perspiration beads along my forehead, and when I brush my hair away from my face to get a better look at him, my stomach dips. He's handsome. So incredibly handsome. It quite literally takes my breath away.

Suddenly remembering he asked me a question, I nod my head slowly. His brows draw together, and the muscle in his jaw flexes as though he's suddenly angry. He looks around us, glaring at the ass-holes in the distance who knocked me over.

"You sure?"

"Y-eah," I whisper. My mouth is painfully dry. The saliva feels like sandpaper as it goes down. He places his hand between us and helps me to my feet. The second I place my hand in his, I feel a tremor wrack my body. Lightning slithers down my spine, damn near electrocuting me.

My knees ache a little when I stand upright, and he must sense it. His gaze homes in on my exposed knees, and he frowns. "You're bleeding. Fucking assholes."

Warmth settles in my cheeks, and I avert my gaze, unable to look at him for too long without feeling like I'm in a cartoon and have hearts floating above my head. I can feel his piercing gaze in the depths of my soul. I tighten my grip on the book in my arms, and he takes notice.

"What's that?"

"It's a mythology book."

"Pretty big book for a little thing like you."

Fighting to tamp down my shy smile, I lift my shoulder in a non-committal shrug. "It's interesting. I don't mind carrying it around."

He smiles then, and hell, it leaves a permanent mark on my soul. It etches itself into every fiber of my being until the very end of time. Endymion jerks his head over his shoulder. "C'mon, I'll walk with you. Maybe this time you won't get trampled."

I bite the inside of my cheek, so I don't grin like a lunatic as I step in stride beside him. We walk in silence for a little while until he asks me more about the book.

"So what is it you like about mythology?"

I shrug. "The stories, I guess. The ability to believe in higher beings. Shooting for the stars, you name it."

He grins. "My mom's family was the same way. Hell, it was why she named me Endymion."

"I like it. Your name, I mean. I think it suits you."

He raises a brow. "How so?"

"He was a handsome shepherd, and you're…" I trail off, the words getting caught in my throat when I realize what I almost let slip. He knows, though, because he chuckles. The sound is warm and deep, and it travels through me in waves.

I suddenly have the urge to reach for my necklace. I grasp it, rubbing my thumb along the silver to breathe past my nervousness.

"It's a nice necklace. I take it you like the moon?"

My gaze shoots to his. "How can you tell?"

His lips twitch as if he's fighting a smirk. "The necklace. Your shirt. The design on your backpack. Kinda gave it all away."

I smile, despite myself. I forgot about all that. Not many people ask why I dress the way I do or why I'm so obsessed with the moon. No one has ever truly cared. Until now.

"I do like it. The moon. My name...my name belonged to the moon goddess. Guess I've just always been a little obsessed."

"Ah. Yeah. That makes sense. What did this goddess do?"

I want to tell him. It's on the tip of my tongue to say she drove the moon across the sky and fell in love with a handsome shepherd by the name of Endymion, but I don't say that. I don't get the chance to because I'm suddenly nudged from the side, and when I hear the high, lilting laughter, I cringe.

"Endy! There you are. Why didn't you wait for us? You know we hate walking alone." Holly Matthews pouts. Her best friend Reina pouts right along with her. She's also the one who bumped me out of the way with her hip, nearly knocking me down. Again.

I'm all but forgotten now that Holly and Reina are here. I slow my pace, falling back as I watch him walk away with them, a sharp ache slicing through my chest. Why does it hurt so much? Having crushes shouldn't cause this much pain.

My heart shrivels in my chest when Endymion glances back at me with his brows drawn in. I sense he's going to say something or maybe call out to me until Holly's manicured hand forces his gaze back on her. Always her.

I spend the rest of the walk home gripping my mythology book and fighting back my tears with a sinking sensation in the pit of my gut. I'm a few blocks away from my street when I feel a presence behind me. The hairs at the nape of my neck stand at attention, and when I glance over my shoulder, my brows draw in, realizing no one's there. Shaking the odd sensation off, I chalk it up to me being alone instead of me being followed.

As I round the corner of the block, I suddenly crash into something and let out a surprised shriek. A husky laugh follows, and my gaze treks up to the source. My eyes widen when I realize who it is.

"Thomas?"

He chuckles, his dark, inky locks hanging haphazardly in his face, as though he hasn't had the time to brush it away in days. Thomas Wentworth has always been town royalty. Though it seems that title has never really sat well with him, so he became the town bad boy instead. I think he thrives on the attention and loves that the women in this town think he's an unattainable miscreant. That is, until Endymion showed up in town. All the attention he basked under slowly went from him to End, and it's obvious he doesn't like it.

"Ah, always so formal. Always so sweet, aren't you, Selene?"

I force a swallow. "I'm not always sweet."

He smirks, clearly knowing better. "Coming home from school?" he asks, his gaze trailing up and down my body, taking in my outfit of choice. I adjust the strap of my backpack on my shoulder, feeling uncomfortable with his scrutiny.

"I am." I make it a point to look at his clothes and quirk a brow. "Are you?"

Something glints in his eyes at my sass. He rubs his mouth absentmindedly, covering his grin. "Nah, I skipped today. Had some other things to do. You should try it sometime."

"Try what?"

"Skipping school." He steps closer to me. Close enough I can smell him and the distinct scent of marijuana. "With me."

My gut clenches and not in a good way. "I can't do that."

He rolls his eyes as if I'm annoying him. "Fine, what about now? Instead of going home, come back to my place with me. We'll hang out."

Something about his proposition seems off. Everything about him right now seems off. Heck, we're almost four years apart. I'm the last person he should be asking to hang out with him. I'm young. A nobody.

"You want to hang out with me at your place? To do what?" I ask dubiously.

He smiles then. It's not soft or warm. It's the opposite, actually.

It has fear rippling down my spine. "Guess you'll just have to wait and see, won't you?"

I take a wobbly step away from him, glancing around the quiet neighborhood, searching for help. Conveniently for him, there's no one to be found. "Sorry, but I can't. My mom and dad are waiting for me."

I try to hurry past him, but his hand shoots out, pressing up against my sternum to halt my progression. "Haven't you ever lived a little, little moon?" he asks, stepping into me. I swallow the sudden lump in my throat and work to control my heavy breathing.

"Bye, Thomas."

Rushing past him, I nearly run home as fear swirls in my gut. I force myself not to look back at him, not even once.

Chapter Two

Selene

JULY 2011-PAST

TODAY IS MY FIFTEENTH BIRTHDAY, AND I FINALLY FEEL LIKE I'M AT AN age where I can keep up with Endymion and stay on his radar. I've spent years watching the girls and women in this town gush over him as though he's a piece of meat. I've nursed my battered heart time and time again as I watched him go out on dates with undeserving girls—just waiting, hoping, and praying he'd eventually take notice of me.

Sadly, he never did.

A few months after he turned eighteen, he left town for work, and I was sure I'd never see him again. Without having him in town, I felt the suffocating weight of my homelife creep in on me. I didn't have anything to look forward to anymore with him gone. I didn't have anything to distract me from the constant fights and bickering. There was only so much tension a teen could handle. I felt like I was walking on eggshells every day, trying to do everything I could to keep things civil between my parents.

Half the time, it didn't work.

Since my parents got in a huge fight about money last night, any thought of sharing cake or dinner at the table together for my birthday was out of the question. So instead, I told them I was going to hang out with some friends. I wasn't really interested in the party everyone planned on going to tonight. I was more interested in the man who, I'd learned only a few days prior, was back home for a few weeks. Since we share a birthday, I know today Endymion is turning nineteen, and even though the years between us might be a cause for concern to some, I don't think it matters. I've loved him since I was kid, and that won't change anytime soon.

I've never been more sure of anything.

I spend most of the night looking for him at Seth Ferguson's party, but he is nowhere to be found. Even though I just started at Dunsmuir High, and, normally, attending parties is a rite of passage, they aren't exactly my scene. It's too much chaos for a girl like me. I prefer to be at home curled up with a good book or outside, staring up at the moon.

I finally give up and decide to head home. And almost as though it was meant to be, as I am crossing the street on my way home, too busy staring up at the moon distractedly, I don't notice the guy running in my path. An *oompf* of air escapes my lungs and echoes down the quiet street. When I glance up, all I'm able to process is the blood rushing through my veins and my heart pounding violently in my chest. It is like the organ is trying to break free at the sight of a sweaty Endymion.

He's shirtless, his broad muscles on display, and it's an impossible task not to stop and gawk at all the muscles, protruding veins, and the droplets of sweat rolling down each rivulet.

"Shit, sorry," he breathes out, plucking a white earbud out of his ear. The music on his iPod must be on full blast because I can hear the strains of rock music screeching through the earbud, even from here. His hair is a drenched mess, the longer strands sticking to his damp forehead in these cute little swirls that have me itching to reach up and tuck them back.

"No, you're fine. I'm sorry. I wasn't paying attention," I ramble, and instead of brushing past him and continuing on my way home, I stand there, still gawking at him as though he's a Greek god. His brows suddenly dip, his face clouding with a frown as he glances around us.

"What are you doing over here? It's not exactly safe to be walking home alone at night."

My stomach does somersaults and backflips at the fact he cares about my well-being. Heat creeps up my neck and settles on my cheeks, but I force a nonchalant shrug, shifting on my feet.

"Nothing has ever happened before. Plus, I know everyone in the neighborhood. I only live a few more blocks away."

He still looks uncomfortable with the thought of me walking on my own. And be still my little heart, I don't think I've ever felt this giddy.

"Which way are you headed?" I point behind him, and he follows the trajectory of my finger and nods. "C'mon, I'd feel much better if I knew you got home safely."

It's a struggle to pull air into my lungs as I walk alongside End. His breathing is still heavy from his run, yet it's controlled, much more controlled than mine would be if I went for a run.

"So you run at night?"

He shrugs. "It helps me clear my head when I need to think. And there's more privacy."

I snort under my breath. "Too much fanfare during the day?"

He shoots a bashful smirk my way. "Noticed that, have you?"

A grin pulls at the corners of my lips. "You've been here, what, four years? I think everyone has noticed."

He shakes his head, his gaze focused ahead of him. "I hate it. The attention."

Surprise flits across my face. "You do?"

His gaze narrows as he stares off into the distance; the corners of his eyes pinching, and for a fraction of a second, he almost looks pained. "With all that attention comes expectations of me and what I'm doing with my life. I graduated high school, yet…I'm still here. In this small town I swore I wouldn't stay in, no matter how much my family loves it."

My heart cinches at the thought of him leaving again. He was gone for a while to community college a few towns over after he graduated high school, but he didn't last long. His dad needed help in his automotive shop, and I heard through the grapevine here in town that his parents couldn't afford the extra expense of college.

"What do you want to do?"

"I don't know." He lifts a shoulder noncommittally. "That's the problem. I considered football, but that's not a plausible career. At least not anymore. College is out of the question. I guess the second-best thing would be to continue working at the automotive shop with my dad, but the thought of fixing cars every day for the rest of my fucking life? I can't stand it."

I fall silent. In all the times I pictured myself talking to him, I never thought the conversation would get so serious. I like that he doesn't have it all together—that he has higher aspirations for himself. A part of me also feels bad for him because, at nineteen, one would think you have everything all figured out, but Endymion? He doesn't even know who he is at this point.

Dread settles in the pit of my stomach once we turn down my street, closing in on my house. The walk was too fast. There's never enough time when it comes to being with Endymion.

"Well…" I let out a breath. "Whatever you do decide you want to do, just make sure it's something you love. Something that'll make you happy. Reach for the stars, Endymion."

We pause in front of my house, and I fidget before him, anticipation swirling through my veins as I wonder what will happen next.

Nothing apparently.

End smiles. "Thanks, kid. I needed that." He lets out a loud yawn, jerking his head back toward my house. "Well, good night. And maybe stop walking around in the middle of the night, yeah? The crime rate might be low here, but that doesn't mean everyone in this town is a saint."

With that quick parting statement, he breaks into an unhurried jog. I can feel the moment between us slipping away, so much so that I begin to panic. Swallowing thickly, I call out after him, causing him to jerk to a quick stop.

"End!"

He turns, brows raised in question.

"I just wanted to say…Happy Birthday."

He smiles then, and it's the most beautiful sight. It settles in my stomach, causing warmth to filter through my veins.

"Happy Birthday, Selene," he calls out, his gaze pinned to mine. I feel a current travel between us. It's electric and damn near shocks me. He has to feel it, too. Right?

Severing the connection, he turns, and I'm left standing there, completely deflated as I watch his form disappear into the night.

Kid.

Would he ever see me as anything else?

Once inside, I head straight for the bathroom in the hallway. Flicking on the light, I cringe at my reflection. With long, boring, wavy brown hair, alabaster skin that makes me look like I'm a vampire, and a face that won't stop anyone in their tracks, I can definitely see why Endymion isn't exactly falling over himself for me. When I was younger, my hair had a lighter tint to it, more like my father's dirty blonde, but as I've gotten older, the color has evolved.

Placing my hands on each side of the vanity, I lean forward and scrutinize every part of my face. Making comparisons between myself and every other girl he's dated. My skin is smooth, like porcelain, which means my cheeks are always unnecessarily rosy. My brows, though shaped and plucked, are still dark and bushy. In my younger years, my "caterpillar brows" were the cause of incessant teasing. My eyes, a simple caramel brown with a ring of green, are identical to my father's, and I have a slender nose that upturns the slightest bit at the tip, just like my mother's. My lips are much too big for my face, and when I smile, it only makes it worse. I usually try to keep my mouth closed when I smile, just so I don't blind everyone by looking like Jim Carrey from *The Mask*. Even without lipstick or colored lip balm, my lips are naturally a pinkish red, which is annoying since half the popular girls in my class think I'm trying to one-up them. The icing on the shit-cake that are my looks? The smattering of freckles I was cursed with that decorate the bridge of my nose. My grandparents think it's cute. Me? Not so much.

With one last self-depreciating glance at myself, I blow out a discontented sigh before heading upstairs. I jerk my gaze up at the sound of stomping feet. My mom's face is twisted with anger as she flies past me without really seeing me.

"Fucking asshole," she mutters under her breath, no doubt referring to my father and the fight they must've had. My grip tightens on the railing, and my chest squeezes in an agonized vise. Slamming my eyes shut, I force myself to remain impassive and think about anything else but my parents and their problems. Adult issues should be the very last thing on my mind. A tired huff slips past my lips as I head into my bedroom. For once, I wish I could go to my mom with my problems, instead of always worrying about hers. I wish I could ask her for advice, but chances are, that'll never happen because her problems and her unhappiness consume almost all her thoughts.

Pacing around my bedroom for a while, I find my thoughts returning to the events of tonight. Still stuck on Endymion. I'm damn near wearing a hole in my carpet until I can't stand it anymore. I need to talk to him again. About anything.

I make an excuse to my mom that I'm heading to my friend, Julia's, to borrow her notes on an assignment for class. She only lives around the corner, so it's not a big deal. Mom agrees, without question, because here in Dunsmuir, you don't have to worry about your child walking around the corner to their friend's house. Everyone in this town knows everyone and keeps their eyes out for the entire community.

I start down the street at a brisk jog, my gaze darting around, wondering where he could've headed next. If he was jogging around the neighborhood, I'd need to turn left on Stone Creek, but he was heading toward his house to finish his jog. Or at the very least, that's what it seemed like. I opt to turn down Elm Street anyway and head toward his house, just to see if he's home. Elm Street turns off Sunflower Lane, the road I live on, a few blocks ahead. If he is, I'm sure his window at the top of his two-story will be lit up, much like it usually is when he's up there.

At fifteen years old, it's no secret that I'm as unsuspecting as they come. And I've never truly known heartbreak until tonight. I jog down Elm Street, closing in on his house, and that's when I see it.

I see *them*.

I thought we might actually be getting somewhere after what I thought was a meaningful conversation, where he actually saw me and I was no longer that invisible girl anymore, but I couldn't have been anymore wrong. He actually didn't see me at all. I was nothing to him, and chances were I always would be.

The knife plunges in my heart when I hear the moan. I glance at Holly Matthews' house, who lives a few houses down from Endymion, and blanch at the shadows I can make out on the side of the house. I pause along the sidewalk, and my eyes widen, my chest cracking open when I realize what I'm looking at. There at the side of the house are Endymion and Holly, damn near going at it. I can see her tan, golden skin peeking out from the shadows and his strong, bulky frame as he holds her up against the side of the house. I shouldn't be all that surprised. Back in high school, Holly and Endymion dated and often couldn't keep their hands off each other. It's obvious that hasn't changed.

A piercing ache settles in my chest, making it hard to breathe. It feels as if someone is taking an ice pick to all my vital organs and jabbing, tearing open my flesh and letting me bleed out.

I can't believe I actually thought one stupid conversation between us tonight would turn into something more, something I've always dreamed of, but of course, that didn't happen. This isn't like the grand scenes in the books I read or the swoony moments in my favorite movies. This is real life, and it fucking sucks.

Grappling for the moon chain around my neck, I tighten my fist around the crescent shape and slam my lips together, holding in the sob that threatens to escape. I let my gaze linger for a few seconds longer before I turn on my heels, nursing my broken heart.

The entire walk back home on my fifteenth birthday is spent with hot trails of tears carving their way down my cheeks as I feel sorry for myself. I tell myself it doesn't change things. I tell myself it just isn't our time, but the little voice inside my head knows better.

Endymion and I were ill-fated and doomed from the start. I should've figured it out sooner, what with all the mythology I read, but I get it now. We are star-crossed lovers, never meant to be. He is the sun, and I am the moon. I'll always chase him, and he'll always run.

I wonder if there will ever be a day when he'll chase the moon?

Chapter Three

Selene

JULY 2014-PAST

It's my eighteenth birthday, and I'm off to college in just a few days. As far away a college I can get in order to escape my parents and their bickering. Pasadena is almost a whopping ten hours away, and I couldn't be more relieved. I got into Caltech and had a grant and a scholarship. It wasn't a full ride, like my parents had hoped, but they promised they'd figure it out financially. I, of course, planned on finding a part-time job out there, once I was settled, to help with the costs.

I've spent years listening, years pretending everything is okay in our home, but it's not. Couples who love each other don't act like my parents do. I don't even know what love looks like. I don't have anything to go off of, but I know with utmost certainty, their marriage isn't it. Don't get me wrong, they have their good days, the days when they're cordial and they seem to get along well enough. But that's all it really is. It's a façade. It's the surface of their relationship. It's what they want everyone else in town to see and believe. *I'm* the only one who truly knows what their relationship is like. I know that Mom, at least five times a day, when my dad isn't around, tells me to never, *ever* get married. She always says, offhandedly, that she wishes she wasn't married. And my dad, well, he's not really any better. I think a part of him is lonely, and I don't really blame him, but I do wish I hadn't heard some of the stuff I did. A few years back, I heard him speaking in hushed tones on the phone one night.

I only know this because I was sneaking back inside from Julia's house after curfew. It was obvious he was speaking to a woman who wasn't my mother. I was angry at first, but then the next morning, when my parents' argument cycle started all over, it definitely made sense. I still don't know why they don't just get a divorce. They can't stand to be in a room together for longer than ten minutes at a time, and I refuse to believe I am the reason they are still pretending to be a happily married couple.

I'm relieved to be headed off to college, and that, I am sure of. I don't know how my parents will survive with just the two of them once I'm gone, but I hope to God they'll somehow figure it out.

Without having to worry about impressing anyone in high school, since Endymion graduated years prior, I've focused all my attention and energy on academics. My crush on him never wavered, and no other boy my age ever came close. I had a few boyfriends here and there, obviously at my best friend Julia's pestering, but the most we ever did was hold hands. Which worked out in my favor in the end. If I didn't have a crush on Endymion and if I was wasting my time dating in high school, I'm positive I wouldn't have gotten into Caltech. I'd always had a strong interest in science, and since my dad was obsessed with all things engineering, I found myself gravitating toward the subject throughout high school. I was captain of the Academic Pentathlon Club, vice president of the student body, a member of the debate team, and I worked for the student newspaper, too. I made sure I was involved in enough clubs and extracurriculars to be college ready, and after all the studying, it's finally paid off.

I'm proud of myself for getting into one of the top ten schools in the US, but a small part of me is bummed I won't be studying anything in literature that has to do with mythology—more precisely, the moon. There is no career in that. Hell, I know this, but it doesn't make the reality of it any easier. Sometimes in life you have to compromise, letting go of the things you love for the things that make sense. I'll have a good life with a career in chemical engineering. I enjoy the science aspect of it, so I'm sure, with a little patience, I'll be fine settling. I'm sure the money won't be too bad either.

When the arguing between my parents starts up again, this time about an overdraft fee in their shared bank account, I leave the house without a word. It is easier to leave and pretend everything is okay than it is to stay and try to make myself believe love is a real, tangible thing. It isn't. Love is a destroyer. It destroys everything in its path. I'm only eighteen, and after watching my parents, I know this. After pining after a guy who's never noticed me, I know this better than anyone. Love is blind. And fucking stupid. It's an emotion I refuse to waste my time on.

With my hands tucked into my jean pockets, I walk along the sidewalk toward the creek. Sometimes I like to sit out by the creek and stare at the water, listening to the small ripples lap at each other. Here in Dunsmuir, the waterfalls are a tourist favorite, but I prefer the hidden gems not many people know about like the creek. Hidden in the hillside a few blocks away from my house, the creek is beautiful in the winter. It freezes over and inches of snow cover the long blades of grass on the banks. It's a winter wonderland. It's beautiful to look up at the mountaintops and see the snow-peaked ridges and the pines covered with white and surrounded by a fine mist.

In the summertime, like tonight, it's the opposite. A slight breeze is enough to keep the sweat from rolling down my spine. The air smells of fresh grass, and in the creek, the lily pads float, crickets chirp, and the silver glow of the moon highlights the water, reflecting the sky.

With my backside perched in the grass, I lean back on my elbows and stare up at the sky to gaze at the moon. From here, I can make out the divots and dark spots. By the size and shape, I'd say tonight is a waxing gibbous. The waxing gibbous is usually the adjustment and refining period. Just as in many aspects of life, things don't always work out the way we plan or want them to, and with this phase of the moon, it helps you realize what you need to re-evaluate—so to speak—to give up or to change direction on whatever it was you set as your intention. During the waxing gibbous, you have to give in to change, you have to change course and sacrifice what you want for what you need.

I stare up at the bright silver light and change course on my intentions, no longer resisting the change I've been fighting. For so long, I thought my place was here in Dunsmuir. I thought for so long I wanted one boy to love me back, but I see now that it was never meant to happen. It's time I accept the fact that those desires will never come to fruition. Instead, I think about my desires for the future, in college and with my family. I brush all unbidden thoughts of Endymion aside, promising only to look forward from here on out.

No more looking back.

Out of habit, I reach for my necklace and rub my thumb over the 3D moon. The action is second nature at this point. I can't remember when my obsession with the moon started. Don't get me wrong, I love the stars and the like, but the moon—so many things are affected by the moon. The moon has many phases, and each phase means something new for everyone, spiritually and scientifically. It's beautiful. I love everything about it.

The moon is a wonder. Not only is it the largest and brightest object in the sky, but, just like the stars, it has always inspired awe in many people. From scientists, to the mythologists, to regular people like me, who look up and wonder what the significance is on nights like this. It's always radiated an air of mystery and magic, love and, obviously, unattainable beauty. It's been used to measure time. The waxing and waning have made it a symbol of change in cycles around the world. One cycle being the constant alternation of birth and death, creation and destruction. The moon belongs to things that transgress the boundaries of astronomy, astrology, and even religion.

I feel a connection to the moon in the myths and legends. The moon gives me a friend when I feel like I have no one—when I am lonely. On nights when things seem bleak, as if nothing in life will ever go according to plan, staring up at the moon brings me a sense of peace. Because when I stare up at the sky that's lit up by the stars and silver light, I know I'm not the only one. I know I'm not the only one who feels invisible or lonely.

For all intents and purposes, it feels like I am the moon, and Endymion is the sun. Our non-present love affair was condemned from the beginning. When I was younger, I wondered why my parents named me Selene. My mother always said it was a random choice, a name both she and my father fell in love with. She later changed her story and said it was because my birth was the light in my father's and her lives. Of course, that always inspired an eye roll because, really?

I always thought it was strange that I was named after a mythical being and so was Endymion. When I was younger, I thought it was fated. I mean, it had to be kismet, right? But as I got older, I realized Endymion and I were a lot like our mythical beings. According to the legends, Selene and Endymion were ill-fated. And in real life, that seems to have transpired.

I startle at the sound of grass crunching behind me, and when I crane my neck to look back, my eyes widen and my breath escapes me in a ragged rush of air.

So much for re-evaluating and giving up on old intentions, right?

Standing there, tall and handsome as ever, illuminated by the glow of the moon is Endymion. I glance behind him toward the street, my brows taking a nosedive when I don't see his car.

Did he walk here?

I was so lost in thought, I didn't even hear him coming.

He looks ruggedly handsome dressed in a simple pair of jeans, a black T-shirt, and a pair of black boots. His eyes seem a little unfocused. I can't tell if it's the lack of light or if he has a lot on his mind. He points at the spot next to me.

"This spot taken?"

My brows shoot up. "What?"

His mouth quirks into a semblance of a grin. "Can I sit?"

I frown at him, completely taken by surprise.

Is he…is he grinning at *me*?

After years of going unnoticed. Years of wishing he'd notice me, he chooses tonight of all nights to finally do so?

I'm sure if this was anyone else, they would have washed their hands of Endymion Black by now. They would have moved on and forgotten about these childish notions of love and fate. But they don't know. They don't know what it feels like when a guy you've loved for years finally shows you a lick of attention. They don't know what it feels like to have his charming grin aimed right at you and it feels like everything in your world is right again.

They don't understand the way you lose your breath.

They don't understand the way you lose all your sense.

People like that will never understand how a girl can love a boy for years, even with a promise of a broken heart.

"Oh, no, sorry." I shake my head, and when his brows raise in question, I realize what that probably sounded like to him—he *can't* sit. "It's open. You can sit. There's no one there. I mean, obviously." The words spill past my lips in a nervous stream of word vomit.

He chuckles. The sound is deep and gravelly as it rolls through me. End lowers himself next to me and blows out a tired breath, as if he hasn't sat in hours. I fidget in the grass, suddenly feeling like the air is stifling. My skin is overheating with his proximity, and suddenly, my brain is going haywire. Whereas, only seconds before, I felt calm as I stared up at the night sky and was chilled to the bone by the brisk air.

His clean, woodsy scent overpowers the smell of the grass and the creek, infiltrating my senses. Sitting next to him, it's hard to ignore his overwhelming presence, just how larger than life he is. Out of the corner of my eye, I trek my gaze up and down his broad shoulders, taking in his profile. The height difference between us is evident even while sitting. He's this big, bulky man.

That's exactly what he is now.

He isn't just a boy or a teen anymore. He is all man.

And at twenty-two years old, he is sexier than ever.

We sit in silence, soaking up the sounds of the creek and the nature around us. I can't help but notice the weird energy radiating off Endymion. In all the times I've been near him, he's always seemed so calm and collected, but right now? He's the opposite. I may not know much about him, just what I know from afar, but whatever is bothering him is affecting his mood.

I open my mouth, trying to find a way to get him to talk, but he beats me to it.

"Happy Birthday."

A smile tugs at the corners of my lips. "Thank you, um, Happy Birthday to you, too."

"Do you spend all your birthdays sitting out here alone by this creek?"

I smile. "I do, actually. What about you? I would think you prefer doing something a little more extravagant on your birthday."

He shrugs. "I like sitting here with you just fine."

My heart stumbles at his words. It's not like he's professing his undying love to me or anything, but hell, tell that to my battered heart that has waited years for this man to show me an ounce of his attention.

Another period of silence lingers between us. Me, thinking about him and the years I may have wasted lusting after him, and him, sitting there, staring off into the distance, stuck in his head.

"You ever feel like life is moving too fast and you can't catch ahold of anything?"

I glance at him fully, no longer pretending I don't notice he's sitting next to me. "All the time. I leave for college soon, and there's this part of me that is scared to leave everything I've ever known behind, but you know what? I'm so tired of dealing with the same crap at home that I *need* a break. I'm looking forward to leaving this place."

"I hate this town. I hate the fucking people here. I hate working at the garage with my dad. I never wanted this to be my life. I never thought that this, *this* is what I had to look forward to."

I pause, processing his words. The last time I had a conversation with Endymion that lasted longer than a moment, he stressed just how badly he didn't want to work at the garage with his dad. Sadness blooms in my chest when I realize he was never able to get out of this town. He ended up working at the very place he hated, the very place he wanted to avoid.

"What did you want?"

Slowly, he turns to look down at me. Like a spotlight shining down on him, the moon highlights his features, making it hard to do anything but beam at him in awe. For a moment, we just sit here in the long blades of grass with the rolling sounds of the creek as the moon stares down at us, studying our interaction as we watch each other. A long moment passes between us, and a startling vibration travels down my spine at the way he stares so deeply into my eyes. It's an awareness of sorts. His heated gaze roams my face, and it's like the first time he's seeing me.

He shakes his head ever so slightly, breaking contact, and glances down at the small sliver of space between us. "It doesn't matter anymore. The only thing I can tell you is to get out. Get as far away from here as you can."

Summoning the brazen courage I didn't realize I had, I look down at his larger than life hand resting in the blades of grass between us and tentatively place mine over his. It prompts him to swing his troubled gaze to mine. "For what it's worth, I think you have the potential to do anything you want, End."

A crease forms between his brows as he stares down at me. His bright, beautiful gaze travels over my features. His stare is a texture I can feel as it traces the lines of my face, down my neck and its slow descent back up. Gooseflesh suddenly covers every inch of my skin at the way he's looking at me. Endymion has seen me around town many times, but he's never truly seen me until now. He's never stopped to stare. And his stare has never looked as heated or as sexual as it does now.

"You're so beautiful," he says quietly, almost to himself, as if he's in a daze. He slides his hand behind my neck, slowly dragging me toward him. The instant his hand is on me, I'm putty in his hold. I fall into his touch, my eyes fluttering shut at the myriad of sensations swirling through my body.

Then after what feels like a lifetime of waiting, we're kissing. His warm, soft lips are on mine, working in tandem, coaxing me to open for him. A swarm of warmth explodes in my belly, and something else tugs low, much deeper. It flutters and pulls just behind my navel. I moan into his mouth, tentatively threading my fingers through the soft hair at the nape of his neck.

The first time I've been kissed, and it's by the boy I've been in love with for years. The boy I've wished endlessly on every star would finally notice me—would finally want me. As our kiss grows heavy, his tongue tangling with mine, my teeth nipping at his plump lips, and my hands traveling across his overheated skin, I realize he's not that boy anymore. He's all man now.

Endymion rolls over on top of me, and I gasp into his mouth when I feel his erection digging into my hip. My core throbs painfully, causing an ache to bloom between my legs. My body is on fire. With every stroke of his tongue and firm glide of his hand, I lose myself in him, falling deeper and deeper into this man until I can't possibly find my way out.

This is what I always wanted. This is all I've *ever* wanted.

He suddenly pulls his mouth away from mine, both of us gasping for much-needed air, our chests heaving, working to accommodate the heavy breathing. End stares down at me with such fire and wonder in his eyes that I want to bottle this memory up and keep it forever. And I know without a shadow of a doubt that I'm not leaving here with my virginity intact tonight. He's the only person I've ever wanted to have any part of me, and I'm certain that I'll never have an opportunity like this with him again.

A bright smile lights my face, surprising him. He opens his mouth, more than likely to ask why I'm grinning like a loon, but I beat him to it. Sliding my arms around his neck, I jerk him down to meet me halfway before I dive in for another kiss. He groans into my mouth, and my sex clenches at the sound. Heat swirls in my belly, and unable to stop myself, my hips thrust up toward his, seeking some type of friction as my hands roam his muscled back.

Knowing exactly what I need, End aligns his hips with mine and thrusts his erection over the seam of my jeans, rubbing against the bundle of nerves. I let out a breathy moan that gets lost in the cool night breeze.

"More," I pant out between heated kisses.

Endymion trails his mouth from my lips down to my neck, swirling his tongue there, making me moan louder. My hips swivel harder now, and I let out a whimper when I feel him work his hand between our bodies and pop the button on my jeans. The sound of the zipper gliding down the metal teeth gets lost in my moans as he kisses my neck. He traces his mouth down, lower, his lips toying with the top of my tank top. My nipples strain painfully against the material of my bra, begging for attention.

At the same time Endymion slips his hand inside my pants and underwear, he pulls the tank top down with the shell of my bra to expose my erect nipple. He makes a hungry sound in the back of his throat as he takes my nipple into his mouth, his warm tongue swirling around the peak. I gasp, my back arching off the grass, when I feel his fingers glide through my wetness. There are too many delicious sensations happening at once for me to focus on. He grazes his teeth over my nipples, alternating from one nipple to the next, driving me insane.

I dig my nails into his back, enjoying his sharp hiss, and the way he slides his fingers inside me, curling them, pumping them in and out, just like I do when I think of him at night. I blink my bleary, lust-hazed eyes open and stare at him hovering on top of me. Thick strands of his rebel curls fall along his forehead, but it's his face, his expression that has me enraptured. He looks like sex. Like the hottest man on the planet. With his plump bottom lip trapped between his teeth, he's enjoying my reaction to him—enjoying the way my body responds to his touch.

"I need more, End, please," I breathe into the night air, arching my back again when his fingers continue pumping in and out of me while he swirls his thumb around the bundle of nerves. With a new brand of impatience, I reach down and start working my jeans down my legs. End follows suit, working down his jeans and freeing his cock. I try not to balk at the sight of his penis, but seeing as this is the first time I've ever seen one in real life, it's hard not to. Especially when his just looks so…long and thick. My core clenches again, this time with anticipation, as he lines himself at my center. We stare at each other, suspended in this moment, and then he's kissing me again. Or I'm kissing him again.

I can no longer tell where he starts and I end.

A groan tears from my chest when he dips the head of his cock in and out of my entrance, lubing himself up. He then brings the tip up to my clit and swirls it there, sending my brain into a tailspin. I can already feel my orgasm looming, and he hasn't even slid inside me yet.

"So beautiful," he whispers near my ear as he trails kisses down the side of my neck, heading back to my chest. My nails dig into his back when I feel him enter me. My body tries to fight the intrusion, instead of welcoming it, and I coach myself through it, trying to focus on his mouth. His tongue swirls around my nipple as I arch my body into his, breathing through the pain, moaning in his ear.

"Fuck, you're so tight," he grits out, as he pushes past the barrier of my virginity. I clutch him and lose myself in the way his hips pump into mine. The way his cock feels sliding in and out of me. My body feels so full, there's an unbearable stinging pang, but behind it is a delicious tug of something deep in my gut. That something has me bringing him closer to me, begging for more.

Endymion lifts my leg over his shoulder, changing the angle of his thrusts, and I lose myself in him. My eyes roll back, and sounds I hadn't even known I could make leave my lips. He's everywhere. His mouth is on mine, stealing the breath from my lungs, and the only sounds are our bodies meeting, coming together as one, and the distant lapping of the creek.

"God, you're fucking perfect," he pants out between kisses as he slides his hand between our bodies. My moans grow in volume when he rubs my clit. It all becomes too much—his thrusts and the way he's working my clit—and I fall apart beneath him, my walls clenching around him, making the sting between my legs more pronounced. Endymion pumps quicker and deeper now, and when a sensual groan spills from his lips and I feel him come inside me, I moan, tugging his lips down to mine, and kiss him, losing myself in him.

We stay like that for a while, our lips and bodies connected, but each of us no longer moving. Slowly, he slides out, and I hiss in pain. I feel sore between my legs. It suddenly feels oddly barren and empty down there without him inside me. Such an odd sensation.

He hovers over me, each hand planted on either side of my head, effectively caging me in. Endymion stares down at me with such heat and a lingering softness in his eyes, it's a complete contradiction, but regardless, I feel myself falling deeper and deeper into him. Both of our chests are still heaving, and I take this time to commit every part of this moment to memory. The way his hungry eyes rake across my face, taking my features in. The way the light of the moon catches on the perspiration dotted along his forehead. The way the entire night suddenly seems as if it belongs to just the two of us.

Unable to contain it, a bright smile spreads across my face, and my heart skips a beat when his does the same. He's always had the most handsome smile. Dipping his head down, he kisses me gently, his tongue parting my lips and softly stroking my tongue. He's hypnotizing. He's all-consuming. He's everything I knew he would be, yet somehow, he's so much better. So much bigger. So much *more*.

With a final peck, he drops down beside me, pulling me onto him. I go willingly, relishing in the feel of his warm chest beneath my head. After sometime, we both dress, and much to my surprise, he falls back onto the grass, taking me with him. My eyes flutter closed, and I listen to the sound of his pounding heart and his heavy breathing slowly returning to normal. I don't know how long we spend lying there, staring up at the sky, stargazing.

At some point, while his fingers are running through my hair, I must've fallen asleep because I come to when I realize I'm being lifted into someone's arms. Slowly, I rouse, blinking up at End through sleep-bleary eyes as he carries me from the creek. The trees and the sky hang above him like a beautiful backdrop, and the moon follows him as though she, too, is chasing him, trying to get a glimpse of what comes next.

"What's happening?" I ask, my voice groggy with sleep.

His answering chuckle is raspy. It hits me in places that take my breath away. "It's getting cold out. I should probably get you home." He presses a kiss to my forehead, and I nuzzle back into the warmth of his chest, never wanting him to let go.

"I live on Sunflower Lane." I yawn.

"I know, beautiful girl."

I don't even remember my head hitting the pillow after he carried me home. One second, I was walking inside the house, wearing a huge smile on my face, and the next, I was crawling into bed feeling like a brand-new person.

I lost my virginity to the man I've been in love with for what feels like all my life. I can't wait to wake up tomorrow and see what comes next—where the future takes us. Sure, he doesn't have a lot in his life figured out, but I am sure that what happened tonight has changed everything.

The next morning, after showering and eating breakfast, I make my way toward End's house. There is an extra unsuspecting pep in my step, not to mention, a sting between my legs. With each throb, I think of last night. I swear I can still feel him inside me. The moment was magical; it was what I had waited years for. A constant heat swirls in my chest, billowing and spreading with each breath. A lasting impression from last night, I suppose.

I pause on his doorstep, flattening my hair to make sure I look okay before summoning the courage to ring his doorbell. I spent a little extra time getting ready this morning. I don't usually bother with makeup, mainly because I tend to look like I have a perpetual blush and red lip going, but today, I took extra time with my hair and put on mascara. I didn't put too much thought into my outfit and just settled on a pair of shorts and a loose V-neck. With my heart pounding violently and butterflies roaring in my belly at the thought of seeing him again, I raise my hand to ring the doorbell. My eyes widen when the door suddenly swings open, and there, in all his handsome glory, is Endymion. His brows pull down when he sees me.

"Hey?" He walks out, shutting and locking the door behind him. I tuck loose strands of hair behind my ear, shifting on my feet. I can already feel the heat rising to my cheeks as I think about last night. My stomach clenches at the memory.

"Hey, you. I just wanted to stop by and see how you were doing after last night."

If possible, the crease between his brows deepens, and he comes up short, his footsteps faltering.

"Riiight." He nods, rubbing at the back of his neck. It's such a boyish mannerism that it makes my stomach flip. "You're, uh…it's Selene, right?"

The smile that was on my face slowly tapers off. A sinking feeling enters my stomach, leaving the hairs at the back of my nape standing at attention. "Yeah," I reply cautiously, a frown now marring my features. "I'm sorry. Am I missing something here—"

"Endy!" Holly singsongs, grabbing our attention. "Are you ready to go? I start my shift in thirty."

That sinking feeling turns into a pit that I feel taking over, swallowing me from the inside out.

"Hey, kid, look, I gotta give Holly a ride, then head to work, but, um, I guess I'll see you around? Talk to you later?"

Pain slices through my chest, creeping into the center, making it hard to breathe. I nod jerkily, fighting back tears as I watch him head toward his truck. My chin quivers, and I bite my bottom lip until all I feel is burning pain. Anything to hold back the tears that are so close to falling. Holly tugs on the back of his shirt as he passes her, bringing him closer, and plants a kiss on his lips. That crater in my chest grows when he pulls back, chuckling down at her like she's his whole world.

"What happened to you last night? I thought we were going to hang out."

End shakes his head as he makes his way around his truck. "I got so fucking drunk that I blacked out. I don't remember a damn thing."

My heart shatters at his words.

Right there on his porch, I feel the walls close in on me. White noise fills my ears. A cold slicing ache spears into my chest. It shoots down the center, making everything tight and hard to breathe. A dark tunnel swims and ebbs, threatening to pull me under just as my lungs squeeze as though in duress.

End glances back at me one final time as they climb into the truck, that crease between his brows ever-present.

They drive off, and I finally let the floodgates free. I stumble off Endymion's porch with tears streaming down my cheeks. My vision is so blurred by tears that I end up tripping on the sidewalk and scraping my knees, but my heart is in so much pain that my body doesn't process the burning from the ripped flesh. There's a gaping hole in my chest where the organ should be.

So I lost my virginity to the man I've loved through my adolescent years, and he was so drunk that he doesn't remember any of it. He doesn't remember the moment we shared. He doesn't remember taking my virginity. Hell, he doesn't remember me at all.

He doesn't remember.

I place a trembling hand over my stomach to settle the sudden bout of nausea I feel. How could I be so stupid? How could I not notice? I internally berate myself for my stupidity.

Was I so blinded by my own lust for him that I didn't realize he'd been drinking? He tasted like mint, not alcohol. How could I be so foolish?

I'm not even surprised that when I walk into my house with tears streaming down my face, my parents are too busy arguing about money and my college funds to notice. I slink into my room and crawl into bed, my body wracking with sobs. All for the broken-hearted, foolish girl who gave herself to a man who doesn't even remember. A man who doesn't even know she exists. I gave Endymion my heart when I was eleven years old, and all he's done in the seven years since then is break it.

I tell myself it's a good thing I'm leaving.

I won't have to see him anymore.

I won't have to see him and Holly anymore.

I make a vow to myself as I sob into my sheets. I won't backtrack this time. While I'm in Pasadena, I'll put my feelings for Endymion in the rearview, and I won't look back. He had his chance, but I will never, ever let him have any more power over me than he's had these past seven years.

Endymion means nothing to me.

I just wish I knew then that forgetting about him would be easier said than done.

Chapter Four

Selene

PRESENT-SIX YEARS LATER

"Luna, baby girl, shoes now!" I yell from the front door for the third time. I finally hear the pitter-patter of her feet, and when she rounds the corner, I see the attitude written all over her face. She slips her tiny feet into her unicorn Vans, whipping her long chestnut hair over her shoulder.

"I heard you the first time, Mommy."

I prop my hands on my hips. "Then why didn't you come the first time?"

She sighs as she walks past me, almost as though I should know better. And honestly, at this point, maybe I should. If there was ever a poster child for a kid with attitude, it would be my daughter. At just five, almost six years old, Luna is probably the sassiest child I've ever met. If I hadn't birthed her, I wouldn't even be sure she's mine. She sure in the hell doesn't have my features. She's a clone of her father. I think that's what makes looking at her every day so hard. It reminds me of that young, doe-eyed girl who harbored a crush on a boy who never returned said crush. Instead, he just unknowingly broke her heart at every turn.

My sweet Luna is my blessing and my painful reminder all wrapped in a beautiful, sassy package.

After that night at the creek, I thought for sure that was it for us. After all the years of trying to get him to notice me, I thought Endymion had finally seen me. In the heat of the moment, I'd given in to him, giving him everything I had to offer by losing my virginity to him. I was so stuck in the moment that I didn't realize we didn't use a condom. I was a virgin, so it's not like I was worried about spreading anything, and I thought I could trust him. But I was wrong. The next day was a nightmare. The way he treated me as if I was a stranger, just a "kid," and the way he could so easily forget about the night we shared together was a stab to the heart. How was I so infatuated with him that I missed his slurred words or unfocused stare? For someone drunk, he seemed so…normal.

A part of me died that day. A piece of my soul shattered when he kissed another girl right in front of me, forgetting about me entirely.

I don't know why I convinced myself that night was any different. Why did I feel like it was magical? It obviously wasn't because he acted as though I was invisible to him—just as he always did. I gave the guy my heart, my virginity, and still, he acted like I was that little kid from the bakery.

It's taken me a while to look past the heartbreak and my anger to gather some perspective on the issue. He was drunk. To him, the night never even happened. I can't fault him forever, and I know that, but it doesn't lessen the blow of his rejection. I can still feel the phantom pangs in my chest. The organs squeezing in a bind. Sometimes, when the loneliness becomes so suffocating, I think back to that first time with him and all the chaos that came after it.

I was well into my first semester of college when I realized I was pregnant. The sickness, I chalked up to homesickness. The weight gain, I chalked up to the late nights and junk food while studying. When my roommate talked me into taking a pregnancy test and it came back positive, I cried. I sobbed so hard, it rivaled the night after losing my virginity. This was almost worse than a broken heart because this baby was a reminder of the guy who never noticed me.

I called my parents and broke the news because, even at almost nineteen years old, I had no idea what the hell I was doing, and quite frankly, the thought of being a mother scared me shitless. I had just barely started college. I wasn't ready to give life to another human being, let alone raise him or her.

Except I didn't tell them the whole truth about the night I got pregnant. For reasons that, even now, I don't quite understand, I never told my parents it was End who got me pregnant. That he was the father of my child. Subconsciously, I think saying it aloud would only hurt more, so I kept it a secret. My own shameful secret.

As expected, the news of my unplanned pregnancy only caused the fighting back home to worsen. I was just glad I wasn't there to witness it firsthand. My mom took a flight out to Pasadena to see me. When she rented a duplex out there, it didn't take long to realize she had no intention of going back home. Apparently, the years of constant fighting had caught up with her. She was done and over it.

My mom was quick to jump into full-on grandma mode, but my dad…he had a harder time accepting it. We didn't talk for three whole months because of how disappointed he was in me. Our relationship over the years dwindled. I was always a daddy's girl, but I guess for a father, watching your baby having a baby was a hard thing to accept.

Mom stayed out in Pasadena with me for a few years. She helped me with the baby while I went to school. I had to drop out of Caltech for Pasadena City College. With a baby, it changed things. The road to becoming a chemical engineer seemed out of reach, so after much consideration, I decided not to pursue it. Instead, I lowered my aspirations to something more doable. Because reaching for the stars? That wasn't an option anymore.

It wasn't until I got my business degree that I knew what I wanted to do. I wanted to open my own metaphysical supply store, fully equipped with crystals, custom-carved candles, and the like. Moonchild did well for a while, but where we lived, a small business that wasn't popular or part of a chain didn't really see too many customers. After twenty months of staying open, I had to make the tough executive decision to close. We slowly started to fall behind on our house payment. Then, because bad news always comes in threes, my world was turned upside down when my dad called my mom and asked her to come home. Though it wasn't because he loved her or missed her. It was because he was sick, and he needed help.

Gavin Drake was as stubborn and prideful as they come. I know this well because I'm the same way. I knew him reaching out to Mom for help couldn't have been easy, which meant he must've been really sick. And I wasn't wrong.

My dad was diagnosed with pancreatic cancer, and it was like a blow to the chest, realizing someone you thought would be around forever wouldn't be around for much longer at all. It made me realize how foolish I was to let our relationship dwindle, especially when I didn't know how much longer I'd have him in Luna's and my life.

So Mom and I made the decision to go back to Dunsmuir for a while. I hadn't kept up with the town since I'd washed my hands of Endymion and everyone else when I left for college. The only person I kept in touch with was my longtime friend, Julia.

We made time for weekly calls and Sunday FaceTime chats. Next to her grandfather, Julia is Luna's favorite person on the planet. Not that I blame her. Julia has always been the loud to my quiet, the vibrant to my dull, the goddamn peanut butter to my jelly. She's flown out to Pasadena on rare occasions. Though I don't see her half as much as I'd like to. Whenever we talk, we steer clear of the subject of Endymion. She's known about my crush since the moment I came home from the bakery and called her, word-vomiting every single detail. Julia knows all about my heartbreak. She just doesn't know the man who fathered my child is, indeed, Endymion Black.

To avoid dealing with the mistakes of my past, my father almost always flew out to see us. It was too hard to go back there, but now, we had to. Luna doesn't know much about her papa, but she knows enough. During major holidays and FaceTime calls are usually the only time she gets to see him, and believe me when I say, they're practically inseparable during those times. She adores my dad, and my dad adores her. Even though our relationship is still somewhat strained, there isn't a doubt in my mind that he loves his granddaughter.

So that is where we are, packing up our lives from the past almost six years and heading to the one place I promised I'd never step foot in again. I have no idea if Luna's father is still there or what he's doing with his life. I can only hope all this won't explode in my face.

To top it all off, I'm moving back in with my parents. I'm not sure how we'll all survive.

"Mommy?"

"Yeah, baby?"

"Is this our new house?"

I pause, my hand hovering over the cardboard box filled with most of our belongings. Since we got here, I've been trying to unpack as quickly as possible, just to help smooth the transition. Luna spent most of her time with my dad. The second we walked through the doors, she screamed out, "Papa!" and ran straight into his arms. My little Luna has always loved spending time with my dad. Whenever we were together for the holidays, she stayed seated on his lap from the time he got there to the time he left. The bond they share is a lot like the bond I had with my dad before the distance and my pregnancy came between us. When I watch them together, I get this twinge in my chest. It's equally beautiful and heartbreaking all at once.

Because even though I hate to give it any more thought than necessary, I don't know how long he'll be around for Luna, and I can only imagine how devastated she'll be when that time comes.

I hate that the only reason we're back here is because my father is sick. I should've done more to bring us together as a family. I should've made more time to fly out here and see him instead of making him come to us. *Why hadn't I tried harder?*

The thought of losing my father makes me sick. It turns my stomach and stops my heart all at once. I'm not ready. I don't think I'll ever be ready to deal with that kind of loss.

Snapping out of my thoughts, I remember the question Luna asked. Settling the stack of shirts on the bed, I shift toward her and blow out a sigh.

"In a way, yes. We're going to stay here with Nana and Papa for a while."

She looks thoughtful for a second, her head cocked to the side. "Can we stay here with Papa forever?"

I trap my bottom lip between my teeth, trying to stop the quiver of my chin and hold it together. Turning back to the box, I blink rapidly, forcing the moisture out of my eyes.

"Yeah, baby. We'll stay here as long as Papa wants us to. Deal?"

I can practically hear her unsuspecting grin in her voice. "Deal."

"You want to help me unpack now?" I ask, glancing back at her.

She purses her lips, shaking her head. "No. Papa said he was gonna take me to get ice cream and then some cake from your favorite store. He even said he'd take me to the store to pick out an early birthday present soon!"

I grin. "Oh, really? You haven't even had lunch yet. And your birthday isn't for another two weeks, little miss."

May first is right around the corner, and with the new move, I'm still not sure what I will do to celebrate her birthday. I had it all planned out the year prior, but it's funny how quickly the course of life can change. I never thought I'd be here, celebrating my daughter's sixth birthday in a place that quite literally makes me queasy when I think about it.

She laughs and skips away. "I know, Mommy."

I shake my head, going back to unpacking.

Kids.

The house is eerily quiet without my dad and the sound of CNN playing in the living room, or Luna's vivacious little voice trailing about, constantly asking questions. I swear that girl is a sponge. She soaks in everything anyone says, and she's as nosy as they come.

I pad down the stairs, gripping the familiar railing, feeling another sharp pain in my chest. Everything in the house looks the same, almost like a shrine of when I was growing up, but at the same time, it doesn't. Over the years, my dad has added his own twists and flairs—you know, bachelor life and all.

His recliner still sits directly in line with his flat screen with the round coffee table off to the side holding his newspaper and sports magazine. There's even his half-empty coffee cup resting on the table right next to the coaster. The sight itself makes me smile. It used to drive my mom crazy that he wouldn't put his mugs on the coaster, especially when it was right there in front of him.

A frown suddenly pulls taut across my face when I think about my mother.

I should probably see how she's handling all this.

I pad into the kitchen, not surprised when I find her searching through Dad's fridge, likely trying to find something to make dinner with.

"I don't think anything new is going to pop out just by staring in there, Mom."

She shoots me a glare over her shoulder. With a sigh, she shuts the fridge door and slaps her hands along her thighs helplessly.

"There is nothing of sustenance in there. We'll need to go grocery shopping. There's no way we can live off jelly, Spam, and sandwich meat. I mean, seriously, how has your father made it this long without starving to death?" She starts throwing open cabinets and cupboards, clearly exasperated.

I lean against the back counter, scrutinizing her closely, knowing exactly why she's blowing the food situation out of proportion.

"It's okay to feel weird here, Mom. It's okay to feel…however it is you're feeling. You haven't been back in this house for years. I get it. This is a weird change for all of us."

My mom pauses in front of the cupboard that holds the mugs. She grips onto the handle so tightly, I'm afraid the polished silver will crumble in her grip. When she hunches forward and a raw sound escapes her throat, my heart cracks open.

Oh, Mom.

"Why didn't he tell me sooner? Why did he wait so fucking long to ask for my help? That stubborn, stubborn man. Did you see him? God, if he would've reached out sooner, I could've…we could've done something."

I do my best to blink back my tears, but they fall anyway. Because I know exactly what she means. I didn't realize how bad my father was looking until I saw him in person today. It's been about two months since we've last seen each other in person, and the change is drastic. He looks tired and skinnier than I ever remember my father being. He doesn't look like himself, and the reality that the man I've looked up to my entire life is slowly deteriorating breaks my heart.

Closing the distance between us, I wrap my arms around my mom's middle, hugging her from the back. I feel her shaking in my arms, and I know she blames herself for not being here. I don't think either of us anticipated how difficult it would be to come back here.

"I hate him. But I still love him, you know?" she chokes out. I slam my eyes shut, tightening my grip on her.

"I know, Mom. I know."

It takes her a few minutes to gather herself, and when she does, she pats my hands secured around her waist to silently let me know she's okay now. When she turns to face me, her eyes are red and puffy, but she sails through, wiping the remnants of her tears away.

"I'll start making that grocery list. I think your father said he wanted pizza tonight, so we'll call that in."

She slips out of the kitchen in search of a pad of paper and a pen, and I release a heavy sigh now that I'm alone. We are only one day in, and I already feel emotionally wrecked. I'm not sure I can handle any more sadness for today.

Chapter Five

Endymion

I scratch at the back of my neck, brows furrowed as I try to figure out what the fuck I'm looking at. When my mother asked me to stop at the store and pick up "lightly sweetened" frosting for my sister's birthday cake, I didn't think this shit was going to be this hard.

I've been standing in this aisle for the past ten minutes rereading labels, looking for anything that sounds like what my mother is asking for. I have not found one label that says anything about sugar-free or lightly sweetened. I'm so close to saying fuck it and buying her a whole new goddamn cake from the bakery. It's what we used to do all the time for my birthdays anyway. But, of course, my sister is a bit more…extra. She's all about the healthy living, clean eating, let's eat kale for breakfast, lunch, and dinner type of lifestyle.

In a nutshell, she's a complete psychopath, who doesn't have taste buds.

Since moving to Dunsmuir from Lake Tahoe, my parents have always sent me to this grocery store to pick up a cake before heading home. It doesn't matter whose birthday or what occasion it is; it's become a tradition. It wasn't until recently that my sister started this healthy lifestyle, then to top it off, she went and reeled my parents in, too. Mom suddenly decided she wanted my dad to eat better, so she cut back on a lot of store-bought shit in favor of making it all herself. Their home has changed a lot since I was living there as a teen.

I'm startled out of my thoughts when a little hand reaches out in my peripheral. When I glance to my left, I spot a little girl, balancing on the shelves, reaching for the pink frosting. Her brown hair curtains her face, shielding her from view, so I can't gauge how old she is. But guessing by how tiny she is, she can't be older than four or five.

"Hey, kiddo. Do you need some help?"

She pauses and slowly lifts her face up toward mine, causing the curtain of hair covering her face to unveil her. My brows disappear into my hairline as I stare at the little girl. She looks almost identical to my sister's daughter, my niece, Valeria. With light brown hair that curls at the bottom, bright green, almond-shaped eyes with thick lashes, she looks like another little Black child running around.

I don't know if it's my imagination, but she looks so much like my niece did when she was younger, I find myself doing a double take, frowning down at her.

Her little nose, which is lightly dusted in freckles, crinkles. "My mommy says I shouldn't talk to strangers." Her tone is sassy, and it's all I can do not to laugh at her. Instead, I cross my arms over my chest, holding back my smirk.

"Your mommy sounds like a smart woman. Where is she?"

The little girl shrugs. "She's at home."

My brows pull down, and I glance around us. "So…how did you get here?"

"My papa took me."

"Okay, kid." I sigh, raking a hand through my hair. It would be just my luck that I run into a lost child at the grocery store while I'm supposed to be here picking up *one* thing. "You're gonna have to start making more sense. Where is your papa then?"

She shrugs. "I think he's buying a cake from the cake lady. He promised I could pick frosting to dip my strawberries in. Back home, me and Mommy always dipped our strawberries in frosting."

My mouth drops open, then closes as I try to process the heap of information she just dropped on me. *Whose kid is this?*

When she continues staring up at me expectantly, I glance toward the frostings, then back down at her sassy little form. "So the pink one?"

A grin spreads across her whole face, and once again, I frown, thinking about my sister and my niece. With a shake of my head, I reach for the pink frosting and hand it to her.

"Luna?"

We both turn at the deep voice. A crease forms between my brows when I spot Gavin Drake from the two-story on Sunflower Lane. Over the past few years, Gavin has become a close friend. I've helped him with a few minor repairs in the house, and we make a point to grab a beer together whenever we get a chance. Hell, I've worked on his car a few times, back when I used to work at the garage. I only managed to work there a few years before I had to quit. I couldn't stand working there a second longer, and it was exactly the nudge I needed to do something else with my life.

I've always been good with my hands, so my parents suggested I do something in carpentry. I worked with a small company a few towns over for about two years before I went back to school and got my business degree. I've never wanted to answer to someone else, especially not when it comes to a job that I know I can do myself, so I decided to start my own company. About three years ago, I started my own construction company with a few of my buddies from high school. Landon, Griffin, and Bishop have been longtime friends for years. Each of us brings something different to the company table. Griffin is our contracts guy, Landon is our numbers guy, Bishop and I are all architecture and brawn, and together, we're an effortless team that always gets the job done.

We've been the main construction company in the county for the past three years, a year after opening. The good news about our work spread like wildfire, and the jobs started coming in left and right. For the most part, we keep our clientele local to avoid travel costs, but the company has been doing so well that Griffin suggested we expand after he received numerous inquiries about bigger contracts.

Now, we keep the small stuff local, and we travel for the bigger contracts with our team of guys. It's a dream job, one I never thought I'd be able to accomplish. For a long time, I thought my father would be upset about me not working with him at the garage, but he understood better than anyone how important doing something meaningful with my life was.

A smile takes over Gavin's face, and he pulls me into a hug, slapping me heartily on the back.

"Endymion, son, how are you? Thank you again for dinner and beers the other night. I appreciate it."

I wave him off, hating how fragile the man felt in my arms just now. I don't remember exactly when it happened, but at some point, Gavin became a big part of my life. I care about the man like he's family. Hell, my parents love him, too. They invite him over for Sunday dinners and family gatherings, and most of the time, he shows up. Lately, though, everyone in town has been whispering about his health, and there's no hiding it now. I can clearly see Gavin truly is sick.

It first started off as little favors. I don't know what happened, and it's not something he's ever up to talking about, but one day, I remember Gavin having it all—a beautiful family, a beautiful wife and daughter—and then the next, he didn't have any of that. I knew his daughter, Selene, went off to college, but gossip started around town when his wife, Cece, just up and left and never came back.

It was tough to watch him fend for himself. He looked sad and lonely, and when the company was first starting out, he was one of our first projects and customers. I'll always be grateful to him.

After that, I went out of my way to make sure he had dinner or even just a place he could come hang out when he was tired of staying inside. Once we'd both get off work, I'd come over with a six-pack of beers, and we'd sit there on his newly refurbished porch and shoot the shit. We talked about trivial things, always steering clear of ourselves, but after growing more comfortable with one another, we delved deeper.

I learned he and his wife, Cece, didn't have the best marriage, and when she left, he always knew it was for the best, even though he regretted not fighting for her. Selene, who had a full ride to Caltech in Pasadena, had gotten pregnant and had to drop out in favor of community college. I could see the disappointment, but when he talked about his grandchild, I could also tell just how smitten he was with her, too.

The times he'd get back from visiting his family in Pasadena were always the hardest to witness because even though he was happy, a lingering loneliness always clung to him, because he was here, and they were there. It's been especially hard to watch the decline in his health. He tried to hide it at first and pass it off as not feeling well or a new diet, but after some time, I started putting two and two together. When he was frequently missing Sunday dinners with my family, my dad told me about some whispers he'd heard around town regarding Mr. Drake. It was the dreaded "C" word.

After one night of drinking together on his porch, he'd stumbled while getting inside and busted his chin. I drove him to the ER where he had to have stitches, and he finally came clean about the cancer. I could see the fear in his eyes. I could also see that he had no intention of fighting it, which I guess, I could understand. He didn't want to suffer any more than he already was. He just wanted his last moments here on earth to be his. I could respect that, but it didn't make that pill any easier to swallow.

I wave his thanks off for the other night. The nights we spend together are just as much for me as they are for him.

"I'm doing pretty good. I was just here to pick up some frosting for Freya's birthday when I ran into little miss here. She needed help getting down some pink frosting."

He grins, looking down at his granddaughter lovingly. The happiness radiating from him is something I haven't seen in a long while. It brings a smile to my face.

"Yeah, my daughter, Selene, is back in town from Pasadena, so little Luna will be around more often."

Once again, hearing the name Selene strikes something in the back of my mind. Flashes of green grass, the soft sound of the creek, and the distinct scent of something floral and fruity are there, but it's faint, tickling at the back of my mind. This happens often when I hang out with Gavin. I remember her from around town. She was younger and smart. Incredibly beautiful in a shy, wallflower kind of way. Oh, and she was obsessed with the moon. I remember specifically she'd always wear a moon necklace. It was her quirk. Really, it was the only thing that reminded me of her. The girl with the beautiful doe eyes who loved the moon.

"Did you get the strawberries, Papa?" The little girl's voice echoes.

Gavin chuckles. "Sure did, squirt."

"She's a cute kid."

"Yeah." He sighs, a small smile twisting across his lips as he watches her hop in place with excitement. "Her dad isn't in her life, but I swear, if you knew Luna, you'd know that doesn't slow her down."

A chuckle escapes my lips. "Oh, I believe it."

"See you around, End," Gavin says, taking Luna's hand in his and turning back down the aisle where he came from. Because his granddaughter is such a character, as they're walking away, she shoots a smile my way, mimicking her grandpa.

"*Yeaaah*, see you around, End."

With a quiet chuckle and a shake of my head, I turn back toward the frostings, and say to hell with it, grabbing the same pink frosting that Luna wanted, and head to the checkout.

After dinner and cake at my parents' place for my sister's birthday, I opt to call it a night and head home. I have to be up early for a job tomorrow. We have to work on the foundation for an add-on on a home renovation. They're expanding by about a hundred feet, which leaves more wiggle room for us to work.

On the drive home, I slow the company truck as I near the creek. For whatever reason, I've always been inexplicably drawn to this creek. There's nothing super special about it. There are some large logs scattered across the greenage, and wildflowers decorate the grass during the spring or summer. During the winter, it's nicer to look at in my opinion. Once the snow covers the thick blades of grass and the creek freezes over, it looks like a painting of what one would envision a winter wonderland to look like.

Over the years, though, the water has changed in color from a dark blue to a murky green. The Dunsmuir teens have taken to throwing garbage in it instead of the fucking trash cans.

The moon gleams over the water, practically calling to me for reasons that are unknown. I make the quick decision to park the truck on the roadside and hop out, wading through the long blades of grass toward the sound of rippling water. I pause upon the figure lying in the grass. My steps slow as I get closer. Part of me wonders if it's a homeless person—I wouldn't be all that surprised if it was. But when I make out the small, feminine figure, I toss that thought out altogether. At the sound of my footsteps, the woman shoots upright, glancing at me. I jerk to a halt, my eyes widening at the sight of who it is lying there.

"Endymion?" she whispers, shock written all over her face. I'm slightly taken aback by her face. I remember a lot about the young girl I share a birthday with. She was the town's good girl, quiet and beautiful with her obsession for the moon, but was she always so... ethereal? So goddamn beautiful? I can't help the way my eyes devour every inch of her skin, the planes and contours of her face. With long, brown hair that looks like it would be silky to the touch, and skin so white it almost looks porcelain here under the moonlight, she's captivating. In a white sundress that brings out the delicateness of her features and the red in her bee-stung lips, I can't seem to look away from her.

I startle, suddenly realizing how odd I must look, standing here, staring down at her without saying anything. "Uh, yeah." I clear my throat. "It's...Selene, right?" She nods, her pouty mouth still gaped in shock as she stares up at me.

"Mind if I sit?"

The second I ask the question, her face twists with disdain. If possible, she looks paler than ever. The pallor of her skin is a ghostly gray now. My brows tug down into a frown at her odd reaction.

"I can come back another time." I point aimlessly over my shoulder.

"No, no. It's fine." She shakes her head, plastering a fake smile across her perfect porcelain skin. I may not know everything that makes up Selene Drake, but she has one of those smiles. That's what I remember most, the way her smile could light up a whole room, but right now? That's the exact opposite of what she's giving me. I know a fake smile when I see one. Her color slowly starts to come back to her face, the majority settling in her cheeks, making them tint with color.

I don't know if it's the moonlight or the fact that I haven't gotten laid in weeks, but I suddenly find myself inexplicably drawn to this woman. I don't remember Selene being this grown up. She's fucking gorgeous here under the moonlight. The way the silver light bounces off her skin and hair is captivating.

I may not have paid much attention to her then, but I am now.

Lowering myself onto the open space of grass next to her, I prop my forearms on my knees and stare out at the creek. I fight the urge to shift toward her and stare, but I'm sure all that would do is freak her out. I can't help but want to look at her again, though, because I swear my mind is making her much more beautiful than she is. There's no way anyone can be that gorgeous or inspire such sudden whimsical feelings in a man.

As the silence and sounds of nature echo around us, I feel oddly more content sitting here beside this woman who I hardly know than I have in a long time. For so long, I've been so focused on work and the company, I don't remember the last time I've taken a moment to just sit and be.

It's different on the nights when I'm with her father because those nights are his. Those are his moments to vent and not feel so lonely, and I'm happy to do that for him.

"You back in town for a while? I ran into your dad at the Grab-N-Go earlier."

She clears her throat, tilting her head down a fraction, causing her curtain of silky dark hair to shield most of her face. It's like she's trying to hide from me. "Yeah. He's…he's not doing so well, so we're staying until further notice."

My brows dip, and I lean forward slightly, trying to look past the dark curtain. I can still make out the delicate features of her face, and there's no mistaking the worry that's pulling taut across her features.

"Yeah, I'm…I'm sorry. Your dad is a good man. It's really shitty."

She nibbles on her bottom lip anxiously. I can't tell if it's from my presence or the topic of discussion.

"He kept it from everyone for a while. Had to take him to the emergency room before I could pull anything out of him."

Slowly, she cranes her neck to look up at me through her thick lashes. Her dark hair and dark brows are such a contrast to her pale skin, and it's absolutely captivating.

"So you guys are…close?"

I nod, my gaze sweeping across her features. She has a light smattering of freckles that run across the bridge of her nose. Everything about her is so different from most women I know and most women in this town. From what I can tell, it doesn't look like she has on a speck of makeup, and where most women draw on their brows and cake their faces with that shit, Selene doesn't. Her brows are dark, thick, and bushy, yet they're shaped and cleaned up so well, they complement her face in ways that would never work on any other woman. Her eyes are large, almost too big for her face, but they give her an innocence that most women lack.

I realize I must be staring at her too hard because she quickly looks away, tucking a thick lock of hair behind her ear. "Yeah, well, we just found out ourselves. And if you don't mind," she says, turning to glance at me, "can you keep that between us? I don't know if he's officially told anyone in town yet, so just…just don't say anything."

I should probably tell her that half the town already knows, but the words never come. There's a long beat of silence as we stare at each other. And as I do, I'm reminded of the little girl from the store. Luna.

As I stare at her mother, I can see the resemblance, mainly the shape of their faces, the freckles dusting across their noses, but above all, whoever the father is, that's who she takes after. I start to wonder what kind of guy she'd found in Pasadena. What kind of guy would leave her, let alone leave his own kid?

As I drink her in and think of her daughter, the bright little ball of sass, I can't imagine any sane man would willingly walk away from either of them.

"You have my word. I won't say anything."

She smiles. It's a closed-mouth grin, but the effect it has on me is still impressive. It's breathtaking. *She's* breathtaking.

Lately, I don't spend much of my free time with women, and when I do, they're usually one-night stands. It's all I have time for these days. But Selene's smile starts in one corner of her mouth and tugs into a full-blown masterpiece that has me questioning my sanity. It has me wondering what it'd be like to have that smile directed at me, day in and day out.

How could I have missed her?

Was she always this enchanting?

Was she always this beautiful?

Slowly, the smile drops off her face when she whispers, "Why are you staring at me like that?"

The truth is, I don't know why I'm staring at her like this. I don't know why I can't seem to act like a regular person around her at this moment.

I consider kissing her, grasping her beautiful face in my hands and taking her red pouty lips with mine. And as I imagine it, I get this strange tingling at the back of my neck, a sense of déjà vu. My brows pull in as I regard her. There's a familiar tug in the air, one I'm unable to place. I can't help but wonder why she seems so familiar to me, but at the same time, she's not.

Why do I feel like if I were to kiss her, she'd taste sweet, like honey, and smell like strawberries? Her skin would be soft, fucking painfully soft, and her moan—

I shake my head, internally berating myself for that train of thought. What the fuck is wrong with me? Why can't I stop thinking of tasting her and touching her?

"Sorry." I chuckle, rubbing at the back of my neck. "You're just so…beautiful."

Once again, she nervously tucks loose hairs behind her ears, avoiding my gaze. We go back to looking out at the creek, but it only holds my attention for a little while. Unable to help myself, I look back at her, trailing my gaze across her profile. She looks deep in thought and upon closer inspection, maybe even a little sad. Her lips are tugged down into a small, barely there frown. I don't even think she realizes she's doing it.

"I met your daughter today. She's cute. How old is she?"

I watch it happen, the way her entire body goes rigid. The muscles near her mouth tighten, and the blood drains from her face for the second time in one night. I open my mouth, wanting to ask if she's okay, but when I drop my gaze down to her hands, I realize they're trembling. She's suddenly an anxious ball of fearful energy.

"I should probably get going," she murmurs, a slight edge to her tone.

A crease forms between my brows. "Yeah, all right. I'll see you around, I guess."

Without another word, she scrambles up from the grass and hurries away. She doesn't look back, not even once.

I spend a while just sitting here, staring out at the creek, trying to figure out why being here feels so familiar—feels so right. I've never actually sat out here. It's quite peaceful. I can clearly see why Selene would want to sit out here and look up at the moon.

Why is this place so familiar? I ask myself again.

When the answer doesn't come to me, I head home, needing to push all thoughts of this creek and the beautiful woman sitting in the grass out of my mind.

Chapter Six

Endymion

IT TURNS OUT, THE JOB I NEED TO WORK ON TODAY INVOLVES THE OBJECT OF my fantasies from last night. I had no idea the contract we'd be working on today was for Gavin. He didn't mention anything to me the other night or at the grocery store. He probably knew if he went through me, I wouldn't charge him, which definitely explains why he went through the other guys and purposely kept it hush-hush.

Last night, I couldn't get Selene out of my head. No matter how hard I tried, I couldn't force her from my mind. I thought about the way her gorgeous hair spilled over her shoulders and the way her smooth porcelain skin looked like it was begging to be touched. The freckles on her nose and her beautiful smile plagued me and my dreams. Though in my dreams, she wasn't wearing what she wore last night at the creek. She was dressed in jeans and a tank top, and she was receptive to my touch.

She begged me to touch her, to kiss her, to make her feel good. I woke up with a permanent hard-on after last night. The dream felt so real. I could practically taste her skin on my lips. I was imagining in vivid detail the rosy color of her nipples just before I took them into my mouth. The way her lower lips glistened for me, begging me to slide through them with my tongue. Her body was so tight, so perfect, I felt like absolute shit when I woke up because I knew it wasn't real life, and the chances of all that happening were slim.

Not only does she already have a kid, but she's also Gavin's daughter. He'd probably chop my balls off if I ever tried anything with her. He's damn right to be overprotective of her. She's gorgeous and has obviously been fucked over by the previous men in her life. I don't blame him, and I'm also not interested in pushing my luck with a sick man.

I hop down from my truck, slamming the door behind me, just as my buddy Bishop meets up with me as we near the porch landing.

"Why didn't you tell me the job was for Gavin Drake?"

He frowns, shooting me a look that clearly says *you know why*. When I raise an expectant brow, he blows out an agitated sigh.

"I didn't really think it mattered. Gavin asked me not to say anything because he knows how you are, so I respected the customer's wishes. This way you could just come in, no questions asked, and get the job done."

I avert my gaze, focusing on the two-story structure, without even bothering to deny it. He's right. They all know exactly how I am. There's no way I would've made Gavin pay for any of our services. I've never cared who the jobs belonged to when I took them before. It's always more money for the business, or helping someone in town and doing something I love. I see his point.

Shaking it off, I knock on the front door, and when Gavin answers, he's wearing a smug look on his face. He's obviously proud of himself for keeping this a secret. Noted.

I let Gavin show me around his place, though I'm familiar with most of the layout already. I listen to him as he explains what he wants while I go over the blueprints Griffin drew up for him. He wants to make the back section of the house bigger, and now, I understand why. It's for Selene and her daughter. It seems they'll be staying in town much longer than I originally thought. I make note of it, already tweaking possible ideas in my head. A lot of unnecessary walls take up extra space toward the back of the property, so if we knock those down, we can create extra space. With three bedrooms and two bathrooms, Gavin's place isn't the worst I've seen in terms of an expansion.

We head out to the backyard and go over a few more basic things with the rest of the guys before Gavin leaves us, letting us get to work. He walks back inside with a bit of a limp in his step. I can't help but frown after him.

"Let's get to work, man," Landon says, purposely slapping me on the back.

Bishop and I take measurements, and I start making a rough draft on the exterior blueprints of how far things would need to come out. If we knock down the back wall to extend, we'll need to get a permit if we extend too far. I'm deep in focus, running numbers through my head, when I suddenly hear the pitter-patter of small feet. With my pencil hovering over the prints, I glance up, and despite myself, I grin when I catch sight of the bleary-eyed little girl with the sleep-mussed hair.

She pushes through the screen door and pauses on the deck, taking in all the men working in the backyard. Gavin's also looking to landscape the backyard, no doubt for his granddaughter. Her face scrunches in dismay, and she furrows her brows when she looks at me, more than likely recognizing me from the grocery store. Padding down the steps, she pauses in front of Bishop and me. He watches her with a confused expression on his face. I don't blame him. The kid is an absolute trip.

"Hi."

"Hey, kiddo."

"My name's Luna."

I fight my grin. "I know. I met you yesterday, remember?"

She pouts, clearly not liking that I've corrected her. I cough back a laugh, correcting myself for her sake. "Hey, Luna."

She grins victoriously at how quickly I gave in. "Whatcha doing?"

I glance around pointedly. "Trying to work on the house for your grandpa."

"Why?"

"Because he wants more space for you and your mom?" I say it as more of a question than anything else. I shoot a wary glance at Bishop and Landon, who look as much out of their element as I do.

I obviously don't know much about kids. None of my buddies have them, and I only have one niece who's already closing in on nine years old.

"Can I have a playground?" She looks directly at Bishop when she asks this.

"Uh…" He shoots a chary glance at me, begging for my help.

"And what about a swimming pool? It can be my early birthday present." This time, she asks Griffin, and he looks just as uncomfortable as Bishop. It's comical.

"It snows here, Luna," I tell her, holding back my laughter. The look she shoots me is so dry, I feel like my skin is being chaffed with sandpaper.

"*Annnd*?" She raises her brow sassily, and all I can do is shake my head because Christ in heaven, this little girl is something else.

"Luna!"

We all turn at the sharp sound of Selene's voice. Her face, clean of any makeup, is just as beautiful as it was last night. Though now that I'm paying attention, she looks stricken. When I glance down, I can understand why. Four people who are practically strangers standing right next to her daughter outside would likely freak anyone out. If I were her father, I'd be a little concerned too.

Selene hurries down the back deck steps toward us. She must've just woken up because she's dressed in her nightgown with a flimsy robe tossed over it, and a pair of flip-flops are the only things adorning her feet. She skids to a halt in front of me and pulls Luna into her side. It doesn't escape my notice how she angles herself in front of her daughter as though she's shielding her from us.

So she's a momma bear. *I like that.*

Selene nervously licks her lips, darting her gaze around me and the guys, and subconsciously, she pats her hair, probably just now realizing it looks a little wild and untamed. It doesn't deter from her beauty, though. If anything, she looks hot in an ornery way.

"Your dad has us back here taking measurements for the expansion, sorry."

Her gaze darts to mine, and we stand there, staring at each other for a few suspended seconds. I feel Bishop, Landon, and Griffin looking back and forth between the two of us. Their gazes are drilling holes into the side of my head, and their unspoken questions swirl in the suddenly tense air between us.

Bishop clears his throat, and it seems to snap us both out of our daze.

"No. I'm sorry," Selene says quickly, shaking her head. "Don't apologize. I just…I just freaked out." She looks down at Luna, who's completely oblivious. Luna's too busy studying the rest of the guys, probably trying to come up with a plan in her head to get one of them to agree to build her a playground or a pool.

The kid's a fucking shark, I tell you.

"I get it. I was just going to walk her back inside with Gavin."

"No, you weren't," Luna singsongs, making us both laugh. Selene's lips twist ruefully, and I soak in everything about her. I follow the sudden trajectory of her hand. Delicately, she reaches around her neck for something, but it's bare.

I'm struck by the sudden realization that she's not wearing the necklace she constantly wore when she was a kid. That was the most vivid memories of our past. That damn moon necklace and that damn thick book she constantly carried around. Her hand flutters away, and she shifts on her feet, clearing her throat almost nervously.

"Well, we should probably head inside and leave you guys to it." She quickly glances at the rest of the guys, before looking back at me, her cheeks turning a bright shade of red. It's a struggle to hold back my grin at how cute she is.

"Mom," Luna groans at the realization that she won't be able to stay out here, and Selene rolls her eyes, sighing under her breath. I wonder how many times a day she does that? It wouldn't matter. I'd probably never tire of seeing it.

They leave as quickly as they came, and the guys and I stand around for a beat, trying to process how odd of a start our morning is off to.

"She's hot. That is a MILF I wouldn't mind becoming a stepfather for. I would let that woman ride my cock until—"

I can't help but glower at Griffin's comment. I shoot daggers at the side of his head, his gaze still intently focused on the door Selene and Luna disappeared through. In a knee-jerk reaction, I smack him upside the head. Instead of being angry with me, he laughs.

The fucking bastard.

Internally, I berate myself for my reaction to what Griffin said. I chalk it up to my friendship with Gavin. I respect the man too much. There's no way I'd ever allow anyone to disrespect his daughter. It has nothing at all to do with the fact she's gorgeous as all hell, and I don't want any of my men near her. Not even my best friends.

"Little girl looks familiar, no? I can't for the life of me figure out what it is."

I perk up at Bishop's comment. His gaze is also solely fixed on the back door she disappeared through, but at least he's wearing a confused expression instead of one filled with lust.

I nod absentmindedly. "I know. The first time I saw her, I swear I thought my sister had a kid she kept hidden from us."

"Weird," Bishop mumbles as he walks off.

Weird, indeed.

After measurements are confirmed, we break ground on the project. A few of the guys get to work on knocking down that back wall, and Griffin and Bishop are off to the side, cutting and measuring boards for the foundation we'll need for the expansion. I've been running back and forth from the truck, carrying supplies and doing my damnedest not to think about Gavin or his daughter.

This is such an odd situation. I've grown close to Gavin over the years. The man is like family to me, so why am I suddenly thinking about his daughter, his pride and fucking joy, sexually? It's wrong on so many levels. A part of me feels as though I'm disrespecting him with the thoughts alone.

I glance toward the back window again, and I don't even bother hiding my smirk when I spot the curtains bunched up in the corner from where Luna keeps peeking through. She's been doing it on and off, trying to get a better look at what we're doing. She tried to sneak out a few times, but Gavin, his wife, and Selene seemed to catch on to her sneaky ways. Plus, they understand how dangerous it is to have a kid back here. It's best she stays put and watches from there.

My smile slowly drops when I spot who's behind Luna, and instead, a foreign sensation builds in my chest. Selene stands there, behind her daughter, observing the guys working on the landscape. When her gaze finally lands on me, her eyes widen, and I swear, even from here, I can see the crimson staining her creamy cheeks. I wave at her because I'm suddenly back in high school, and it seems I have a fucking crush. And said crush seems to be just as taken aback. Selene is quick to snap the curtains shut, shielding me from view, and I can't help but chuckle, shaking my head as I get back to work.

After another hour and a half, we break for lunch, most of the guys leaving to eat, while the rest of us hang back. Griffin left to get us food from Rita's Diner. It's a staple here in Dunsmuir. No one does burgers like Rita.

We pause at the sound of soft, lilting laughter, and we all turn toward the source. Holding a tray filled with glasses of water is Cece, Gavin's wife.

"Hope you guys are thirsty. I brought my little helper with me."

And there, a few paces behind her, is Luna, her footsteps slow and sure. Her pink little tongue is peeking out between her lips in concentration as she tries not to drop the glasses of water. For whatever reason, the kid makes me smile.

"Is the heat getting to you boys yet?" Cece asks, when she finally reaches us, the remaining guys taking the offered glasses. Cece is a beautiful woman for someone in her late fifties. If it wasn't for the deep-set laugh lines and crow's feet around her eyes, you'd never guess her age. It seems the time away from her husband wears well on her. It's still hard to believe their relationship wasn't what the town always thought it was.

"Nah, not yet. We're managing, Mrs. Drake." She seems to come up short on the use of the name but recovers quickly.

"This weather make you miss the Pasadena weather?" Griffin asks. She arches a single brow at the question.

"Boy, you haven't felt heat till you've lived in Pasadena during the summer."

A slight tugging on my jeans has me glancing down to the little girl at my side. Luna stares up at me with those big doe eyes, an extra glass of water still in her hands.

"Here," she says, thrusting it at me, spilling some over the lip as she does so. I don't mind, though. I take the water with a gracious smile, and just to really drive the thirsty act home, I finish the whole glass for her, and her entire face lights up.

"Nana, look! He drank it all!"

Cece smiles down at her indulgently and shakes her head as she looks back and forth between us. "That one is just like her mother. Can't seem to steer clear of you. This little one has been yapping inside about you all day."

I ruffle Luna's hair, and she laughs like it's the funniest thing in the world. It takes me a few seconds to process her words, and when I do, my brows pull down, and I turn back toward Cece.

"What do you mean?"

"I just mean like mother like daughter. Selene always had the biggest crush on you, and now it seems our little Luna has grown attached to you, too."

The expression I'm wearing on my face must be one of confusion because Bishop and Landon laugh behind me. Bishop even goes as far as slapping me on the back as though he finds the situation hilarious.

"Oh, come on. You had to have heard talk around town over the years. And even if you didn't, it's always been kind of obvious. Well, at least to her father and me it was."

If possible, the frown on my face deepens. "What exactly?"

"The day you moved into town, Selene damn near fell in love with you."

If I had water in my mouth, I would've done a spit-take. *What the hell is she talking about?*

Cece frowns. "You mean you never noticed? Hell, I think my little Selene thought you two would get married one day. She had the biggest crush on you. Since that first night you rolled into town, she'd been doodling your last name in notebooks till she turned eighteen. Funny how life works out, isn't it?"

With a parting smile, she calls after Luna, who goes running after her grandma, and I watch her leave, trying to process her words.

Selene used to have a crush on me.

Well, damn. Ain't that something?

How did I never see it before? And why didn't I ever notice?

Chapter Seven

Selene

"Mommy!" Luna yells as she runs inside the house. She went on a water run for the guys with my mom, and obviously, it didn't help her burn off any of this extra energy she seems to have today, of all days.

I should probably take her to the park, but I still have so many boxes to unpack, and with the guys working on the back, there's no way I can take her back there to play.

And honestly, with how close we are to Endymion, it's making me anxious. I'm pushing my luck here, I know this, but I don't know what else to do. He just keeps popping up when I least expect him to. I mean, honest to God, how was I supposed to know he was going to have his own construction business? How was I supposed to know he and my father have built some weird sort of bond while I've been away? How was I supposed to know he decided to stay in Dunsmuir for good?

It's all too much to process. I'm starting to get a headache from all of it.

And that is just the start of the issues suddenly presenting themselves left and right. Another is my crush I thought I buried six years ago when I had my heart broken. It seems I was wrong, because the way my heart and body react when I'm near Endymion now? That's not the way people act when they're around someone they don't care about. My stomach dips and flips when he's near, and I can still feel his hands on me, his lips on my bare skin, and his firm body hovering over mine as though I'm being transported back in time. My eyes slam shut as the memories flood my brain. It's been so long, you'd think they'd be grainy at best, but the feel of his lips against my skin is as clear as if it were happening this instant.

Those are definitely not the thoughts of someone who has moved on.

It doesn't help that he looks better now than he did when we were younger, if that is even possible. Everything about him is different, yet it's still the same. Though matured, his features are the same as they were six years ago, just somehow better now, a little more rugged. He seems taller, broader, and I am sure he has muscles in places one shouldn't even need muscles. His arms are thick and muscular, the veins protruding from his tan skin. I'm sure he probably stays in shape from his job, and even though I try to stop the train of thought, I can't help but imagine him at work, his hot, sweaty body, the muscles rippling—

Stop it! I chide myself internally. *Now is not the time to be fantasizing about this man.*

His voice is deeper and raspier than I remember it being all those years ago, too. If I thought he had a sexy voice then? He has the kind of voice now that probably has women dropping their panties with one word.

And I hate him for it.

Why couldn't he have gotten fat and ugly in the past six years?

Does he really have to be so handsome?

It all feels so unfair.

I worked so hard to forget about him—to bury my feelings, my torment, and all my hurt—to care for our daughter and give her a good life, but it feels as though the universe is somewhere looking down at my predicament and laughing at me by bringing us together like this again.

Because I'm sure if he ever finds out the truth, I'll see a side of Endymion I never thought possible.

Over the years, I considered reaching out to him and explaining, but each time, I'd talk myself out of it. I mean, what was I really going to say to him?

Hey, we had sex one night when you were blackout drunk, and you took my virginity and got me pregnant. Oh, and meet your daughter, Luna.

Throwing that on him like that never felt right to me. Though it's not like hiding it from him has made it any better. A part of me worries about what he'll think of me. Will he think I'm lying about him being drunk? What if he doesn't believe me? He doesn't even know who I am, so what if he misinterprets my crush on him as something obsessive?

It also didn't help matters that, at the time, when he was still with Holly and I was nursing a broken heart, I didn't know how to explain it to him without making him out to be a scumbag cheater.

Because in my adolescent mind, that's exactly what he had morphed into.

I didn't know it at the time, but supposedly, Holly and Endymion weren't together the night it happened. Sure, they were friends with… benefits, but apparently, Holly had a lot of those, and End was just one of them. Julia told me all this one night when I broke down, needing information on everything that was going on back home. Julia and my father were the only ties I still had to Dunsmuir, to Endymion, and it wasn't really like I could ask my father anything about End.

Things are getting messy, and I can quite literally feel the train going off the tracks. We're derailing, and I have no clue how to fix this. How to fix any of it. Because, even though I know all hell will break loose when I do it, I *want* to tell him. I want him to know Luna is his daughter. I just don't know how.

How do you tell someone he's missed six years of his child's life and it's all your fault?

"Mommy, guess what?" Luna skids to a halt in front of me, vibrating with energy.

"Hmm?" I pause, tapping my pointer finger on my chin and looking up at the ceiling for answers. "Chicken butt?"

Luna tosses her head back and laughs. "No, silly. Nana says you were in love with End!"

My eyes widen, and I choke on air.

End?

End?! When did my daughter start calling Endymion by his nickname, End? I scan the room for my mother, who's standing off to the side, rolling her eyes.

"I said no such thing."

"Yeah, you did!" Luna retorts, snitching on her grandmother. "You told him that Mommy had a *huuuge* crush on him when she was little."

My stomach revolts and mortification weighs heavily on my chest, making it hard to breathe. "Mom!" I gasp, enraged that she'd feel the need to say anything at all. So what if I had a huge crush on the guy when I was younger? Does she really think I want him to be reminded of that? Especially now, years later?

It's not totally her fault since she doesn't know the truth, either. Everyone thinks Luna's father is a guy from Caltech. No one bothered to do the math or question who it could have been. Why would they? It was me we were talking about—boring Selene who no one noticed. Sweet Selene who would never lie about anything. My parents were so consumed by the rocky state of their marriage that they didn't question the logistics. They didn't question me or any of it.

Oh, how times have changed.

"My goodness, Selene. What's the big deal? Your crush on him wasn't exactly a secret."

"Yeah, it was, Nana."

My mom narrows her eyes down at Luna. "All right, little girl. That's the last time you go on a water run with me."

"Awww!" Luna groans, and I can tell by her tone that she's close to throwing a tantrum. I should probably stop the fit before it begins, but I'm too fixated on my mother to do so.

"What does she mean?" I cross my arms over my chest.

"Endymion didn't know you had a crush on him all those years ago." She shrugs like it's no big deal when, in fact, it is a big fucking deal. I feel my body flame with anger. I glance toward the window where the guys are sitting around on their break. My stomach jolts violently when I realize End is looking at the window, too. He's shirtless, the tan lines of his body are on full display, and I can make out his six-pack even from here. *Jesus Christ*. My mouth goes dry the longer I stare, so I move away from his distracting body, dragging my gaze upward.

That's a mistake.

Our eyes lock, and suddenly, this strange current of electricity zings through my body. Now that I know he knows, I can't help the way my face heats with embarrassment. I wish the ground would just swallow me whole.

Want to know what's worse than your longtime crush never knowing how you felt about him?

Him finding out years later.

Yeah, that's worse.

I quickly look away and do my best to ignore the way my body is suddenly trembling over this news. This is bad. He knows I had a crush on him.

God, this is so damn embarrassing!

"What's going on in here?" Dad asks, walking into the kitchen. Luna runs into his arms, and when I see the wince and hear the hiss of pain that leaves him when he catches her, I make a mental note to speak to her tonight about being careful with her grandpa.

"Oh, nothing." I sigh. "Mom is just hell-bent on ruining my life."

My dad shoots a questioning glance at my mom, and she shakes her head at him, having a silent conversation. "I brought up her crush on Endymion, and now she's acting like it's the end of the world."

My dad chuckles. "Well, hopefully it won't be too awkward for you tonight then, Selene. We're having dinner with Endymion at the steakhouse."

My mouth gapes.

Heart pounds.

Bile rises up my throat.

Oh, joy.

Kegman's Steakhouse is one of the staples here in Dunsmuir. Usually when tourists are here during the winter months to see the snow or during the summer months to see the multitude of waterfalls, this place is packed. Locals normally steer clear during those times. At other times throughout the year, like tonight, it's not too bad.

I'm a sweaty, nervous ball of energy while I try to mentally prepare myself for how tonight may go. My heart pounds wildly in my chest as we're led to a table big enough to seat all of us. Of course, End is already here, looking as handsome as ever. Dressed in a red and black flannel over a white T-shirt that shows off his broad chest, he looks effortlessly casual. There's something so rugged and manly about him now that he didn't necessarily have when he was a rebel teen.

I remember so many things about End, but after spending so many years trying to forget the details, trying to forget every part of him, now that he's here in the flesh, all those thoughts and feelings are rushing back. They're bombarding my brain at full speed, filling my headspace with the most confusing thoughts.

Under the dim lights of the restaurant, his hair looks more of a sandy blond rather than its usual light brown, and it's long enough now that it curls at the ends, near the nape of his neck, where his flannel collar is. There's a light smattering of scruff dusted along his prominent jaw that I didn't notice earlier. It's almost as if he missed one day of shaving, and this is the outcome, a perfectly stubbled jawline.

When we approach the table and his emerald gaze locks with mine, my stomach flips. An airy sensation fills my chest, like someone is blasting cool air into my lungs. I quickly avert my gaze, clearly unsettled by how handsome he is.

"Hey, End. Hope we didn't keep you waiting too long," Dad says, as he sits next to him. Endymion waves him off.

"Not at all. Just got here myself."

I pause when it comes time for me to sit. With my hand tightly gripped around Luna's, I only have two options: sit across from Endymion or make my mother sit across from him. One would think their own mother would take the seat across from Endymion to make things less awkward. Of course, that's too much to ask.

"Selene, sweetie, hurry up and sit." I shoot a nasty glare at my mom over my shoulder, and my anger with her only grows when I notice the knowing gleam in her eyes.

What a shit.

I slide into the seat across from Endymion, and I settle Luna into the spot next to me. I suddenly feel like my skin is itchy and on fire, and I can't seem to stop fidgeting. I have to keep fighting the urge to look up at End and stare, but instead, I force my gaze down, opening my menu and pretending to be deep in thought.

Dad and End start talking logistics of the expansion on the house, and I pretend the sound of End's voice doesn't stir something deep and primal inside me.

He broke your heart, Selene.

He is not a swoony character in a romance novel.

"Mommy, can I sit with End and Papa?" Luna asks, snapping me out of my fake menu browsing.

My head jerks up at her question, and without permission, my gaze swings to End. He's scrutinizing me much too closely for my liking. I feel his gaze burning into my flesh, marking me. I break out in a sweat and quickly look away, back down at Luna.

"Oh, I don't know, baby. I think he wants to eat in peace—"

"I don't mind," Endymion cuts in, and I hear Luna's victorious hoot as she fist bumps the air. It's on the tip of my tongue to tell her no. This isn't a good idea for so many reasons. I glance back up toward End, and my stomach dips. He seems sincere, as though he actually wants to have my daughter bug him while he eats.

Err—his daughter.

God, this is so screwed up.

What have I done?

I nod down at Luna, unable to voice my answer because of how guilty I'm suddenly feeling. It's suffocating. I feel like I can't breathe. A heavy weight sits on my chest, and it feels like if I make one wrong move, the weight will crack my sternum open and kill me. It only gets worse as I watch my daughter—our daughter—settle between her father and my father. It strikes me then, just how much she really does look like Endymion. They're practically twins sitting there next to each other. And the smile gracing Luna's face as she talks his ear off? It's wider than I've seen in a really long time.

Lately, she's been asking more and more about her father, and each time, it's like a chip to my battered heart. It's killing me to keep the truth from everyone, especially now. It all feels so…wrong. I thought I'd made the right choice, but clearly, I was wrong, and I see that now. Sitting across from Endymion and lying to them both is breaking my heart.

Pressure builds in my nose, and my eyes start to water when

End says something to Luna that makes her laugh. It's such a beautiful, lilting, carefree sound—it's so her. When I feel a sudden wave of emotion roll over me, I rapidly blink, trying to keep the tears at bay.

"I'll be back. I need to use the restroom," I just about choke out.

The legs of my chair scrape the floor as I push away from the table and hurry into the bathroom. Thankfully, it's empty, because the minute I step over the threshold, I fall apart. I cup a hand over my mouth and slam my eyes shut, letting the tears roll down my cheeks in hot torrents.

I've fucked up.

I kept a man, a good man, away from his child.

I kept my daughter away from her father.

All for what, my pride? Because I had a broken heart?

Even if I do try to fix this now, everyone will hate me. I'll be turned into the monster. The woman who kept Endymion's child from him. He's going to hate me. And what will happen when he tries to fight me for custody of her? How am I going to justify my actions in court? I'll lose her.

And I can't lose her.

That little girl is my entire life and then some.

My hands tremble as I place them on the edges of the sink for support. I bow my head, trying to figure out how to fix this. I just need to take a few days to figure out how to break the news to Endymion, then to Luna. My parents are going to be so disappointed in me when they find out, but I can't think about that right now.

Inhaling a shaky breath, I stand upright, squaring my shoulders and wiping my face clean of tears. I look like a mess. My eyes are puffy and bloodshot, and my nose is red. I look like Rudolph. There is no way I can hide my mess of a face from anyone, once I step foot out of this bathroom.

Thankful that my purse is still strapped around my shoulder, I dig through it, searching for anything that can help me look at least a fraction more put together than I do now. The universe must feel bad for laughing at me as often as it does because I get lucky when I find a tube of mascara and some tinted moisturizer. I squirt some lotion and rub it into my skin, breathing a sigh of relief when I see it covers most of the redness. I'm a little wary when I apply the mascara. I have no clue how long it's been in my purse, and I wouldn't be all that surprised if I woke up tomorrow with a sty on my lash line.

Would serve me right, I guess.

With one last glance in the mirror, semi-satisfied with how I look, I walk out, trying to remind myself to hold my head high and just focus on getting through tonight. I don't need to worry about anything else other than getting through the rest of this dinner—

My breath gets knocked out of me when I slam into a hard wall. Only I realize when I glance up that it's not a hard wall at all. It's Endymion. His hands shoot out, gripping my upper arms to steady me, and my breath leaves me in a whoosh, like someone sucker punched me in the gut and stole the air straight from my lungs. His hands are like hot coals, burning through every layer of my skin, incinerating my flesh. When our gazes clash, I feel a shock roll through my system, part painful, part enticing.

There's a long beat when we stand there, his hands still on me, and we just stare at each other. I lick my suddenly dry lips, and his eyes dip, following the movement. My heart pounds an aggressive staccato, a riot of emotions happening inside my body. I take a sudden step back from End, and his hands fall away from my arms. I miss the heat of his touch immediately.

He suddenly frowns down at me, taking notice of my face and the puffiness around my eyes. Taking a step toward me, he bends just a bit, trying to meet my eyes. "Hey, you okay?"

I trap my bottom lip between my teeth and bite down while I nod my head. I don't trust myself to say anything. It's best if I keep my mouth shut. Because the way things are sounding in my head at the moment? I'm on the verge of telling him everything right here, right now in the hallway of a steakhouse outside of the bathrooms.

He deserves better than that.

Luna deserves better than that.

"Did something happen—?" he starts to ask, but we both startle at the voice a few feet to the right of us.

"Selene? Is that you?" My brows tug down at the inquisition, and I turn toward the source. "Hell, it is you. I thought you left Dunsmuir years ago?"

"James?" I cough, choking on my saliva.

What the hell is happening right now?

James was one of my first boyfriends in town, even though we never shared a kiss or basically did anything other than hold hands. He always knew about my crush on Endymion, which makes me standing here with Endymion, of all people, so damn awkward. The breakup wasn't on the best of terms. He called me an idiot for pining after someone who'd never love me back, and honestly, he wasn't wrong.

"God, how long has it been?" he asks, grinning at me. It seems he hasn't taken notice of Endymion yet.

"Almost six years. I was in Pasadena for a while. I'm back now but not sure for how long."

James's grin widens. "That's great. You look…wow, you look beautiful, Selene."

His gaze travels up and down my body, lingering on my face, and a tremble wracks my body with embarrassment. I quickly glance at Endymion out of the corner of my eye, and he's watching the entire interaction with an odd glower on his face. He crosses his thick arms over his chest, scrutinizing James.

I tuck stray hairs behind my ear, feeling uneasy. Everything about this interaction feels awkward. "Thank you," I mumble, shifting on my feet.

"We should get together sometime. Hang out and catch up."

At this, Endymion clears his throat, and James finally takes notice of him. His eyes widen, and they dart back and forth between us, as though he's slowly processing the situation.

"I don't have much free time on my hands these days. I have a five-year-old to keep up with," I say, trying to let him down easily.

His brows shoot up into his hairline, shock registering on his face. "Holy shit, you have a kid?" He looks down at my body pointedly. "Wow. I mean, you'd never be able to tell. You look great."

Universe, please just swallow me whole now. Please, for the love of God.

"Wait, are you two...Did you two finally get together? I guess that crush you had on him finally paid off, right?" James points at Endymion and me. My mouth drops open in shock, and when I look at Endymion for help, he's biting back a smile, as though he suddenly finds all of this funny. He peers down at me, and I can clearly see the mirth dancing in his gaze.

"No. We're...He's just...No." I shake my head, unable to form a single articulate sentence. James frowns at this, obviously noticing how flustered I am.

"Well, if that's the case, and you really are single, I'd love to take you out sometime." Without giving me a chance to respond, James pulls me into a hug that lingers about five seconds too long. "I'll see you around, Selene." I watch him walk away, my jaw still unhinged as I work to process what just happened.

What are the odds of running into James while I'm with Endymion, of all people?

God, I hate small towns.

I risk a glance at Endymion, expecting to find him smirking still, but he's not smirking now at all. His gaze is narrowed on James's retreating back as if he's angry.

What the hell does he have to be angry about?

"We should probably head back," I mumble, drawing his attention back to me. Instead of moving, he just stands there, his gaze searching mine. The way he regards me makes me feel exposed. It's unsettling. I feel as if he's seeing everything when he looks at me. And when one is hiding as many secrets as I am, that is a dangerous thing.

Figures.

For once in my life, I feel like Endymion is finally seeing *me*, and surprisingly, it's not what I want anymore.

Or at the very least, that's what I tell myself.

"Right," he breathes, nodding his head, as if he's having an intense conversation with himself.

On the way back to our table, I swear, conversations cease as we pass others. I can feel their eyes on us. It has my neck prickling with awareness and discomfort.

"Everyone keeps staring at us," I whisper under my breath, suddenly feeling panicked. I feel Endymion step closer as we weave through the tables. His body heat warms me from head to toe, and his proximity and distinct smell percolate around me, making my heart skip beats dangerously.

"Not looking at us," Endymion murmurs, bending near my ear. His warm breath ghosts across the back of my neck, and a quiver rips down my spine. A small, inaudible gasp escapes my lips. "They're looking at you."

Goosebumps.

I swing my gaze up to his as we near our table, unsure if I heard him right.

"Me? Why would they be looking at me?"

The corner of Endymion's mouth quirks, and the effects of that small movement hit me square in the chest. "Why wouldn't they be looking at you?" he counters, with so much heat in his eyes that I break into a sweat and have to look away.

I damn near scramble back into my seat once we reach our table. I can feel my parents' questioning gazes on me, but I pretend not to notice.

Just act natural.

Be normal.

"Mommy. You look like a tomato," Luna announces to the whole table.

My eyes slam shut, and I have to fight the urge to slide down the chair and hide underneath the table.

Oh, my sweet girl. You're too honest sometimes.

Chapter Eight

Selene

THE REST OF DINNER GOES OFF WITHOUT A HITCH. WELL, FOR everyone else at least. I'm still a nervous, jittery mess. Every time Endymion looks my way, I'm quick to look at anything and anyone else, and I pretend I don't notice. Though it's obvious I do because the flaming in my face gives me away. Every. Single. Time. I can tell he tries to fight his laughter where I'm concerned.

I notice the multiple times his mouth quirks up as though he's enjoying the way he's making me fidget in his presence. As much as I try not to pay it any mind, I can't help but notice the way he stares at me unabashedly during dinner. It obviously doesn't escape my mother's notice either. She's grinning like the Cheshire cat.

My parents try to engage me in conversation throughout the night, but for the most part, I keep it short and simple, not wanting the spotlight on me. I'm just trying to make it through the rest of the night unscathed.

I'd say the highlight of tonight is studying Endymion and Luna together. He's effortless with her, and she seems drawn to him. That's the peak and downfall of my night, watching the way he interacts with her. I get a dull throb in my chest when I see his smile or hear his laughter. It's so carefree. It hurts because he has no clue the little girl sitting next to him is his daughter.

At some point during the night, I glance at my mother, who is darting her gaze back and forth between Luna and End. I expected her to have that annoying grin on her face, but color me surprised when I realize she's frowning at them. And when she looks at me, I can see the wheels churning in her head.

This is not good.

Thankfully, Dad keeps the conversation moving throughout dinner. It doesn't escape my notice, though, how he pushes the food around on his plate. He's been doing it at almost every meal, pretending to eat, making his plate look like he's touched more of his food than he actually has. Worry seizes my gut. It's the little things like this that make his illness seem more daunting. It really is happening and there is nothing I can do to stop it.

It feels as if it's life's curse—watching the person who brought you into this world fall apart. It's a simple and painful reminder that life is so much shorter than any of us imagine.

My dad asks Endymion about his family, checking on them to see how they're doing. Apparently, Dad spends a lot of time with them for birthdays and family barbecues. It makes me feel guilty for leaving him here on his own.

How lonely was he without Mom and me here?

Why didn't he reach out sooner?

Those are just a few of the questions that run through my head during dinner. I also learn a few things about End that I didn't know before tonight. It's weird. I spent so much time crushing on this man, trying to steal moments and time with him, and now that I'm not vying for his attention, he's everywhere. I spent so much of my time chasing him, trying to get him to notice me, and now that I've given up that pursuit, he's fallen back into my life, almost on a silver platter of sorts.

He has a niece of his own. His sister, Freya, got pregnant at a young age, too, though, unlike me, she eventually married the baby's father. It made me equal parts happy and guilty to learn about his niece. I tried to make myself believe that at least I didn't have to feel too bad about keeping their granddaughter a secret and depriving them of a grandchild because they already had one. But as soon as that thought passed, the guilt slammed into me because, yes, I should feel bad about what I'm doing. I am depriving grandparents of a grandchild. I am depriving End of a relationship with his daughter, but I think what hurts me the most is realizing I am depriving my pride and joy of so much more love. She has a slew of other people out there who would love her fiercely.

It only makes me hate myself more by the time the night comes to an end.

I am exhausted when we all say good night. I've spent so many years suppressing my emotions that they all seemed to bubble to the surface during dinner. It was tiring to pretend everything in our little orbit was okay, when really, nothing was. And chances are, when the truth comes out, nothing in our lives will ever be okay again. With a lingering stare, that lasts a few beats too long, I say goodbye to End, hoping that, somehow, I'll be able to make this right.

When I tuck my sweet girl into bed, I lie beside her and watch her sleep, tracing the planes of her soft features that are identical to Endymion's. The only attributes she got from me are the freckles and her nose. Everything else is all Endymion.

She doesn't have the blinding pale skin that I have. There is a golden tint to her skin that comes from Endymion. Endymion's mom was born in Greece, so he truly is my version of a Greek god. Her beautiful eyes are a shade darker than her father's, but the resemblance in color is still striking. Her hair color and texture are another thing she inherited from him.

With a soft lingering kiss on her forehead, I keep my lips rested against her skin. A smarting sensation pierces my heart and a shot of lightning strikes my soul.

"I'll make it right, baby. I promise."

Quietly, I close the door to my old bedroom, leaving it cracked. Everything feels so heavy. There's so much on my mind; I just want to sit in peace for a little while and think. Think about the future. The past. What comes next.

I ask my mom and dad to keep an eye on Luna while I head to the creek. They don't even bat an eye, since it's what I always did as a kid. The creek has always been a safe place for me. That's the only thing that hasn't changed in all these years.

The creek is the one place in this world where I feel right. I feel content here. It is easy to soak in the night sky. It is easy to talk to the moon out here because I feel like she listens. Out here, I don't feel the pressure. The pressure to find the parts of me I left hidden between pages of a story I never wanted to forget, but somehow, End is always in the place I looked. The sun sees what I do, but the moon, the moon knows all my secrets. Even the darkest ones I'll never be able to admit, even to myself.

Out here, with the rippling sounds of nature and the smell of fresh grass, I never grow tired of the moon. It's cratered with imperfections, visible from light years away. And, at times, I feel like a walking, talking imperfection. The moon has a dark side, just like so many of us, and it sits alone in the sea of stars. For all intents and purposes, I feel like I am the moon.

There's a cool breeze out tonight that ruffles my hair, warding a slight chill through my body. When I pass the hill and get to the creek, my mouth turns down as I take in all the garbage, just as I did the night before. I also can't ignore the flashes of memories that slam into me as I stand near the dark, murky water, watching it move back and forth in a dance of sorts. Running and chasing. Reaching and falling back.

The creek has always held some of my best memories, but now, as I stand here, there are new memories, ones I've tried like hell to forget over the years. I close my eyes, thinking of that night with

Endymion. I picture that foolish doe-eyed girl, thinking she finally had a chance with the boy who had always put those stars in her eyes. I was so reckless that night. I put so much faith in a love I so desperately thought I wanted. But that is just the thing about chasing love—you can't. Love comes to you when it's ready. Love comes at the most inopportune times. And if you are lucky, love won't find you at all.

For a long time, I wondered if I ever really loved Endymion. Could love truly be one-sided? Could you have so much hope and love for a relationship, for a future that wasn't promised, even if the other person didn't know you existed? I didn't think so. It wasn't until I gave birth to Luna that I learned what true love is. It is smiling in the face of agony. It is counting my lucky stars that out of all the souls in the universe, the moon brought her to me.

My obsession with the moon is obvious, but I named Luna after the moon because the it is magic for the soul, and it is light for the senses. The second I held my daughter in my arms, that's exactly what she was to me. She was a wonder. She was my moonchild.

Plopping down on the grass, I rest back on my elbows, just as I used to do when I was younger, and I stare up at the dark indigo sky. There's a smattering of stars dusted along the dark blanket, and the moon, without fail, casts a bright silvery glow along the ground.

"Give me a sign," I whisper to the moon. "Please tell me what to do."

I close my eyes, waiting for the answer to come to me. I'm not surprised when it doesn't. Not even the moon can help me out of this predicament.

"Figures," I mumble under my breath.

"What does?"

I let out a startled yelp at the sound of the deep voice. I swing around, toward the source, eyes wide with surprise when I spot Endymion eating up the distance between us. He slows to a stop a few feet beside me, staring down at me.

He's wearing the same clothes he wore to dinner, and somehow, they look even better on him in an outdoor setting.

"What...how..." I trail off, unable to form a coherent sentence. Endymion chuckles. The sound drifts down to me, swirling through my body, raising the gooseflesh on my skin. If this were a cartoon, his laughter would have a stream of music notes attached to it, and those notes would encircle me.

"I had a feeling you'd be out here."

My brows jump. "Why would you think that?"

He shrugs, dropping down on the grass next to me, looking out at the water. "You came here last night, so I guess I was hoping you'd do the same tonight, too." He leans back on his forearms and elbows, mirroring the pose I had adopted minutes before. "It's oddly peaceful out here."

"It is," I whisper, still trying to wrap my head around the fact that he's here, sitting next to me again.

"It's weird. I've always been drawn to this creek. I've just never understood why. But I guess I can see why you come out here. It's quiet. Helps you think."

My heart lurches for multiple reasons, one being the fact that he feels drawn to this place. The place we created a child together. And also, because he admitted he came here in the hopes of seeing me.

"Why?"

He turns to look at me with his brows pulled together in a questioning gaze. I feel his eyes sweeping across my face, lingering on my lips, then back up to my eyes.

"Why?" he parrots. "Why it helps me think, or why something else?" There's a knowing gleam in his eyes. He knows exactly what I'm referring to. The corner of his mouth kicks up, and he puts me out of my misery by answering for me. He shifts, distributing his weight, so he can face me. I feel his gaze burrow beneath my skin. There's an odd current in the air as we stare at each other. "Because I wanted to see you again."

My stomach dips.

Butterflies that I haven't felt since I was a young girl take flight, flapping their wings recklessly. The way he's looking at me…the way I'm feeling…it's all so dangerous.

"But why?" My voice is nothing more than a whisper. I'm surprised he even hears it.

"Because I can't get you out of my head, Selene." Ever so slowly, he starts leaning toward me. My eyes grow wide, and my breath gets caught in my throat. Part of me wants to push him away and run from this, but the bigger part, *that* part wants his lips on mine again.

We're like magnets, a negative and a positive drawn together. I feel my body leaning in to meet him, even when I know it's wrong. Even when I know this is a mistake, I can't seem to stop it from happening.

Just before our lips touch, our breaths intermingling—on the verge of getting reacquainted—the soft pants blow across each other's faces, breathing each other in, clarity smacks me on the forehead. I freeze, and like a bucket of ice was dumped on me, my entire body grows unbearably cold. With quick, jerky movements, I back up, darting my gaze away, looking at anything but him.

My chest burns as I stare out at the water. I can feel his gaze searing into the side of my skull. I press my lips together tightly, fighting to breathe past the tight fist around my lungs.

"You can't do that," I scold.

"Do what?"

My heart pricks with regret. "You know what."

Silence descends between us as we just sit and stare out at the rippling creek, avoiding each other.

"Can I ask you something?" he asks, after some time passes.

Tightness blocks my airway. "Sure."

"That guy at the restaurant tonight…were you considering his offer? Of seeing him?"

"I—well, no…I'm not exactly in a good place to be dating right now."

"*Hmm.*" If I'm not mistaken, the sound is a pleased one. "So, you wouldn't make an exception for anyone?"

"What? What do you mean?"

He laughs. The sound, so warm and raspy, that it travels from my fingertips down to my toes. "I mean, if I wanted to take you out, what would your answer be?"

Slowly, I turn to face him. I search his eyes, looking for his angle, trying to figure out if this is some sick joke. But all I see reflected back at me is genuine interest.

"I…no…we couldn't…I couldn't…"

A wide grin spreads across his face. It's slow in its descent but blinding, nonetheless. He's enjoying this.

"Give me one good reason."

"I can give you several."

His mouth quirks. "Fine. Let me hear them."

"I—" I choke on all the reasons I should say. A disbelieving sound bubbles up my throat at how ludicrous this whole situation is. A heavy moment hangs between us. Him staring at me, waiting for me to tell him all the reasons this isn't a good idea, and me, staring at him, knowing all the words I need to say, but none come forth.

"One date, Selene. One date," he says, growing serious. His warm gaze sweeps across my face, lingering on my mouth and eyes. It's like he can't decide where he wants to split his time.

My chest squeezes painfully, and sadness enters my heart. "I can't."

He doesn't say anything for a while. We just continue staring at one another, soaking each other in.

"That's fair," he finally says after some time. My younger self is screaming at how stupid and idiotic I am. "Doesn't mean I can't change your mind."

I raise a brow at him, waiting for him to elaborate. "And how do you plan on doing that?"

He shrugs, a small, confident smile stealing over his handsome features. "Courting you, of course."

A loud laugh bursts past my lips. My eyes widen, and I slap a hand over my mouth, trying to take it back. If possible, his grin widens. "Give me more of that, Selene."

"More of what?"

"More of your smiles. Your laughter. More of everything. I'll take whatever you're willing to give me."

A heaviness settles between us—a brand-new form of tension created by the man sitting next to me.

"I'm serious, Endymion. We can't…*I* can't."

A frown steals over my face when he pushes to his feet and smirks down at me. "I heard you, but that doesn't mean I can't change your mind. Good night, Selene."

I watch slack-jawed as he crosses over the hill, leaving me to my own turbulent thoughts. Just before he disappears, he shoots an impish grin over his shoulder that I feel down to my bones. It has my pulse skyrocketing, and my heart threatening to burst out of my chest, squeezing between my ribs.

Once he's out of sight, I flop back on the grass, staring up at the starry sky. The moon is still there, hanging just as proudly as she was before. I lie there for a while, trying to process what just happened.

Endymion asked *me* out.

He wants to court *me*.

How the hell am I going to say no?

Chapter Nine

Endymion

It's been two days since the night at the creek with Selene, and I've yet to accomplish any kind of courting. I never had to go out of my way to chase after a woman before. I wasn't expecting her to agree right away to the idea of a date, but hell, I didn't expect the flat-out no I'd gotten either. That was a first.

And oddly, I found I liked it.

It was a challenge.

There was a thrill there, something I haven't felt with a woman in God knows how long. It was thrilling, knowing I held so much space in her mind in her younger years. It makes me wonder if she still has those lingering thoughts. Does she still harbor any of those feelings toward me? Is any part of that crush still there?

The real kicker for me is how blind I was in my youth. How did I miss it? How did I miss her crush on me? If it's as obvious as everyone is making it out to be, how had I never noticed?

I am still trying to process, trying to think of a way to court her. I know next to nothing about her. None of the guys know anything about her either. It seems my best sources of information are her family, and I'm not sure how to broach the subject.

As if on cue, I spot her little shadow before I see her. Luna, for the third time within the last two hours, slips outside again and finds a spot for herself next to me on the board I'm sitting on. The kid is an absolute riot. She's an entity of her own. And I find I enjoy her presence more than I should.

"Hey, End," she says calmly, a Red Vine hanging out of the corner of her mouth.

"Miss Luna," I reply in greeting. She adopts my exact pose. Her brows pinch together as she stares out at the guys working. Apparently, that's the severity of my face out here as I look after the guys.

A thought suddenly strikes me since I have her sitting here next to me. I shift on the board, turning toward her the slightest bit.

"Hey, you know, since I have you here, I thought I'd pick your brain."

She grunts, taking a bite of her Red Vine. "Eww. I don't want you touching my brain."

A chuckle gets caught in my chest. "No, it means I have questions for you, specifically about your mom, that I'd like you to answer."

She purses her lips and raises a single brow at me. "What's in it for me?"

I choke as I try to stifle my laughter. God, this kid is pure comedy.

"That playground you wanted? Consider it done."

Her eyes narrow as she looks up at me, as if she's gauging just how serious I am. "Cross your heart?"

"Hope to die."

Her grin is calculating. "What do you need to know about my mommy?"

"Anything and everything. But let's start with her favorite flower."

Luna pauses her chewing. Her brows furrow. "Well, my mommy doesn't get flowers. So, I don't think she has a favorite. Her favorite food is Mexican, but she told my nana once that she doesn't like to eat that too much because it makes her fart a lot."

A laugh bursts past my lips at that one. God, I can only imagine how red Selene's face would look right now if she heard her daughter.

"You're a funny kid. You know that, right?"

Luna shrugs. "It's a gift."

"Luna Bella!"

Her eyes widen at the sound of Cece's yell. It seems she's been discovered.

"Bye, End!" she hollers over her shoulder, running back inside. Once she's out of sight, I call out to Griffin and Landon.

"I'm heading downtown. I'll be back."

"What the hell for?" Bishop shouts back from somewhere, having heard my conversation.

"Got some flowers to buy!"

"What the fuck, man?"

"Endymion, what brings you in here? This is the last place I would've expected to see you."

I laugh, dipping my head sheepishly. I'm so out of my element here, and it shows. "Yeah, I know. I'm here for some flowers."

"Okaaaay," Dalia, the owner of Dalia's Flowers, says, crossing her arms over her chest, waiting for me to elaborate. "I'm gonna need a bit more to go on here, son. What are the flowers for? A special occasion?"

"Sure. Got a bouquet specifically for courting women?"

I'm only half-joking.

Her eyes widen, and her brows disappear into her hairline. It's obviously a shock that I, of all people in town, am here buying flowers for someone.

"Who are they for? If you don't mind me asking."

"They're for Gavin's daughter, actually. Selene Drake."

"Wow," she breathes, a wide grin stealing over her features. "I never thought I'd see the day."

"What?"

"Do you know how long this whole town has been dying for you to pull your head out of your ass and get with Selene? It's about damn time, son."

That gives me pause. "The whole town knew about her crush?"

"I think the whole county knew. Everyone except you, it seems. C'mon. We'll need to cook up something extra special if you plan on winning her over now. You better hope those feelings are still there, or hell, you'll need a miracle to get her to fall for you."

"Tell me about it," I mumble.

I follow Dalia into the back, where she has rows upon rows of flowers, ranging from color and size, in various buckets.

"So, what's her favorite flower? Let's start there."

I have the decency to at least look ashamed. "I don't know her favorite flower. I was just kind of hoping to surprise her."

Dalia shakes her head, mumbling under her breath something about me still being foolish even all these years later.

"All right, son. Here's what we're going to do," she says, turning her back on me as she moves through the aisles toward the red roses. "We'll do a bouquet of red roses with some baby's breath. You can't really go wrong there."

When I walk out of Dalia's with the bouquet of a dozen red roses, I pause on the street, unsure of what to do now. This whole courting thing is new to me, and it's a lot harder than I anticipated. I start heading back toward my truck, trying to figure out how I'm going to get the flowers to Selene without looking like a complete idiot. I still haven't even talked to Gavin. Hell, I don't even know if he'll be okay with me trying to court his daughter. I'd bet my money on a hell no.

I guess once I get back to their house to finish work, I can ring the doorbell and give the flowers to her. If Gavin happens to answer the door, I'll finally talk with him. About my plans. About dating his daughter.

I'm just about to round the front of my truck when I hear it. The laugh is soft and lilting. It's the kind of laugh that you feel settle in your chest. The kind of laugh you can picture listening to for the rest of your life. It's one of those laughs that is like fucking music to your ears. It's the exact reason I turn around, trying to find the source. I'm not even all that surprised when I spot Selene. Her arms are full of grocery bags as she shifts them from arm to arm as she talks with Mr. Jackson, owner of Jackson's Hardware Store that's right next to the Grab-N-Go.

What are the fucking odds?

My grip tightens around the bouquet of red roses as I take her in. She's dressed in another of those loose dresses she had on last night. She's a tiny little thing. She can't be over five-two. Her hair is in a loose braid that hangs over her shoulder. Stray hairs frame her gorgeous face, and I have a hard time looking away. She must feel the weight of my gaze. After she says goodbye to Mr. Jackson, she turns around with her brows pulled down in confusion. When our gazes collide, I see the shock register. Her mouth opens and then closes, like that of a gaping fish.

I watch as her gaze drops down to the bouquet in my hands and then back up. A myriad of emotions crosses her face. I swear one of them is even jealousy that I spot.

Closing the distance, I stop just a few feet in front of her, and unable to help myself, I grin. I can feel the gazes of everyone in town. Or maybe it just feels that way now that I know everyone in town knew about her crush on me. I had no idea so many people were rooting for me—rooting for us.

"Selene," I say by way of greeting. I watch it happen, the way the soft pink tint of embarrassment starts at her chest, slowly creeping up, coloring her neck, until it travels up to her cheeks, flushing her entire face pink. "You look beautiful."

A crease forms between her brows, and she looks down at

herself, then shakes her head as though what I'm saying can't be true. "No. What? No, I don't."

I chuckle, quite enjoying the way I frazzle her. "You have a hard time accepting compliments, don't you?"

Her mouth pinches. "That's not true."

I quirk a brow that clearly says I don't believe her. I decide to change the subject. "Out doing some shopping?"

She clears her throat, and when she opens her mouth to speak, a croak leaves instead. She starts coughing and banging on her chest as she tries to pull herself together. "Yeah. My dad had nothing in the house to eat. And as much as we'd like to eat out every night, we can't."

"Let me guess, all he had in the fridge was some Spam, sandwich meat, and pickles?"

Surprise alights her eyes. "Close. It was jelly, not pickles."

I smirk, shaking my head. It definitely sounds like Gavin. I usually made a point to drop by with some groceries. He'd get mad, but thank me anyway. I've been out of town, closing up a contract for the past two weeks, so I didn't have a chance to stop by before his family showed up.

"That's probably my fault. I usually take him some groceries when I have time. Work has been a little hectic, and time got away from me."

Her brows dip, causing the cutest little crease to form between them. She looks down at her feet, then back up at me through her lashes. "You do all that for him?"

"Yeah. I mean, it's not really a big deal."

"That is a big deal, Endymion. So, thank you. That can't be easy. Especially when you have your own life and your own family to worry about."

I shrug, suddenly uncomfortable with the praise. "He's like family."

With her head cocked to the side the slightest bit, Selene regards me with quiet curiosity. Her gaze darts down to the bouquet in my hands, and something passes over her features briefly before I can figure out what it is. She steels herself, adopting a passive expression and a smile that doesn't quite reach her eyes.

"Those are nice," she mentions, nodding toward the bouquet.

"You like them?"

"Yeah. I mean, sure. They're pretty."

"I actually planned on giving them to you at your house, but here. They're for you."

If it's at all possible for her eyes to get any bigger than they already are, they do. Surprise is written all over her face as she looks from me to the bouquet.

"Wait. What? Those are for me?"

I smirk. "I told you I was going to court you. Figured flowers were the best way to start."

Something warm enters her eyes. It softens her whole face and gentles her entire demeanor. She sighs, but I can see her fighting her smile. I can tell it's just itching to spread across her face.

"I told you I can't date. *We* shouldn't date."

I shrug, thrusting the bouquet toward her. She takes it with caution, staring down at the flowers with wide, disbelieving eyes.

"I guess I'll have to stop by every day with flowers until you give me a yes, won't I?"

Her laughter finally breaks free, and it's so beautiful. It transforms her entire face and takes my fucking breath away.

"You can't be serious? That's…that's insane."

Shaking my head, I step into her, causing her breath to hitch. "Not insane. That's courting, babe. And I'm just getting started."

Unable to help myself, I reach out, tucking the thick strand of hair hanging in her face behind her ear, settling it just above the braid. I haven't touched her yet, but I can feel the tremor that rolls through her body. She quickly darts her gaze around us, taking in the few people watching what will happen next. Her flush brightens the color of her cheeks, and she traps her bottom lip between her teeth.

I fight my grin. "Need a ride back home? That's where I'm headed anyway."

She pauses, looking unsure for a beat, but then shakes her head. She tips her chin toward the parking lot.

"I have my dad's car. But thanks."

"See you later, Selene."

I start walking back toward my truck, but I pause, turning back at the sound of her voice.

"Thank you, Endymion. For the flowers." The grin that's on her face is one I want to keep there forever. One I want to bottle up and remember. Because *I* put it there. And I've never seen a more beautiful sight.

As I drive off, I spot her getting into her father's car, but not before cradling that bouquet to her chest and sniffing the flowers.

I smile the entire way back to her house.

Chapter Ten

Selene

"WHERE DID THE FLOWERS COME FROM?" IS THE FIRST THING I hear when I walk inside the front door. Forget offering to help with these grocery bags. Apparently, the flowers are much more important.

I ignore my mother's question, and instead, I pretend I don't hear her at all. I set the bouquet down gently and start putting away the groceries. My ignoring her only gets me so far when I hear the soft, lilting laughter of my daughter echoing off the walls. Her bare feet slap against the hardwood floors the closer she gets.

I stand in front of the fridge with the carton of milk in my hand. "Slippers on now, Luna Drake."

She skids to an abrupt halt, then I hear her frustrated growl before her feet stomp back the way she came as she looks for her slippers.

Children.

I can feel my mother's gaze on me as I empty the bags and put everything away. In my peripheral, I spot her lift the roses and sniff. She props one hand on her hip, and it's the *start talking* stance.

"So, who are the flowers from?"

"What flowers?" I ask, my voice high-pitched with the lie.

"Don't give me that, Selene. You know what flowers I'm talking about. Are they from…Endymion?"

I swing to face her, my brows slanted in confusion. An odd sensation brews in my gut. It is one thing to process the idea of End buying me flowers of his own volition, but it's another entirely to think he only bought them because someone else suggested it. I feel…special today. I've never been pursued so thoroughly before, and the last person I would've expected the sweet gesture to come from would be Endymion. I spent years hoping a day like this would come, and now that it's here, I have no idea how to handle it. That light billowing sensation shooting through the center of my chest suddenly dissipates at the thought of someone else putting the idea in his head. "What would make you think that? Did you put him up to this?"

My mom's grin starts in one corner of her face and quickly spreads all the way across. "So you admit it? He bought the flowers for you?"

I narrow my eyes at the smug look on her face. I stupidly fell into her trap without meaning to. I rack my brain, trying to think of something that'll get her off my back. The last thing I need is her asking questions that I most certainly don't have the answers to. I don't need her getting her hopes up where Endymion and I are concerned because we can't be together. Not when he doesn't know the truth.

"Mom." I turn toward her, my voice a warning. "Don't do that. Don't get your hopes up over something that isn't there."

"Isn't there? Honey, were you not at the same dinner I was? I watched you two, the way you looked at each other. There was so much tension in the air the other night—hell, it makes me hot just thinking about it."

I groan. "Mother. Please, stop it."

"What is the big deal here, Selene?" She slaps her hands down at her sides in exasperation. "You've been in love with Endymion for years. Why are you suddenly pushing him away?"

"Things are different now. I'm not that same hope-filled girl anymore."

"You're telling me you feel nothing for him at all? That crush of what, seven-plus years is suddenly gone, just like that?"

"Yes. No. I don't know, Mom. I haven't thought about him in years. I never thought I'd see him again. I have Luna now. I can't—"

"You can't what?" my mom asks, crossing her arms over her chest. "You can't be happy? Honey, you're a great mother. Don't think you don't deserve happiness, because you do. What could one date with Endymion hurt?"

It could hurt everything. One date could be my downfall.

"You don't get it." I sigh, avoiding her gaze.

"Why do I feel like I'm missing something here? Is there something you want to share?"

My heart lurches. I keep my gaze fixed out the kitchen window, working up the courage to say what I should've said six years ago. This is my chance. I know I should come clean now. Maybe my mother can help me figure out the next steps. But when I open my mouth to reply, nothing comes out.

"Are those your flowers, Mommy?" Luna yells, as she runs into the kitchen, startling both of us. I snap my mouth shut. I can't tell my mother now, not with little ears here. Shifting, I plaster a smile on my face for my daughter's sake.

"Yes, they are."

She picks them up off the counter and sniffs. Luna pulls a face, jerking her head back. "They stink."

I laugh. "That's just the smell of roses, honey. Some people like it."

She shrugs and spins on her heels with the bouquet still in her hand. My brows pull down when I see where she's heading. I break into a quick run after her.

"Luna, we already told you, you can't go back there right now. They're working."

Ignoring me, my daughter throws open the back door and waves down Endymion, who's talking to my father and a few of his buddies he works with.

"End!" Luna yells loud enough to gain the attention of every person in our neighborhood. "My mommy loves them!" She waves the bouquet around recklessly. I shift my gaze between her and End, who's staring at her with a smirk on his face. I can practically hear him chuckling under his breath even from here. She gives him a thumbs-up, and my gaze narrows as the pieces suddenly click. So it wasn't my mother's idea. It was hers?

I glance at my dad, who's watching the entire scene unfold with a blank expression on his face. I can't tell what he's thinking. How does he feel about End, the man he's grown close with over the past few years, giving his daughter flowers? If it bothers him, he's good at hiding it.

End says something to my dad, but he's too far away to make out whatever it is, then he's heading toward us, dodging his men who are working. My heart kickstarts in my chest. As if someone attached spark plugs to the organ, it pounds to life, beating erratically as he closes the distance. There's sweat glimmering on his forehead, and his T-shirt clings to his skin in the best of ways, showcasing the defined muscles hidden beneath. I swallow hard, trying to avert my gaze.

"Hey, kid," he says, smiling down at Luna.

Hearing him call her "kid" does strange things to me. The effects of it have my stomach turning sharply while the steel drums pound in my chest.

She gives him a big toothy grin, shooting him a thumbs-up. "She loves them! But I hate to tell you, they kinda stink."

Endymion and I share a look, both of us burst out laughing at what a character she is.

"Luna Bella!" my mom yells, sticking her head out of the door. "Is that playdough on your papa's carpet?"

"Crap," Luna hisses. She hands the bouquet back over to me, before spinning on her heels and running to clean up her mess. End and I watch her until she's gone. The flowers in my arms suddenly feel like they weigh a hundred pounds.

"So I'm guessing the flowers were her idea?"

"Not exactly. I asked her some things about you. She seemed like the best source for information."

"Information for what exactly?"

"On how to get you to agree to that date. I had to know your favorite. But it seems she couldn't even help in that department."

I flush, glancing down at my feet to avoid his gaze, and shift, feeling heat crawl across my back. I'm instantly annoyed with myself. Why is it that whenever I'm in the presence of this man, he turns me back into that flushing, shy fool from our childhood? I know I'm a different person now. I've gone through heartbreak, birthed a child, and even opened my own business. Running into Endymion again shouldn't still affect me this way, but it does. Goddammit, it does.

"Well, I'm sure she didn't give the information up freely. What did you have to promise her?"

Endymion laughs. The warm sound swirls through my chest, curling around my heart. "A playground. She's a shark, that one. Hell, I wouldn't be surprised if she grows up to be a lawyer."

I twist my lips, fighting my own smile. "I have that same thought all the time."

For a moment, we just stand there staring at each other as something heavy circulates between us. Guilt slams into me as I stare into his eyes. How can I joke around with him about Luna when he doesn't even know she's his daughter?

"You never did say what it was. Your favorite flower."

"Oh, I, umm, I don't really have a favorite."

Endymion's mouth twists ruefully. "Noted."

One of the guys, Bishop I think his name is, calls out to End, asking for his help with something. I don't remember a whole lot about Endymion's friends, mainly because my sights were always so set on End that no one ever compared. From what I recall, Bishop has always been the rugged bad boy, through and through. He was the boy fathers warned their daughters about. There's no denying how handsome he is now, with dark, almost inky black hair and sleeves of tattoos that cover his arms. I'm sure he's a walking, talking wet dream for most women.

Landon was always the cleanest cut out of the guys. With an Army-style cut, tan skin, and bright blue eyes, he's handsome to most women's standards. His father worked at the sheriff's station for years, and I was always so certain he'd follow in his footsteps—guess not.

The only friend I really know nothing about is Griffin. Back when I lived here, he was never around, so it makes me wonder how he became part of their group. I make a mental note to ask Julia for the scoop on that. She's the only one who ever stays up-to-date on all the drama and gossip in town. It only makes sense she'd know how he met Endymion.

"I gotta head back, but I'll see you tomorrow, Selene," End cuts in, snapping me out of my thoughts.

"Tomorrow?"

He smiles. The effect of it is a defibrillator to the heart. It sends a course of lightning through the organ. "Your daily dose of courting."

An amused sound bubbles past my lips. I trap my bottom lip in my mouth, and much to my horror, I realize I'm staring up at him fondly, with an expression a woman would use with her lover. One that is entirely too smitten. "You don't have to do this, Endymion. I'm serious."

He shrugs, walking backward, keeping those gorgeous leafy greens on me. "I know I don't. It doesn't mean I'm going to stop any-time soon. I told you, Selene. One date."

With that, he turns, walking back toward the guys and my dad. When my gaze clashes with my father, my stomach churns anxiously. I can't tell what he's thinking, and honestly, I don't want to know. I hurry back inside, sliding the door shut behind me. I rest my weight against it, staring up at the ceiling.

What the hell am I supposed to do now?

"Wait, you're telling me he asked you out on a date, he bought you a freaking bouquet of red roses, and you *still* said no? Are you dumb? Did you bump your head in Pasadena so hard you no longer have a shred of common sense?"

I shoot my best friend, Julia, a glare. Her face is just as made up as it always is. That's Julia in a nutshell. She takes her appearance seriously. I don't think there's ever been a time she's gone out in public without makeup. It isn't that she needs it; she looks beautiful without it. She's dressed in her work attire, a red dress that hugs her slender curves, her platinum blond bob swaying with her frustrated motions as I recount the events of the past few days. She's beautiful inside and out, with striking features that stop men in their tracks wherever we go.

Julia works here at Rita's Diner, one of our constant hangouts when we were younger. We've been meaning to catch up, but with her busy schedule, it's been nearly impossible, so she suggested I come to her—which works in my favor since I'm jobless. If I'm going to stay here for an unknown amount of time, I need to get a job. And I figure, since my best friend works here, this might be the best place to try. I tried putting my business degree to good use, but here in a small town like this? That means nothing at all.

"Jules, I'm not that girl anymore. That crush was six years ago. I moved on. I'm not that stupid little kid anymore, hoping the hottest guy in town will take notice of her."

"Babe. That was no crush. You were in deep with Endymion. That doesn't just go away because you've been gone six years. That much I know."

Why does everyone keep saying that?

I blow out an agitated breath. "It's not going to work anyway. I have a daughter I'm trying to raise, and I'm supposed to be here for my father, not starting a new relationship with someone."

"Selene, babe. I get that, I do. But at some point, you gotta live your life for you, too. I mean, hell, when was the last time you had sex?"

"Shhh!" I hiss, darting my gaze around the diner, hoping no one heard that. "It's been…I don't know. It's been a long time."

Julia narrows her eyes. It's almost like she can read the answer as if it's written on my forehead. "How long is a long time, exactly?" I look down at the table, focusing on the Sweet'N Low sugar packet I'm spinning around. Anything to avoid her gaze. "Selene. How long?" she demands, her voice growing impatient.

"It's been six years," I mumble under my breath. Julia jerks forward so quickly, it looks like someone pushed her from behind.

"I'm sorry, what the hell did you just say?"

My face is flaming in mortification. God, I hate talking about this. I didn't really have too many people back in Pasadena I could confide in, and even when I did, I would still call Julia for weekly updates. But my sex life is something that has never been on the table—a topic *not* up for discussion.

"Six years."

Julia's face pales. Quite literally, I watch as the color drains from her face. "Oh, honey. Are you okay? I mean, does it…does it even work anymore?" she whispers, looking truly worried that my vagina is broken after six years of not being in use. I swat at her.

"Stop it! Of course, it still works." I pause. "I mean, I think it still does. Right?"

"I'm even more confused now than I was before this conversation started. Why the hell are you saying no to Endymion? Endymion Black of all fucking people? His dick is probably huge. Imagine all the incredible sex you guys can have."

My stomach dips and does a somersault of sorts. Hell, it feels as if acrobatics are happening in my gut.

Oh, I can imagine it all right. I can imagine it just fine. I've lived it and done it. It's what got me pregnant in the first place. It's also why I haven't bothered with any other relationships. No one in Pasadena came close to Endymion. Even though I promised myself I was leaving him in the past, that changed when I had Luna. She was my reminder of what I couldn't have.

It's not like I purposely set out to remain abstinent all these years. It's difficult to juggle being a young single mother, trying to finish school and run a business. After I gave birth, I moved in with my mom in her duplex, and we stayed there for a few years, before we were able to upgrade to something a bit better once I opened Moonchild. With the profit I was making from it and the money from my mother's job, it helped pay for the new house, but it was still hard to coordinate our schedules, so we could take care of Luna. While I was in college, my mom stayed home with Luna for me until I got off, then she'd head out for work and come home late at night.

When I opened Moonchild, things were a little more financially stable. Until it wasn't. But none of it never left any room for me to go out and make friends or meet new people. I wasn't exactly interested in starting a new relationship, so I guess I never really went out of my way to look or open myself up to more possibilities.

"I'm living with my parents, Julia. I'm not exactly in the best place to start a relationship with anyone. I need to focus on Luna and my father."

"So what? You think Endymion doesn't understand? He has

his own place for God's sake. It's not like he's going to bang you on your father's couch."

I slam my eyes shut and shake my head at her. And as much as I try not to, I picture just that—him banging me on my father's couch or me bent over, his muscled body pumping in and—

"You're thinking about it, aren't you?"

"What? No."

She smirks with a knowing gleam in her eyes. "Yeah, sure. Neither was I. So what are you going to do, keep turning him down until he moves on?"

"Well, yeah. That was the plan."

"And if he doesn't move on?"

I come up short. I hadn't really thought about that. Can I keep saying no to Endymion forever, even if it is the right thing to do?

My brain says yes, but my heart, that foolish organ, says no.

"Selene! How are you, sweetie?" Rita's voice rings loudly in the diner, interrupting my thoughts as she walks up to our table. I shoot her a smile that doesn't quite reach my eyes. I love her as a person, but I'm not exactly sure how much I'll love working for her.

"I'm doing well. How are you?"

"Oh, you know, just getting old. I hear you have a sweet little girl now. What's her name?"

My smile turns genuine. "Luna."

"My, how time flies. I remember when you were just a little thing. Now look at you, a baby with a baby. Julia tells me you're looking for a job?"

I perk up. "I was actually hoping I could interview here with you."

Rita waves me off. "No need for an interview, honey. You'll start Friday. Just shadow Julia for the day. She'll give you a quick crash course on how everything works at the diner." Her name gets called from the kitchen, and she places a gentle hand on my shoulder. "We're all so glad to have you back, sweetie. See you Friday."

Once she disappears into the kitchen, I turn toward Julia. "Well, that was easier than I expected."

"You sure about working here, Selene? It's not exactly glamorous, like owning your own business."

I roll my eyes. "Yeah, and look how well that turned out for me? I don't really have any other choice. I need to get back on my feet, and if Rita's is my way of doing it, so be it."

"All right." She sighs, pushing up from her seat. "I gotta head back, so bust out that notepad and start taking notes, girlfriend. Oh, and are you still stopping by tomorrow?"

I groan. "Do I have to?"

"Yes! You know how Beth-Ann can be. I refuse to let my sister use *my* house for this dildo party if I don't have any moral support."

I stifle my laughter. "Okay, fine. As long as I don't have to, you know, take any of those things home."

"Those things?" she mocks. "What are you, a virgin? How did you even get pregnant? I will never understand."

With a shake of her head, Julia ties her uniformed apron around her waist and gets back to work. I follow her until she tells me to park my ass down and take notes. She obviously doesn't like the idea of me shadowing her so closely. I sit for a while longer, watching Julia and a few of the other waitresses take orders and bus tables. I try to get a feel for what it'll be like working here. I try to picture myself here in this setting, but I can't. I never thought this is where I would end up—back here in this town, working at Rita's, of all places. Back in college, I got a job at a local bookstore, which is worlds different than this.

Maybe the universe is still laughing at me after all.

Later, after I get Luna ready for bed, I cuddle next to her in my old bed. This is the room we've been staying in until the expansion is finished. The stack of books by my feet is growing heavier and heavier with each one I finish. I think this is the seventh one we've gone through tonight, and still, my girl doesn't seem the least bit tired.

"All right, baby girl. It's time for bed now. No more books."

Luna groans. "Ugh. Fine." She turns into me, snuggling into my stomach. I run my fingers through her soft waves, brushing the hair behind her ear.

"Do you have to go back to work, Mommy?"

My chest tightens. "I do. I'm sorry, baby. But hey, at least you'll get to spend a ton of more time with Papa."

That seems to perk her up. "Can we get ice cream and go to the park?"

"Of course you can."

"And what about End?"

I pause. "What about Endymion?"

"Well, can I hang out with Papa and End?"

I trap my bottom lip between my teeth and chew on it anxiously as I contemplate what to say. "I don't know, baby. He works, and he's probably really busy."

"Oh, c'mon, Mommy. Please."

"We'll see."

There's a long beat, and I think she's starting to fall asleep.

"You really like him, don't you?"

"Mhmm," she hums, on the cusp of sleep, and it only makes me hate myself even more.

Chapter Eleven

Selene

When Julia said her sister Beth-Ann was using her house to host a dildo party, she wasn't kidding. The second I walk through the door, a dick quite literally slaps me in the face. From the ceiling, pink rubber dildos hang around a string, all in various lengths and…girths.

I catch Julia's gaze from across the room, and a laugh bursts from my chest at the expression on her face. If my friend is already overwhelmed by the obscene amount of dicks in here tonight, I'm sure I will be, too.

When I bypass the table in the hall with flavored condoms and dick lollipops, I'm hit with a sweltering wave of wariness. There are phalluses everywhere. Idly, I wonder if I turn back now, maybe no one will notice. Except for Julia, of course. She'd definitely have my ass if I try to leave. Summoning the courage to step into Julia's living room that sounds like it's filled with women, I slam my eyes shut and inhale a deep breath.

It's just a room full of women from my past—no big deal.

The second I cross over the threshold, it definitely turns into a big deal. Conversations dwindle, then the whispers start as if I'm not even there. I can feel gazes from my past drilling holes into me. Heat prickles my skin, settling in my cheeks, uncomfortably so. My steps falter when I spot Holly Matthews sitting next to her best friend,

Reina Holloway. Reina rakes her gaze down my body, from head to toe. She leans into Holly and whispers, but it's still loud enough that I can hear it.

"She had a baby, and the father left them. It's just so sad."

A tight cinch squeezes my chest, and I hurry across the room, settling next to Julia. I can feel everyone's curious eyes on me, and for reasons I can't even explain, I'm embarrassed and ashamed. How many of them are looking at me like I'm a failure? How many of them are feeling sorry for me because my daughter's father isn't a part of our lives?

I'm sure all they see is the quiet and awkward Selene, who is now all grown up and still can't keep a man. She couldn't capture End's attention, and she couldn't even keep her baby daddy's attention. I can practically hear their thoughts blending together as one. They're a riot in my head, pounding against my skull, hammering into my fractured soul.

Little do they know, it's my own fault my daughter's father isn't a part of her life. It isn't because I can't keep a man; it's just because I'm an idiot. I'm a horrible person.

"Ignore them. They're too bored with their own lives to mind their own damn business." Julia bends near my ear, whispering the words reassuringly. She pats my thigh, trying to make me feel more comfortable about this whole awkward situation.

It's not working.

I haven't seen Holly Matthews since that morning after the creek when my heart was ripped to shreds. She's still gorgeous as ever. Though now, her hair is a bright platinum blond. It's not the natural platinum like Julia's. Hell, Julia and her sister were born with an almost silver hue to their hair. But Holly's? It's obvious this is the work of a salon. She wears much more makeup than I remember her wearing years ago, and clothes so tight, I know they can't be comfortable. Even though I shouldn't, I can't seem to stop staring at her, taking in everything about her.

Flashes of the past keep slamming into me, one after another. Holly and End at their prom. Holly and End groping each other in the shadows. Holly and End driving off together the morning after he took my virginity.

There's a burning in my chest. A green spill of envy spreads into the cavity, making it hard to breathe. I'm jealous of her. I've always been jealous of her because she's had pieces of the man I've always wanted. And now…now that *he* wants to go on a date with *me*, of all people, I just can't seem to wrap my head around any of it.

When did things in this town get so ass-backwards?

I quickly look elsewhere when Holly glances my way, staring straight at me. My crush on her boyfriend was obviously no secret to anyone here in town. Holly always knew about it, and I'm positive she's always hated me for it. I try not to think about her and End, but I must enjoy pain because I can't help myself. Part of me wonders what happened between them. When I left town, how much longer did they stay together? Or how much longer did they continue their friends-with-benefits relationship?

What made them call it quits?

Do they still have feelings for each other?

I'm all too thankful when Beth-Ann finally takes her place centerstage in the living room. She claps her hands together excitedly.

"Thank you all for taking the time out of your busy schedules to be here today. I really appreciate it. If you haven't already guessed why you're here, this is a sex toy party!" She throws her arms in the air and accidentally slaps one of the hanging dicks. I clamp my lips together, trying like hell not to burst out laughing.

"I've teamed up with a local brand to be a sponsor for their products. I'll host these parties every few months to keep you all up-to-date on the newest and hottest products we have in store and online. All participants today will receive a goodie bag, and using my discount, you'll get ten percent off any item of your choosing.

Now," she says, clasping her hands together, "I know you all didn't come here today to hear me talk, so without further ado, I'm going to have Julia pass around our first product, a version of the famous Jack Rabbit. Feel free to pass it around and get a good look at it. You can turn it on and watch how it works. There's also a catalog in front of you where you can mark the products you're interested in."

Most of the party is spent doing just that. I watch as sex toy after sex toy is passed around, each one more intricate than the previous one. There's a permanent flush on my cheeks that I'm sure will never leave after seeing the things I've seen here today. I'm not a prude. Or at the very least, I don't think I am, but I'll also say, I've never used any kind of sex toy before.

For one, I've lived with my mother for the past five years, so having a dildo or anything of the like hardly seemed appropriate. And two, I have a curious five-year-old who is much too nosy for her own good. The last thing I need is her finding a dildo and running around the house with it. That seems more like a nightmare than it would be pleasurable.

I can admit that by the time we near the end of the party, I'm sort of enjoying myself. I've missed Julia. She makes me laugh, even in the worst situations, like this current one. We play a few games, and sadly, I'm the lucky winner of one of the products. I try to pass it off on Julia, begging her to take it from me, but she just laughs, pushing the box back toward me.

"Oh, no, that's all yours, girlfriend. You'll be needing it since you've been turning down a certain someone left and right."

I shoot Julia a glare, drilling holes into the side of her head with my eyes, begging her to shut it. It's too late, though. The women closest to us have caught on.

"Who have you been turning down?"

"Someone's been showing interest?"

"Oh, my. Who is it?"

My grip tightens around the box, and I have the sudden urge to chuck it at Julia's head. I mouth the word, "Asshole," to her, but she just grins cheekily in response. I try not to let it bother me that a few women seem surprised someone is showing interest at all.

"It's Endymion. He's been asking Selene here out on dates, and because Selene is a complete psycho, she keeps turning him down. He even brought her flowers."

A handful of gasps sound around the room, and suddenly, I'm the focus of everyone's attention. Reina chokes on a scorn-filled laugh.

"I'm sorry, did you just say Endymion as in Endymion Black?" There's disbelief in her tone. It has me wishing this couch would just swallow me whole—anything to get out of this room. I risk a glance at Reina and find her glaring at me. When I glance to her left, Holly is staring at me with an odd expression on her face. It's not quite anger, but she's obviously not happy about this news. She sniffs, turning her nose up at me, and she pretends not to care. But it's obvious she does.

That's just another reason I need to steer clear of Endymion.

"Well, I say it's about damn time you two get together," Beth-Ann says.

I shake my head. "Oh, no. We're not…I'm not…I said no."

"Why the hell would you do that?" everyone damn near shouts in unison.

"No offense, but why would he bother with you? You have a kid?" There's no mistaking the disgust that laces Reina's tone. I press my lips together, holding in the cold retort that's on the tip of my tongue.

That's my cue to leave.

"Ignore her. Some people don't understand what fate is," Julia tosses back at Reina. I force a smile on my face and push up.

"I should probably get going anyway. I do have a daughter to get home to. It was so great seeing you all again. And Beth-Ann, I had fun. Thank you for…this." I raise the box that's in my hands, still not sure how the hell I'm going to get rid of this thing.

Julia walks me to the front door, her face colored with anger. She keeps muttering under her breath, and I can only imagine what has her this upset. Julia has always been the momma bear in our friendship. Where I'm the quiet wallflower, she's the outspoken one who's not afraid to tell anyone what's on her mind, or more like, put someone in their place.

"Who does that bitch think she is?" she hisses. Snatching the box from my hands, she shoves it inside a nondescript bag, then gives it back to me.

I blow out a sigh. "It's fine. I'm used to it."

"You shouldn't have to be used to anything. People should just be decent human beings instead of assholes who weren't raised right."

I grin at her. "You know I love you, right?"

That gets her to calm down some. "I love you, too. Do me a favor. Bring my niece over soon? I'm kind of dying to fill her head with some mementos she can keep forever."

I roll my eyes, edging toward the door. "Oh, yeah, because that's exactly what my five-year-old needs. Mementos from you, of all people."

"What? I'm great!"

I can't even hold back my laughter on my way out. "Bye, Julia. See you tomorrow."

"Seven sharp!"

"Got it," I toss back over my shoulder, as I make my way down the porch steps. I glance to my left since that's the way back home, but I pause, my head automatically turning right toward the creek. It's already late. I should probably head home and get to bed early before work tomorrow, but I find myself taking the detour anyway. Almost like the creek and the moon are calling my name.

I pass over the hill, and my steps falter when I near the water. I notice something lying in the grass, and when I close in on what it is, my heart trips over itself in my chest. My stomach dips, those pesky butterflies taking flight when I spot the bouquet of daisies. They look a bit wilted as though they've been sitting out here for a day, which makes sense since I didn't have a chance to come sit out here last night. End must've stopped by, thinking I'd be here, and left them for me.

Glitter bursts in my chest at the thought. It's billowy and airy. Like an explosion of sparkles.

I plop down in the grass with a permanent grin etched on my face as I stare down at the flowers.

"I take it you like them."

I startle at the sound of his voice, whipping around to face him. My eyes widen when I finally spot him closing the distance between us, taking in every muscular inch of him. "Oh my God! How do you keep doing that?"

He's dressed casually again in work clothes—only that's not all. He's holding another bouquet. This time, it's peonies.

"Endymion…you shouldn't have."

He shrugs, taking a seat on the grass next to me. He hands the second set of flowers off to me with a grin. "I wanted to. I plan on going through every flower until we find the one."

"The one?"

He leans back, showcasing his incredible body in that shirt. "The one that makes you say yes, of course."

My laughter comes out embarrassingly close to a giggle. "You're insane. Seriously. How did you even know I'd be here?"

"I didn't. I hoped you would be, though. I came last night, stayed for a while, hoping you'd show, but when you didn't, I left the flowers, figuring it was too late to drop them off at the house. I didn't want to scare Luna or piss Gavin off."

I snort. "You really waited?"

"Yeah. Figured I'd try again tonight. I stopped at your house first, but I heard you were out, so I was hoping you'd be here."

At the mention of me being out, I think of Holly and try to ignore the jealousy filling my veins at the thought of the two of them together. I have no right to feel that way. She had him first. He was never even mine to have in the first place. There's a myriad of contradictory emotions rioting inside me at the moment. I'm shocked and pleasantly surprised that he's gone through all this trouble just to see me. I'm angry and jealous because he has a past with a woman I'll never be able to compete with. I'm feeling incredibly guilty because I want to come clean with him about everything, but I'm afraid. I'm so afraid of losing this, of losing my daughter, of letting everyone down.

"Wow. I'm…shocked you did all that."

"Why wouldn't I?" he asks, his brows drawn in, those vibrant greens searching mine for answers. I press my tongue to the roof of my mouth, working through how to respond to that.

Clearing my throat, I glance down at the wild grass between us. I don't know what to talk about or say, so I ask the first thing that comes to mind, even if I already know the answer to it. "So you have your own construction company now?"

He nods, his intense gaze still drilling holes into me. "Yeah, it's been a few years since we've been up and running. It's great. I've always been pretty good with my hands, so it just made sense. Haven't looked back since."

Oh, I know you are, I think to myself. Hell, I can practically feel the heat of his touch on my skin. The memory is both a blessing and a curse.

I smile, glad he was able to find his place, find that perfect something he was always searching for. "I'm happy for you. I always knew you'd go on to do something amazing."

A softness enters Endymion's eyes. There's a warmth there that rolls through my body in waves, making my throat clog with emotion for unknown reasons. He's looking at me like I wished he always would. I always wondered what it would feel like, having his heated gaze caress my flesh.

"What about you? I heard you got a job at Rita's?"

I drop my gaze, blindly picking at the grass between us. A sharp ache drizzles throughout my chest. Why do I feel like a failure all of a sudden? Shame wraps heavily around my shoulders, weighing me down.

"Heard about that, did you?" My voice is a low murmur.

"Small town. News travels fast." As if sensing I'm not exactly proud that I'll be working at a diner, he tries to make me feel better. "There's nothing wrong with working at Rita's, Selene."

I expel a shaky sigh that rattles my chest, my hold on my emotions threatening to crumble. "I guess part of me feels like a failure. Back in Pasadena, I had my own store. Something that was mine, and now, I'll be bussing tables at a diner I frequented as a child. When I thought about where I'd be in life, I didn't think it'd be here. I thought I'd be doing amazing things by now."

"Just because you don't own your own store anymore doesn't mean you aren't doing amazing things. You're raising a daughter on your own. That in itself is amazing."

Slowly, I drag my gaze up, meeting his stare. My heart aches dully against my sternum. He doesn't even know, doesn't have a single clue, and it's all my fault. I force a smile on my face that doesn't quite reach my eyes. It's meant to appease him—anything to steer away from this heavy subject.

"Thank you, End. I needed that."

He nods, and for a second, I think he's going to say more on the subject, but he decides not to. For that, I'm all too thankful. As much as I appreciate him trying to make me feel better, I still feel like a horrible human being. Not to mention, a failure of an adult. This train of thought is better left for the moon and me when no one else is around.

Silence descends between us as we stare out at the creek, each of us thinking about something different, I'm sure. Endymion shifts, and when he glances down at the bags sitting between us, near our legs. I feel my entire face go up in flames. *Oh, hell.* He pushes himself upright, reaching for the bag. Dread settles in my gut, and I silently curse Julia for making me go there tonight.

"Did you do some shopping?" he asks, picking up one of the smaller bags with all the favors inside.

"Wait, don't!" It's too late. I can see the second understanding dawns on his face because his eyes widen and jerk to me. "Oh, God." I groan, dropping my head into my hands, trying to hide from him.

"Well…I wasn't expecting that."

A mortified laugh bursts past my lips, and I pull my hands away from my face, using it to shove at his arm. That's a mistake, though, because in doing so, I can feel all the hard muscles beneath my palm. I have to fight the urge to curl my hand around his bicep and squeeze the muscle there.

"I can explain that. All of it. I swear it's not mine."

He raises a brow, amusement crinkling the corners of his eyes. There's a crooked grin on his face that's doing strange things to my core. He has a slight dimple in his right cheek that is so adorable that I have a hard time looking away. "Oh, it's not?"

I come up short. "Well, it is. But technically, it's not. My best friend's sister was having some…sex toy party with dildos hanging from the ceiling. It was…it was hell on earth."

Endymion tosses his head back and laughs. It's a no-holds-barred kind of laugh. I watch his Adam's apple bob as he works to accommodate his hysterics. "Ah, that certainly makes more sense." He pulls out a six-inch dick-shaped gummy, and we share a look, then we both suddenly collapse into a fit of laughter. I fall into his side, resting my head on his shoulder as we chortle until tears threaten to fall from how hard I'm cackling.

"Let's see what's in this one," he says, once his laughter is partly under control. He starts reaching for the bigger bag, and I toss myself back on the grass, anything to avoid having to look at him as he opens that one. When he does, I hear him choke back his amusement.

"Christ…this is…" He trails off, and I peek one eye open, raising up on my elbows to see what he's referring to. And sure enough, the toy I won just had to be this monstrosity of a curved cock, fully equipped with beads inside that light up and roll around once it's turned on and there's even a clit massager. "Interesting," he murmurs, eyeing the toy as though he's offended such a thing exists for women. I stare at him, taking him in, the way the silver light shines on him like a spotlight. I'd take having him over that thing a thousand times over.

"I'm sure you measure up just fine."

I don't know what makes me say it, and I immediately regret it. Slowly, End turns to look down at me, something dark and hot passing over his eyes. He stares down at me, heat filling his gaze. It has my core clenching and throbbing, and a thrill coursing down my spine.

I open my mouth to correct myself. "I just mean, I'm sure you're fine. I'm sure women enjoy you just fine. I mean, not that I would know. Because I don't. And I don't want to. I just mean not everyone wants that instead of the real thing."

If it's possible, his eyes grow a few shades darker, and his lips twist ruefully as he tries to hide his grin.

"No, wait. That came out wrong again. I'm not saying I want the real thing. From you. Or anyone, for that matter. But I'm not saying I don't *not* want it either."

When End raises his brows, and his smile breaks free, I slam my eyes shut and toss myself back on the grass again. "That's not right either, is it? God. This is the most embarrassing day of my life."

My heart lurches, and my stomach clenches with desire when I feel him shift. I don't even need to open my eyes to know he's leaning over me. I can feel his body heat and smell his scent. Something clean and minty mixed with something that is inherently End—all testosterone. My heart is pounding in my chest when I hear his question. He's so close.

"And why is that?"

I peel my eyes open, not surprised to find him leaned toward me. He isn't completely hovering over me, but he's close enough that all it would take is for me to reach around his neck and pull his mouth down to mine. And I find that I want to do that more and more with each passing second I stare up at him. His eyes are a dark forest green right now as they take me in, moving from my eyes to my lips.

I find myself leaning up toward him slowly, hoping he'll close the distance and kiss me. Like we're drawn together, like two strings being tugged slowly, we grow closer until I feel his breath ghosting across my face.

"I think you know why," I whisper. We're so close, mere inches apart, all it would take is one small movement, and we'd be kissing. I feel the barest hint of his lips against mine, and I almost moan and fall into him. That is, until we hear the sound of loud voices. We jolt apart, just as some random teens come strolling over the hill. They pause when they see us. No doubt these assholes are the ones constantly making a mess out here.

"Aw, fuck. Let's go, man," they say to each other, going back the way they came. Endymion and I share a look. There's a moment when we stare at each other doused in silence.

"I should probably go. It's late," I mutter, pushing up from the ground. If I'm not mistaken, he looks disappointed, but he still helps me stand, nonetheless.

"Want a ride?"

"I shouldn't. *We* shouldn't."

He frowns. "You shouldn't be walking alone out so late at night, either."

I can tell he isn't going to give in on this, so I acquiesce. "Okay, fine. Just a ride." I start walking toward his truck when I hear him from behind me.

"Can't forget this one."

When I turn, my lips are thinned into a grim line. I roll my eyes, stomping toward him, and snatch the bag from him. "I'm going to kill Julia," I mumble on the way to his truck.

The ride is mostly silent, a thick tension swirling in the confined space between us.

When he pulls to a stop at the curb, we both just sit there, not saying anything. That was too close tonight. I almost risked everything for one kiss. What the hell was I thinking? I have to be stronger. I can't keep doing this.

"Thank you. For the ride. And the flowers. And just…thank you, Endymion."

He smiles. It causes the corners of his beautiful, vibrant eyes to crinkle softly. "You don't need to thank me. I'll see you tomorrow, Selene."

I pause with my hand gripped around the door handle. Unable to help it, I smile. "Right. Good night."

"Good night, beautiful."

Those words drip down from my pounding heart and settle somewhere low in my belly, like a warm dose of nectar or sunshine. They echo on a boisterous repeat as I unlock the front door and shut it behind me. I rest my back on the wood and sag against it.

God, he's even more charming than I thought, I think as I look down at the two bouquets in my hands. I want to believe I can be strong enough to keep saying no to him, but if tonight is any indication, I obviously can't.

Before this escalates any further, I need to come clean. I need to tell him the truth about that night at the creek and about Luna. He's not going to like it, and it's going to hurt, but it has to be done.

I can only hope tomorrow I'm a stronger person than I was today.

Chapter Twelve

Endymion

We finally break the entire wall down outside of Gavin's house. For safety purposes, Cece and Gavin took Luna out around town. The kid is too slippery, and I didn't want to take the chance of her getting hurt.

I didn't get a chance to see Selene this morning, but I learned she started her job at Rita's. I make a mental note that once I get done here, I'll stop in for a visit. A wry grin twists my lips just at the thought.

"What the hell are you smiling about?" Griffin asks, nudging me on the arm.

I shrug noncommittally, getting back to work. "I wasn't."

Everyone suddenly stops short. "Okay, something is definitely off here. You're lying about smiling now, man? Who is she?"

I don't bother with a reply, not that I need to, though, not when I have Bishop around. The asshole.

"Oh, I'll tell you who it is. It's the MILF, isn't it?" Landon pipes in. Griffin crosses his tattooed arms over his chest, a smug grin now in place thanks to Lan. Fucker thinks he knows everything.

The rest of the guys go wild over this news. "She won't even agree to go on a date with me. Let's not jump the gun."

"What do you mean she won't agree on a date? Wasn't she in love with you when she lived here?"

My brows rise incredulously. "You guys noticed it, too?"

"It was hard not to," Bishop says, clapping me on the back.

"Seriously. You were such an idiot back then, letting a girl like her slip through your fingers. Isn't life crazy? She chased you for years, gave up, got pregnant by some random dude, and now all of a sudden, you're the one chasing her. If you weren't such a shit, I bet that'd be your kid."

After Landon's speech, we all get back to work, and I remain silent the entire time, stuck in my thoughts. He wasn't wrong. His observation hits much too close to home.

Why didn't I notice her then? And why can't I seem to look away from her now?

Something about Selene draws you in. It makes me want to get closer, stare longer, and know everything there is to know about her as a person. I want her to let her walls down and show me the real her. The one that sits in that grassy field, gazing out at the creek. She's not the only one I find myself drawn to—it's Luna, too. I've never met a kid with more spunk. She's adorable. I'm not all that surprised. Her mother is Selene, after all.

Once we call it a day and as the guys head out, I inform them that I'll be late for beers and the game at Griffin's house. I have a woman to woo, and the last thing I need is to hear more of their shit.

When I push through the diner doors, the bell chimes, and all eyes swing my way. I rake a hand through my hair that is still damp from my shower. I'm used to this—the women in this town staring for far too long. The whispers about my past, about my present, and of course, my future. That is the main thing I still hate about living here in Dunsmuir, even after all these years. It is a small town, and all people like to do is talk. It doesn't matter if the shit they are spewing is true or false; they spread it anyway.

Ignoring the glances, I find an open booth in the corner, and I set another fresh bouquet down on the table. This time I went with a mix of lilies and calla lilies. I lean back, slinging my arm over the back of the open booth, looking around, trying to find the woman I came here for. Almost like it was meant to be, she stumbles out from the back double doors, juggling a tray filled with glasses.

On anyone else, this uniform looks plain and boring, but on Selene? She looks like a fucking goddess. Her hair is in another one of those loose braids, her face clean of any makeup. Her cheeks have a pink tint, probably from running around and standing on her feet all day. The uniform here at Rita's is a simple red dress with a black apron. And for some reason, I can't stop staring at her perfect, shapely legs. Her long, brown hair and her creamy skin is a balm I never knew I needed.

She's beautiful. I've never been surer of anything.

Off to the right, she serves a table the drinks from her tray. She turns around, blowing out a deep sigh. Stray strands of hair have fallen into her eyes and billow around her face with that gust of air. It's fucking adorable. That's about the time she notices me sitting there, and she freezes. Those gorgeous doe eyes widen, and her face flames. She glances down at herself, around the diner, then back at me. Slowly, she wipes her hands down her front apron, then she squares her shoulders and makes her way toward me. The whole time, her gaze drifts from the flowers on the table, then back to me, like she can't seem to decide where she wants to look.

Selene pauses in front of my booth, and she wrings her hands in her apron nervously. In a nervous tic, she traps her bottom lip between her teeth, chewing on it. And, fuck me, I love it when she does that, too.

"Selene," I say by way of greeting, unable to hide my grin. Her gaze drops to my lips, then back up to my eyes, like she doesn't want to get caught staring for too long.

"Endymion." She clears her throat, her face flushing. Her bottom lip has popped free, and my eyes are riveted to her pinkish red plump lips.

I reach for the bouquet of lilies and hand them off to her. "Your daily dose of flowers, as promised." That gets a smile out of her. It slowly spreads across her face, brightening her features. She grins down at the bouquet, taking them in with a soft look in her eyes. I do a quick scan around Rita's and realize everyone has stopped talking and eating, and instead, they're gaping at us.

"God, Endymion," she breathes. "These are beautiful." She suddenly frowns, glancing around her, as if she's just now realizing how quiet it's gotten in here. Her mouth opens as if she's going to say something, but then she snaps it shut.

"Thank you," she mumbles quietly, as though she doesn't want everyone around us to hear. I grin up at her, unable to help myself. I don't know how it's possible—I shouldn't even be able to smell it, what with the delicious savory scent floating around Rita's—but somehow, I can still smell her. Her scent is so distinct. Even out in the field at the creek, her presence overshadows everything. It's an alluring scent, all soft and sweet. Like coconut milk and cedarwood. Like flowers and honey.

"What do you say about that date?"

The creamy expanse of her chest goes up in flames. I hear a sharp intake of breath from someone in the diner. Selene glances over her shoulder and shifts on her feet, obviously uncomfortable with the close scrutiny. She gets a nod from Rita herself and leans down to speak near my ear.

"People are going to talk," she whisper-hisses.

Cocking my head to the side, I regard her for a beat. She's never really struck me as someone who cares what others think, but obviously, she does care. Or maybe, she just hates being the focal point of conversation or the spotlight of gossip here in town. I eventually shrug. "Let them talk, babe."

The concept seems insane to her because she looks at me like I'm crazy. She shoots another quick glance over her shoulder, and I grin at her.

"Go ahead. I know you have your hands full."

Selene pauses, and it looks like she wants to say more, but she nods, offering me a gentle smile. "Did you…did you want anything?"

"I could go for a coffee."

Her smile is shy as she dips her head, trying to hide her face. I get the sense this is a protective gesture. One she uses to hide. Doesn't she know it only makes me want to delve deeper?

She suddenly clears her throat, feigning bravado. Squaring her shoulders, she nods. "Right. Okay. A coffee. I can do that."

I milk my time in the diner. It gives me the perfect view of Selene as she works. She sends furtive glances my way often, probably wondering when I'll leave, but I'm enjoying myself far too much. It doesn't escape my notice the way men in the diner watch her. She's beautiful, so it's not like I blame them, but I can't ignore the ball of anger that turns my gut at their coveted glances. I try to rationalize what the hell the sensation could be, and I realize it's jealousy. I'm jealous of every man in here who gets to stare at her. I'm jealous they get any of her time at all. I want it all. I want all of her.

I'm a selfish fucking bastard, and I don't give a damn.

I think about the man she had a kid with. I try to envision what he would've been like. Did she love him? Was it serious? And my biggest issue is, will he ever come back? Is that who she is waiting for—Luna's father to pull his head out of his ass, so they can finally be together? I hope not.

When the guys text me, asking where I am, I decide to call it a night. I've spent enough time sitting here, thinking about all the ways this woman invades every part of my brain.

I pay the bill and leave a tip on the table, which is more than triple the bill. The bell chimes as I walk out toward the truck, and once I'm about to climb in, I hear the door chime again, followed by soft footsteps.

"End, wait!" Selene calls after me. I pause with my hand still gripping the handle on the truck and turn. Her lips are pursed, the lines around her eyes tight with frustration.

"Here. I can't take this," she says, passing the hundred-dollar bill back to me. I keep my hands just where they are, refusing to take it back.

"Yes, you can."

"End," she says, her voice growing stern. "This is a hundred-dollar tip. All you had was coffee that was left untouched."

I shrug. "And it was the best damn coffee I've ever had."

She growls in frustration. "Would you have given Rita this same tip if she was the one serving you?"

A smirk twists the corner of my mouth. "No, I wouldn't have, because Rita isn't you."

"I—wait, what?"

My grin widens. The effect of it seems to catch her off guard, and her slender throat works a thick swallow. Slowly, I close the distance between us and wrap my hand around hers, softly tucking the money back into her palm. Her skin is soft, so fucking smooth, and I find myself wanting to hang on. Hang on to that electricity coursing through my veins. Hang on to that look in her eyes. Hang on to everything about her.

"It's yours, Selene." She stares up at me, hazel eyes so soft, I practically fucking melt into a puddle right then and there. "See you tomorrow." Before I can think better of it, I lean forward, and as much as I'd like to aim for her bee-stung lips, I decide not to. Instead, I press a soft kiss on her cheek, enjoying the way her skin feels against mine. I get a whiff of her scent, and fuck me, she's absolutely divine this close. In every shape and form.

I hear her soft intake of breath, and if I'm not mistaken, I swear she even leans into the kiss like she wants more. That could just be my mind playing tricks on me, though.

I step away, my grin still glued to my face as I back up toward the truck. She's frozen in place, still standing there, mouth agape, staring after me as though I've done the craziest thing in the world. And hell, maybe I have.

"Can someone please tell me why we're here in this shithole instead of back at my place, watching the game?" Bishop complains for what feels like the tenth time within the past few minutes. The guys—and by *the guys*, I mean Landon—wanted to come to the bar and shoot the shit, play pool, and watch the game instead of at Bishop's place like we normally do. I personally think he's here for other reasons.

"Probably because our boy Landon here wants to get laid, and he can't do that hanging out at your place all night."

Landon shoots me a glare for calling him out. Now, if we can just figure out who he's trying to seal the deal with tonight.

"How about you fuck off, yeah? You've been buying the same chick flowers for what, the past ten days, and she still keeps saying no. Don't give me shit. You guys should be giving End shit."

I roll my eyes.

"He's not the one that dragged us here tonight, asshole," Griffin retorts.

"Thank you!" Bishop slams a meaty hand down on the bar top, happy one of us has some sense.

"What the hell are y'all even complaining about? The game is on right here!" Landon points at the TV with frustration.

We all shoot him a glower.

"Bert hasn't upgraded this TV in years. So, yeah, excuse me if I'm pissed off that I have to watch the game on this shit box instead of on a flat screen like a normal person. I mean, Christ, who doesn't own a flat screen? It's fucking 2020!"

I can't really argue with that.

Bert, the owner of Bert's Pub, has owned this place since what feels like the dawn of time. His father, Bert Sr., opened the pub years ago, and Bert took over for his father when he passed. I'm not kidding when I say everything is the same as it was years ago. There have been minor changes we've done for Bert, but for the most part, this place is like stepping back into the 80s sprinkled with a dash of 70s flavor.

It's a goddamn time machine.

It has character, I'll give it that. It's a staple here, just like so many other places. A part of this town's history, a core place where the locals flock for good conversation and a fun night out. I glance around, taking in everyone crowded at the bar and the surrounding tables. There are about five pool tables in total, each one in use, including the one we're using. The bar is made up of worn oak that gives it character, telling the story of just how long Bert's has been around. The stools are black and red, the red cushions are a bit worn, but they're still comfortable, nonetheless.

The décor is much as you'd expect—local sports teams' banners hanging, a Bud Light neon sign hangs in the front window right next to the open sign, and the TVs are all these old, pieces of shit that no one hardly looks at. Do the people in this generation even know what it's like to go most of your childhood watching something in SD? Before HD was even a thing? Probably not.

Music floats from the speakers, and I'm just glad it isn't country. That's where I draw the line in this fucking town.

Bishop cues the balls on the table, before taking the first shot. The loud crack reverberates between us, scattering the balls along the velvet surface.

"So, who is she? Might as well tell us now. We're going to find out eventually," Bishop demands with a bit of an attitude. If there was a surefire way to piss off Bishop, it would be ruining baseball for him, and tonight, Landon has committed a cardinal sin in his world.

Landon sighs. Picking up his pool stick, he angles himself over the table and takes his shot. Just as the white ball connects with his intended solid color, he mumbles a name under his breath. We all pause, our eyes widening. I share a look with the rest of the guys, and they burst into laughter. Bishop clutches his stomach, howling with hysterics, and Griffin damn near has tears rolling down his cheeks. I hide my laughter behind my hand, thinking about the other night with Selene and the bags of dildos she got from Beth-Ann's party. I guess Landon's in for a treat with her.

"Well, tonight just got interesting," Griffin mumbles aloud, gaze pinned to the entrance. When I follow the trajectory, I see why.

Beth-Ann, her sister Julia, and Selene, of all people, step over the threshold. Something weaves its way through the air, a static electricity I can feel swimming through my veins. I straighten on the stool, my gaze glued to Selene. Her hair is down, hanging around her back in a soft curtain of waves that I'm itching to drag my hand through. Her creamy skin is on display in the dress she's wearing. Heat shoots through my body as I take her in. She looks beautiful tonight, but that's not new. She always looks beautiful. Her dress is a virginal white, off-the-shoulder number that's cinched at the waist, making her look tinier than I remember. Her heels make her legs look like they go on for miles.

I find myself sliding off the barstool, weaving through Bert's, just to get close to her. She must sense me coming, or her friends tell her, because she swings her gaze toward me, our eyes homing in on each other. A ripple shoots down my spine, the sensation otherworldly. It's odd and foreign, and I'm certain she feels it, too. Her lips part, and I notice the way her chest rises and falls sharply at my presence. It's that awareness. That current between us that's impossible to ignore.

"Endymion," she greets, and if I'm not mistaken, the sound is raspy. Pink slowly invades her cheeks, and I find myself smiling, despite my better judgement.

"Funny running into you here," I mumble, raking my gaze across her flesh, soaking in every inch of her while I can. She smiles, the corners of her eyes crinkling with the laughter she's holding in. "You look…you look beautiful."

"My heart. I think I've just had a heart attack from cuteness overload."

Selene and I turn toward the source, finding her friend Julia staring at the two of us with hearts in her eyes. Her hands are splayed over her chest, across her heart, as if she quite literally can't take it.

"Julia," I greet, unable to hide my grin. She's funny; I'll give her that.

"Greek god of Dunsmuir. It's always a pleasure." She curtsies, and I choke on my laughter. In my peripheral, I catch Selene pinch the bridge of her nose, likely embarrassed by her friend's antics. "Also," Julia says, pausing to look at me pointedly, "don't give up on this one just yet. She'll give in to you soon enough. Lord knows this has been years in the making."

"Okay, Julia. Thank you," Selene rushes out, shooing her off. Her face is the cutest shade of red, and she shifts in those heels.

"Years in the making, huh?"

Her mouth turns down, and she rolls her eyes at me, nudging me on the arm, but I still see the humor lurking there. "Don't push it, End."

We both turn toward our friends. Beth-Ann has taken my spot at the bar next to Landon, and Julia is being introduced to Griffin and Bishop.

"We should probably head over there before the guys try to get an easy win in pool."

Selene scoffs. "Julia is a shark at pool. She'll definitely hold her own against your friends."

"And what about you?"

She pauses, then, a smirk steals across her face. It's damn beautiful. "I guess we'll find out, won't we, Mr. Black?"

She turns, heading toward her friends, and the entire way I watch her go, riveted to the sight of her. And if I'm not mistaken, there's an extra sway to her hips. Fuck, if it doesn't make me rock hard.

Two seats open at the bar, a few feet away from our friends, so we take them. She settles in beside me, and I get a whiff of her perfume. It's that damned honey and sweet flowers scent - something that is inherently her.

"I take it you're a baseball fan?" she comments.

I realize I've been sneaking glances at her and the TV, unsure what I want to look at more. Who the fuck am I kidding? It's her.

"I prefer football, but baseball is a close second."

She cranes her neck over her shoulder, glancing at the screen. "I've heard about that guy."

"Liam Falcon?" I ask, referring to the Giants pitcher.

She nods. "Watched an interview with him and his wife. Kind of incredible, their love, and his passion for the game."

I know what she's referring to. A few months back, news leaked of Falcon's wife being assaulted. It was plastered on every celebrity news channel and website. When questioned about it, he went off on a few reporters and then later did a string of interviews with his wife, Bea, where they confronted the rumors of their past.

The guy didn't play when it came to his wife. He was extremely protective. That showed through whenever they were spotted together in public. They looked at each other like a couple deeply in love. With a kind of passion you longed for. It's exactly what's been lacking in all my relationships. I didn't date or have girlfriends because no woman ignited something inside me so deep and sharp that I wanted to know more. That I wanted to keep them around for more than just sex. Until Selene.

"How was work?" I ask her, changing the subject. "If I'd known you were going to be here, I would've brought more flowers."

Her eyes light with amusement, and her lips quirk. "You already bought me flowers today."

I shrug. "Who's to say I can't get you flowers twice a day?"

"You're enjoying this, aren't you?" She shakes her head, fighting back a smile. A chuckle spills past my lips, and I lift my shoulder noncommittally. I'm not even going to bother denying it.

"I am. More time with you is always a good time, beautiful."

She ducks her head down in a bashful way, tucking a thick lock of hair behind her ear. Her mouth twists ruefully.

"You're good at that."

"At what?"

"This." She aims a pointed look at me. "You're so…I don't know, charming, I guess. As though this all comes naturally to you."

"And you're telling me it doesn't come naturally to you? I don't believe that."

She scoffs. "Believe it. I think that's what makes this so hard. I have no idea what I'm doing, Endymion."

I pause, taking in the heaviness that has suddenly settled around us. Her shoulders are tense, and I realize now, this *isn't* easy for her.

"Look," I breathe out, twisting toward her. "You don't have to know what you're doing. I don't need any other version of you than the one that's sitting right here. We can figure it out together."

Her face falls. She obviously doesn't like that answer. "No, we can't."

"Why not?"

"Because…because my life is difficult. I have a child, End. I have responsibilities. Nights like this? A free night out with friends is one in a million. Dating you, or…whatever it is you want, it's not possible with someone like me."

"I think it is possible. We can just take Luna out with us." I shrug as if it's no big deal. "I get that dating you comes with its own set of obstacles, but for me, Luna isn't one of them."

Selene looks away. Silence wraps around us, filling the air with tension. Sadness overtakes her features, and I know what she's going to say before she does. It's deflating to the ego, and it's disappointing. Why now? All those years, she harbored a crush on me, and now, suddenly, she wants nothing to do with me.

"What are you so afraid of, Selene? Did the last guy hurt you so much, you're not even willing to try again?"

Slowly, she looks up at me. Something in her eyes gives me pause. It's a storm of emotion, blending and swirling that I can't seem to pin it down to one.

"Yes," she whispers in response, staring me directly in my eyes. I get an uncomfortable stitch in my chest at the look of torment in her eyes. I want to know her. I want everything.

But most of all, I want to take that look away.

"I'm not him, Selene."

She scoffs and shakes her head harshly. "I don't even know who you are anymore."

I press my lips together at that answer, stumped, unsure of what to say. No one has ever really known me. The town saw what they wanted. But I want that to change with Selene. I want her to know me. The real me.

When Bert remains holed up on the other end of the bar, I tell Selene I'll be right back, so I can get us some drinks. Hell, there's gotta be something to cut the sudden tension between us. I decide to cut myself off after this last beer for tonight, and I grab Selene another cranberry and vodka, though, I'm sure it'll go to waste. She didn't seem all that enthused while drinking the first. I don't imagine she drinks very often, and I'm sure when she does, it's sparse. She doesn't really strike me as the kind of mom who dies to get out and party.

As I'm headed back toward Selene, I notice the barstool I was just sitting on is no longer empty. It's now taken by someone dressed in a black shirt with long unruly black hair I'd know anywhere. I grind my back teeth together when I get a look at Selene's face. She looks uncomfortable. I catch the tail end of his sentence.

"Well, look at you." He whistles. "Anyone ever tell you that you grew up real nice?"

Selene forces a thin smile. "More than I'd like."

"You here with anyone, *little moon*? What do you say we get out of here?"

Setting the drinks on the bar top, I clasp a hand on Thomas's shoulder, gripping tightly. He stiffens beneath my grip. "She's with me."

Slowly, Thomas rises from the stool, turning to face me with a scowl firmly in place. "Well, if it isn't Endymion, the great."

"Isn't your girlfriend at home waiting for you? This is the last place you should be."

"Holly could give two shits about where I am, but you know that already, don't you?"

I press my lips together in a grim line, sparing a quick glance at Selene, who's watching on, a frown marring her face. Thomas has always hated me. The moment I moved into town, and he was no longer the only guy women flocked to, he became angry. After I dated Holly for a few years, he went ahead and did the same, but Holly has never been the kind of girl who wants to be tied down, and I was never that guy who wanted to be tied down either. Our friends-with-benefits arrangement worked for us. Until it didn't.

It seems Thomas still isn't over it.

"Tommy, boy, you better not be starting no shit in here tonight," Bert yells from the other side of the bar, obviously realizing this situation could get ugly.

Thomas shoots me a scathing glare, glances back at Selene one last time, letting his gaze linger on her exposed legs for a beat too long, before he's gone. I have the sudden urge to clock him for looking at my girl.

My girl? Christ. I internally chide myself.

I take the now empty barstool and pass her drink to her. "You all right?"

She nods. "I'm fine. He hasn't changed at all over the years."

I scoff. *You got that right.*

"Can I ask you something?" I ask, after a beat of awkward silence passes.

She nods, sipping from the dainty straw.

"Why didn't you ever tell me?"

I see it, the moment her eyes flare with panic, and her body stiffens on the stool. I watch as all the blood drains from her face. "Tell you w-what?"

"About how you felt all those years ago?"

She breathes out a huge sigh, and her body sags in relief. I eye her warily, wondering what that was all about.

"What did you think I was going to ask?"

Avoiding my gaze, she sets the glass on the bar top, looking down at the rings of condensation on the oak.

"There were so many times I wanted to tell you, but…I don't know. I think I just hoped you'd see me one day, and when you didn't, I didn't think professing my lov—professing my crush was the smartest decision."

"How long?"

A crease forms between her brows. "How long what?"

"How long did you have the crush?"

"Oh, God." She darts her gaze back down, avoiding me. "I don't really remember."

I chuckle, nudging her in the arm. "Just say it."

Peeking up at me through her lashes, she inhales a deep breath and summons the courage to say whatever it is. "Do you remember the first time we ever met?"

I frown. She's going to dodge my question with a question?

"The Grab-N-Go on our birthday."

Her eyes widen. She's obviously surprised by my memory. "Wow. You remember? I didn't think you would."

"So that was it?"

"Pretty much. You were the first guy I'd ever really taken notice of. This town…it was so quiet and boring before you got here. And it felt like I was the first of the town to ever lay eyes on you. In my small, childish mind, it felt like fate. Same birthday, buying the same cake. I guess, in my head, I convinced myself something with you would eventually be a possibility."

Understanding begins to dawn on me. She'd harbored a crush since the moment we met. How could I expect her to profess her feelings when she always felt like she was just someone in the background?

"I wish you would've told me. Said something. I might've been able to pull my head out of my ass sooner."

Her lips quirk in amusement. "Don't give yourself too much credit, now."

The grin that steals over my face makes my cheeks twinge with unused muscles. I haven't smiled this often in years, if not ever.

"I did notice you, you know. That first day in the store. I thought you were beautiful in a wallflower kind of way. You intrigued me. The one thing I remember most is your moon necklace. How much the moon meant to you."

She smiles. "Yeah, I had the necklace for a while. The chain broke a few years back while I was in Pasadena, and I just never bought a new one. It's funny, I went so many years feeling like that necklace was a talisman of sorts, and when I didn't have it, I chalked up all the bad things in my life to that specific cause. And now, without it, sometimes I feel bare, naked. For years, I relied on that necklace for strength."

"How did you become so…moon—"

"Moon obsessed?" She laughs and shrugs, a seriousness taking over her features. "It may not seem like it, but my parents fought a lot, and it was hard to deal with as a kid. I didn't want to have to choose a side. I didn't want to have to love one parent more than I loved the other, because, at times, it felt as though I was expected to pick. When they weren't on speaking terms, I was always the middleman. I had to make my dad dinner when Mom refused to. And when Mom couldn't figure something out, she had to come to me, because both of them were too prideful. It was tough. I spent a lot of time locked in my room, trying to ignore the sound of their shouting. It was always about the same thing. Money."

Something heavy settles over my chest as I listen to her. She seems deep in thought. Lost in her own mind.

"I remember one night while they were arguing, I opened the window and considered leaving. Not for long, because, obviously, I was just a child, but I thought just to get some fresh air and get away from their constant bickering. When I opened the window, I spotted the moon, and I don't know what it was about that night, but I stopped and really looked at it. So many times, we look up into the night sky and just skim over the moon. What's so special about something that's there every night, right? But that night, it was different. I felt like, for once, I had someone I could talk to. Someone I could confide in. Someone who would be there to listen each night.

"After that night, I started doing my own research on the moon, the phases, and what they meant in terms of spirituality. I was always interested in mythology, and it seemed the two intertwined. Then I became fascinated with the mythology behind the moon and the moon goddess. I felt like a kindred spirit with her since her name was Selene, too. I wanted to feel like there was a reason I felt so attached to the moon. Maybe there was; maybe there wasn't. But that's what I loved about the moon. The ability it has to change lives. Change the earth. It's stronger and much more resilient than people give it credit for.

"After all that, I started becoming obsessed with using the moon to manifest my intentions. Which I know, it sounds crazy, but you'd be surprised what believing in something can do for you. I learned about crystals and chakras, all the ways the earth gives us the tools to heal ourselves, without medication but our own divination. I even opened my own shop in Pasadena. It was a healing store."

My brows shoot up. So that was the business she lost out there? I wasn't expecting that.

"Wow. I had no idea your love for the moon began all those years ago. What happened with the business, if you don't mind me asking?"

She sighs, clearly still deflated by this. "Moonchild did well for a while, but where we lived in Pasadena, we needed more customers than my few regulars and some tourists. People would come in and look, but it was hard making a profit when there are bigger chains people flock to. Healing and 'magick' stores are often overlooked. People tend to think they're only there for hippies or witches, but that's not true. I don't practice witchcraft, but just like them, I do believe in manifesting your own intentions by using your own power. We were open for a little over a year and a half before I had to close. One day, I'd like to try again, but right now, making a decent living and taking care of my dad and Luna will have to do."

"You never thought about opening one here?"

She shrugs, glancing around at the lively bar-goers. "I never had any intention of coming back here."

"Why not?"

"Besides my dad being here, I didn't feel like Dunsmuir held anything for me anymore."

"He's missed you guys. He probably won't say it, but the times I've been with him, all he ever talked about was you and Luna. Felt like I knew her before I ever even met her."

She smiles, but her eyes swim with emotion. "I feel bad for being gone all those years. But when I got pregnant..." She pauses, quickly darting her gaze to mine. "My dad and I didn't have the best relationship. It was tough for him to come to terms with. There was a rift, and when push came to shove, my mom was there when he wasn't. I guess over the years when our relationship dwindled it was easy to put him in this box as the man who didn't step up to the plate. It was tough and unfair of me. It wasn't until maybe Luna's second birthday that we started doing things as a family again. It's still tough, but Luna…she loves him."

"He loves her, too. And I'm not blaming you for the decisions you made. Families are tough. Mine isn't perfect either."

"Is this where you expect me to believe your family was worse off than mine?" she asks, raising a single brow.

I chuckle. "No. Definitely not. I guess a part of me just understands you a bit better now. I understand why he was here, and you guys were there. I always wondered, but I never wanted to ask him. Felt like I would be pouring salt into his invisible wound."

"What made you start hanging out with my dad, anyway? When did that happen exactly?"

"Maybe about a year after your mom left? It sort of happened. Small projects here, offering each other beers or takeout there, and then we eventually made it a weekly thing. He'd always been good friends with my dad back when he'd bring your guys' cars to the garage for maintenance, so we decided to invite him over and treat him like family."

Her eyes grow misty. "I know I said this already, but thank you."

"Don't thank me. Anyone would've done it."

She shakes her head. "That's not true, and you know it."

A beat passes between us, and I have the urge to take her face in my hands and kiss her. Taste her lips and let my hands disappear into those long strands. But the sound of her phone chiming is our only saving grace. She quickly pulls it out of her purse, glancing at the screen.

"Everything okay?"

"Oh, yeah." She waves me off. "My mom was just letting me know Luna fell asleep with my dad. I'll just carry her into bed with me once I get home."

"How old is Luna?"

She smiles at the mention of her daughter. I don't even think she realizes she's doing it. It's just something that comes naturally when discussing Luna, I assume. "She's five going on twenty-five. I swear, that little girl is something else. She'll be six in a few days, actually."

A chuckle bursts past my lips. "Oh, I can only imagine. She's… sassy. I find I quite like it."

Selene rolls her eyes. "Yeah, because you don't have to parent her." As she says it, she suddenly deflates, a guilty look passing over her features.

"And her dad? Is he still in her life?"

Her brows tug down, slanting over her face, causing shadows. "Why?"

"Guess I'm just trying to figure out if he's my competition."

Selene looks away again, studiously avoiding my gaze. "There's no competition. Not with him and this…this version of you."

"This version of me?"

"Forget it."

"Have you…dated since him?"

She pulls a face. "God, no. Well, there was one guy I dated about a year and a half after she was born, but there was no spark. I felt like I was trying to make something work just to say I did it, you know? I blame Julia. She was the one who suggested I get out and date to help me move on. To help get my life back on track."

At the mention of Julia's name, it's like summoning over the beast. She sashays toward us.

"You guys down for pool? You two against Griffin and me?"

"I'm not very good. I don't even know how to play."

Julia smiles, patting her on the shoulder. "Oh, I know. That's why I'm assigning you to play. You'll help me look nice and sporty in front of Griffin. Now c'mon, hurry up."

I let out a chuckle when Julia is out of earshot. "She's perfect for Griffin."

Selene purses her lips. "My thoughts exactly. You sure you want me as your partner? I really suck at this. I'm not even kidding."

I grin, pushing up from the stool. I place my hand between us, palm up. "C'mon, I'll show you how it's done."

When she places her hand in mine, I do my best to ignore the way the currents of electricity stroke my palm at our point of contact.

Chapter Thirteen

Selene

When I place my hand in his, a thrill shoots up my arm, and the heaviness percolates in the air between us. Whatever the sensation is, it's potent. My tummy flips when we walk hand in hand toward the pool table. Julia and Griffin are already choosing their sticks. Off to the side, I notice Beth-Ann and Landon flirting in the corner of the bar, standing very, *very* close.

"Here, give this one a try," End says, handing one of the smaller sticks to me. I grab it warily, unsure of how to hold it and "give it a try." He chuckles at my attempts.

"Let me show you what I mean. Set your stick here," he says, demonstrating with his own on the edge of the table. "Place these two fingers on top and just glide the stick through. Feel the stick move in your hands; it should feel smooth and easy. Nice and controlled."

My stomach clenches at his words. They sound oddly erotic, even though this is the furthest thing from sexy. But coming from Endymion's mouth? Anything is sexy.

I shake my head, trying to clear my mind of those muddled thoughts and do as he instructs. It feels the same, even with his pointers, but I don't tell him so. I just don't think I have the skill for this. Some people are born to do stuff like this and get it on their first try. I'm not one of them.

"Feel okay?" he asks.

I nod, forcing a smile. His own smirk tells me he sees right through it. Leaning into me, he places his mouth near my ear to whisper his next words.

"I'll do all the heavy lifting, don't worry."

A flutter works its way through my body. I try to focus as Griffin cues the balls and takes the first shot. After he hits, he lets Julia go before it's our turn. I'm up, and my nerves suddenly make me tremble. I have a hard time keeping the stick still, that's how nervous I am. I feel End's heat behind me as he hovers around me.

"Here. Let me help."

He reaches around me, setting my hand and fingers exactly where he wants them. His skin on mine feels absolutely incredible. I find myself leaning into his touch, smelling his skin, and trying to soak in as much of him as I possibly can.

"Perfect. Now push it forward and aim here."

I do as he says, and surprisingly, I hit the white ball into our solid colors, pocketing a red one. I turn around, a grin spreading across my face. This is the first time I've ever played pool, and I've actually sunk a ball. Nothing like this ever works in my favor, and I'm sure I have Endymion to thank for that.

When it's his turn, he pockets one and lets me try for another, and again, he leans into me, trying to help. I feel the strong contours of his body against mine. His pecs, his biceps as they brush the outside of my arms. The heat emanates off his body in waves, rolling through me. It makes me feel dizzy and off-kilter. I can feel myself practically falling back under his spell. Being so close to him, having him show so much interest in me, it's a strange turn of tables. It makes me want to throw caution to the wind and just give myself over to him.

But like being doused in cold water, I remember why I can't do that.

Because I'm a liar.

A horrible human.

I'm the woman who's kept his child away from him, and he doesn't even know it.

I have everything I need to say all worked out in my head, but every time I try, nothing happens. The words never come forth. It's almost as if they're trapped, and my subconscious won't let them go.

I try not to enjoy the way his body feels against mine. The way his hands curl around my hands, the way his body seems to align with mine so perfectly. It's cliché; the way it feels like we're puzzle pieces finally becoming one.

My heart lurches, and my throat closes when I feel his lips near my ear. With his front pressed to my back, his heat, his smell, I have to hold my breath and trap my bottom lip between my teeth, trying to hold in the moan that's dying to escape.

"Okay, this is our last chance to end them. You ready?"

My stomach dips. My eyes flutter closed, and I don't realize I'm doing it until I hear his sharp inhale. I realize I'm fully leaned against him, making him take the brunt of all my weight.

Slowly, I shift in his arms, craning my neck to look back at him. My eyes zero in on his lips, and I lick my own, dying to know what it would be like now. Would it be as good as it was years ago?

Would I still feel all the same things I felt then?

My heart knows that answer better than anyone.

That string between us tugs us closer. He's staring at me with eyes that possess a shade of green that I've never seen on him. They're filled with heat and desire. Slowly, we both inch forward, and he searches my gaze. I can feel his unspoken questions.

"Are you sure?"

"Should I stop?"

I don't say yes.

But I also don't say no.

Because even though I know this a disaster in the making, I want him. I want him like I want the stars and the moon. I've wanted him for thirteen years. That's not going to change just because I spent years away from him. If anything, I feel more drawn to him now than I ever have before.

"Are you two going to take your turn or what?"

I jolt away from End, my gaze swinging toward Julia. She has her brows raised, clearly impatient with how long we're taking. She may not realize it, but she just saved me from making a huge mistake. She unknowingly just cut through what would've surely been another fall down the rabbit hole for me.

What is it about this man that makes me act so irrationally?

I adjust my stick with jerky movements and hurry up and hit the ball. Without even trying, I sink the eight ball, and everyone eyes me.

Figures, doesn't it?

"It's getting late," I announce to the table, hoping Julia will get the hint that I need her to give me a ride. If I stay here with Endymion any longer, I'm not sure if I'll be able to keep myself in check. I *cannot* let this happen.

"I can give you a ride back if you want," End offers.

Julia hoots, tossing her arms in the air. She's obviously too buzzed to drive me anyway. "Look at that! Perfect. You can catch a ride with End, and I'll catch one with Griffin, if you know what I mean," she says in a loud whisper that everyone hears. She does this twitchy thing with her eye. I think she's trying to wink at me, but honestly, I can't be too sure. She could just have an eyelash stuck in her eye. Because that's exactly what it looks like.

My lids slam shut.

You can do this.

Just a few more minutes.

You can hold it together that long.

Inhaling a breath for strength, I turn and face End, giving him a smile that doesn't quite reach my eyes. It's filled with nerves.

"Thank you."

The walk out to his truck is quiet and filled with tension. Like the gentleman he is, he helps me into the passenger seat. He places one of his hands along my waist, giving me a boost of sorts. I feel the heat of his hand burn through my clothes, branding my skin with his touch. It has my body breaking out in gooseflesh, just from one touch alone.

My eyes flutter closed, and I drop my head back onto the leather headrest, trying to pull myself together. But in doing so, my senses home in on End. The truck smells like him: a minty, clean scent with a hint of sage and something woodsy. It wafts in the confined space, infiltrating my senses.

My eyes fling open when he hops in. I try to keep my gaze trained on the dashboard. Anything to avoid looking at him. He starts the truck and pulls out of the parking lot, letting me get lost in my own thoughts.

The ride is quick, but I'm still antsy. I keep shifting on the leather, crossing and uncrossing my legs. It doesn't help that my feet are throbbing. It's been far too long since I've worn heels. It's not like I have many opportunities to wear them anyway.

When the truck rolls to a stop at the curb in front of my dad's house, it feels like a repeat of the other night. I tell myself I just need to thank him for the ride and be done with it. But that's not what I do.

I turn toward him, and that's my first mistake. My heart jumps into my throat when I realize he's already watching me with heavy, intense eyes that are wreaking havoc on my breaths. His bright-eyed gaze searches mine, scouring across my flesh. Tonight, his eyes look like a deep emerald green. The intensity with which he regards me has me swallowing thickly.

"Thank you. For tonight."

The corner of his mouth lifts ever so slightly. It's the smallest tic of movement, but it's still a wonder how it has the effect on me that it does. I feel it in my core.

"Anytime. I'll see you tomorrow, Selene."

I pause with my hand on the handle. My brows tug low into a frown. "You really aren't going to give up, are you?"

He shrugs. "You're worth the wait."

My traitorous heart skips a beat at his words. My chest squeezes with emotion, and guilt clogs my throat. "Why me?"

He twists, leaning across the center console, just enough that he's able to tuck stray hairs behind my ears. His fingers graze my cheek in the process. It has my heart pounding, trying to pump its way out of my chest, between the bones of my rib cage and into his hands for safekeeping. There's a roaring in my gut. It's the sensation of thousands of angry bees swarming. Buzzing so violently, I have to place a trembling hand over my stomach to calm the riot of sensations.

For so long I thought I was over this. Over him. I was wrong. I thought I left my love for him somewhere between the stars and the moon. But it turns out, my love for this man never left, it never waned. It's always been there, lying dormant, waiting for him to wake me from this eternal slumber.

"Why not you?" As he says this, his thumb finds its way to my lips, and he traces my lower one ever so softly. It's incredibly erotic and oh, so enticing. Without meaning to, I lean into his touch, closing the distance between us. My gaze is riveted to his lips. They're plump, and if memory serves me right, they have the capacity to drive a girl insane with lust. He's skilled. I remember that. So beyond skilled. My core throbs as images from the past surface, slamming into me. Begging me to do it again. To feel him inside me again.

I dart my gaze from his mouth to his eyes, and he does the same.

We lean in closer. So close, I can practically taste him. His breaths ghost across my face, intermingling with mine. Frissons of electricity pass through my body, into my veins and bloodstream as we close the distance. At the last minute, he turns, his lips connecting with my cheek and the corner of my mouth. He pulls away gently, staring down at me with so much heat in his eyes, I'm molten lava.

"If this isn't what you want, I need you to get out now. Because if you stay in here another second, I won't be able to stay away. I won't be able to stop myself." I feel him writing those words on my skin.

Slowly, I process. My mind is still boggled over that half-kiss. With slow ease, I pull away the slightest bit. Disappointment passes over his eyes, but it's brief. He shoots me a crooked smile, so much heat still lingering in the depths.

"See you tomorrow, Selene."

I nod, swallowing the sudden lump in my throat. A beat passes between us where we stare at each other before I jump into action. I get out of the truck and all but run into the house. My heart is banging against my chest, making it heave as it works to accommodate my heavy breathing.

I press a shaky hand to the side of my mouth where he kissed me. Without permission, a giddy grin spreads across my face. It makes everything feel lighter as though I'm floating on cloud nine. Pushing off the door, I walk past the kitchen and am about to head down the hall to check on Luna when I spot someone in the living room.

"Mom?"

She's covered in a blanket, her gaze fixed out the window. In this position, she has a clear view of the front of the house, where End just dropped me off. There's no doubt in my mind she saw what happened. I would think she'd be excited. She's the one who's always pushed for me to try my luck with him, but she seems quiet and reserved tonight. Almost pensive. As if something heavy is weighing on her mind.

"What are you still doing up?" I ask, taking the seat next to her. She finally turns to look at me. The lines around her mouth are deep as she purses her lips.

Something is definitely wrong.

She searches my gaze, looking for something. But I have no clue what.

"I want you to be honest with me if I ask you something."

My heart drops at her tone. Something is most definitely off here. My heart pounds and a stone settles in the pit of my gut.

"Okay," I say, my voice trembling with wariness.

"Who's Luna's father?"

My heart does something weird at that moment. As panic fills my chest, my heart stops beating, yet pounds a violent rhythm all at once. It's almost like I'm having an out-of-body experience. I can see the moment happening, but I can't grasp it. I can't grasp anything. Dread settles, cold and heavy over my shoulders, digging its claws into my skin.

I can slowly feel the blood drain from my face when she starts speaking again, obviously realizing I'm not going to answer.

"While you were at work earlier, I took Luna to the park with your father. We ran into Freya, Endymion's sister. Her daughter… her daughter is the spitting image of Luna. It was all we could talk about—Freya and me—just how much they look alike."

A sinking feeling enters my stomach. It feels like all the walls are closing in around me. Like someone is quite literally stealing the air from my lungs, making it impossible to pull in a single breath.

"That's…that's…" I trail off, unable to form a coherent thought. I have no more lies. I have nothing left.

My mom gives me a look. It's one that's filled with disappointment and something else I can't quite put my finger on. That look alone has my heart shriveling, dropping onto the carpet between us and shattering. I place a trembling hand over my mouth, trying to hold in the impending sob.

I collapse into a heap next to her, dropping my head into my hands. The dam finally breaks free. A sob tears from my chest, and I feel my mom's warm hand slide around my back, trying to comfort me.

"Talk to me, Selene. What's going on?" she implores.

"Before we left for Pasadena, I was at the creek one night. I just wanted one more night there before I left because I wasn't sure if I'd ever come back. That night, Endymion came by the creek." I pause, replaying the events of that night. My heart squeezes uncomfortably as I replay it all, frame by frame. I was so dumb. I was just a stupid girl in love. "That was the first night I felt like he finally saw me. We talked, and it was…it was different. I-I don't know how, but one thing led to another, then…"

My mom clears her throat, obviously understanding where I'm going with the story. Tears trail down my cheeks when I look back up at her.

"The next day, I went over to see him and talk to him. I thought that night had changed things. I was so caught up in him that I considered leaving the idea of college behind just to be with him." My mom's lips thin into a grim line. She obviously doesn't like that—doesn't like where my head was. It's crazy; the things love will make you do. "He didn't even remember. He was so drunk that night that he didn't remember me or what we did. I saw him with Holly, and it felt like…it felt like a betrayal. I felt like I had given him every piece of me, and he wasn't even of sound mind to notice."

Pity enters my mom's eyes, and I hate it. I hate that she pities me. "Oh, honey," she whispers.

"In Pasadena, I didn't notice the symptoms at first. It wasn't until my roommate talked me into taking a pregnancy test that I realized what had happened. I was pregnant with Endymion's baby, and he didn't even remember how it happened. I should've said something. I know that." I pause, wanting her to hear me and understand why I did what I did. Trying to justify my actions, just so I can have one person on my side. Because I know once this gets out, no one will be on my side. "I was just…I was so embarrassed. I was so hurt. I didn't know how I was going to explain that we slept together while he was drunk, and I was now pregnant. Then there was Holly. I didn't know if they were a couple. I didn't want to be the talk of the town. My crush wasn't exactly a secret, so I didn't want other people to think I did this intentionally. I just…I wanted him, and at the moment, it seemed like a good idea. Giving him my body, sharing something with him that I'd longed for, for years."

My mom heaves a deep sigh, nodding as she processes the information. I swipe the tears off my face, waiting for the reprimands to start. Waiting for her to tell me what a horrible human being I am.

She doesn't do that, though.

"That's why you keep turning him down, isn't it? You feel guilty."

"We'd never work anyway. He doesn't know the truth. He doesn't know that I've kept his daughter from him for years."

"This…God, Selene. This isn't good. You have to tell him."

I look down at the floor solemnly. "I know. I've been trying to find a way, but he's so…he's so persistent. Each time I think I'm ready, he storms into my life, charming me, buying me flowers, being sweet to Luna, and I don't know how to handle it. I've been in love with him for years. All I ever wanted was for him to see me. And now, now that's all he seems to be doing. He's seeing me, Mom."

My mom smiles sadly. "He's finally chasing the moon."

My chin wobbles and pressure builds behind my eyes. "I don't know what to do anymore. Luna's birthday is in a few days. How am I going to tell him?"

She pulls me into her arms, placing a chaste kiss on the top of my head. "You do know what you need to do. You just need to build up the courage to do it. I know you don't want to spring this on everyone and ruin her birthday, but she'll have many more, Selene."

"He's going to hate me," I whimper.

She's silent as she heaves a deep sigh. "He'll be angry with you. There's no doubt it. But I don't think it's possible for anyone to hate you, Selene. You're the sliver of light we long for. You're our moon, brightening our sky when everything is dark."

"How am I going to tell Luna?"

"Talk to Endymion first. You can both decide how you want to tell Luna. This isn't just your decision anymore. This is his, too. It's time to start including him in his daughter's life."

That night, I crawl into bed beside Luna and pull her into my body, hugging her to me so tightly, I fear I might hurt her, but I don't let go. I'm so scared of letting go.

I don't want to lose her.

For so long, it's just been her and me against the world. I never considered what it'd be like if that dynamic changed. I whisper sweet reassurances to her under my breath as I look out the window at the moon. So many things could go wrong. He could try to take her from me. He could try to keep me from her permanently. My heart clenches painfully at the thought, causing tears to leak out of the corners of my eyes. I squeeze my lids shut, praying for the strength it'll take to do the right thing.

The thing I should've done years ago.

Endymion deserves it.

My beautiful little girl deserves it.

I think of how sweet End has been lately, how hard he's tried to get me to open up, and I mourn the loss of a relationship that can never be.

He is the day. I am the night.

He is the sun. I am the moon.

We're opposite souls, yet we've found our way to each other despite that. I just hope there is a way to coexist peacefully.

Chapter Fourteen

Endymion

I watch her climb the steps into her house, and as she goes, I can't ignore the tingle reverberating from my lips. Every time I'm close to kissing her, I can't help but get these flashes of that previous dream. The one of us by the creek. My mouth on her skin, her hands roaming my body. Her soft, delicate moans. I swear, I can taste her. In the back of my mind, it's like I know what she'd feel like beneath me. She'd be incredibly smooth and smell like coconut, flowers, and honey. She'd feel like heaven.

My imagination is running wild with all these images and sensations. It feels like I have every part of her memorized, and I didn't even realize it. In my mind, I know the lines of her thighs, know what she feels like beneath my fingertips.

Shaking my head, I brush off the oddness of my thoughts. I've never felt this way about a woman. I've never been this persistent. I've never wanted to have anyone as badly as I want Selene. All of her. I want the light parts that emanate off her. I want the dark parts people take for granted. I want mornings with her. I want the days when I get to know her daughter. I want the days when I'm the reason she smiles.

I don't know when it happened, but at some point, I started falling for the moon. For her beauty. Her light. I started falling for Selene, and I find the sensation I've been running from my entire life isn't as bad as I once thought.

I had to drive out of town the night after I gave her a ride home from the bar. I had some contracts I needed to get signed before the start of our next projects. The guys were still hard at work at Gavin's place. Today, when I pull the truck up beside the curb, I take a peek in the back, noticing most of the crew has left for the day. It's after seven, so it's not really a shocker. My eyes linger a little longer on the random streams of decorations. It hits me then. Selene mentioned it was Luna's birthday soon. I must've missed it while I was out of town.

I grip the bouquet. This time, I went with daffodils. I don't plan on stopping until I get my yes. I ring the doorbell, and when Cece answers, I'm surprised by how…reserved she's acting.

"Endymion, hey. Didn't catch you here earlier."

"Yeah, I had some contracts to take care of in Redding. I just wanted to stop by and leave these for Selene. Wasn't sure if she was working or she'd be here."

Cece smiles, but it doesn't quite reach her eyes. "She just got in a little while ago. I'll get her for you." Just as she's inviting me in, I spot Selene over her shoulder. She looks beautiful, but that shouldn't really be a surprise at this point. She's dressed in a loose shirt that hangs off one shoulder and a pair of jeans. She smiles at me, but just like her mother, it doesn't reach her eyes. She seems nervous as her gaze darts from me to her mother. She's wringing her hands, almost as though she can't stay still.

"Hey," she croaks out and coughs into her hand to clear her throat. "I was hoping you'd come by. I actually…" She pauses, and it looks like she's sucking in a deep breath. "I actually wanted to talk to you about something."

My brows shoot up. This was unexpected.

She whispers something to her mom and shuts the door behind her, meeting me outside.

"Want to, um, go to the creek? Give us a little more privacy?"

I smile. "Lead the way."

Before we leave, I hand off the flowers to her, and her eyes brighten. But they dim just as quickly as if she remembers something.

"You okay?" I ask, as we walk toward the creek in silence.

She blows out a deep breath, turning her head to look up at me. "Yeah, I will be."

I grin, and just as I knew she would, she darts her gaze away, those cheeks heating.

"You look beautiful tonight."

She scoffs, unable to keep the smile off her face. "You know, I think you're just saying that to say it now."

I laugh. "I'm serious. You're beautiful."

She rolls her eyes, but I still see the hint of a smile on her lips. "Have you seen me? I just worked a full shift. My hair permanently smells like grease and fries, and I'm pretty sure the bags under my eyes have the capacity to swallow me whole."

Once we climb the hill toward the creek, I take the spot next to her in the grass. I shift to look at her, and I mean *really* look at her. I try to see all the bad things she's talking about. I'll admit, she looks tired, but she still looks beautiful. She smells even better. Like her usual honey and floral scent. It's her. It doesn't matter how long she's worked or what other smells have clung to her because I still smell *her*.

"I am looking. And want to know what I see?"

She tucks her legs into her chest, setting her cheek on top of them as she looks up at me.

"What do you see?"

"I see a gorgeous woman. I see a woman who I spent years overlooking and now? I'm taking in every piece of you like it's going to be my first and last time because I refuse to make that mistake again."

Her lips part in shock. Those beautiful doe eyes soften, and I can't tell if it's the gleam of the moonlight, but I swear her eyes start to water.

"Why couldn't you do this six years ago?" she whispers, her voice trembling with emotion. I press my lips together, angry with myself for letting her slip through my fingers all those years ago. Unable to help myself, I stroke my thumb across the freckles on the bridge of her nose. I relish the way her skin feels beneath my flesh. She feels like mine.

"Because I was an idiot. But I'm here now."

She sniffs, looking away from me. Her gaze is focused on the rippling water in the creek. She looks deep in thought. She always seems like she has a lot on her mind, but tonight is different. She seems different. As if she's waging some internal battle.

"I need to tell you something," she finally says after some time passes. "It's something I should've told you a long time ago." When she turns to look at me, I'm struck by just how beautiful she is. The way the moonlight gleams on her skin, like liquid pearl. She's porcelain. Perfect in every way, and I want nothing more than to be careful with her.

Those frissons are back. That string is being tugged. And those magnets are being drawn together. It's so forceful this time, and I have no way to stop it. My hand suddenly finds its way around the back of her neck and into her hair. She lets out a soft sound. It's a cross between a whimper and a moan, and I realize then that I can't hold back, not even if I tried. Tugging her mouth toward mine, I seal my lips over hers, falling into the kiss. Into her taste. She moans into my mouth, her hands coming up to my shoulders and gripping on for dear life. I work her bee-stung lips, getting lost in her sweet taste. I pause, though, when a flash hits me.

It's a moment of déjà vu. More than just déjà vu. I'm kissing her in the dream. I'm tasting her. It feels like heaven, a familiar heaven I haven't been able to fully forget. And how did I know she would taste like this? Like strawberries and cream. How did I know the exact way she'd feel in my arms? It's almost as if I've done this before. Almost as though—

When my tongue strokes hers, I'm transported back in time, and the images that flash behind my closed lids send a chill down my spine.

What the...

Her hot little body beneath my hands.

The strong smell of grass and the ripples of the creek behind us.

The moon illuminating her beautiful face beneath me as she pants, tossing her head back.

Feeling her tight, wet heat around my cock. Feeling her nails dig into my skin, her soft pants in my ears.

My eyes fling open, and I jerk away from her. I try to process what my brain already knows. I try to rationalize and chalk it up to chemistry, but it's not. My eyes grow wide, realization dawning on me. My imagination cannot be that vivid, and as I search her features, her soft hazel eyes that suddenly look guilty—the look on her face says it all.

We've done this before.

There's no other explanation.

My eyes slam shut, and I try to rack my brain for answers. There has to be a logical explanation. Surely, if I'd slept with her, I'd remember in full detail, wouldn't I? Why wouldn't she tell me?

Ice spreads through my veins as I think about the dream. I focus on what I was wearing and what I was doing out at the creek. Then it hits me. I vaguely remember the night years ago when I got drunk. Feeling frustrated and overworked at the garage, I left in a shit mood. I was tired of dealing with the bullshit, so I drank myself stupid, and like an idiot, I stumbled home.

Dread settles in the pit of my stomach as I put the pieces of the puzzle together. They still come in flashes, but I remember stopping by the creek to rest. I remember a beautiful girl lying there. I remember wanting to kiss her so badly, so I did. Then I remember the way she moaned into my mouth, clutched onto me.

Christ in heaven.

I fucked her.

While I was drunk.

Fuck!

"End—"

"This isn't our first kiss, is it?" There's an edge to my tone. Her stricken eyes grow wide.

"I can explain," she whispers, her bottom lip trembling.

"We've done more than this, haven't we?"

Her chin quivers with emotion. "I didn't tell you because I was embarrassed and ashamed. She doesn't even know. No one does."

My brows furrow. Who the hell is she—

An ice-cold twinge slithers down the center of my chest, stopping my heart.

I shoot to my feet unsteadily, taking a wary step back. My gaze narrows on Selene. Is she saying what I think she's saying?

No.

There's no way.

I try to do the math in my head. Try to remember how long it's been. How old her daughter might be in comparison.

"Are you telling me..." I trail off, trying to catch my breath. "Are you telling me that that little girl might be mine?"

Tears start slipping down her cheeks. "You're the only man I've ever slept with, End. There's no might about it."

Bile rises, threatening to expel at my feet.

"What are you saying right now, Selene? What the hell are you telling me right now, because it sure seems like you're telling me Luna is my daughter, and that can't be. She's fucking *five*. Five years old!"

Selene flinches at my tone. "She turned six yesterday."

Everything inside me crumples at her words. My chest caves, and my nostrils flare. Selene drops her face into her hands, and her body shakes as she sobs.

"Tell me right now. Is she mine? Is that little girl mine?"

She picks her head up, and I know the answer before she even utters the words. I feel it deep in my soul.

"She's yours."

My eyes slam shut. Emotion slams into me like a wrecking ball. It seizes my chest, squeezing my lungs in a vise. I should've known. When I first spotted her, it's no coincidence I thought she looked like my sister and niece, but now I get it. It's because she shares my blood. It's because she is *mine*.

A flash of anger and betrayal suddenly rips through my veins. Does Gavin know? Why hasn't he ever told me?

As if reading my thoughts, she answers my internal questions.

"He doesn't know. No one does. I only told my mother the other night. I tried to talk to you, years ago, I really did, I just…" She trails off, lost in her thoughts.

That explains her reaction to seeing me today on her porch.

Slowly, I shift my gaze, looking at her, trying to piece it together in my mind, trying to make it make sense. But I can't. Raking a frustrated hand through my hair, I pace, trying to remain calm.

"I need…fuck. I need to go."

I turn on my heels, leaving her there at the creek while I try to process.

While I try to process the fact that I have a five-year-old daughter—no, wait, a six-year-old daughter. A daughter that her mother tried to hide from me.

Chapter Fifteen

Selene

EVENTUALLY, WHEN I MAKE MY WAY BACK FROM THE CREEK, I WALK INTO the house on autopilot. The tears have long since dried on my face, and instead, I've been beating myself up for my choices. Guilt is a heavy burden weighing on my chest. The way Endymion looked at me tonight, it was the lowest low of my life. He looked disgusted and betrayed. The ache in my chest flares uncomfortably.

"Are you okay?" I jolt at the sound of my mom's voice. The words were whispered, but for some reason, they blared like an alarm in my ears.

Am I okay?

No. No, I'm not.

"He knows," I croak, tamping down a fresh wave of emotion.

"How did he take it?"

"Well." I blow out a shaky sigh. I feel drained of all energy, and I have nothing left. The shrug I give my mother conveys just that. "He left. I-I don't know what to do. I don't know what happens next."

"We'll figure it out tomorrow, okay? Right now, I think it's best if you just...go to bed. Give him time to process." I nod, though I know my chances of actually getting any sleep tonight are slim. I'll never forget the look in his eyes tonight. It was a painful mix of betrayal and anger.

"What's going on?" I freeze at the sound of my dad's voice. He sounds groggy and tired, and I'm sure this is the very last thing he needs to hear right now. I squeeze my eyes shut, mentally preparing myself for how I'm going to break the news to him.

"I-I…there's something I haven't told you. Something I haven't been honest about with anyone." Dad darts his gaze back and forth between my mother and me, a slow frown making itself at home on his face.

"What is it?"

"Luna's…" I choke, looking at the ground. Pressure builds in my chest, making it hard to breathe. I can't even look him in the eye and say it. "Endymion is Luna's dad. I never told anyone. It's a…a long story. And it's one he doesn't remember."

When I look up, my dad is staring at me with shock. Something passes over his features, but it's too brief to dissect it. "Did he…did he hurt you?"

The lines around his mouth are deep, and I realize then what my explanation probably sounded like to a father's ears.

"No! God, no. It wasn't like that. He was…drunk. He didn't remember any of it the next day, and I never told anyone. Then when I was in Pasadena, I found out I was pregnant. I made the wrong decision back then. I decided to keep a father from his child, and I know that was wrong." I sniff, trying to keep the pressure in my nose and eyes at bay. "We can talk more tomorrow, but right now, I think I just want to lie down with Luna and stop thinking just for a little while."

Without waiting for a response, I head down the hall and fall into bed next to my sweet girl. Silent tears trek down my face well into the morning. Regret is heavy and unbearable when I do eventually fall asleep.

I wake to the normal sound of End's crew working in the backyard. My heart does a sudden, traitorous jolt, and my stomach churns when my brain processes what happened last night. I spring up from the bed and run to the window, looking out toward the street, trying to see if I spot his truck.

Part of me wonders if he'll show up today at all.

Will he demand to take Luna?

What will happen next?

Padding into the bathroom, I brush my teeth and wash my face, taking in my swollen eyes and everything else I hate about myself. I'm having a hard time looking at myself in the mirror today, more so than usual. The weight of my past decisions is suffocating. Coming face-to-face with my poor choices is a slap in the face. I thought I was doing the right thing all those years ago. Hell, that's a lie. I always knew it was wrong, but I wasn't strong enough to face my faults head-on.

Heading back into the bedroom, I notice Luna stirring, and I can't help the smile that takes over my face. She's the one good thing in all of this. The only good thing I've ever done in my life. As I stare at my sweet girl, her little cherubic face soft with sleep, my heart aches, worry burning in my gut.

I don't want to hurt her.

The sound of something slamming shut outside has me edging toward the window. Ice floods my veins, and I freeze, watching as Endymion makes his way toward the house, gait stiff with barely restrained anger. Lurching into action, I snatch my cotton robe off the hanger and run out of the bedroom with my heart in my throat. In the narrow hallway, I pass my mom, who is eyeing me as if I'm insane.

"Stay with Luna. Keep her inside. Endymion just got here, and I'm not exactly sure what to expect."

I'm already running toward the door when she shouts after me.

"But you're still in your pajamas!"

I have bigger things to worry about.

I throw the front door open just in time, because Endymion is there, his hand raised like he was about to ring the doorbell. There's a moment when we both stand there, saying nothing as we stare at one another. The air crackles with a tension that is so potent, it's a live wire between us. Apprehension snakes its way through my veins, and my stomach turns uncomfortably.

That moment evaporates when I shut the door behind me, meeting him on the porch steps. Those lips that kissed me senselessly only hours prior now thin into a grim line and the muscle in his jaw fastens with frustration. His breathing turns heavy with whatever emotions he's feeling.

"Hey," I offer timidly, testing the waters. If possible, his face becomes more severe at the sound of my voice. "How are you?"

Endymion's brows raise incredulously. "How am I? *How am I*?" The tenor of his voice ramps up in volume, and his thunderous expression has fear skipping down my spine. He takes a threatening step into me, and on instinct, I stumble back. My senses are on high alert. "How the fuck do you think I'm doing, Selene?"

Tightness spreads through my chest, making my throat tight. "I know. I'm sorry. That was dumb. I just…I just didn't know where your head was after last night."

"And where the fuck would you expect it to be?" he bellows, and I flinch at the ire in his voice. A sob builds in my throat. I've never had anyone talk to me the way he is right now. I've never done well being yelled at. Maybe it's from years of living in a home with parents who fought the same way, but my stomach tightens, and I grow uneasy. I risk a glance back at the house, worried Luna will hear his raised voice. A few of his men have stopped working and are glancing our way, likely trying to figure out what's happening between us.

"I'm so sorry, End," I whisper.

"You're *sorry*?" He scoffs. The sound is a finely crafted blade to the heart. "You stole my daughter from me, Selene, and you think your sorry makes it all fucking better?"

"Please, just calm down and let me explain."

"Calm down?" He takes another step into me. This time, when I look into his eyes that are filled with anger, I finally see the other emotions. The sadness. His frustration. And the fear. He's confused and angry with me, rightfully so, but he's also scared. I just wish I knew about what.

I made a mistake, and chances are, I'll never be able to make it right.

"There is nothing you can say that will justify this." He clenches his jaw against the words, the veins in his jugular protruding against his tan skin. End rakes a frustrated hand through his hair, tugging on the ends. He looks like a feral, caged animal that is unable to handle his emotions. "What the fuck did you think my reaction was going to be? Did you think I wouldn't find out? I've missed six fucking years of her life. Six years!"

My eyes slam shut as I work to keep the tears at bay, but it's futile. "I'm sorry, Endymion. There's so much you don't understand… so much—"

"The only thing I don't understand is what kind of cold-hearted person could do this," he grits out coldly, taking another step forward. My back is flat against the front door. I sink into the wood, sagging against it to hold me upright. I wish it would swallow me whole. I feel the anger radiating off Endymion. He hovers just mere inches from me, his scent infiltrating my senses, making it hard for me to think clearly. "Just tell me why. Make me understand what was going through your head when you decided to run off to Pasadena and have my baby without telling me."

His tone gets my back up. He knows he's bullying me. He knows just how guilty I'm feeling, and he wants to tear me down. Fire burns through my veins, and I narrow my gaze, holding on to this sudden burst of anger.

"You were drunk, Endymion!" I snap. "You were so drunk you

don't remember taking my virginity. That next morning, I came to you so we could talk, and you ran off with Holly. I didn't know, okay? I didn't find out until much later, and by then, it'd been months since that night. I didn't know how to explain what happened. I didn't know how Holly would take the news. The idea of her boyfriend getting someone else pregnant while you two were together. I was confused and scared!"

"We weren't even together!" he shouts back.

"How was I supposed to know that? I didn't care about those facts. All I wanted was to get the hell away from you and this town after that night. When I found out I was pregnant, I was already four months along. I couldn't even believe it. And I wanted to reach out and tell you, but the first time I called my dad to break the news, our relationship fell apart, and I no longer had any connections out here, except Julia, and when I asked about you, you were gone. I had no way to tell you."

"You could've found out where I was if you'd asked my parents."

"I didn't think about any of that! I didn't know how you'd take the news. I didn't know if you knew about my crush, and I worried you'd think I was insane. I worried about what everyone was going to say and think once they found out the truth."

"So, all that was more important to you than telling me about that night? Telling me about the pregnancy?"

"At the time, yes. It made sense in my head. I rationalized it. But over the years, that changed. Especially now."

"You know what you are?" he asks, looking down at me with a look of utter contempt. "You're selfish. You're exactly what I thought you were, a fucking child. You let your own pride get in the way of me meeting my daughter."

Pain slices through my chest. My ears are full of static. I open my mouth, stuttering out words, trying to refute the claim, but it's true. I was being selfish when I made those decisions. "I-I..."

"You what? Is this the part where you lie, and you tell me you tried to tell me?"

I never wanted it to come to this. I never wanted it to get to such an ugly place where he's this angry with me. I place a trembling hand over my lips, trying to hold in the sob. I hate myself at this moment because he's right. As much as I hate to admit it, I did act like a child. Luna has lost years with her father because of me. All those times she's asked about him, I should've told her the truth. I should've tried to reach out to Endymion earlier, and maybe…maybe it wouldn't be as bad as it is now.

"No," I choke, swiping the tears under my eyes. "You're right. I was childish. I was so hurt by…" I pause, keeping the words locked inside, not even going to bother repeating them out loud. He doesn't need to know how deep my feelings went for him. That will only make me look more like a fool than I already do. "I shouldn't have let that happen," I say, pushing the words past my quivering lips. "I should've been the bigger person. I know I can't make up for the years you lost, but she's here now, and I promise you, I won't get in the way of you being a father to her."

"You're right, you can't. The only reason I came here today was to look you in the face when I tell you I'm hiring a lawyer. You're not keeping her from me any longer."

My blood runs cold at the admission, fear wrapping around my heart with a deadly grip.

"Wait. Endymion," I choke, clutching onto his arm as he turns away. He shakes my hold off him, and the look he pins me with me chills me to the bone. I let go of him immediately. There's no heat in his gaze. Not like there has been the last week or so that he's been courting me. No, instead, it's just ice. It feels like dry ice against my skin, burning in a different, more painful way. Almost as if the glare alone is abrading my skin.

My heart withers, and pain laces through my chest as I force the words past my lips. "I wasn't going to keep her from you. Please, let's talk about this."

"We both know that's a fucking lie, Selene. Just like everything else that comes out of your mouth." The way he says my name, with so much venom lacing his tone, it slides its way inside my blood and burns. I can't seem to catch my breath. It's too painful. Everything hurts.

"Are you planning to fight for custody?" The question barely makes it past the panic restricting my throat.

End spears me with a deathly glare. "If I have to, I will."

He storms away from the house, and the first tear slips down my cheek. It's slow in its descent, making a mockery of me and my affliction. I cast a quick glance around the yard and pause on one of his friends, Bishop. He's staring at me, frozen in his spot, shock written all over his face. He must think I'm a monster. I'm sure in no time at all, everyone will. For a split second, I almost think I see empathy in his eyes, but he turns before I can get a better look.

Trying to pull myself together as best as I can, I turn and walk back into the house. My dad is there, pacing the oak floors. He comes right to me when he sees me, worry lingering in his gaze.

"You okay?"

I inhale a deep, rattling breath that makes the ice filling my chest ache even more. "No. He's getting a lawyer. I-I don't know what to do. Lord knows I deserve this after not telling him, but…I don't know. I'm going to talk to Luna. I don't know how quickly all this is going to happen, and I don't want her to be blindsided."

My dad nods slowly as he processes with a concerned expression painted on his face. "What do you need from me?"

"Maybe keep Mom busy? I need to be alone with Luna for a while."

Dad pulls me in for a hug that threatens to crumble the hold I have on my emotions. I'm hanging on by a thread, and I know the minute I see my little girl, I'm going to fall apart because my biggest regret in all this is failing her.

I'm not surprised that when I push through the bedroom door, I can already hear her playing with her toys, her imagination running wild.

"Hey, Mommy," she says, glancing up quickly before focusing back on the task at hand.

"Hi, baby. What are you doing?"

"Playing with the dolls Papa bought me. Nana said they're going to buy me McDonald's breakfast this morning, so we don't have to cook."

I grin down at her, taking the open place next to her on the bed. I pat the spot right next to me.

"Can I talk to you about something for a second? It's really important."

She huffs out a breath, drops her Barbies, and tosses herself into the spot right next to me. Mirroring my position, she turns to face me, setting her hands in her lap just like I'm doing. She looks so much like Endymion at this moment that it's hard to ignore the burn in my chest. Anxiety slams into me, eating away at my confidence as I wring my hands together, trying to figure out a way to tell her.

"I thought maybe we could talk about your dad."

Her eyes widen, and for what feels like the first time ever, I think my daughter is actually listening to me. Her usual sass is nowhere to be found, and instead, she's staring up at me like she can't wait to hear more.

"Your dad and I…well, we don't live close. But now that we're here with Papa, we live closer and—"

If it's possible for her eyes to grow bigger, they do. "You mean, my daddy is here?"

My heart squeezes. "Yes. Do you remember Endymion?"

"Of course, I remember End!" I can see her brimming with excitement already.

"Well, End is…your father. Since we lived far away, and he lived here, it was hard to see him."

Her little face scrunches in an adorable frown. "Why didn't he come to see us? Like Papa does?"

I trap my bottom lip between my teeth, trying to keep my tears at bay. "He didn't come to see you because he didn't know about you."

"Why didn't he know about me?" Her smile slowly slips off her precious little face, and I'm panicking internally. She's too young to understand any of this. I can't tell my child that one drunken night her father got me pregnant and didn't remember it.

"Because I…" My voice trails off as I try to gather myself. Pain has taken residence in my chest. It's a living, breathing entity that is all-consuming. The very last thing I want is my daughter hating me for the decisions I've made, but being honest about her father is what she deserves. It's what they both deserved from the start. Swallowing my pride and my fear, I force the words past my lips. "I never told him. I didn't think I'd ever see him again. And I'm sorry, baby. I'm sorry I didn't tell him sooner. I'm sorry I didn't tell you sooner."

She's quiet as she looks up at me, her little eyes searching my face, watching me. Her little mouth tugs down in a semblance of a frown.

Does she hate me, too?

"Does that mean I'm gonna live with End now?"

My throat closes. I blink away the tears that are building, tamping down the tightness that's squeezing my throat. "Well, maybe. Yes. That's a very good possibility. But first, I think we should focus on you getting to know him better."

"But what about you?" she asks quietly, her eyes suddenly filling with tears. "Where will you go?"

I smile sadly, blinking past the fresh wave of emotion burning the backs of my eyes. "I'll be right here. I'm not going anywhere." I take her little hand in mine and squeeze. "This just means you get double the love."

She looks pensive as she glances down at the bed. "What if he doesn't like me?"

"Hey, none of that," I chide, scooting closer to her and pulling her onto my lap. "Endymion thinks you're the funniest little lady around already. He's going to love you. He already does."

"But what if he doesn't?"

"He will."

She pulls back, raising a single brow at me with attitude. "But what if he doesn't?" She enunciates each word as though I'm deaf, and she's having to spell it out for me. All I can do is laugh because my sassy little girl is back.

"Then I'll love you enough for both of us."

Her smile is blinding. It fills my heart with so much love that I can barely stand it. "I love you, Mommy," she whispers, nuzzling into my chest.

"I love you always, Luna Bella."

I clutch my daughter to my chest, finally letting my tears fall.

After putting my sweet girl to bed, I make a quick detour and decide to see my best friend. I rap my knuckles on the front door. I think I have most of my emotions in check until Julia opens the door, wearing a warm smile on her face. My expression must give it all away because her smile falls, and without me needing to ask, she pulls me into her arms, clutching me against her body.

"What did that son of a bitch do?"

A sob rips from my chest. "It wasn't him. It's me."

Heaving a sigh, Julia guides me inside her house, leading us into the kitchen. I take the seat across from her at the table, unable to stop the tears from rolling down my cheeks.

"Ready to talk now, or should I bust out the chocolates and wine?"

"Chocolates and wine. Definitely."

Once I have a significant amount of wine and chocolate in front of me, I figure it's now or never. I just hope she doesn't hate me for keeping the truth from her, too.

"Luna's father isn't some guy I met at Caltech." Julia freezes with her wine glass to her lips, her brows tugging low. "It's Endymion."

With slow, methodical movements, Julia sets her wine glass down onto the table and narrows her eyes to thin slits. "Elaborate. Right now."

"A few days before I left for college, I slept with Endymion. It was perfect, and everything I've ever wanted, until it wasn't. I didn't know he was drunk, so drunk he didn't remember anything the next day. He didn't remember me, Julia. He drove off with Holly, and it felt like that was the last straw. I was hurt and upset. I wanted nothing to do with him ever again."

Pain grips my chest when I see hurt flare in the depths of Julia's eyes. "I'm your best friend. How could you keep this from me?"

I reach across the table, taking her hand in mine and squeezing. "Because I was so fucking embarrassed. I spent so many years chasing after a guy who didn't even know I existed. I gave my virginity to him, and still, it wasn't enough. I felt stupid."

"Do you really think I care if you look stupid, Selene? I would've helped you. I would've...I don't know what I would've done, but I would've been there for you."

A hot tear leaks down my cheek. "I know you would've, and I'm so sorry, Julia. There were so many times I wanted to tell you, but I just didn't know how. I think I also knew you would've made me tell him."

"Tell him what—" Julia's eyes widen, and hell, I swear I even see the color leave her face. "Oh, Jesus fucking Christ, he doesn't even know. How could you possibly think you could keep a man away from his child like this?" she reprimands.

"I don't know! It wasn't my intention. I just…I didn't know how to tell him the truth. How could I? He didn't even remember sleeping with me."

She begins rubbing at her temples as if all this is starting to give her a headache. "God, Selene, how are you going to tell him?"

Grabbing the wine glass, I tip it back, downing most of it in one go. "I told him, and let's just say…it didn't go well. He hates me, Julia, and I know I deserve it. Hell, I probably deserve to be stoned or hanged or—"

"Okay, let's not get too carried away."

I blow out a sigh. "I know I deserve a lot worse, but it still hurts. His anger toward me. For the first time since I was that idiotic young girl, End was seeing me. *I* was the girl he wanted. He was chasing *me*."

"Just give him time. Let him be angry, Sel. He has every right to be."

"I know. I just wish it didn't hurt so much."

Julia scoots her chair next to me and wraps her arm around my shoulders, pulling me into her side. I rest my head on her shoulder, trying to hold back a fresh wave of tears. "Even though you're an ass-hole who has been keeping major secrets from me, I still love you. You have a good heart and the sweetest soul. He'll see that sooner rather than later. I promise."

"Have I told you how much I love you lately?"

Julia's chest vibrates with a laugh. "Not nearly enough, babe. You got a ton of repenting to do."

"Don't I know it."

I keep my finger hovered over the call button, unsure if I should wait for him to make the first move. He dropped the lawyer bomb on me earlier today, so a part of me feels like I should wait for him to come to me, but if this is going to work, he needs to spend time with Luna. Especially now that she knows the truth.

Well, most of it anyway.

Just do it. For Luna.

Swallowing my pride, I dial the number my father gave me earlier. After my talk with Luna this morning, we had McDonald's for breakfast, then I let her run amok to play. While she was playing, I asked Dad for End's number. I noticed there was a bit of hesitation in his eyes, but I tried not to read too much into it. I've been sitting on the number for what feels like hours, all because I'm afraid of what End will have to say.

With my heart banging against my chest, I call the number and listen as the line rings once, twice, and a third time, before the deep voice erupts on the other end of the line.

"Black Construction, this is Endymion, how can I help you?"

I open my mouth, a hello, or something intelligible is on the tip of my tongue, but all that falls from my lips is a horrendous squeak. He sounds just as handsome on the phone as he does in real life. If possible, his voice even sounds deeper here. "Hello?" he calls again, this time a little louder with a hint of impatience in his tone.

"Endymion. Hi." I pause, slamming my eyes shut as I try to gather my thoughts. "It's Selene."

Silence.

Deafening silence.

"You still there?" I ask, pulling the phone away from my ear. Glancing down at the screen, I check to see if he ended the call. He didn't.

"I'm here," he says, his voice sounding much gruffer than it did before. "What do you want?" I flinch at the ice in his tone. My grip tightens on my cell phone.

"I just wanted to tell you that I talked to Luna. She, um…she knows about you. And I know you've spent time with her before, but I thought it would be a good idea for both of you to spend some more time together."

"When?"

"Whenever works best for you—"

"I can be there in a few," he says, cutting me off. There's a brusqueness to his tone. It's almost like he doesn't even want to hear me speak.

"Okay, cool. Great. This is great. Thank you."

He scoffs. It's such an ugly sound that stabs viciously at my soul. "Don't thank me for spending time with my own daughter."

With that, he clicks off, and I slam my eyes shut. I deflate against the counter, hanging my head. I take a few minutes to compose myself, to prepare myself for more days like today. Hell, probably an eternity.

I get Luna dressed, and true to his word, Endymion is here in just a few short minutes. My parents have thankfully retreated to their own rooms. I think they understood how important this would be for Luna and Endymion, and the last thing they need is an audience dissecting every moment of their time together.

"Is he here?" Luna jumps up and down excitedly, and I grin down at her, glad at least one of us is feeling positive about this experience. Her eyes suddenly grow wide as if she's just remembered something. "Oh, no! I forgot my toys in the room. Wait, Mommy!"

Sucking in a lungful of air, I palm the amethyst crystals in my pocket for strength and open the door. My breath gets lodged in my throat at the sight of him. Dressed in another flannel, a forest green and gray one that brings out the color of his eyes, and a black shirt with fitted jeans, he looks as handsome as ever. His hair is an unruly mess at the top of his head. If my memory serves me correctly, the strands are thick and silky to the touch. Rogue strands fall over his pale green eyes that are so opaque, they're almost like moonstones dipped in an ethereal moss.

His jaw is set in a firm line. The muscles jump, no doubt as he grinds his teeth together. It's obvious he's not happy that he has to converse with me. He couldn't be any colder toward me, even if he tried. I shift awkwardly on my feet, feeling anxiety twist my stomach. I tug at the hem of my shirt nervously, suddenly incapable of speech now that he's here. I had everything I was going to say to him worked out. I planned on playing the part of the strong parental front, but that obviously isn't working.

"Where is she?" he asks, glancing inside, over my shoulder.

As if answering for me, Luna's feet pound along the oak floors as she runs down the hall. She's wearing her favorite dress. It's a white summer dress with sunflowers on it. Her brown hair hangs around her shoulders in little loose little curls that she's had since she was a baby. I added a sunflower clip to each side of her head to keep the hair out of her face. Her little arms are filled with toys. My lips quirk up in amusement as I watch her skid to an abrupt halt, her bright eyes looking up at Endymion.

As I watch my daughter stare up at her father, something happens in my chest. It's a restricting sensation that makes it hard to breathe. I press my palm to my sternum, trying to rub the icy twinge away.

Luna's cheeks are tinged a soft pink, just like mine usually are, as she stares up at Endymion. "Hi," she whispers.

I risk a glance at Endymion's face and find him staring down at Luna, a fierce look in his eyes that displays so much emotion, I internally berate myself. I've never seen him look so uncertain. Finding out you have a daughter you never knew about can't be easy. It's written all over his face.

"Hey there, Luna." His tone is softer than I've ever heard. A voice reserved solely for our daughter.

Luna grins. She looks like a happy, bright-eyed little girl, just like she's supposed to.

"I'm so happy you're here!" she belts out excitedly, dropping the toys that are in her hands, and she throws her arms around Endymion's legs, hugging him. He seems slightly taken aback at first but seems to recover quickly, wrapping his arms around her, then lifting her. Hurt skirts briefly across his face as he holds our daughter before he masks it. The view of them together like this, it has a fresh wave of tears stinging my eyes. They look like twins. She is quite literally a tiny version of Endymion. His hands span most of her back, making my sweet girl look tinier than she usually does in my arms.

When I glance back up at his face, my heart does something strange at that moment. It skips more than one beat. The way Endymion is looking down at Luna isn't the way he's looked at her before. This look is different. It's filled with so much love and emotion that I don't know how to process it. His eyes are soft as he stares down at her, his arms tightening around her like he never wants to let go. My chest caves with a burning discomfort, making it hard to pull in a single breath. I sink my teeth into my bottom lip until I feel the stitch of pain.

I lock eyes with Endymion, and he says so much at that moment without words. There are accusations in his eyes. Anger at me keeping his daughter from him. Depriving him of moments like this. I sniff past the pressure building in my nose, and I glance away. It suddenly feels like I'm an intruder, unwelcome here. I start backing away, but as if sensing that I'm getting ready to leave them alone, Luna whirls around in his hold, her brows tugging low over her cherubic little face.

"Where are you going, Mommy? Aren't you going to play with us?"

I dart a quick glance at Endymion before looking back at her. "Oh, I don't know, baby. I think you two should—"

"I think what your mom means is, we're gonna hang out together in your grandpa's living room."

"Okay!" She scoops up her toys and runs at full speed into the living room.

"Thank you," I whisper under my breath. He turns to look at me, his gaze searching mine. His lips thin.

"I didn't do it for you."

Parting with such harsh words, he follows Luna into the living room while I hang back a bit, trying to pull it together long enough that I won't fall apart in front of them.

I take the furthest end of the couch, and I watch Endymion play with Luna. Or rather, he watches her as she plays and explains how the game goes. She introduces the names of her Barbies and their favorite things. He watches her so closely as if he's committing everything about her to memory. He asks questions about the dolls and their favorite colors as if he truly wants to know the answers. He's so good with her.

Without meaning to, as I watch Endymion with our daughter, I fall a little deeper in love with him. I've tried to pretend I don't care about him anymore, but that's a lie. I've *always* loved him.

"And this one is Moonstone," she says, referring to one of her Barbies with black hair. "I named her that because she kinda looks like my mommy, doesn't she? My mommy loves the moon. Did you know that?"

Endymion glances at me. "I didn't know that," he lies, humoring her.

"Yeah, my mommy is really smart, and she's like the smartest mommy in the world. Oh, and she has all these cool stones she uses to do magic!"

I shake my head, laughing nervously. "Baby, I told you it's not magic. The crystals are just something to believe in. Something to hold on to when you need extra strength. Remember, I said the magic isn't in the stone, it's in *you*."

My stomach drops when I glance at End. He's staring at me with narrowed eyes. I lick my suddenly dry lips.

"It's not magic. I promise. It's just crystals. Like these," I say, digging into my pocket, pulling out the crystals I've been holding on to. His brows dip even more, and he nods slowly. He still doesn't quite understand why I'm carrying them around with me.

Not many people do.

"Oh!" Luna yells. "Do you have any tattoos?"

Endymion chuckles at her brisk change in subject. "I do. Just a few."

She grins. "So does my mommy!"

Again, he glances at me but says nothing. Thankfully, he asks her another question about a different Barbie, so we can get off the topic of me.

"And this one is one of my favorites. Theo bought it for me."

End's brows dip. "Who's Theo?"

"Oh, he was our old neighbor. He always bought me and Mommy stuff." Methodically, Endymion aims a questioning look at me. I feel my cheeks pink because I know what Luna's going to say next before it even falls past her loose lips. "Yeah, he was in love with Mommy."

My eyes slam shut. *Great.*

Just great.

"Luna Bella, that's not true. Don't say that."

She shoots a glare at me. "Yeah, it is! He told Nana and me. He said he wanted to date you, but you always said no."

I press my lips together, studiously avoiding Endymion's gaze. I can feel it burning a hole through the side of my head. I clasp my hands together, pushing to my feet.

"You know what? I'm going to grab you guys some snacks. I'll be back." My voice betrays me, revealing just how nervous I am, and I practically run off.

"Okay, Mommy," Luna says, cheerily oblivious. Once in the kitchen, I rub the crystal more fiercely, cursing myself for not keeping it together.

Theo is handsome. And sweet. But I wasn't interested. I considered dating him, but it was hard. I'd just opened Moonchild, and I didn't have a ton of free time on my hands, and the time I did have, I spent with Luna. We shared one kiss that woke up something inside me that had been dormant for years, but other than that, there was no spark or butterflies. What I felt with him was nothing like what I felt with Endymion, and that was the problem. It would've been unfair of me to go on a date with him, knowing deep down, he'd never measure up to the man I'd loved my entire life.

I was beginning to think no one would measure up. Endymion was a force all on his own.

Gathering some snacks for them, I set everything on a tray and start walking it back into the living room but pause as I listen in on their conversation, still hidden by the wall. Luna is telling Endymion a story about last Christmas, and I can hear his deep chuckle, his prying questions. A small smile turns up the corners of my mouth. I hang back a bit and listen a little longer, not wanting to ruin their moment.

"So, you like sunflowers?" his deep voice asks, referring to her outfit of choice.

"I do! It's my favorite flower. Do you like sunflowers?"

Endymion pauses. "I do now."

My heart squeezes. I slam my eyes shut, gripping the tray of snacks for dear life.

Once there's a lull in the conversation, I drop the snacks on the table and make excuses, saying I need to wash clothes really quick and clean up the bedroom. When I glance at Endymion, there's a knowing gleam in his eyes. He knows exactly what I'm doing, but obviously, he doesn't say anything.

I retreat to the bedroom down the hall and rest on the bed. Flopping back on the sheets, I stare up at the ceiling. A deep sigh expels from my chest as I think about what the future could possibly hold for all of us.

It's selfish of me to feel this way—I mean, hell, I've had six years of interrupted time with my daughter, and Endymion has had none, but I still can't help but worry about the holidays. The times I'll have to share her. The nights I'll have to fall asleep without her. The thought alone is crippling. It squeezes my chest in an unrelenting fist and makes it hard to breathe.

A single tear leaks out of the corner of my eye, rolling down my temple and disappearing into my hair. I hate this feeling. I can definitely see why my parents stayed together all those years, to avoid this, the sharing. Having to go any amount of time without seeing your child is devastating.

I'm running through all the bad scenarios in my head and pause at the sound of light rapping at the door. Hastily, I wipe my face and sniff back the pressure in my nose, thinking it's Luna. I don't want her to see me cry. Getting to know her father should be a happy moment, not filled with my worries and my tears.

Imagine my surprise when my dad pops his head inside. He looks tired, with dark bags under his eyes and worry written all over his face. Some days he seems better than others, but today isn't one of those days. Part of me thinks it has to do with the news I dropped about Endymion and me. I knew the stress would be too much for him.

Guilt is a heavy boulder resting on my shoulders. Not only am I a horrible human being for keeping a man away from his daughter, but I've lost precious time with my father, all because I couldn't put my pride aside and pick up the goddamn phone.

Heaving a tired sigh, I push upright and rest my back against the headboard of my old bedroom, watching him as he steps into the room and perches on the edge of the mattress.

"How're you doing, kiddo?"

I shrug noncommittally. "I'm managing. Trying to give them their space, even if it is the hardest thing I've ever had to do."

"I bet. How's Endymion handling it?"

A dry laugh bursts past my lips. "How is he? I'm surprised you didn't hear him earlier. And if you couldn't tell, he's not good. He hates me," I mumble.

Dad barks out a gruff chuckle. "Oh, I did. I think everyone in Dunsmuir heard you guys out front."

"Oh, God," I groan, dropping my head in my hands. "I can't believe this is happening."

My dad's silent for a beat until he blows out a sigh. "Why didn't you ever say anything to me, honey? All those times you asked about Endymion, I just thought it was because you still had a crush on him. I never even…I never put the pieces together. And I'm sorry."

My brows disappear into my hairline. "You're sorry? Dad…none of this is your fault."

His mouth twists into a frown. "Maybe a part of it is. I haven't been a great father or a great husband. I should've been around more. I should've fought harder for your mother instead of fighting with her. I should've done a lot of things differently, but most of all, I'm so damn sorry I wasn't there for you when you needed me most."

My throat closes at his words. We've never discussed the rough patch in our relationship. We've always avoided the topic, but now that he's mentioned it, it brings up emotions from the past I thought I'd gotten over. A prick ricochets through my chest, and tears burn the backs of my eyes.

"Dad," I choke out against the tightness in my throat, falling into his arms. I clutch at my father, crying for the scared eighteen-year-old girl who found out she was pregnant. All those months that girl was ignored by her father. The one man in her life who was supposed to be there through everything. And I'm crying because now the man upstairs is going to take him from me. Just when I barely got him back. “I love you.”

“I love you, too, honey,” he breathes into my hair. “We’ll get through this. Luna is going to be fine, and as for Endymion…he’ll come around and forgive you.”

I laugh without humor. “I don’t think that’s going to happen.”

“Don’t sell yourself short, Selene. He’ll forgive you in his own time. You’re the mother of his child. He’ll never be able to hate you.”

“Thank you, Daddy,” I whisper into the crook of his neck, never wanting to let go.

Chapter Sixteen

Endymion

I have a daughter.

I have a five—no, six—year-old daughter that I never knew about.

On top of all that, I'm still trying to process the fact that I slept with Selene while I was blackout drunk and don't even remember it happening.

How is that even possible?

I am still trying to unfold the insanity of it all. Before Selene got into town, I hadn't thought much of her. I didn't have much reason to. But the times I did think about her, it was always a glimpse of her soft skin and silver moonlight. That was all I could associate with her and my memory. It wasn't until she showed up back Dunsmuir that I found myself needing to be near her. Something about her called to me. Something I couldn't get out of my head.

Since seeing her for the first time in years, I've had these frequent flashes, quick images that play behind my lids like a movie reel, but I chalked it up to a dream or a newfound fantasy. Never in a million years did I think it was real. Never did I think I was secretly reliving those memories. That the entire time my head was trying to tell me to wake up. Trying to tell me who she really was.

I still don't know how to process how I feel about Selene, after everything that has happened. I'm angry with her, so fucking angry, but a small part of me understands her logic. It was the logic of a teenager, of a brokenhearted girl who didn't know any better. I'm still utterly captivated by her beauty. By her heart and soul. By everything that she is, but after this…I don't know if I can trust her. I don't know who that woman is anymore.

I can't help but replay these past few weeks. The way she seemed drawn to me—there was no denying the attraction between us—but for some reason, she always turned me down, and at the time, I thought it was because she'd been hurt before. And I guess, in some way, she had. But not intentionally. I never intentionally set out to hurt her. I thought I'd be able to wear her down, and she'd eventually agree to that date with me. Now, I just feel like an idiot. Did she laugh behind my back when I asked her out on those dates? Did she think I was a fool? Because I sure as hell feel like one.

And then there's my daughter. The fact that I'm even repeating that sentence and it's factual is…insane. I have a daughter—the most beautiful little girl and she already has my heart beating solely for her. Even though I'd met Luna before, it was different earlier today at Gavin's place. I spent time with her as my child. She is mine. Mine to love, mine to protect, mine to care for. I tried not to think about all the parties I had already missed. All her firsts I'd never be able to get back. There is nothing I can do about that now.

I've made a promise to myself that I'll be there for every first from here on out. There isn't a chance in hell I am missing out on anything else in my daughter's life.

I missed watching her take her first steps and say her first words. I didn't know if she cried a lot when she was baby or if she was always so calm like my niece was. Something tells me, though, that calm isn't in Luna's vocabulary. She has spunk and sass in spades, and I find her to be the funniest little thing on the planet. She's mad gorgeous. I see so many parts of myself in her, but I also see so much of Selene, too, when I look at her now.

"How are you holding up?" Bishop asks, setting a beer down in front of me. My mouth waters, but after the recent knowledge that I created a child while intoxicated, I don't think the best thing for me to be doing tonight is drinking.

I finally told the guys everything after I left Selene's place earlier. Though, I'm sure most of them got the gist of what was going on when I yelled at her the day prior. It was hard to miss. I didn't mean to yell or lose my temper with her. It was wrong, especially taking the risk of Luna seeing, but something inside me snapped. I had zero control over my emotions at that moment.

"Honestly, I still don't know how to feel."

Bishop sighs, plopping down next to me. "You really don't remember?"

My mouth twists into a grimace. "No. Not really. When I saw Selene, there was a spark of a memory, but I chalked it up to a vivid dream. Because I couldn't remember that happening. I can't believe that..."

"This would be just your luck. You have sex with one of the hottest girls in town, and you don't even remember it. And on top of that, you get her pregnant."

I laugh darkly. "Right? I kept wondering why I felt so drawn to her. She's beautiful, that's obvious, but it was something else. She felt so familiar to me. She was easy to be around."

"Does this change things for you?"

I pause, thinking. "I don't know. All I know is, I want to get to know my daughter."

My daughter is my only concern right now. Once I figure things out with her, then I'll deal with Selene.

"The lawyers. Were you serious about that?"

"Shouldn't I be? I'd be stupid not to set something in motion, wouldn't I?"

Bishop shrugs, taking a swig from his beer bottle. "She seems to be agreeable, but I see what you're saying. Do what you gotta do, man. Make the best of a shitty situation."

"I don't want to disrupt Luna's life. Obviously, Selene and her family are all she knows, but I don't want to miss any more time with her."

"Then don't."

"Easier said than done." I sigh. "I'm heading over tomorrow morning to spend the day with Luna. I swear, time with her flies by, and I can't get enough of it. Enough of her laughter, and everything that makes her the little person she is."

"Soak it in, my friend. I know you've missed some years, but that's not her whole life. There are still so many firsts you'll get to experience," Bishop reassures, clapping me on the back.

"Thanks, man."

"Can I just say how jealous I am that you get claiming rights on Selene now? If she didn't fall for your pitiful flower bullshit, I would've asked her on a real date."

I shoot him a glare, my stomach muscles tightening at the idea of anyone else near her, despite everything she's done. "She's off-limits."

Bishop raises a brow, the corner of his mouth quirking with amusement. He knows exactly what he's doing, and fuck him for doing it.

"I guess it would be kinda weird if your daughter started calling me Daddy, too, right?"

"I'd kill you."

He starts choking on his beer through his laughter and raises his hands in surrender. "I'm kidding. Totally kidding. I promise, things will work themselves out, End. Give it time. Get to know your daughter and see where things go."

"Yeah, we'll see."

The next morning, I ring the doorbell at Selene's place, trying to ignore the nervous thrum of energy coursing through my body at the thought of seeing Luna again. Yesterday was a slow introduction for us. I didn't learn much about her, but I did learn a whole hell of a lot about her toys and what she liked to play with. The thing is, I want to know everything about my daughter as a person. Her likes and dislikes and everything else in between.

I can't help but overthink, something I've never done. Will she love me as much as I love her? What if she doesn't like me as a father? I have all these worries at the forefront of my mind that I have to struggle to tamp down.

My grip around the bouquet in my hand tightens just as the front door opens. Selene stands there, looking fresh-faced and beautiful. Dressed in a loose shirt that hangs off one shoulder and a pair of leggings, she's never looked more gorgeous, and I hate that that's the first thing I notice. My anger should be the only emotion I feel when I look at this woman, not desire.

Her bright honey eyes widen when she glances down at the bouquet in my hands. She presses her hand to her mouth to hide the quivering of her chin. The only real thing I got out of my daughter yesterday was the fact that she mentioned sunflowers were her favorite flower. It's obvious that me standing here with a bouquet of sunflowers for Luna makes Selene emotional.

As if my thoughts summon her, giggling echoes down the hallway until Luna pokes her little head out from behind her mother's legs. Her little face breaks out into a smile that hits me square in the chest. Stepping outside, she looks as beautiful and perfect as she did the day before.

Today she is wearing a romper with crescent moons on it and little white Vans on her feet that are, in fact, no longer white. A crescent hair tie keeps her hair secured at the top of her head.

Luna reminds me so much of her mom dressed like this.

She glances at the bouquet clutched in my hand, and her eyes widen. "Are those mine?" she whispers, looking unsure.

"They are." I hand the flowers to her, and Luna takes them, hugging them to her chest so tightly, I'm surprised half of them aren't crushed to a pulp. Her eyes are round with awe as she stares down at them. "Wow," she breathes. "I've never seen real sunflowers before. Mommy, look at them!" She shoves them up, practically hitting Selene in the face with them. Selene laughs, a soft, indulgent smile on her face as she stares down at Luna.

"They're beautiful, baby. Why don't you both sit inside while I finish making breakfast? Go on." She pats Luna's little bottom, getting her moving. Luna runs off with the flowers, her sandaled feet slapping against the hardwood floors as she goes.

Selene shuts the door behind me, and she pauses, looking like she wants to say something, but before she can, I take off toward Luna. I came here to spend time with my daughter, not listen to any more of her apologies.

When I step into Gavin's living room, a space I've sat in countless times before watching the game with a beer in hand, it suddenly feels different. It's odd that I'm here now with my daughter. Yesterday, Selene mentioned her mother and Gavin would be gone most of the day since he had a doctor's appointment. It would give me the time alone with my daughter I need. I don't like feeling as if I'm being judged and watched by everyone while I'm trying to get to know Luna.

She sits there on the couch, legs swinging, staring up at me expectantly as I take the seat next to her. Her happiness seems to have subsided, and now she seems a little nervous. Tightness blocks my airway as I try to find words to put her at ease, but they don't come. What do I say? How do I put her at ease when I'm feeling just as out of my element? I want to ask her so many questions, but I don't even know where to start.

She suddenly reaches for something on the table and pulls it onto her lap. It's a notebook with glitter unicorns on it. "My mommy helped me draw some of my favorite things. Maybe you can do the same?" Luna hands the book to me, those big doe eyes staring up at me with so much innocence it absolutely rips my heart to shreds. Swallowing thickly, I take the notebook from her and open the page she has dog-eared. Emotion slams into me as I stare at her handwriting and her drawings. It is an absolute chaotic mess, but fuck me, I love it. I want to know every second of her life. Every single detail that makes her up as a whole.

I shoot a glance at her, only to find her smiling at me. All because I accepted the notebook. Her smile penetrates my chest, banishing the nervousness I felt mere seconds ago.

"Why don't you walk me through all of this before I start on my list, yeah?"

Luna nods vigorously, scooting closer to me. Her small leg presses against mine, and the light touch triggers an array of emotions inside me. "This here is a bowl of macaroni. It's my favorite food. My mommy makes it for me all the time, but sometimes, she tries to hide vegetables inside, thinking I won't notice." Luna pauses and leans into me, cupping her mouth in a whisper. "Don't tell Mommy, but I do notice. I pretend to eat it, but spit it out when she's not looking."

A laugh bursts from my chest at her honesty. "So, I take it vegetables are no-go for you?"

She shakes her head. "Green stuff doesn't taste good."

I move on to the next drawing in her notebook. "And what about this?"

"Oh, that's a raccoon, but it's pink. Because pink is my favorite color, and raccoons are my favorite animal."

I quirk a brow at her, rubbing at the back of my neck. "That's… different."

"Papa bought me a pink raccoon stuffy for my birthday, even though I told him I wanted a real one."

My mouth twists with amusement. "You asked your papa to find you a real pink raccoon?" She nods, looking dead serious. It squeezes another laugh out of me.

This kid is fucking hilarious.

Luna tells me everything from her favorite book (*Pig the Pug*) to all the things she loves to do (play Barbies and pretend doctor are just some of her favorites). I hang on her every word, entranced by the information she shares and just how smart she is. She says things and jokes around like no other kid I know. She's incredible. The more I get to know my daughter, the more that warmth in my chest spreads.

We finally get through all her drawings of her likes and dislikes.

"And this here is us." She points at the last page. It's a drawing of two stick figures holding hands—a tall person and a little person, their necks longer than their bodies. There are clouds in an array of colors and a sun in the corner, wearing a smile. At the bottom of her drawing is her name scribbled in a mess of letters that has me running the pad of my finger over them.

"You made this for me?" I ask, my voice gruffer than I intend.

She grins, nodding her head. "It's you and me."

I continue staring down at the drawing, unable to find the right words for what I'm feeling. I've never felt so overcome with emotion.

"I love it." Those are the only words I manage to get out through the tightness blocking my airway.

Her eyes glimmer with happiness. "You do?"

I nod, biting back the sudden barrage of emotions. "It's the best gift I've ever been given."

The smile that spreads across her face embeds itself into my soul. She's managed to stitch her name across my heart permanently, and I've never felt more at peace than I have sitting next to this little ball of beautiful, chaotic energy.

A throat clears near the doorway of the living room, drawing my attention away from Luna. Selene stands there with tears glimmering in her eyes. When our gazes clash, heat rises to her cheeks, and she shifts, avoiding my gaze.

"Breakfast is ready. I made enough for everyone. If you're hungry."

Luna hops to her feet, taking my hand in hers. "C'mon! Mommy makes the *best* breakfast!"

I indulge her in a smile and let her drag me into the kitchen. Luna takes the seat next to me at the table just as Selene slides our plates in front of us. Luna wasn't kidding when she said Selene makes a good breakfast. She went all out. Eggs, bacon, potatoes, and homemade waffles.

Throughout breakfast, our daughter chats our ears off, talking about everything and anything. I soak it all in, never wanting her to stop. A few times, I catch Selene watching me, and whenever she realizes she's caught, she quickly looks down and continues pushing the food around on her plate, not eating.

At moments like these, it's hard to ignore how stunning Selene is. How human she is. I'm still incredibly angry with her, but every time I see the look of guilt or torture on her face, I want to take it away.

Today, her eyes look a little more honey than they do their normal hazel blend of colors. When the sunlight seeping in through the kitchen windows catches her eyes, I can clearly see the hints of honey mixed with a blend of other colors. Her eyes are a melt of autumn tones and winter frost. She's a goddess on earth, a blooming flower amongst the leaves.

After breakfast, I spend more time with Luna. She shows me her favorite toys, her favorite channels on YouTube, and proceeds to tell me every story under the sun. When it starts getting late, I regretfully tell her I have to get to work.

"Aw, man!" Her disappointment resembles my own. I wish I could stay all day, but I do still have a company to run, and I need to have a conversation with her mother in private. Luna looks up at me, her big bright eyes filled with hope. "Are you coming back tomorrow?"

I drop down to my haunches before her. Taking her hand in mine, I squeeze gently. "I'll be back every single day."

"You promise?"

"I promise."

Catching me off guard, Luna throws herself into my arms and hugs me. Her little arms wind around my neck and squeeze.

"Bye, Daddy," she whispers in that sweet voice.

The word strikes me right in the fucking chest, reaching places I never knew existed. It takes everything in me to keep my emotions in check as my entire world tilts on its axis.

"Bye, baby," I whisper back. I have no intention of letting her go. I want to soak in every second I can. I'll never be able to make up for those lost years, but I want to hang on to my little girl while she's still little for as long as I possibly can.

When I glance up, fire and ice engulf my heart when I spot Selene staring at us. Regret and torment are in her eyes, but it doesn't even come close to what I feel gripping my chest.

"Luna, start cleaning up your toys while I talk to your dad really quick, okay?"

My little girl groans but still does as she's told, leaving me with her mother. I push up to my full height, squaring my shoulders.

"I think today went well."

Even though I want to say something I know will hurt her feelings, I nod. Instead, I say, "I have this weekend off. I'm thinking about taking Luna over to my parents' place. Maybe out to the movies or something."

Selene rubs her lips together. "She'd like that."

Tense silence resumes between us. She shifts, her mouth opening like she wants to say more, but the words never come. I'm not sure what she could say at this point that could make anything about this situation better. My phone vibrates in my pocket, and I take that as my cue to leave.

"I'll be in touch."

Her crestfallen face is the last thing I see before I turn on my heels, heading back toward my truck.

Chapter Seventeen

Endymion

The next day, after I got back from dropping of a contract for a new project a few towns over, I head over to Selene's place. I'm surprised when Gavin answers the door instead of her.

"End, how are you?" he asks.

I slip my hands into my pockets, lifting a shoulder in a noncommittal shrug. "I've been better."

An unexplainable sadness takes over his face. He glances over his shoulder once before he walks out, closing the door. He jerks his head behind me. "C'mon, son."

I follow in step beside Gavin, remaining silent. I wait for him to say whatever it is that's bothering him. "I'm sorry about all of this, End. I had no idea. I know this can't be easy for you. I imagine it isn't easy for either of you." Tightness grips my chest. "I knew I'd made mistakes in the past, but it wasn't until I learned who my granddaughter's father was that I realized just how much I fucked up. I failed as a father, End. I went far too long without speaking to my daughter, and there has been nothing I regret more. I can't help but think maybe if I was there for her, she would've confided in me."

"This isn't your fault, Gavin." I sigh, hating that he blames himself.

"It is. My daughter is strong, and I know this is killing her, the guilt of keeping you from Luna. And I know right now all you probably feel toward her is anger, but…she means well. Always has. She has the best heart. Even if she made horrible choices, she cares about you."

My nostrils flare. I don't want to hear this right now. Not when I already feel my anger slipping. I need to stay angry with Selene. My anger is giving me purpose. It's a guide through this fucked up new situation. That's the only way I'll get through this.

He pauses when we get to my truck. "I'm sure you're here to see Luna, not listen to me babble. They're out getting signed up for the next school year."

I nod. "Thanks, Gavin. For everything."

His eyes shine with something I can't place. He shoots a tight-lipped smile my way. "Don't thank me. Just trying to right some of my wrongs while I still can."

Pain spears my heart at his words.

He turns, heading back inside the house, his gait slow and stiff. It is the walk of a man in misery. A man with his strength being depleted day in and day out.

Hopping into my truck, I make an educated guess and figure out where Luna and Selene are. The entire drive there, I still feel the lingering effects of my conversation with Gavin. An inexplicable sadness haunts me. He's been a close friend. Not so much a father, since I already have a loving father, but something just as close.

The second I step foot onto the grounds of the elementary school, everyone stops to stare. I let the curious glances roll off my back. Then the whispers start, people wondering why I'm here. Dunsmuir Elementary is a K-8 school and the only one here in the town. It's the same one that's been here since I moved from Lake Tahoe. It wasn't hard to guess where Selene would be signing Luna up.

I find Selene and Luna easily. They're in a long line of other parents waiting to fill out a stack of paperwork. When Luna sees me, her eyes light up, and the smile that ripples across my face spreads over my heart like a warm blanket. She disengages her hand from Selene's and runs into my arms. I catch her effortlessly.

"Hi, Daddy," she says, staring me directly in the eyes. Warmth fills my veins, and my heart stutters at that one word. My grin widens. She is too cute for her own good, and she's all mine. Barely able to contain her excitement, she wraps her little hands around my neck and grins.

"Mommy's signing me up for school."

My chest expands with something light. The sensation is so foreign that it trips me up. Why did hearing the word "mommy" spark something in my chest? I've heard Luna say it before, while referring to Selene, but now that she's mine? The word "mommy" takes on a whole new meaning. I have a whole new connection to this woman that I never saw coming.

"I see that. You excited?"

"Yup." She pops the "p" with extra oomph. "My papa said he'd give me a toy if I learn something new every day once school starts."

"Did he? Sounds like a good papa."

"He's the best. But when can I meet my other papa and nana?" she asks, cocking her head to the side. Her long wavy brown hair, identical to her mother's, slides to the side of her shoulder like a curtain of sorts. My brows furrow.

"What do you mean?"

"Well," she starts, glancing back at her mom. "Mommy told me last night that I have another nana and papa who love me a lot, too. She said that pretty soon I'd get to meet them."

My gaze darts toward Selene. She's still in line, though now, her gaze is glued to us. She's fidgeting, her hands fiddling with the paperwork she's holding as if she can't help herself. She shoots me a shaky smile. It's barely there and definitely unsure.

I don't return it.

Instead, I look back at Luna. "Yeah, those are my parents, and they're so excited to meet you."

With everything going on, I still haven't talked to my parents about everything, which I need to do as soon as possible. If they hear about this from anyone else but me, they'll have a heart attack, and by they, I mean my mother. A part of me is actually surprised Selene talked about my parents to Luna. I don't know why, but I thought she'd try to hold back, try to keep Luna from us, but obviously, that doesn't seem to be the case. So far, she's been fairly accommodating about everything.

Not that any of it makes up for the six years I've already lost.

Taking Luna's hand in mine, I guide us toward the long line Selene's waiting in. I notice her body begin to stiffen the closer we get. I can feel the curious gazes of everyone near us.

"Selene." My voice is gruff and cold.

Hurt lances across her face, and her slender throat works a swallow. "Endymion."

I raise a brow. My full name? Interesting.

"I'm sorry. I should've told you I was signing her up today. It just…it slipped my mind."

I bite my tongue, not wanting to spew hurtful words. Especially not in front of Luna. As much as I'd like to lash out at Selene, I need to practice some self-restraint for my daughter's sake.

"It's fine. I'm here now."

We stand in tense silence while Luna talks our ears off. The line goes by pretty quickly, and before long, we're next. Selene hands over most of the stuff while she finishes filling out the remaining paperwork.

We go through the rest of the motions of getting Luna signed up for school. Most of the families and parents have disbursed, left to do other things, but Luna begs us to stay a little while longer so she can play on the playground.

Selene and I take a seat at one of the benches near the playground and watch her. She's been quiet this whole time, her eyes glued to our daughter.

Our daughter.

That's not something I thought I'd ever get to say. She fidgets again, just like she's been since I showed up here unannounced. There is so much I want to say, so much I want to ask, but I find that I don't know where to start. There is no telling where her head is, or what this means for the future. She uprooted her life to stay here to take care of her father. What happens when that's done and over with? This is my home, where my company is. I can't leave, and I refuse to let her take my daughter from me again.

"How long are you staying?"

She looks down at her hands. "As long as my dad needs me."

A spark of anger ignites in my gut. "You're insane if you think you're going to take my daughter with you."

Her gaze swings to mine, and for the first time since I learned the truth, there's something other than sadness brimming there. Rage. It burns through those big, painfully beautiful hazel eyes in waves.

"Did I say that?" she snaps, anger burning the edges of her tone. Her eyes slam shut, and she rubs at her temple, heaving a tired sigh. "Obviously now, I'll need to find a permanent place for us and figure out what to do from there. I have no intention of taking her from you, Endymion."

Some of the tension I was feeling settles at her words. It's better than I was hoping for. Nothing about our situation has been ideal.

I shift on the bench, watching Luna skid down the slide with a happy grin on her face. We sit for a long stretch of time, my next words like a bomb detonating between us. "I spoke to a lawyer yesterday."

Her gaze swings to mine. Those doe eyes are wide and filled with fear. "What for?"

My lips thin into a grim line. "To get custody of my daughter."

The color slowly drains from her face. "To get custody of your—" She chokes. "Are you fucking kidding me? You're being ridiculous."

That simmering burn of anger in my gut suddenly roars to life, and I shoot to my feet before I say something I regret. This woman pushes all of my fucking buttons.

"Don't you dare walk away, Endymion Black," she barks out, trailing me. When I don't slow my strides, she jumps in front of me, her hand clasping my forearm. I'm sure she thinks her grip is tight and unrelenting, but really, it feels like nothing at all. This woman couldn't hurt a goddamn fly. "You can't just drop a bomb like that and leave!"

I whirl on her. "Why not? It's exactly what you did all those years ago."

Her bottom lip trembles. "That was different, and you know it. Luna is my life, Endymion. I will not let you take her from me. I will agree to everything you say, but I will not give my baby girl up." The pain, fear, and anger she's been keeping locked away all explode at once. Tears soak her face as she lashes out, her finger colliding with my chest in a harsh jab. "I've made horrible mistakes, but I'm doing everything I can to right those."

"Mommy! Daddy! Look at me!"

Luna's excited voice pulls me out of the argument, and I watch closely as she struggles to make her way across the monkey bars. Plastering a grin on my face, I shoot her a thumbs-up. When I glance at Selene, she's wiping the tears off her face and sniffing, trying to pull herself together before Luna sees.

Without a word, she turns on her heels, heading for our little girl. Heaving a deep, tired sigh, I give her a few minutes before I follow. Luna's grin stretches across her face when she sees me.

"Want to go for some ice cream, Daddy?"

I shoot a glance at Selene, who is purposely avoiding my gaze. "I'd like that."

The tension is thick at Sal's ice cream shop. I remember coming in here as a teen after high school and getting the same thing every time—pistachio in a cone. Luna's grip on my hand is tight as she peers into the glass windows, deciding what flavor she wants. Selene is hanging back, giving us space. I don't tell her so, but I appreciate it. I appreciate that she isn't hovering, that she's letting me find my way with our daughter.

"What kind are you getting, Daddy?" As soon as she asks the question, Sal, the owner of the shop, rests his hands on the other side of the counter.

"Did I just hear this sweet little thing call you daddy? Lord, I'm getting old."

"This is my daughter, Luna."

She smiles up at Sal, a cheesy grin on her face. "And that right there is my mama," Luna adds, pointing toward Selene. A blush stains her cheeks, and she waves shyly at Sal. His brows jump into his receding hairline.

"Well, I'll be. Is that you, Selene? How long has it been since I saw you, child?"

Selene smiles. "It's been a while, Sal." She glances around. "I take it you still have the best ice cream in town?"

"In town? Girl, you know good and well Sal's is the best in the *county*."

"How could I forget." Selene laughs. The sound wraps around me, causing my gut to clench for unknown reasons. It's such a harmonic sound. I want to hate it, but I can't.

"So, what are we getting for the beautiful family today? Let's see if I remember this correctly. Rocky road for you," he says, pointing at Selene. "Pistachio in a cone for you," he says to me. "But you, I have no idea what you want, little miss."

Luna smiles. "I'll have strawberry. With a cone. And sprinkles, please."

"Good choice."

Much to Selene's chagrin, I pay for our ice creams, and we find an open booth. Luna slides in next to me, eyeing my cone dubiously.

"Why is your ice cream green? All green stuff tastes gross." Her little nose is turned up in disgust, prompting Selene and me to laugh.

"You've never tried pistachio? You haven't lived." I lift the cone toward her, and she jerks back as if its proximity is offending.

"No way!"

"All right, your loss." I take a big chunk out of the ice cream, and she looks torn.

"Well, wait, don't eat it all."

My upper lip quirks. "Why ever not?"

"Because I want to try it now," she admits begrudgingly.

With a laugh, I tilt the cone toward her, and she takes a tentative taste. Her eyes widen almost immediately. She goes back in for another taste, then another, then another, until Selene and I are laughing at her again.

"I take it you like it?"

"Mommy! I found my new favorite ice cream!"

I glance at Selene just as she's taking a long lick of her ice cream, and Jesus Christ, I may be pissed as hell at her, but my body obviously doesn't share the same feelings. Heat coils deep in my gut, and I have to force myself to look away.

"Little miss, you finished over there yet?" Sal hollers toward our table. Luna glances over at him, wearing an ice cream mustache.

"Yup!"

"Want to come help make the next batch of ice cream?"

Luna slides out of the booth, hopping up and down in front of our table. "Mommy, can I go help? Please, please, pleaaase."

Selene smiles. "Go on. But make sure you listen to Sal, okay?"

She runs off, letting herself around the counter. She stands beside Sal, waiting for instruction, eager to make ice cream.

It doesn't escape my notice that when it came to asking permission for something, she asked Selene first, not me. I'd be lying if I said it didn't hurt. If I didn't feel that sharp laceration of rejection in my chest. I can't help but wonder how long it will be before she feels comfortable enough to ask me permission for something. Or will that only ever be her mother's position? Just thinking about it makes me angry all over again. My gut seizes with frustration, and I see red.

Forcing myself to look at something else and calm down, I spot a table a few spaces down from us. There is a group of people sitting there. Two women and three men. What bothers me is the man at the end of the booth has his eyes glued to Selene. She's completely oblivious to him eye-fucking her as she finishes her ice cream, her gaze glued to Luna. He's not even being sneaky about it either, the fucking bastard.

I grind my teeth together, tension filling my body as I think about Selene with another man. I have no right. I shouldn't even care at all, but I suddenly feel possessive of this woman. The woman who birthed my child. The woman who lost her virginity to me. I can't stop thinking about another man touching her because even though I loathe to admit it, she feels like mine.

Every one of her firsts is mine. I hate that I don't remember that night. I hate that I was such a fucking idiot, and I hurt her enough to drive her away and keep Luna from me. I want to make amends for the past.

Idly, I wonder if she's slept with anyone else since then, and I grow angry over the possibility of it being true.

If she was out with someone, who was watching Luna? And Jesus, the thought of another man parenting my child has red seeping into my vision. My hands fist under the table. For as long as I am walking this earth, no one else will step in as father where my daugh ter is concerned.

I shift back around in my seat, only to find Selene staring at me. She glances away quickly, realizing she was caught ogling. That damn flush climbs up the creamy expanse of her chest to her slender throat, and I'm riveted by the sight. Sneaking another glance at me, she realizes I'm still staring and shoots me a wary smile that doesn't reach her eyes.

As I stare at her, taking everything about her in, I wonder what the past few years have been like for her. I can't imagine she has a lot of friends, not while being a single mother and trying to make ends meet. The sinister part of me hopes she didn't have time for dates or friends. Because if she did, if she did date and find the perfect someone, things right now would be a whole hell of a lot different. To think of Selene having another child with someone else makes me feel fucking violent. It also makes me wonder if she's been with that asshole that Luna was talking about the other day. Theo, she said his name was.

"Who is Theo?"

She seems startled by the question. "What?"

"Luna mentioned a man named Theo the other day. The one who was 'in love' with you. I'd like to know what other men have been around my daughter."

She rears back in the booth as if I've slapped her. The flush that was just coloring her cheeks has drained, and in its place is a pained expression. I don't know why I'm being such a dick about this, but I need to hear it. I need to hear her say that there has been no one else near my daughter.

"Theo was our neighbor back in Pasadena. That's *all* he ever was. I didn't have time to date. So, the answer to your question"—she pauses, inhaling a shaky breath—"is no. There have been no other men around *our* daughter." The frustration drips from her tone like sour nectar. She shoves away from the booth, heading toward Luna and Sal.

That's twice in one day I've gotten a rise out of her.

I didn't think she had it in her, but she's a lot feistier than I thought.

I find I like that—much more than I should.

After knocking on the front door, it doesn't take long for my mom to answer, a frown marring her features when she sees me. It's not out of the ordinary for me to come over and visit, but it is when I don't call ahead of time and tell my parents I'm on the way over.

"Endy, I didn't know you were coming over. I would've made dinner."

"I think I'll pass on the whole vegan diet, or whatever it is you guys are doing now."

My mom rolls her eyes, swatting my arm as she lets me pass over the threshold. My dad is in the living room, laid out on the recliner, watching sports highlights, as usual. When he sees me, he grins.

"Son! Didn't know you were stopping by."

Guilt slams into me. I rake a hand through my hair and pause in the center of the living room, feeling my mother's presence behind me.

"This isn't exactly a social visit. There's something I need to tell you guys."

They both sit, and my mother reaches for my dad's hand, obviously sensing this is serious. "What's going on, End?"

"I have a daughter."

My dad's eyes widen, and my mom's mouth drops open. The stunned silence stretches until I go on, elaborating for them.

"She's six. And her name is Luna."

My mom's hand flies to her chest, her brows drawing together in a frown. "Six? What do you mean, she's six?" Her tone is rising, and I'm sure she probably thinks this is all *my* doing.

I heave a sigh. "I didn't know she even existed until a few days ago."

"Well, who is the mother? Please, for the love of God, do not say it's Holly—"

"Selene Drake."

Both my parents jerk back, stunned by this news. "As in Gavin and Cece Drake's daughter? How did…?"

Shame has me looking away. This is the hardest part to say, the part I played in all this. "I was drunk when it happened and didn't remember any of it. She left for college a few days later and didn't find out until months later that she was pregnant."

"Wow. Okay." My dad blows out a breath.

Though my mom, her eyes are misty. "I have another grandbaby?"

My lip quirks. Of course, this would be her response. "You do. She looks just like Valeria when she was that age."

"Let me see!" She slaps my arm, and I chuckle, pulling my phone out to show her all the photos I've snapped of Luna so far. She gasps, taking the phone from me to show my father.

"Oh, Ermias, just look at her. She's gorgeous. When can we meet her?"

"I was thinking this weekend."

"And how is Selene taking all of this?"

I shrug. "She hasn't tried to fight me on anything. I told her I missed six years of my daughter's life, and I wasn't going to miss any more. I didn't care if she wanted a fight or not."

My mom gives me a watery smile. "That's my boy. Now, c'mon, let me fix you something to eat really quick."

I shake my head, even though I know it's a futile attempt. "I'm not hungry."

"Humor me, son."

She proceeds to warm up the food they ate for dinner, and the whole time she sneaks glances at me. "I imagine this is a hard time for Selene." I grunt. "You have every right to be angry, but I also want to be sure you're treating that woman with respect. She birthed your child and raised her for years without help."

"And whose fault was that?"

"Do not let your anger get in the way of the bigger picture. You have a beautiful family. Not many people have that at all. Go easy on her is all I'm saying."

For the rest of the night, I think about what going easy on Selene would mean. She doesn't deserve my good side quite yet, but my mother's right. I am finding it harder and harder to stay angry with her.

I stare blankly at the television screen, allowing Griffin to talk my ear off. He's been going on and on about ideas for a potential client. I should be listening. Any good business partner would be listening, but I'm not. Instead, I'm thinking about Selene. I'm thinking about the past and what a fucking asshole I have been to her. My moods often swing from feeling bad to being angry with her for keeping Luna from me. I'm at war with myself over this fierce woman who loves our daughter endlessly.

"Are you even listening?"

I take a long pull from my beer. "Hell no."

Griffin sighs. "Jesus Christ, what is it now?"

I shoot him a glare. "I don't know what to do, not about Selene or how to parent our daughter."

Griffin sets his beer down and lets out a long-drawn-out sigh. "What's there to figure out, End? Seriously. You have a daughter and a beautiful woman who is still clearly in love with you. You have it all."

"She kept her from me, Griff. How am I supposed to get over that shit? How am I supposed to look at her and not see all the years I missed?"

"Because what's done is done. Don't forget you're not innocent either. You took her virginity while you were drunk, got her pregnant, and forgot about it. You're no saint here either. You both need to forgive each other and do what's best for Luna. And I know that would mean being a family." I must make a face because he laughs. "Don't even try to lie and tell me you feel nothing for Selene. Hell, even I feel something for her." My gaze shoots to his; eyes narrowed in warning. It only proves his point further.

"I do feel something. That's what makes this tough. The push and pull. The wanting to give in to her while wanting to still hold on to my anger."

"Look, I may not have known Selene back then, but I can say, she's good, man. I see the way she still looks at you, End, and this time, if you brush her to the side like you did back then, you're going to lose her forever."

The thought of losing Selene forever doesn't sit right with me. Not in the least.

Chapter Eighteen

Selene

My heart jumps into my throat at the sound of the loud knocking. I spoke to End briefly on the phone yesterday, and he mentioned he'd be picking up Luna today to take to his parents' house. He left no room for argument, not that I would have anyway. The conversation was painfully short, and his tone was cold as ice. I thought things might slowly start getting better between us, for the sake of Luna, but if anything, he seems even angrier with me now than he was before.

His mood swings are beginning to give me whiplash.

This will be the first time Luna will be on her own with End, and I hate to admit it, but I'm sad. I know Endymion is more than capable and responsible, but my daughter has always been beside me through everything, and today is the startling reality that she isn't just mine anymore.

Sucking in a deep breath, I call out to Luna as I open the front door. End stands there as handsome as ever. His eyes trail up and down my body in a slow perusal. Goosebumps erupt over my skin until they suddenly evaporate at the disgusted look on his face. That seems to be the only expression he wears around me these days, and a glare, of course. He wears that glare, aimed my way, like no one I've ever known.

It's eviscerating.

A shot to the damn heart.

"Hey, Daddy!" Luna croons excitedly. A warm smile takes over End's face; it's worlds different than the way he just looked at me. He drops down to his haunches, opening his arms for her. She runs into him at full speed, hugging him something fierce. An agonized sting shoots through my chest as I watch them. I miss having him look at me that way. But I can guarantee that won't happen, especially not now. He hates me.

Not like I don't deserve it.

It's moments like these when I see how good he is with her, and I see how much she loves him already, that I hate myself for the decisions I've made. I know I can't turn back time. The only thing I can do now is try to make it up to both of them.

"You ready to meet your other grandparents?" End asks her, pulling back slightly so he can see her.

"Yes!" She fist pumps, drawing a wry grin out of me.

"Well, c'mon then, wouldn't want to keep them waiting."

Luna's smile slips, and she glances at me. My chest caves with distress, and I plaster a smile on my face, trying to remain calm for her sake. The thing about being so close to your child, they know when you're barely hanging on by a thread, and I know Luna can sense that I'm about to fall apart.

"But what about my mommy?"

End glances at me, his brows pulling down, prompting me to clear my throat. I run my fingers through her hair, trying to put her at ease. "I have a lot of cleaning to do today, babe. Why don't you go and have fun for me, yeah?"

"But I want you to come with us." Her chin trembles, and Endymion blows out a sigh.

"Why don't we head there, and your mom can meet us when she's ready. Does that sound like a plan?"

The quiver in her chin stops almost immediately, and she seeks out my gaze. "You'll come, right, Mommy?"

My smile is shaky. "Of course, I will, unicorn butt. Let me clean up, get ready, and then I'll meet you there, okay?"

Her grin is back in place, and she high-fives me. "I'm ready to go!"

"I'll send you the address," End mentions in passing as he takes Luna's hand, walking with her toward his truck. I watch from the doorway as he buckles her in her car seat he bought her before taking off.

I didn't need an address. Hell, I've had his address memorized by heart since I was twelve years old.

When I park my car outside of Endymion's parents' house, I have the urge to run. To drive off before anyone sees me. I'm sure Luna is fine. She's probably forgotten all about me. She won't need me hanging around, making things awkward when she's there having fun. My stomach revolts at the image of me standing there in front of his family. They're going to hate me, and they have every right to. That doesn't make this pill any easier to swallow. The last thing I want to do is stand around while a group of people judges me as if I'm wearing a big scarlet letter on my chest.

It's too late for any of that, though, because the front door opens and out steps an older man I recognize from years ago. Mr. Black. He's wearing a warm smile, waving at me from his position on the front porch, but none of that settles the rampant nerves that are turning my stomach.

Gulping a deep breath, I grab my purse and make my way across the lawn. My feigned bravado all but evaporates when Ermias shoots me a sad smile. I damn near crumple right there on the spot. He's the spitting image of his son minus his hair. Mr. Ermias Black is all broad-shouldered Norwegian, with sandy blond hair that has gray interspersed, and the brightest pair of blue eyes I've ever seen. A lot of Endymion's looks come from his father. The set of their eyes, their thick, arched brows, and full lips, but Endymion takes after his mother, Aurora, too. I remember her having a smile that could light up a room—and that's exactly what End's smile does. It's what he passed onto my daughter. He inherited his mother's blond-brown hair and green eyes, and from the looks of it, that's where the similarities end.

I clear my throat painfully before greeting him. "Mr. Black."

"How are you, Selene? It's been a long time."

My brows pinch. I can't tell if he's simply trying to have a conversation with me or if he's taking a jab at me for keeping his granddaughter away all these years. My cheeks heat with embarrassment and shame, and I drop my gaze.

"I'm okay. How are you guys?"

"We're hanging in there. C'mon, Endymion and Luna are out back." He leads the way into the house, and I follow, my gaze eating up the décor surrounding us. In all my years of being here in Dunsmuir, I never stepped foot in Endymion's childhood home, and now that I'm here, under these circumstances, it feels strange. Almost made up.

When Ermias throws open the sliding glass doors to the backyard, my heart flutters at the sight of my daughter running and laughing with a carefree grin on her face. I pause just on the other end of threshold, unable to keep my gaze off her. I've seen happiness written on my daughter's face plenty of times, but this? Never like this. It's a shot to the heart. It has me questioning my capabilities as a mother.

A warm hand settles on my shoulder, and when I look up, I spot Ermias there, a knowing look on his face. "She's been talking about you for the past hour. I know she misses you."

He leads the way into the backyard, and Luna glances over at the sound of the door closing. Her face splits into a blinding grin, and unable to help myself, I laugh. She runs across the lawn, throwing herself at my legs.

"I missed you, Mommy," she breathes against me.

"I missed you, too, nugget."

"Did you meet Grandpa Ermias and Grandma Aurora yet?" she asks, her eyes glittering with excitement.

"I've already met them, but why don't you reintroduce me?"

My little girl does just that, taking me to each of her grandparents to introduce me as if I've never met them before. They stare at her with a love that envelops me wholeheartedly. The whole time, I can feel End's gaze on us, but I work to keep my gaze fixed on anything but him. I don't want to see the anger or the look of disgust on his face anymore. Not when I'm already so close to falling apart where he's concerned.

"Selene, you look gorgeous, and your timing is perfect. We were just about to eat," Aurora says, smiling, as she tickles Luna along her ribs. "C'mon, munchkin, let's get the food for everyone."

"I can help," I offer, not wanting to stand with the men of the family.

Aurora waves me off. "We got it, sweetie."

I deflate, watching as they disappear into the house. Silence descends, and a weird tension cackles in the air. It has me shifting on my feet. Ermias must sense that his son and I aren't going to speak to each other because he tries to strike up a conversation.

"So, Selene, how was Pasadena? I hear the summers there are pretty gnarly compared to here."

I breathe a silent sigh of relief. Now this I can do. Filler conversation about the weather. Awkward silence? Not so much.

I dive into conversation with Ermias. We discuss random things, mainly just conversation fillers to keep from making everyone uncomfortable with the silence.

Dinner isn't much better. We try to have a civilized meal, but you can't miss the tension in the air. Endymion doesn't want me here, that much is obvious. And his parents are doing the best they can to include me in the conversation, but at this point, I wish they would stop and just let the conversation flow between them.

Luna is telling a story about her old kindergarten teacher, and everyone is riveted, absolutely glued to her and her vibrant personality. It makes me smile. Feeling eyes on me, I glance up, and my heart skids to an abrupt halt when my gaze clashes with Endymion's. He's leering, staring at me through narrowed slits. There's something in his eyes I can't quite place, and its intensity sends a tremor down my spine. My mouth goes painfully dry, and I glance away, looking down at Luna then up at Aurora, only to realize her gaze is darting back and forth between her son and me. Her brows dented together.

Crap.

Heat climbs up my chest and settles into my cheeks, and I make a mental note only to focus on my daughter for the rest of the evening. It should be simple. But it's easier said than done. Luna carries the weight of most of the conversation through dinner, practically jumping with energy at the thought of going back outside to play. Endymion built a playground in his parents' backyard for his niece years prior, fully equipped with swings, a sandbox, and a slide, so she's in heaven back here. Especially since my parents' house is currently under construction.

I fidget uncomfortably as I stand on the back patio. My heart twinges, and my stomach tightens as I watch Luna play with Endymion. Her father. I never thought I'd see the day. Honest to God, I never thought this would happen. Yet now that we're here, I can't help but hate myself. I deprived my daughter of a father, and a father of his daughter. I'm trying not to be too hard on myself through this whole transition because what's done is done, but I can't help it. I look back now on those decisions and wonder who that person was? Why didn't I say something sooner? Endymion and his parents are amazing people. Why ever did I think they would shoo me away?

"How are you doing?"

I turn at the sound of Endymion's mom's voice. Like me, she's watching her son play with his daughter. When I look at her, there's a wistful look on her face as she watches them run around together. I wonder how long she waited for her son to give her a grandchild? Did I deprive them, too?

"I'm hanging in there, trying not to hate myself," I tell her, opting for honesty.

Aurora takes my hand in hers and squeezes reassuringly, sending shockwaves through my body. "Don't beat yourself up, Selene. Endymion has always been…angry. About everything it seems like. Even as a kid, he hated change but got tired of routine, not a great combination. I've always been a firm believer in everything happens for a reason. I'd like to think maybe my son wouldn't have been ready for this news all those years ago. Maybe it would've changed the course of his life forever? Just give him some time to process, and know, I understand. I am just glad she's in our lives now."

"Why are you being so nice to me?" I choke out, fighting back my tears. It suddenly feels like every emotion is clogged in my throat, blocking my airway. Luna calls to me from across the backyard, a huge grin on her face.

"Mommy, look at this!" she yells out, going back to playing with Endymion.

Aurora continues. "Because like it or not, we're family now, Selene. And my son is an idiot. Even a blind person could see the way you looked at him, but he just…he's always been too focused. He's always reaching for the stars, and don't get me wrong, that's not a bad thing, but he never stopped to look at the star that was closest to him—the brightest one. I know he overlooked you, but don't let it get to you now. I know you're an amazing person. I know your heart. That isn't going to change because you were gone for six years. It's okay to put the past in the past and move forward."

"I hate that I let my pride get in the way. I hate that after all these years I still feel stupid when I'm near him. I'm like that teenage girl all over again with a hopeless crush."

"Men are dumb creatures by nature, honey. Don't feel too bad." I laugh and use my sleeve to get rid of the stray tears. "C'mon, let's have some pie."

We all settle around the table they have in their backyard while Aurora serves up slices of her delicious apple pie. It's a town favorite. Always has been.

"So, Selene, Endymion and Luna were telling us that you're getting little miss signed up for classes. First grade, how does it feel?"

"Like time is going by much too quickly," I tell Ermias.

Endymion's lips purse in disapproval, obviously not happy that he wasn't able to be a part of her previous years. I deflate in my seat, feeling incredibly guilty. I can imagine it feels the same way for him—as though he'll never have enough time with her because she's growing way too fast.

"I heard through your dad that you're now working at Rita's?"

I nod, plastering an uncomfortable smile on my face. "It's different. I haven't worked customer service since I was in college, but since I'm out of work while here, I thought it'd be nice to pitch in with my dad, help him pay the bills. Maybe save enough to get my own place."

This seems to make them happy. Aurora smiles. She reaches across the table and pats my hand. "You know, we're actually going to have a barbecue here next weekend. I think you should come. I have a friend who is a realtor, and maybe you two can exchange numbers."

"That sounds great."

When night rolls around, Luna and I say our goodbyes. Endymion walks us to the car and buckles her in. I step away, giving them their privacy and hear them speaking in hushed tones. I hear her little giggle, and it makes me smile, despite the constant pit in my gut. He shuts her door, and I know, within a few minutes, she'll be out like a light.

An awkward silence descends as Endymion stands before me, his gaze raking up and down my body. I cross my arms over my chest protectively, feeling unsure.

"You know, about the invite your mother extended to me, I don't have to come."

His gaze searches mine but gives nothing away. His face remains impassive, impossible for me to read. "It's fine. Luna will want you there."

I clear my throat. "Okay. Sure."

"Thank you for coming." The words sound insincere as if they're hard for him to say, let alone swallow. I hate that.

"Of course. And look, I know you're still angry with me—"

That seems to do it. His eyes suddenly flare with pent-up rage, and his lips thin into a grim line. The sinews of his strong body grow taut with tension, making me regret me and my stupid mouth instantaneously.

"Did you think a few outings with my daughter would suddenly take away my anger, Selene?" He takes a step toward me, and I back away on instinct. I don't think he'd ever hurt me, but something in his eyes, a darkness mixed with reckless abandon—it's a pool of heat that is so hot, it damn near incinerates me.

"No. Well, yes. I mean, no. I just hoped—"

"Don't hope, Selene. It gets you nowhere."

He stalks away, gait stiff, the muscles in his back bunched with tension, and I watch the entire way he goes, feeling off-kilter and deflated.

After showering off my shift at Rita's, I get dressed for the party at End's parents' house. It's all the town has been talking about. Apparently, they've been doing it every year in the summertime. Not that I would know, I've been gone and am no longer a true member of this town.

News has spread fast about Luna and her relation to the Blacks. The gossip mill still hasn't changed one bit since I've been gone. It probably never will. I've been getting side-eyes and disapproving stares at work from other town-goers, and my only saving grace has been Rita and Julia. They've been quick to speak up and defend me against the vultures and their harsh words when I can't speak up for myself. I'd like to think I'm not that weak teenaged girl from six years ago, but giving in to the town's antics, defending myself to them, almost feels like I'm fighting back for no reason. I do deserve their wrath, so if this is my punishment, so be it.

With the summer heat at an all-time high, I opt for a yellow sundress and some nude espadrille sandals that buckle around the ankle. I blow-dry my hair and run a brush through it, deciding to keep the natural waves I have going instead of going all out and doing my hair. I'll have enough people judging me as it is. The last thing I want to do is draw too much attention to myself.

Before I left for work earlier, I dressed Luna similarly in a cute little pink romper with unicorns and a bow in her hair. Endymion's smile was so wide when he came to pick her up; it had my stomach flipping, and my heart tripping over itself.

"You ready yet? Or are you on your what, hundredth heart attack of the day?" Julia asks, popping her head into the doorway. I glance away from my reflection and shoot her a glare.

"I'm ready."

She's coming along as moral support, but I'm not exactly sure how supportive she'll actually be. I love her, don't get me wrong, but she's always had this "I don't give a shit what other people think of me" motto that I've never quite been able to adopt.

My stomach twists with unease as we park down the street from their house. There are a ton of cars, and plenty of the town is hanging around. This is definitely going to be a packed shindig. That is what I hate about small towns.

"C'mon, it's probably not as bad as you're thinking," Julia assures, dragging me along with her. When we walk into the backyard, and I see everyone seated around at the multitude of tables, my breath gets caught in my throat. It is exactly what I was fearing.

Only so much worse.

As soon as everyone takes notice of us, there is a lull in the roaring conversation, and I can feel everyone's gaze on me. Some with looks of contempt and others with looks of pity. I don't need their pity, and I certainly don't need their anger. I have enough of that from End to last a lifetime.

One look, in particular, has my stomach souring, and my heart shriveling. Freya Black is beautiful and has always been incredibly sweet, but the way she's glaring daggers at me right now? You'd never believe it. She hates me. It's written all over the soft planes of her face. I kept her brother's daughter from him, deprived her of a niece, a cousin for her daughter to play with—I get it. I'm sure she thinks I'm the devil incarnate.

"There you are!" Aurora cheers, pulling me into a warm hug that takes me by surprise. "Ignore them. They have nothing better to do than gossip," she whispers into my ear, trying to put me at ease. I give her a wobbly smile that doesn't quite reach my eyes.

"Thank you, Aurora."

"Come. End and Luna are just over there." She points over toward them, and my stomach drops at the scene before me. It's like I'm reliving the agony of the past and the hurt of being invisible and insignificant in the eyes of Endymion Black. Holly Matthews is standing there with Endymion and our daughter. A sharp ache shoots through my chest. If things were different, this would be their story.

Suddenly, the thought of sharing my daughter with Holly makes me sick to my stomach. I place a trembling hand over my gut, trying to inhale deep, stabilizing breaths, but my lungs have suddenly forgotten how to work.

Julia must sense my pain because she grips my arm, being the supportive friend, and drags me toward my daughter. She doesn't say it, but I feel it in the squeeze of her hand on mine. *"Everything is fine."* and *"You're okay."*

When Luna notices I'm here, a smile breaks out across her little face, and it slowly ebbs away the pain-filled throb I feel wreaking havoc in my chest.

"Mommy!" she yells. I close the distance between us and glance at Endymion and Holly once more. They're both laughing with each other, looking like the perfect couple I remember from my teen years. My heart cracks open at the realization. At the sound of Luna's excitement, they both glance my way just as I drop to my haunches and throw my arms open for my little girl. She squeezes me in a bear hug, peppering my face with kisses.

When she pulls back, she cups my cheek, staring into my eyes. "You look really pretty, Mommy."

I smile. "Not prettier than you."

Her laughter is like music to my ears.

Looking over her shoulder, I spot Holly with her hand on Endymion's arm, and a surge of envy roars through my veins, knocking the wind out of me. It borders on possessiveness because as much as I hate to admit it, I wish he were mine. It'll never happen, though, this I know. Ignoring the iciness that's shooting down the center of my chest, making me feel numb, I coach myself through my breathing techniques.

Deep inhale. Long exhale.

This is what I wanted to avoid. This sick feeling right here. Holly smirks as though she knows exactly what seeing them together is doing to me. I avert my gaze, soaking in my daughter. She takes my hand and Julia's hand, showing us how she goes down the slide. I welcome the distraction with open arms.

I feel eyes on me, and I know without looking who it is. There is that damn tension in the air, that thickness that makes it hard to breathe. It's the Endymion effect. I feel his presence come up behind me. I can also tell by the squeak that leaves Julia at his nearness. I don't bother turning. I don't want to see Holly with her paws all over him in front of our daughter any longer.

"You came," is all he says when he steps beside me. I have to fight the urge to turn and look at him and all his handsome glory.

"I did."

"You know what? I'm going to say my hellos. I'll meet up with you later, Selene," Julia offers, sounding unsure. I curse her in my head the entire time.

So much for having my back.

In my peripheral, I spot him cross his arms over his broad chest. "You look nice."

"Thanks," I mumble, still refusing to look at him.

As Luna continues to play, I make an excuse, anything to get away from him. After seeing him with Holly, I suddenly feel sad and angry. The emotions are rioting inside me, demanding to be heard—or more accurately, felt.

"I'm going to see if your mom needs help with anything."

I don't bother waiting for his response. I bypass table after table of whispers that cling to me like they've dug their talons into my flesh. Despite all that, I'm holding my head high even when my chest feels like it's going to explode at any given second. Aurora's face alights with surprise when I step into the kitchen, a perpetual redness coating my cheeks.

"Selene, is something wrong?" she asks, sounding truly concerned. As if she cares.

I shake my head. "Everything is fine. I wanted to see if you need help with anything."

She pauses, studying me for a few suspended seconds, warmth seeping into her gaze. "Here, why don't you help me bring these trays out there? And thank you, Selene. I appreciate it."

I begin dropping off the glass trays of various foods to the table they have set up out there on the patio. My feet falter as I'm bringing out the last tray. It's heavier than the rest, the glass still unbelievably warm against my palms from the food inside. Holly is off to the side of the table with her group of friends.

"We're going out on a date. I knew time wouldn't change anything between us. We're still as good now as we were then," I hear Holly gloat to Reina. My stomach cramps and pain shoots through my chest. It wraps cold and savage around my heart. A sick sensation brews in my gut.

The glass tray I'm holding tumbles from my hands and falls at my feet, shattering against the pavement. Everyone stops what they're doing to look at me, eyes wide, judging me. My face flames, the attention making me uncomfortable. My chin trembles, and I trap my bottom lip between my teeth, trying to stifle the tears.

I will not cry here.

I will not cry here.

My baby comes up running to me, stopping before the mess. "What happened, Mommy?" she asks in her sweet little voice.

I sniff past the pressure in my nose, and I force a smile for her sake, avoiding everyone's probing gaze. "It just slipped from my hands, that's all, baby."

I bend to start cleaning the mess of glass and splattered food. I rush to do it, hate feeling like I'm under a microscope of this whole damn town. *Why won't everyone just look away?* I glance up quickly, and my stomach twists with anguish when I see how close Holly is now standing to End. When he even got near her, I don't remember, but seeing them so close, after what I just heard, it has my heart shriveling. She's laughing under her breath, resting her hand on his firm bicep, obviously finding my clumsiness hilarious. My stomach revolts, and I fear I might vomit right here in front of everyone.

Pain slices through my hand, and a sharp gasp suddenly falls past my lips. Luna makes a mewling sound before yelling, "Oh no!"

While cleaning, I accidentally cut myself on the shards of glass. Blood drips from the wound, stinging as the open air hits it. I hurry to cover my finger, not wanting to freak her out. Endymion comes running over, leaving Holly, obviously thinking something happened to Luna instead of me. When he sees the blood, he scoops up Luna, trying to distract her. I blow out a sigh and cradle my finger to my chest, heading inside.

In search of the bathroom or a first-aid kit, I spot Freya, who is no longer glaring at me, but this time, staring after me with a look of pity in her eyes. I find I much prefer the anger.

"Down the hall, on the right," she calls out to me.

I keep my hand cradled to my chest, opening up drawers in the bathroom, looking for something I can cover this with. I'm not sure a Band-Aid will hold, but I'll take what I can get. I opt to wrap it in toilet paper for now while I search for what I need.

I'm so caught up in my own thoughts that I don't hear the footsteps until his voice echoes from beside me, making me squeak in surprise.

"Let me take a look," End says, glancing down at my hand pointedly. The blood is already soaking through the botched toilet paper wrap-job I did. He is larger than life. His body takes up all the space in this small bathroom, making it hard to breathe. I shake my head.

"No, it's fine. I'm just looking for a Band-Aid or something."

"Selene."

The way he says my name gives me pause. Slowly, I glance up at him through the curtain of my hair, and our eyes connect. A moment passes between us, and I hate the way my stomach flips at all in his presence. It's not like he feels the same way. Maybe if I was Holly, he might, but I'm not. I'm me—plain ole Selene. Nothing special, and the likelihood is, I never will be.

His jaw is dusted lightly with stubble, and I have to fight the urge to caress his handsome face. He reaches his hand out between us, clearly telling me to place mine in his, so he can have a look. Blowing out a resigned breath, I do as he says, and he unwraps the bloody toilet paper from my finger, taking a look. The second his skin is on mine, a tingle travels through my body. It's an awareness I wish wasn't there. One I wish I could ignore. One I should not be feeling at all. His touch is gentle and soft, and I can't help but admire everything about him at this moment. I'm sure he can feel my gaze on him, but I can't seem to bring myself to look away.

"You all right?" he asks as he cleans the wound.

I wince a little at the sting but try to shrug it off as nothing major. "It's just a small cut. I'll be fine."

"I wasn't talking about the cut, Selene."

My brows pull together in a frown, and I pause. "What were you talking about then?"

He sighs. "She was talking to me. Not the other way around, if that's what you're thinking."

I don't respond, mainly because I'm unsure how to. He doesn't have to explain. He owes me nothing while I owe him everything.

"You don't owe me anything," I mumble.

"You're right. I don't." My eyes slam shut, an ache ricocheting through my chest. That one hurt. "But that doesn't mean I want you to think there's anything between Holly and me because there isn't."

I nod slowly, trying to process the torment in my chest with the reality of his words, and make sense of what I heard Holly say. I hate that his words invoke any kind of hope in my chest.

"She said you asked her out." I clear my throat, despising how weak I sound. Because as much as it pains me to admit, I hate that he's moved on from me so quickly. Not long ago, he was chasing after me, trying to court me, and now he's all but ready to fall back into old habits with her. "Look, I know you hate me. I get it. It's fine, you know, if you want to. Just as long as Luna isn't involved."

"I don't hate you," he murmurs gruffly.

I scoff. "Really? I'd like to see how you treat people you do hate."

Endymion heaves a deep sigh. "I'm upset with you, sure, and as much as I'd like to, I don't hate you."

I sneak a glance up at him, and he's searching my gaze, something akin to heat brewing in his colored eyes, but I know that can't be right. My mind must be playing tricks on me.

"Well," I clear my throat. "Whatever your feelings are, just know it's okay. You can date whoever you want."

"And what if I don't want her? What would you say to that?"

"Want who?" I ask, my heart pounding in my chest.

"Holly. What if I don't want Holly?"

My heart is a steel drum in my chest as it pounds recklessly. I swallow past the golf ball-sized lump in my throat. "Who would you want then, if not her?"

I wait with bated breath for his answer. He searches my gaze, and I don't know if I imagine it, but I swear he steps closer. His grip on my hand gets a little tighter. The heat in his eyes kicks up a few notches.

"Everything okay over here?"

A surprised squeak tumbles past my lips at the sound of Aurora's voice. I jerk away from Endymion as if we were caught kissing. Heat settles in my cheeks, and my chest heaves violently as it works to accommodate my breathing.

"Fine. We're fine," I pant out in a panic. "I was just about done in here. I can help you clean up out there."

She smiles, her gaze darting back and forth between her son and me. "Don't worry about it. We've already got it cleaned up and don't feel too bad. Everyone hates Mrs. Wallace's casserole. I think you did everyone a favor today. Though, she might be a bit upset about her tray. But don't you worry yourself about that."

"I'll pay her back. I promise."

Aurora laughs softly, pulling me in stride with her. "You're too sweet for your own good, you know that?"

For the rest of the evening, I stay near Luna and Julia, avoiding Endymion at all costs. I made Julia promise she wouldn't leave my side, so no more awkward conversations would pass between us. Part of me wishes my parents would've come. Maybe then I wouldn't feel so out of place. I understand why they didn't, though. The last thing my father wants on him is the pitying eyes of everyone in town.

I keep thinking back to what Endymion said earlier, or really, what he didn't say.

"What if I don't want Holly?"

If not Holly, who else?

It couldn't be me, could it? Especially not after everything that has happened. There is no way he can still feel anything for me. It also doesn't escape my notice the way he dodges and avoids Holly the rest of the night. It makes me unreasonably happy—much more than it should. I have no right to feel this way. It's stupid. I'm setting myself up for failure. Plunging face first into heartbreak, and I can't stop myself.

I am only realizing now how dangerous being in love with a man like Endymion is for the mind, body, and soul.

He's already destroyed me once, and I'm determined not to let it happen again. Not after all the progress. Not now that Luna is involved. This time around, I need to be smart.

Endymion is off-limits.

Chapter Nineteen

Endymion

"WHERE ARE WE GOING, DADDY?" LUNA ASKS FROM THE backseat.

Selene dropped her off earlier before she went to work at the diner. For the last week and a half, we've finally found somewhat of a routine. With her working at Rita's and me running the company with the guys, finding enough time to spend with my daughter has been a challenge. Luna has been a welcome joy in my life. Working around the business and making time for her has been my top priority.

"Want to visit your mom for a little bit? Thought we could get some lunch."

Luna squeals in the backseat, obviously liking that idea. It warms my heart, seeing how much she loves her mom. Selene is incredible with her. She's beyond patient and incredibly loving. Both of them together are a vision. It does something strange whenever I see them together. Hell, even my anger is slowly dissipating. And in its place is desire, because even after everything that has happened, I still want Selene. She's beautiful. Inside and out. I have to force myself to look angry or portray this cold façade that gives nothing away because when I'm near this woman, all I seem to do is *feel*.

I was so close to telling her that day in my parents' bathroom. It isn't Holly I want; it's her.

I'm tired of the bullshit.

I know what I want, and that's my daughter and Selene.

I want them both.

If my mother hadn't walked in when she did, I would've kissed her. Damn the consequences, damn my anger. I would've kissed this woman because she's all I can think about. All I want.

Taking Luna's hand in mine, I help her out of the truck, and we walk hand in hand into Rita's. The patrons dining inside turn around when the bell announces our arrival. Rita, the owner of the place, smiles when she sees us.

"Well, hey there," she greets us, getting us seated at a table. It's a corner booth near the register, away from the craziness of the diner. "What are we getting for you today, little lady?"

"Hmm. A cheeseburger with French fries, please. Oh, and my mommy."

Rita laughs. "Okay, little miss, I'll get right on that for you. What are you having, End?"

"I'll have my usual. Thanks, Rita."

With a soft, familiar smile, she leaves us, and I search the diner for any sign of Selene. I spot her taking orders at a rowdy table. When I see who is sitting there, my back teeth gnash together, and the muscles along my jaw jump with frustration. Thomas—Holly's boyfriend or ex-boyfriend, whatever the hell they are now—and his friends are all seated there, and the way they're looking at Selene, damn near eye-fucking her in her work outfit, doesn't sit well with me.

"Is Papa sick?" Luna suddenly asks, dragging my attention away from her mother and the guys at the table.

My brows pull together in a frown. "What makes you ask that?"

My happy little girl grows serious. "At the party, that lady you were talking to said something to her friend. She said the only reason me and Mommy are here is because Papa is sick. Then she said he's going to die."

Fury burns in my chest. The flames lick at my organs, incinerating me from the inside out. I press my lips in a hard line and my nostrils flare, working to tamp down my anger. What the hell am I supposed to say to that? The only reason I spoke to Holly was because I didn't want to be a dick, especially not in front of my daughter. We are still getting to know each other, and I didn't want to tell Holly to "fuck off" in front of Luna. Some other part of me wanted to forget about the awkwardness between us. We were once friends before anything else.

I haven't thought about her in years. She was a close friend, but sometime during high school, that changed. I've never been in love, and I think that's what bothers Holly the most about our previous relationship. The fact that I was never able to let myself go and fall for her. I came to the conclusion long ago that she just wasn't the right girl for me. I didn't feel a spark when I was with her. All I felt was comfortability. It was easy being with her. I didn't have to think twice about anything.

But with Selene? I've feel that spark, that tug of magnetism when we're in the same room. It's as if my body knows her frequency the second she steps into a room. I think that spark has always been there; she just doesn't know it. I felt it that first night I got into town. When I locked gazes with a beautifully soft girl who was standing amongst a sea of sugar, it was a jolt to the system, the fact that I wanted to know more about her. She doesn't know this, but over the years, when we'd run into each other, I could recall every moment spent with her. Hell, the only instance I don't clearly remember with her is the night at the creek.

This is what they call fate, I think. This electricity, this magnetism. This strange feeling in my gut.

She was always so quiet and soft-spoken. So goddamn beautiful. She had this purity about her, this light that made you want to leave her untouched and merely watch and admire her from a distance.

That's exactly what I did all those years. She may believe she was invisible to everyone all those years ago, but she's wrong. It was painfully obvious Selene was the most beautiful girl in town. That hasn't changed.

The fact that Holly would let that slip in front of my daughter says a lot about her. She hasn't changed one bit since high school. This is exactly her MO. She's immature, doesn't care about anyone but herself, and obviously doesn't know when to keep her mouth shut. The whole town knows Gavin is sick, but that doesn't mean they're gossiping about it in front of him and his family.

I grip at the back of my neck, trying to find the correct way to tackle this. I may be her father, but Gavin is Selene's father. I don't know if they plan on talking to Luna if things begin to deteriorate, or if they'll keep her in the dark until he's ready. Hell, I don't even know what I want to do. I don't want to lie to her, but I don't want to break my daughter's heart either. I've seen how much she loves her Papa Gavin, and losing him will be devastating for her.

"Why haven't you asked your mom?"

Luna shrugs. "I think it might make Mommy sad. I told Papa last night that I wanted a little brother or sister to play with, and he looked like he was gonna cry."

It takes me a second to process her words. "You want a little brother or a sister?"

She nods. "I want a real family."

Her innocent words are a puncture to the heart. Pain seeps into my chest, and I swallow. "We are a real family."

Luna shakes her head. "At my old school, all the other mommies and daddies live together, but you and Mommy don't. I want a family like that. A real family with a mommy, a daddy, and a baby sister. But I'll take a little brother, too."

I choke on a laugh at her truthfulness. "I want that, too."

"You do?" she asks, eyes wide.

"I do."

My back tingles with awareness, and when I glance at the back doors of the diner, I see why. Selene is headed toward us; her hair pulled back into a messy braid that does nothing to take away from her beauty. That little red dress doesn't hide her legs and the curvy backside there. The one I'm itching to get my hands on. She looks beautiful. She always looks so fucking beautiful.

She places our plates before us, a smile on her face as she stares down at Luna. "A special cheeseburger for my special Luna Bella."

"Thank you, Mommy."

Selene then slides my plate in front of me, avoiding my gaze. She's been doing it a lot lately. Hell, she's always been shy. But it's like now, she purposely tries not to look at me and I hate it. I just want her to look me in the fucking eyes *once* so she can see everything I'm unable to say out loud in front of our daughter.

"Guess what Daddy bought me today?" Luna singsongs between bites of her food.

"What did he get you?"

"He bought me the Barbie Dream House I've been wanting, *and* he bought me more dolls to go with it." Luna is practically vibrating with excitement on her side of the booth as she tells her mom.

If it weren't for the amusement glinting in her hazel eyes and the smirk twisting her lips, I'd think she's mad at me.

"You spoil her."

She doesn't say it like it's a bad thing, just merely stating a fact. I can't hold back the grin that takes over my face. I shrug my shoulders. "She makes it hard to say no."

Selene laughs, and fuck me, the sound hits me square in the chest. She's so goddamn beautiful when she smiles, which is obvious because no man in this joint can keep his eyes off her. We share a moment, her standing there, staring down at me with the best smile

I've ever had the pleasure of witnessing, and me, looking up at her like she's every fucking star lighting up the darkest sky.

There's a sharp whistle followed by, "Hey, sweet cheeks. Can we get some service over here?"

Selene's smile falters, and her shoulders stiffen. Color settles in her cheeks. I glance around her, and my eyes narrow when I realize whose table the shout came from. Seeming embarrassed by the attention or being called out, she tucks a few hairs behind her ears and drops down to press a kiss to Luna's head.

"I should really get back to work," she whispers.

The entire time I watch her go, glaring at the table of rowdy men. The biggest asshole of all is sitting there, looking sleazy as shit, arms slung along the backs of the booth with his eyes glued to *my* fucking woman. I can't hear what he's saying to her from here, but whatever it is, it has Selene's perpetual pink cheeks turning a bright shade of red, and she shifts on her feet, obviously uncomfortable. The men around the booth laugh hysterically, and I grip the edges of the table.

"They laugh a lot," Luna observes, her gaze glued to their table, just like mine is.

"Yeah, they do." My voice is all gravel and displeasure.

"It happens all the time around Mommy."

"What does?"

"That." She points toward them. "Nana says the boys love Mommy because they can't have her." She shrugs. "Whatever that means."

Hearing that come out of my daughter's mouth only drives me closer to the edge. I want to stake my claim on Selene right here, right now. I want to march over there, pull her into my arms, and kiss her. Let all those bastards know that she's mine. She carried my fucking child. No one else's. It's only been me, and fucking hell, I plan on keeping it that way.

Rita stops by our table. "We still doing okay over here?"

I'm nodding when I glance behind her and see fucking red. That slimy bastard is toying with the hem of Selene's dress while she tries to push him away, looking around for help. A growl rips from my chest, a wave of possessive anger I've not felt before firing through my veins. I shoot out of the booth, stalking across the diner, consequences be damned. Thomas sees me coming, and the fucker has the gall to smirk at me. Egging me on.

"Well, look who it is, the baby daddy."

Selene whirls around, her eyes going wide when she sees me. My anger reaches new heights when I realize her face isn't red with embarrassment anymore. No, instead, her face is drained of all color. She's afraid. They've fucking scared her.

"C'mon, Black, share the love. You've already fucked her—"

My hand shoots out, and I slam him against the booth. I curl my fist into his shirt, getting into his face. "Come near her again, and you're done. Understand me?"

"Well, I'll be. Never thought I'd see the day End Black cared about anyone other than himself." He's pushing my fucking buttons, and it's working. "Tell me one thing, man. Does she taste as good as she looks?" I raise my fist back, ready to clock him, but sweet honey and bergamot infiltrate my senses, and when soft warmth closes around my bicep, I pause and turn.

Selene is trying to hold me back, her eyes pleading with me to stop. She pointedly looks toward our table, and I spot my little girl, mostly being blocked by Rita, but still watching with curiosity.

Slowly, I release Thomas, tamping down the anger that's nearly bubbling over the surface. "Get the fuck out. Don't ever come near Selene again. I mean it."

A burly voice pipes in behind me, and when I crane my neck to look, surprise raises my brows. Bobby, Rita's husband, is the cook here. He's a tall, burly man who has a no-nonsense aura about him.

He's definitely someone you do not want to fuck with. "All of you, out."

The guys at the table share a look before they shove away, spilling their drinks and making a mess for no other reason than to be dicks to Selene and the rest of Rita's staff. Once they're gone, the tightness in my chest ebbs away, but my anger is still there, flowing like the force of the falls. I open and close my fists at my sides, dying to plow my knuckles into the son of a bitch's face.

"End, can I talk to you for a second?"

There's an edge to Selene's tone that I know can't be good. I nod rigidly, and she glances over her shoulder at Bobby. "Can you ask Rita to stay with Luna for a sec?"

"Of course." He shoots me a sympathetic look, likely knowing where this is going.

Fucking hell.

As soon as we're out back, Selene lays into me. Jabbing her strong little finger into my chest, she has anger written all over gorgeous fucking face.

"What the hell was that back there? Are you insane?"

"Probably." I shrug, slipping my hands into my pockets.

Selene begins to pace, rubbing at the back of her neck in frustration. Every time she walks, that little damn dress rides up her thighs, fueling the little embers left from my anger.

Rita couldn't choose an uglier goddamn uniform? Christ.

"You can't do that," she suddenly blurts, stopping a few feet away from me. "You can't go around fighting people trying to…trying to defend my honor, or whatever that was. You'll scare her!"

Guilt bears down on my shoulders. Heaving a deep sigh filled with remorse, I rake a hand through my hair and nod. She's right. I'm a father now. I can't just start fights whenever something upsets me. Luna will see everything, and that's the very last thing I want.

But was I supposed to let him grope her in public? It was obvious no one else noticed, and she wasn't going to get any help elsewhere. I had to step in.

"You're right. I'm sorry. But if you think for one second I'm going to let a man touch you, you're out of your damn mind, Selene."

Her brows raise, damn near disappearing into her hairline, and her mouth drops open in shock. "What man touches me is no concern of yours, Endymion. We share a daughter together, and that's it."

That beautiful pink flush is now staining her neck and cheeks again, and I can't help but wonder how far it extends. I don't remember much about the night we slept together, and Jesus Christ, I hate my younger self for allowing this woman to slip through my fingers.

I step closer to her, and she takes a wary step back. Her chest is heaving, the pulse at the base of her neck is pounding, and fuck me, all I want to do is swipe my tongue across her flesh and taste her. She's wrong. We don't just share a daughter together. We share a lot more. We have chemistry. There's an inexplicable spark between us, even when we were younger, even when I did everything I could to run from it and pretend I didn't notice her. But I'm not running from it anymore. I want her. I want this. I want my fucking family.

"You and I both know there's a lot more than that between us. Luna isn't the only reason we keep finding ourselves here. I want—"

"Selene, honey, Rita is asking for you," Bobby hollers from the back door, ruining the moment. She's still staring at me, wide-eyed, her chest rising and falling in rapid motion. I didn't get to finish saying what I wanted to, but she gets the gist. She's going to hear me out. I'm not doing this anymore. Not when I have a beautiful woman before me and a beautiful daughter in there waiting for me.

"Let's go." She clears her throat. "I have to get back to work."

When I walk back to my table, Luna is staring at me curiously, and my lungs squeeze in a vise. Fuck. I hope she isn't afraid of me. I take the seat across from her, giving Rita a smile in thanks.

"I'm sorry about that, Luna. I shouldn't have—"

Surprising the shit out of me, my little girl leans forward, wearing a conspiratorial grin on her face. "That was awesome, Daddy. But you really should've punched him."

I choke on a laugh. Jesus Christ, this kid.

I love her to death already. I have since the moment I found out she was mine, maybe even before that.

I've just tucked Luna into bed, and I perch on the edge, setting down the book she wanted me to read to her. Four times.

"I gotta get going, Luna. But I'll see you tomorrow, okay?"

She smiles up at me, eyelids drooped with fatigue, and spreads her arms, indicating she wants a hug.

"I love you, Daddy," my little girl breathes into my chest, stopping my heart midbeat. I clutch her body to me even tighter. I slam my eyes shut, despising Selene and caring for her in equal measure. I want to hate her. Hell, I have every right to hate her, but I can't. Because at the end of the day, she gave me my daughter. Something about her makes it impossible for me to hold on to my anger. Something so heavy that it makes it hard to breathe or think when I'm near her.

Luna settles back in the sheets, and as soon as her eyes close, her little chest rises and falls deeply as sleep pulls her under. I quietly make my way out of the bedroom, saying my goodbyes to Gavin and Cece. I am still giving Luna time to adjust, but I don't want to do this forever. I want to be able to sleep under the same roof as my daughter.

After the eventful lunch at the diner, I spent the evening with Luna at Gavin's. It didn't escape my notice how tired he looks. Every day, he seems to look thinner and thinner. I can see why Luna asked what she did.

My mind drifts to the conversation I had with Gavin in his living room after the diner incident. We watched Luna play with her toys on the far end of the room, each of us stuck in our own heads. He was watching her with sadness in his eyes. It was one that hit me square in the chest.

"When are you guys going to tell her?" I ask quietly.

His nostrils flare, the muscles in his jaw jumping with barely restrained emotion, and he clears his throat. "Selene doesn't want to tell her yet."

My gaze narrows on Gavin. "You haven't told her how bad it is yet, have you?"

A sheen of tears builds in his eyes as he watches his granddaughter. "It'll break her heart. She blames herself for a lot of the time we went without speaking. She'll never recover from this."

My eyes slam shut. I feel a deep throbbing coming on at the base of my skull. "It'll break her if you don't tell her, Gavin. Does Cece know?"

He's quiet for a long beat. "She knows. The woman hates my guts, and even she isn't handling it well." He laughs, but the sound is pained and filled with remorse. "I just need a little more time. A little more time to break the news to my daughter. Then to Luna."

I nod, even though I don't agree. How can I go against a sick man's wishes? It seems like all Gavin Drake wants is time, but I don't have the heart to remind him that his is running out.

After that painful conversation with Gavin, we spent the rest of the evening with a looming black cloud hovering over our heads.

I'm snapped out of my thoughts when I spot Selene pulling into the driveway. Tucking my hands into my jean pockets, I trudge through the grass on the front lawn, crossing the distance between us.

Her gaze keeps flitting to my face, then back to the windshield. I swear I see her lips moving, though I can't be sure what she's saying to herself. She seems to square her shoulders before she climbs out of the car and strides toward me with a look of pure determination etched on her face.

My gaze trails from those gorgeous doe eyes down to her dirtied shoes, and even though she's been working on her feet all day, I've never seen anyone who has looked more perfect, more beautiful. Selene jerks to a halt before me, eyeing me through narrowed slits. Her plump lips purse as she works through something in her mind.

"Funny story," she starts to say, not looking all that enthused. "Spotted Thomas after work walking to the bar. I couldn't help but notice his black eye. Especially since he didn't have one only hours prior." She crosses her arms over her chest, and I glance down at the creamy expanse, wondering if the freckles there dusting across the bridge of her nose extend anywhere else. When her foot begins tapping, I realize she's waiting for me to fess up.

I shrug my shoulders noncommittally. "That is a funny story."

Her lip twitches, making it obvious she's trying to hold back a smile. "You wouldn't happen to know anything about that, would you?"

"And if I did?" I challenge her.

She swallows, searching my gaze. "I'd tell you that it was stupid and irresponsible. Especially since you have a daughter."

My gaze narrows. "I told you, no man is going to touch what is mine. Thomas overstepped his bounds today, saying what he did about you. He was embarrassing you on purpose to be a dick. And I'm well aware I have a daughter now. She was nowhere near us when it happened."

"Why do you keep saying that?"

"Saying what?"

Heat settles in her cheeks. "You said 'what's mine.'"

I eat up the distance between us, staring down at her, heat swirling in my gut. Her slender throat works a swallow, and for every step forward I take, she takes a step back, until her back collides with the passenger side of the car. Her eyes dart to the house behind me. All the lights are already off inside, Luna out for the count. The stars have long since scattered across the sky.

"Because you are mine, Selene. I've never been more sure of anything."

Her breath hitches. Those plump lips part.

"You don't mean that." Her voice is a mere whisper. It almost sounds like a plea. She wants this to be a lie. She *needs* it to be a lie.

"Oh, I do, babe. I may not have been thinking clearly all those years ago, but I am now. I want you, Selene. In all this mess, that's the one thing that hasn't changed."

She averts her gaze, unable to look me in the eye any longer. She's so small that she barely grazes my chest, so she keeps her gaze settled there, trained on the material of my shirt.

"What if I don't want you, want this anymore?"

I press my lips together in frustration. "Who do you want then?"

"Julia's thinking about setting me up on a date with one of her friends."

My hands fist at my sides, and I step into her. Her soft body grazes mine, and I hover above her, caging her against the car.

"Look me in the eye and tell me you don't want this."

Slowly, she flicks her gaze up to mine, that bottom lip trapped between her teeth in contemplation. "I…I…"

"Say it," I grit.

"I can't," she whispers, and my composure snaps.

Chapter Twenty

Selene

"I can't." The words fall from my lips, and my heart jumps into my throat at the look on End's face. It's pure animalistic hunger.

He grips my wrists and pins my body against my car. Before I can anticipate his next move, his mouth slams down on mine, dominating it in a way only he can.

My struggle comes to a stop instantaneously, and I gasp, the earth rocking beneath my feet. He uses the opportunity to thrust his tongue inside, taking what he wants, infecting my heart with his disease like no one else ever has. The kiss is furious and punishing, stoking the fire and fury between us. His potent taste, the one I've never forgotten, settles deep into my bones.

My fingers find purchase in his hair, and I fist the silky strands as I match every angry stroke he delivers. His strong thigh wedges between my legs as he grasps my arms pinning them against the car, stroking the one spot that sends shockwaves through my body.

My hips lift, grinding indecently as I greedily reach for that mind-numbing pleasure.

It's been so long—too long.

The orgasm washes over me like a hurricane, flooding every nerve ending in my body. I drown in it, crying against his mouth, too lost in it all to be embarrassed by the quick thrill.

He grips my jaw with one hand and forces my head back against the passenger side of my car, his teeth sinking into my bottom lip with a sharp bite. A slight metallic taste of blood touches my tongue before he pulls his mouth away.

His furious face hovers before mine, eyes wild with lust, but the anger is still there, just as prominent as before. "There is no one else. Just us."

My lungs heave for air as I gaze up at him, heart beating painfully with every breath I take. "Just *us* or Holly, too?"

His jaw tightens. "You know better than that. Holly is my past, Selene, and as much as I'd like to change the past, I can't. But you, you're..."

My brows pull down. "I'm what?"

"You're the only woman I see in my future. The only one I want there."

My heart jumps into my throat, and my stomach does somersaults at his words. A thrill shoots down my spine.

"Endymion...we can't just...we can't do this. We have Luna to think about."

"I am thinking about Luna. I'm thinking about a little girl who told me she wants a real family. A little girl who deserves more than just being tucked into bed by her dad and having to watch him leave. She's my kid, too, and I will take what belongs to me." His fingers brush my swollen lips. "All of it."

My heart just about explodes as I watch him walk away, hopping into his truck. When his taillights disappear down the street, I finally feel like I'm able to breathe. Endymion Black is intense. He still has the capability to steal the very breath from my lungs.

After showering off the grease from working at the diner, I climb into bed beside Luna and pull her into my arms. With my gaze riveted to the ceiling, I try to think of what to do next. There is no going back after what happened tonight. Either I can let this play out with End and see where it takes us, or I can be the mature adult and put a stop to this before I get hurt again. This time, I'm sure the damage will be a lot more extensive than the last. Weighing the pros and cons, I mindlessly rub the pad of my finger over my swollen lips, remembering the way he felt. Heat coils deep in my gut, and my core clenches and throbs just thinking about the way he kissed and touched me. He was like a man starved. Like he couldn't get enough.

And me.

Jesus.

The way I dry humped his leg will mortify me for the rest of my life. I was so caught up in the moment, in him, and the way he was making me feel that I couldn't think clearly.

I never seem to think clearly when I'm near Endymion. That should be answer enough for me.

The next morning, I take Luna with me to have breakfast with Julia. Even though we work together at the diner, we haven't had a chance to hang out as often as either of us would like. My heart thumps unsteadily, and my core clenches when I see who is across the street from the restaurant, doing construction on the building. Dressed in frayed work pants and a shirt that does nothing to hide the ripped body beneath, End looks like a wet dream—the very star of mine, in fact. Even from here, I can clearly see the muscles in his arms bulging as he carries long pieces of wood to and from a truck parked along the street. Hell, his skin looks like it's glistening. I can practically see the beads of sweat rolling down his arms and neck.

I think about last night. The way his tongue stroked mine. Then my mind conjures images from the past, memories of that night at the creek, his tongue circling my nipples, his long, thick cock—

"You're drooling. Isn't your mom drooling, Luna?"

"Yup."

I whirl back around and clear my throat, feigning innocence. "I'm not. I'm just hungry."

Julia scoffs loudly. "Oh, I bet you are. You're hungry for his di—"

"Okaaay." I clap my hands together loudly, trying to drown out whatever Julia was going to say. "Enough about me. What about you and Griffin? Is there anything happening there?"

Julia rolls her eyes, waving me off. "Not even close. He's fun, hot as all hell, but he's also a manwhore. I don't do those. A one-time ride with him to Spank Town was more than enough."

My lips thin at her lingo. I shoot a quick look down at Luna, but she's not paying attention. She's much too busy dousing her waffles in more syrup and chocolate. As if they didn't already come with enough.

"Do I sense some intimidation here?" I goad. Julia aims a scathing glare my way, which tells me I'm not far off. She's always been the strong, speak your mind type, so the fact she's getting pissy over this? It says a lot more about her "relationship" with Griffin than she wants to admit.

"Don't play this game with me, Selene. I know all I have to do is mention Endymion's coc—"

My stomach dips incessantly as I think about End and a certain appendage. I haven't told Julia about last night, though I'm not sure why. It's not like she'll judge me, but a part of me wants to keep it a secret. For now, at least—just between the two of us.

I steer clear of boy talk, deciding it's best to leave that talk for a girls' night, definitely not in front of my daughter. "Luna, baby, how are the waffles?"

She smiles with a mouthful of food and chocolate syrup around her lips. "Really good."

Out of the corner of my eye, I peek once more across the street at Endymion. His words from last night ring loudly in my head, making me feel guilty. I wait for Luna to finish her food before I broach the subject, unsure of how she'll react. I'm not even sure I'm ready, but End was right. This isn't fair to him, and this isn't fair to her.

I want to believe that kiss yesterday changed things, but I can't let myself back into his orbit. I need to stay strong and think about doing what's best for Luna, and that means giving her and Endymion the chance to be a real family. It may not be in the same way he suggested last night, but this is the best I can do—until I can come to a decision about us.

"Luna Bella, how would you feel about staying the night at your daddy's house. Does that sound like fun?"

Her little eyes widen. "Really?" she coos excitedly, vibrating in her seat. "Will you be there?"

I sober, tightness pulling taut across my chest. "No, I won't. But if you need me to pick you up, I'll only be a call away."

She seems pensive, almost as pensive as I feel about this whole situation. "Well, I do miss Daddy a lot when he's gone, but I'm going to miss you, too."

My smile is borderline sad. "I'll miss you, too, but I'll be at work anyway, so technically, it'll be like every other day when you're hanging with Nana and Papa. Maybe when I get off, I'll even stop by and kiss you good night?"

She mulls that over in her head, likely sifting through her fears. After a few solid beats, she says, "I like that idea, Mommy."

It has a smile tugging at the corners of my lips and warmth curling around my heart. *Such a strong girl.*

Looking out the window, I feel somewhat better about my decision when I spot End. He deserves this. I may not be able to offer him a relationship, but I can give him this. They both deserve it.

"I don't care what anyone says. You're an incredible mother."

I roll my eyes at Julia. "That doesn't exactly make me feel great. Knowing this whole town hates me."

She waves me off. "They'll get over it."

I hope so. If this is where I'm forced to stay, I don't want to deal with hateful glares any longer. As much as I hate to admit it, I'm waiting on another scandal to come forth, so everyone will leave me alone.

After paying for breakfast, we all file into the car, and I'm just about to drive off when I realize I left my phone. Julia stays in the car with Luna while I run inside to look for it near our table. I'm in such a hurry, I don't pay attention to where I'm going—or who's in front of me, and I slam into someone.

"Ouch!"

My body goes rigid at the sound of Holly's voice.

Once I regain my footing, I run a nervous hand over my hair, trying to flatten it. "Holly, crap—I'm so sorry. I didn't see you."

Her gaze narrows on me. She drags her eyes up and down my body, her upper lip curling in obvious distaste. "You know, I didn't get it at first, but I think I do now."

My brows tug low over my face. "Get what?"

"End's anger with me. He's never forgiven me for breaking things off with him for Thomas. It's why they got in a fight yesterday. Everything about last night makes so much more sense." She scoffs, and my stomach churns unsteadily. Seeing as Endymion kissed me last night, I suddenly have a bad feeling. It worms its way down my spine in a cold chill.

What does she know about last night?

"What do you mean?"

There's a gleam in her eyes that doesn't quite sit right with me. "I saw you two last night. And I'm saying this to help you, sweetie, this is End's MO. He doesn't care about anyone but himself. He's getting back at me through you, don't you see? I planned on stopping by to tell you myself."

Acid burns the back of my throat and my lungs clench, restricting air. "Tell me what?" My voice is pensive. Reminiscent of how I feel.

She smiles now, and it's a dagger to the chest. "After he left you and your sweet little daughter, I went to his place."

My heart is a dull throb in my chest as I process. Tears burn the backs of my eyes, but I refuse to let them fall. Not when that's clearly what she wants to happen.

"I need to go." I brush past her, and with each step I take, I feel my heart shattering at my feet, crumbling to pieces.

"Bye, Selene," she calls out after me, victory ringing loudly in her tone.

I damn near run out of there, phone all but forgotten. My feet skid to a halt when I see who is standing outside of the car, talking to Luna through the window. My heart throbs at the sight of him. Anger and something else I'm too afraid to dissect run through me.

"I was just about to head in there and tell you your phone was in the cup holder this whole time. Wait—what's wrong?" Julia calls out through the open window as I round the car.

I bypass End, ignoring him completely. I can't look at him right now, not after hearing what Holly just told me. I'm sure most of it was fabricated to make me angry, but the problem is, it worked. I'll never feel secure enough with this man. There is too much baggage on my side. I'm not confident enough for this. I went years being invisible to this man. Why should now be any different?

"Selene, you all right?" End asks.

A burning sensation slithers down my throat, slowly seeping into my chest. It's agonizing.

Just then, Holly walks out with a self-satisfied grin on her face. My gut cramps with anger. Endymion glances from me to her, his brows creasing, obviously sensing that something is wrong.

Suppressed rage bubbles to the surface. "I don't know, End. Why don't you ask Holly?"

The muscle in his jaw clenches, making him look severe. "I don't want to ask her. I'm asking you."

"I think I know what's happening here, Endy. See, I told poor little Selene about last night, and I think I upset her."

Endymion's gaze swings to hers, fury written all over him. "What the hell is wrong with you?"

I glance back toward the car to check on Luna. Through my haze of hurt and anger, I didn't even notice when Julia turned the car and music on to drown out our voices for Luna. I turn back around to face them, my heart squeezing painfully when Endymion begins to close the distance between us. I put my hands up between us, halting his progression.

"Just tell me she's lying."

He sets his jaw in a hard line. "She came to my house."

My brows jump into my hairline, and that pit in my stomach threatens to swallow me whole. "And that somehow makes it better?"

"She showed up there, and I told her to leave. That's all."

Holly laughs. The sound is like nails on a chalkboard for me. "Keep telling yourself that's all that happened, End."

Not wanting to hear any more of this, I grip onto the handle of the car and freeze. With a glance over my shoulder, I forget to mask the pain as I let the words fall from my lips. "I listened to what you said last night and was going to tell you today that I think Luna should try staying the night at your place."

With that, I get into the car, and I'm thankful Julia is in a much better headspace than I am because she drives off, taking me far away from what will always be Dunsmuir's golden couple.

It doesn't matter how much time has passed. It will always be Holly and End.

My ears ring from the deafening sound of the waterfall. I sit perched on the boulder that overlooks the stream. I keep my gaze fixed on the white froth of liquid that bubbles at the force of the falls. The stream of water flows from the moss, and the sight is riveting. The stark green and vibrant blue are such a contrast, and it's breathtaking.

Dunsmuir is known for its waterfalls. It's one of the many reasons we get so many tourists here. I used to come here a lot with my dad—whenever he needed to get away from my mom—before it got too crowded. I wanted to go to the creek but everything there reminds me of Endymion. The creek is my place to go to stare at the stars and dream, but here…this is the place I can come to when I don't want to think or dream. I just want to be left alone with my thoughts. There's something about the noise here, about not being able to hear your own thoughts, that gives you a peace of mind you never truly knew you needed. There's tranquility in the cascading roar of water.

My dad showed me this place, Mossbrae Falls, years ago, before the tourists ever found it. The water that runs behind Mr. Jackson's property connects with the Sacramento River. Sometimes it feels like he has the waterfall all to himself. There are plenty of other falls nearby that tourists can visit, but this one, it feels like ours. Reserved solely for the town folk.

"What are you doing here?"

I startle at the sound of the voice. It takes all my energy not to turn and face him. I can't even bring myself to look at Endymion. I'm still angry, but underneath all that anger is hurt. So much hurt.

I promised myself years ago that I'd never let another break my heart, let alone the same man who had done it years prior. What is it about Endymion Black that turns me and this town into complete fools?

I shrug my shoulders noncommittally, avoiding his gaze. "I came here a lot with my dad when I was younger."

I sense him take the spot next to me on the boulder. Feeling his gaze on me, I keep my focus trained on the water. He's quiet for a beat, processing that. "I did, too."

That was also why I loved the falls so much because Endymion was always here, too. Even though he didn't know I existed, I enjoyed being close to him. But that was before the area here changed. Before it became just another tourist attraction.

"I know. I used to see you out here all the time."

"Why didn't you ever say anything?"

I shrug off the strain in my heart. "Because I was pathetic."

He blows out a heavy sigh. "No, you weren't."

I don't reply. I don't have the energy to.

Luna is at the house with my parents, helping my mom with dinner. I asked her if she could stay with her for a while. I just needed to get out and think after what transpired today.

"We need to talk about earlier."

My lips press together in a grim line. "There's nothing to talk about."

Endymion grunts irritably. "Jesus, Selene. Nothing happened. I don't want Holly. I've told you that already. I just want you. I shouldn't feel anything for you at all, after everything you've done, but I do. I can't stop thinking about that goddamn night at the creek all those years ago, and what a fucking idiot I was for letting you go—for letting you slip through my fingers. I can't stop feeling when I'm near you, and that's the fucking problem."

My chest tightens with emotion, drawing a tear out of the corner of my eye. "I don't want to do this. I can't. I meant what I said about Luna. We can figure something out. Visits. Splitting the time between us, but…I don't want this, Endymion. I've had my heart broken by you once and barely survived. I won't be able to do it again."

A barrage of emotions slams into me at what I just let slip. I've told him too much. I need to leave before I make an even bigger fool of myself.

"In everything that has happened since that night, I don't think I've told you the one thing that really matters, Selene. I'm sorry. I'm sorry for that night. I'm sorry for leaving you and Luna. And I'm sorry for the way I've been acting. The very last thing I want to do is hurt you."

Pain spears through my chest. It's hot and cold as it spreads, like a disease, or an infection of some sort. This is everything I've always wanted to hear. He's saying all the right things, but why does it still hurt so much?

Pushing to my feet, I try to put some distance between us, so I can think clearly. Why does he have to be so goddamn consuming?

He's silent, offering me time to gather my thoughts. There's only one thing keeping me from falling back into him. I know it deep within my soul. It's fear. I've had my heart broken by this man, and now that Luna is in both of our lives, I can't let that happen again. I won't.

I turn to face him, and that hopeful look there, the look of understanding in his eyes absolutely shatters me.

"I can't do this, End. I'm sorry." A tear slips out of the corner of my eye, and I leave him. I don't bother looking back because I know if I do, I'll crumble.

When I get back home, I'm surprised when I find my dad seated on the front porch, waiting for me. My brows furrow as I take the spot next to him, worry tightening my gut.

"What are you doing out here? Is everything okay?"

He jerks his chin toward the setting sun. The sunset casts rich hues of red blended with oranges, purples, and pinks. "Just getting some fresh air. Trying to see what you like so much about sitting out at the creek, staring up at the sky for answers."

I smile tiredly. "It's peaceful. And believe it or not, I actually went to the falls today. It made me think of you."

My dad is silent for some time. It's so long that it prompts me to cast a glance his way, realizing something is on his mind.

"There's something I've been meaning to talk to you about."

"Okay, shoot." I try to tamp down the sadness of today and focus on my dad instead. I might be emotionally spent, but I'll make time for him. When he shifts toward me, meeting my gaze, my stomach drops at the look shining there in his eyes. I've never seen my dad cry. Never seen him get teary-eyed or emotional, and seeing it now unsettles me. My lungs squeeze as though in duress, and my heart begins racing in my chest. The skin of my palms is slick with sweat.

"What's happening?" I whisper.

My dad tries to smile to put me at ease, but it's wobbly, and he ends up sobbing instead. The sound tears from his chest, shocking me into silence. He drops his head, and I watch as my father breaks down in front of me, right here on the porch. My chest caves with pain, and my heart crumbles. I know what he's going to say before he even says it. I feel it. And I feel like my world is shattering because of it.

He gathers himself. His next words steal the breath from my lungs. "I'm dying, Selene."

My chin quivers with emotion, and tears well in my eyes. "Don't talk like that. We can fight it, can't we? We still have time, Dad."

He shakes his head, setting his hand on top of mine. The broken man from just a few moments ago is gone, and in his place is the father I remember. The man who has always been well put together. Stoic and strong. My protector.

"There is no more time, baby. This is it for me."

I shake my head, feeling my tears carve hot trails down my cheeks. "No. No, we'll find a new doctor. We'll get a second opinion. We'll do whatever it takes."

My dad squeezes my hand, another round of tears welling in his eyes. "It's too late for a second opinion. I waited too long."

Rage sparks in my chest. "Why did you do that? Why would you wait?" My bottom lip quivers.

"Because if I'm going to die, I'm going to do it in my right mind. Not with countless drugs passing through my system where I won't even be conscious of what's happening around me. I want to be here for you and Luna, not stuck somewhere in a bed waiting to die."

Everything he's saying makes sense, but it doesn't make it any easier to swallow. It hurts. The torment battering against my chest is crippling.

Sniffing past the pressure, I wipe at the tears soaking my face, trying to suppress the quiver of my bottom lip.

"I get it…I just…it feels like I just got you back," I choke out, pain lancing through my heart, tearing the organ to shreds.

My dad's eyes slam shut. When he opens them again, he looks like he is on the verge of crumbling again.

"I've made a lot of mistakes in my life. I went about our relationship the wrong way, and that's no one's fault but mine. I regret so many things, but you…you've always been the one thing I did right. I love you, Selene. Like the sun loves the moon. Like *you* love the moon. Years from now, don't ever forget how much I love you. How much I regret letting so much time pass without speaking to you."

A sob rips past my lips, and I fall into my dad's arms, squeezing him to me. I grapple at his back, feeling like he's going to slip away from me at any given moment. I want to turn back time. I want him to stay. For me. For Luna. For Mom.

Doesn't he know how lost we'll be without him?

My dad holds me for a while longer, and we sit together out on the porch, both of us sniffling as we stare up at the blanket of stars in the dark velvet sky. The moon gleams, and unlike every other night, she brings me no comfort tonight.

Chapter Twenty-One

Selene

I RING THE DOORBELL WITH MY HEART IN MY THROAT, AND MY NERVES shaking chaotically. I don't know what I'm doing here. This is a stupid idea. He's not going to be happy to see me, but after the mess in the parking lot the other day and at the falls the other night, I need to talk to him.

He's been away the last two nights, having to run contracts for work, so we haven't had to deal with each other, and he hasn't been able to see Luna. She's been asking about him like crazy, so we've opted to do phone calls and FaceTime until he gets back.

He mentioned he'd be back sometime tonight or tomorrow morning, so after Luna fell asleep, I left her with my parents and decided to drive to his place and try to have a civil conversation with him. I need to clear the air of any awkwardness between us. Because I can't handle it. I need to do what's best for Luna, and that means keeping my distance from Endymion, but that also means keeping the peace. Whenever I'm near him, I don't think straight. He's always had this hold over me, and being so close to him, seeing him with our daughter, has only heightened my attraction to him.

I wish I didn't love him. I wish I didn't feel anything for him at all. That would make all of this much easier. But that's not the case. There has never been a day that I haven't loved Endymion Black. From the first moment I laid eyes on him, he imprinted himself on my heart, leaving a mark that promised to last a lifetime, and since then, I've never truly let go.

Standing here on his doorstep, I glance out at the quiet street behind me. Amusement tugs at the corners of my lips. How fitting is it that Endymion lives on a street named Stardust?

The door suddenly opens, and a gasp gets caught in my throat at the sight of a shirtless Endymion. Something is happening inside me. My heart is pounding uncontrollably, and my legs suddenly feel like they're going to give out on me. Warmth pools in my core, and electricity buzzes through my veins. I feel hot. There is an incessant throbbing between my legs that should not be there as I stare at my daughter's father.

Endymion's brows furrow, his gaze raking up and down my body as he takes me in. He's obviously taken aback by the sight of me on his porch. I shift awkwardly, suddenly feeling like this was a bad idea.

"Hi."

"What are you doing here? Where's Luna?"

My heart takes a beating. I refrain from flinching at his cold words. Of course, he wouldn't care that I'm here. He only cares about our daughter. I need to remember that. This is what I told him I wanted, after all. He's giving me exactly what I want. Still, that doesn't make it sting any less.

Then why does it hurt so much?

"She's fine. When I left, she was already in bed asleep. I actually came here to talk to you."

There's a long beat where End just stands there staring at me before he moves. Stepping back, he opens the door for me, indicating I walk in. I do so cautiously, feeling out of my element. It's never just been the two of us. Luna is always between us as the buffer. Without her here, the air is thick with tension, making it hard to pull in a single breath. All I can smell is him. Everything about him and his very essence percolate around us.

Closing the door behind him, Endymion crosses his thick arms over his broad, tan chest, causing the muscles to jut out. It's a painfully beautiful sight. The veins in his forearms and hands protrude, and I find myself swallowing thickly, struggling to look away.

"What did you want to talk to me about?" His tone is all grit and no-nonsense. His hand has a white-knuckle grip on the door, as if he's holding himself back from something and barely keeping it together.

Tucking a lock of hair behind my ear, I square my shoulders, searching for the courage to get the words past my lips.

"I thought we should talk about what happened. A few days ago." His jaw clenches, but he doesn't say anything else, so I proceed. "I overreacted in the parking lot about Holly. And I apologize. That's what I should've said to you at the falls that day. But…I meant what I said about everything else. I can't do this. That kiss from the other night can't happen again. I think we're all in a good place. We've found a good balance, and I think it's best if we forget it ever happened."

Endymion scoffs. He drops his arms, taking a step toward me. "You want me to forget it ever happened, Selene?" His eyes are molten pools of lava, and I'm the ash at his feet. My heart lurches when he closes the distance between us, backing me into a wall. Literally and figuratively. "What if I don't want to forget?"

My heart stalls, and my stomach dips at his words. Something that feels dangerously like hope blooms in my chest, and before I can tamp it down, End crowds me, caging me in until all I feel is him. All I can smell is him.

Everything about this moment is wreaking havoc on my nervous system. My chest is heaving wildly to accommodate my breaths, and my nipples pebble against my bra, vying for attention from this godlike man.

I shake my head, trying to clear the lust fog he's induced. "What are you saying?"

"I'm saying I'm still so fucking angry with you, but goddammit, I can't stay away,"

Before I can comprehend his words, his mouth slams down on mine, crashing through the last barrier I had in place. A cry of longing pours from my lips, his kiss possessing me right down to my very soul. There's no fighting it. This need, the magnetic pull between us is stronger than both our wills combined, and I succumb to it, letting it drown me in my own desire.

End curls his hand possessively around the nape of my neck, yanking me into him. My hands fly to his warm chest, and I moan into his mouth at the feel of his hot, smooth skin beneath mine. He's all hard muscle and pure unadulterated male. His other hand grips and kneads at the flesh of my hip and backside. The pads of his fingers on his free hand toy with the material of my shirt as he slowly drags it up over my head. My first instinct is to curl in on myself, but when he glances down at my chest, he growls like a wild animal, taking in the see-through lace demi-cup bra. Taking one of the straps, he slides it down my shoulder, his eyes following the movement. He lets it hang there, his fingers toying with the tantalizing soft skin of the top of my breast. My breathing is ragged. That and the sound of my pounding heart are all that echoes around us.

When Endymion finally meets my eyes, my core clenches painfully, and my mouth drops open in a gasp. He's eye-fucking me. There is no better way to put it. The emerald green in his eyes is burning and licking at my flesh as he sweeps his gaze across my face. And Jesus, I've never wanted anything more than his mouth on me. Almost as if he can read my innermost thoughts, Endymion tugs on the other strap of my bra, causing the cups to peel down and expose my nipples. The points harden immediately at his heated gaze and the cool air.

"You are fucking beautiful, Selene," he murmurs appreciatively, rubbing the pad of his thumb back and forth against my nipple. A moan falls past my lips without permission, and it seems to spur him on. With a growl, End drops down, taking my breast into his mouth, and I become putty in his hands. The moans that spill from my lips are embarrassingly loud. But he doesn't seem to mind.

Heat swirls through my stomach, tugging at that place deep inside me. I'm struggling to catch my breath. The way his tongue is swirling and his teeth are nibbling at the hardened peak is driving me wild. My sex clenches, demanding to be taken care of.

"End-d, we can't," I pant out, still trying to hang on to some sense.

"Tell me you don't want this, Selene. Tell me, and I'll stop. But just know, if you say no, this is it, Selene. I won't be toyed with. I've shown my hand; now show me yours."

"I can't say no," I whisper. "Not after years of waiting for this."

"Neither can I." Swooping down, he takes my mouth again, his hands sliding under my backside, kneading the globes. He hauls me into his arms, and my legs wrap around his waist of their own accord. Our mouths fuse, and I shamelessly grind my center against him. "Jesus Christ," he rumbles between heated kisses.

His mouth trails down my neck, sucking and nipping at the skin there. Before I realize what's happening, I'm dropped back onto his bed, and he strips me of my clothes. When End drops to his knees before me, spreading my legs, I throw myself back, gripping the comforter in anticipation. His mouth continues its tormented path, leaving its mark until he's kneeling at my feet, his warm breath fanning over my hot center.

"End," I breathe, thrusting my hips toward his face in an uncontrollable motion. The need burning inside me is combustible, searing me from the inside out. He spreads me open for his viewing, taking a long, leisurely lick of my most intimate part.

"Oh, God!" The heated whimper flees me, my legs trembling as desire floods every part of my body.

"Easy, baby," he croons, gripping my thighs to keep me from crumbling to pieces.

With slow, methodical movements, he trails kisses up and down my thigh, toying with me. He kisses me everywhere except the one place I really need his mouth again.

"Please."

That must be the magic word because his tongue does a long swipe down my center and swirls around my clit, causing my back to arch off the bed. His licks are slow and attentive, and the skill, the finesse with which he eats me with should make me angry, but I'm not. I'm suddenly thankful. He flutters his tongue over my folds, and my back bows. Sliding a long digit inside me, he strokes my inner walls, toying with me, hitting someplace deep inside me that has me gasping for breath and clawing at the sheets.

"Christ, you're beautiful," he groans, as he watches me writhe.

Something hot coils deep in my gut, and when End adds a second finger, the sound of my arousal smacks around us. When he arches his fingers inside me and sucks my clit into his mouth, I fall apart. My body shoots off like a bottle rocket, spasming on the bed as the orgasm rips through me.

Endymion trails hot, wet kisses up my stomach, between my breasts, until he reaches my mouth. His hard body covers mine, my back kissing the cool sheets as his hot lips descend on mine. I can taste myself on his tongue, and I find myself savoring him. His tongue swirls against my skin, down my neck. When his lips curl around a throbbing nipple, I jerk against him, another cry ripping from my throat.

He blows on the stiff peak, soothing the sting before taking the other one into his mouth and inflicting the same exquisite pleasure.

My head drops back, fingers gliding through his hair. Every tug and sharp bite of his teeth against my flesh makes my pussy clench and ache for more. As if sensing that's what I need, End strips out of his remaining clothes and climbs between my legs. As I stare up at him, I get flashes of that shaggy-haired End, hovering above me in the field.

"I never thought I'd be here with you again, like this."

Warmth swirls behind those intense moss-colored eyes. "I'm committing every moment of tonight to memory. I let you slip through my fingers once, babe. It's not happening again." End chooses then to slide inside me, and we both groan. Him with pleasure, and me, a slight sting of pain. My walls stretch to accommodate his length, but it's a burn I welcome.

With each deep thrust of his hips, I lose myself a little more. I fall into him, down the rabbit hole, seeing no way up. Perspiration clings to his skin, making his muscles glisten under the moonlight seeping in through his bedroom window. And the way he stares down at me? It's different. A world away from our first time. He's really here with me. Not inebriated or stuck in his head about the issues in his life.

Keeping one hand flat on the mattress beside my head, he wraps the other around my waist, changing the angle of his thrusts. His cock slides in and out of me. The sound of smacking wet flesh echoes around us, percolating the air with the scent of my desire. The tip of his cock hits something inside me at this angle. It has my mouth dropping open in a silent scream and pleasure rippling down my spine.

"That's it, baby. Let go for me. Let me watch you come on my cock."

As if my body lives to serve him, I follow his command. The muscles in my stomach clench violently, and my sex grips his cock like a clamp as the first wave of pleasure slams into me. It takes my breath away, spreading through my chest like embers from a wildfire and flowing through my veins like I've been lit on fire. Every one of my nerve endings is vibrating.

"You're so fucking beautiful when you come," he praises. My body spasms beneath his, and he keeps going, his cock sliding in and out at a pace that takes my breath away until he finds his own release.

He hangs his head, resting his damp forehead against mine, and I can't help the smile that takes over my face. Tentatively, I rest my hand on his muscular back and let myself explore his body while I still can.

Endymion grunts hotly when I palm his backside. He has the best ass on a guy I've ever seen.

"Jesus Christ, Selene," he growls, making me laugh. Pushing upright, he hovers above me, staring down at me with an unreadable expression on his face. "I could listen to you laugh all day."

My heart flips in my chest, almost bursting at the seams. "I'm sure that would get annoying."

He shakes his head, obviously disagreeing as he brushes my hair out of my face. "You're the most beautiful woman I've ever laid eyes on."

My heart jumps into my throat, on my tongue even. "Thank you," I whisper back. "You are, too." A crooked grin steals over his features, making him look even more handsome. That ever-present electricity, that tension is there, lingering between us as we search each other's eyes.

No words are needed at this moment. Everything that needs to be said is done with our eyes. Endymion places a warm kiss to my lips before lying back and pulling me into his arms. I rest my head on his chest and close my eyes. A smile steals over my features as I listen to the synchronized beat of his heart until it beats with my own.

I wake up the next morning to hot dreams of Endymion's body on top of mine. His tongue trails across my flesh as his delectable mouth places fevered kisses on my sex. My core clenches as if I can actually feel his tongue on me in real-time.

I'm on the brink of an orgasm, but I'm certain it's just a dream until my eyes spring open, and I find Endymion's face buried between my thighs. A moan rips past my lips at the sight of him, and I swear, he grins.

End takes a languid lick, making a show of the way he's eating me. That tongue doesn't miss a single spot, swiping across every nerve and crevice of my slit. With one hand fisting the sheet, the other finds purchase in his hair, and I tug, silently begging him for more.

With a growl, he delves deeper into me. He tongues my clit, swirling faster the louder I moan and the more I writhe. A thick finger nudges my entrance. The teasing makes me whimper. Everything feels so tight, so sore from last night, but for the life of me, I don't want him to stop this. I want more. I need more.

"Christ, you're so fucking swollen here, babe," End groans, while his finger pumps in and out of me with lazy strokes. It's a slow rhythm that drives me wild with lust.

"More, End. I need more."

Endymion slides in another finger, shushing me. "Shhh. I know what you need." With two of his digits stroking my upper walls, he delves down, his mouth finding purchase on my clit, and he sucks the bundle of nerves with a ravenous need. My hips arch off the bed, and heat consumes my body. I feel like I'm on fire. His tongue alternates between sucking and licking at my clit with rapid bursts. It's so much, so many sensations at once, that I feel like I am going to explode. End snakes his hand up my torso, landing on a peaked nipple. My knees lock around his ears as I buck into him, my orgasm ripping into me with a fervor I've yet to experience. Liquid nirvana blooms through my core, spreading beyond reach.

My chest rises and falls sharply as I come down from my high.

I sense him moving around, but I'm so boneless and dizzy after that orgasm, I can't bring myself to open my eyes and look.

"Good morning." He chuckles, climbing into the open space next to me.

A wide grin steals over my face. Blinking my lids open, I turn to face him, warmth filling my chest. "Good morning, indeed."

He smirks at that. With the morning sun filtering in through his bedroom window, it brings out the bright green in his eyes and the light strands of his hair. He's beautiful, painfully beautiful.

"Let's do something today. As a family." My heart flips wildly at the suggestion. "I was thinking we can take Luna to the zoo. Together."

There's a damn furnace in my chest. "She'd love that."

"And what about you?"

"What about me?"

"I meant what I said at the falls, Selene. I want you. I want this. You're mine, babe." His thumb swipes across my lower lip slowly, and the movement goes straight to my core.

I kiss him. Slamming my mouth against his, I kiss the man I've loved for what feels like an eternity.

Chapter Twenty-Two

Selene

As I lie in bed, my body wrapped around Endymion's like I'm a contortionist of some sort, I smile thinking about the day we had. It was beyond perfect. It was everything I could've asked for. And Luna, my sweet girl, I don't think I've ever seen her so happy. She smiled and laughed with her dad as they walked from exhibit to exhibit, looking at the animals.

Watching their relationship blossom is beautiful. The way End looks at our daughter makes my heart soar. With every moment we spend together, his eyes remain glued to her as if he's committing everything about her to memory. As if he was trying to recognize each of her smiles and each of her expressions.

By the time we got home from the zoo, Luna was out cold, and End suggested we let her sleep at my parents' place. Apparently one night wasn't enough. He needed more, and so did I. After three orgasms, I've been lying here, wrapped in his arms, trying to soak it all in.

I try to stay here in this perfect moment with him, but my mind begins to wander. The worries slowly flood in, making me wonder if this is all just a fluke. It doesn't feel like one, but we have a daughter now. We can't make these reckless decisions anymore. He must sense where my thoughts are heading because he presses a kiss to my temple and breathes out a sigh.

"Tell me what you're thinking."

I nibble on my bottom lip, wondering if I should settle on the truth. "I was thinking last night and today were amazing, but…but what are we doing? What happens now?" I shift on the bed, tilting my body, so I can face him. He does the same, craning his neck, so he can look down at me.

In this new position, I feel something trickle out of me and drip between my legs, remnants of what just transpired between us. It hits me then. My eyes widen. I sit upright, glancing down at the bed, then back to Endymion. His eyes are heated, darker than they were only moments ago, as he stares down between my legs.

My heart kickstarts, racing in my chest, and I swallow thickly. "I'm not on birth control, Endymion."

Slowly, he glances up at me and quirks a brow. "And?"

My lips press together in disapproval. "*And*? And this is exactly how I got pregnant with Luna in the first place. Because we didn't use protection."

Jesus, why does sex with this man always turn my brain into mush when it comes to protection?

He grinds his teeth together, causing the muscles along his jaw to jump with frustration. "I take it this is a problem for you?"

My eyes slam shut. A spark of anger flicks to life in my chest at how obtuse and nonchalant he's being.

"We can't do that, End." I sigh. "We have to be responsible and think about Luna."

He grunts. "I am thinking about Luna. She told me she wants a sister or a brother. She told me she wants to be a real family, and I want to give it to her."

My chest squeezes. "You can't give a child these things if you're not even sure you want them. It isn't fair."

His brows tug low, anger passing over his features. "Who said I wasn't sure I wanted them? I've never been more sure of anything in my life. Yeah, we have plenty of things to figure out as a family, but I want you. I want you and Luna. Not just because it'll make her happy but because it'll also make me happy."

I'm stunned into silence by his words. I wasn't expecting that. I mean, I knew Luna wanted a bigger family, but that was always a topic I avoided broaching, but now, it may be unavoidable. Everything he's saying sounds so perfect and easy, but can it really be that simple? Can we just live happily ever after, especially after everything that has happened?

"I don't know how to do this, Endymion. And the last thing I want is Luna hurt in all of this."

A protective gleam enters his eyes. "We'll figure it out together. And she won't get hurt. Neither will you. I won't allow it."

"How can you be so sure?"

"Because I'd protect you both with my life. I'm all in with you, Selene. Mess and all, I want you." He reaches out, caressing my bottom lip with the pad of his thumb. "Move in with me."

I stiffen, my eyes growing wide at the suggestion. "What?"

His lips quirk. "I said move in with me."

"I know what you said. I'm just trying to make sense of it. I can't just move in with you."

"Why not? Would it really be such a bad thing?"

I sputter. "Moving in? Having another baby? Yeah, it might. I don't even know how Luna feels about all of this. About us. Kids say one thing one moment but change their minds the next."

His face pinches in a scowl. "She wants us to be a family. I want this family with you. What's the problem?"

"The problem is, you hated me just a few days ago, and now you're suddenly trying to impregnate me *and* get me to move in with you."

"I've never hated you. Am I angry? Yes. That's going to take some time to go away, but that doesn't just rest on your shoulders.

I'm angry with myself, too. I've made just as many mistakes. The fact of the matter is, I can't get you out of my head, Selene. I want this. I want you. And I want our daughter. All of us under one roof."

I search his gaze, trying to tamp down that bursting sensation in my chest. I don't need to get my hopes up. He could just be saying all this now, in post-coital bliss, but what about tomorrow, or the next day? We'll need to talk about this when he has a clear head, and sex isn't involved.

"I'll have to talk to Luna about it tomorrow."

"*We'll* talk to Luna about it tomorrow," he corrects.

I smile. "Deal."

We lie there in a comfortable silence, each of us dissecting the other in our own ways. His eyes are warm as they travel the length of my naked body. There's the slightest twinge of self-consciousness, but the way he's staring at me, as if I'm the most beautiful woman on the planet, ebbs it away. The need to cover myself, to hide my body from him disappears.

The muscle in his jaw suddenly tightens, and his brows pull together in a frown of sorts. "How many dates have you been on since Luna was born?"

My stomach dips. "A few."

His lips thin. He obviously doesn't like that answer. His stare is unnerving. And strangely, it feels perpetual. "And how many have you slept with?"

My lips part in shock at how up front he is. He asks the question without an ounce of shame. If it were anyone else, I'd be annoyed or put off by this line of questioning. But it's not anyone else. It's him. It's the boy I've spent most of my life loving. The boy who is now a man. A man who is the father of my child, and a man who wants me.

I swallow thickly, averting my gaze. I feel the heat settle into my cheeks, and I hate it. It's always a dead giveaway. "No one."

"Repeat that."

"I haven't slept with anyone but you. Until now."

My gaze flicks up at the sound of his growl. The breath whooshes out of my lungs at the heated expression on his face. It's lethal. He leans in, dragging his warm hand around my hip and pulling my body flush with his. I settle my hands on his muscular shoulders, my chest heaving at the look in his eyes. It's a look that sends a bolt of electricity straight to my core.

"Do you know what that does to me, Selene?" he asks, kissing a warm path down my neck that awakens my body. My nipples pebble against the cool air, and my sex clenches, throbbing with need. "Knowing that I'm the only man who has ever been inside you?" End's hand glides down from my hip, slipping between my sticky thighs. He pauses when he reaches the apex. I'm damp between my legs. I'm a mess with his cum and my arousal, but he doesn't seem to mind. With the pad of his finger, he traces gentle circles on my skin, and my core clenches painfully. He's so close to my sex. All it would take is him moving up a few inches, but he seems content to torture me. He continues as if his proximity doesn't drive me wild.

A ragged gasp rips from my chest when his finger stills on my lower lips. I'm wet everywhere, and by the look on his face, the heat simmering in his eyes, I take it he likes it. He licks his lips and swipes his finger through my folds, rubbing my wetness over my clit, then dragging it back down to my entrance, which is still leaking with his cum.

His gaze flicks up to mine, something dark, hot, and wanton burning there that takes my breath away. Slowly, he toys with his cum and begins pushing it back inside me. His finger slides in and out, and his gaze flits from our point of contact back up to my face, as if he can't decide where he wants to look more.

It's wrong.

It's so, so wrong and risky, but Christ, it feels so good. Everything about this moment feels so right, and I can't tell him to stop. I don't want to tell him to stop. "Knowing that I'm the only one who is ever going to be inside you makes me possessive, babe. So fucking possessive of what's mine," he grits, out over the sound of my arousal smacking against his finger. I should be embarrassed, but all I can focus on is the pleasure. The warmth building at the base of my spine and the desire pooling low in my belly.

I feel his erection against my hip, and my eyes widen. I raise my brows, silently asking, "Already?"

He doesn't need to answer. He slides his finger out of my pussy and drags it up my body to my lips. A shudder wracks through me when he rubs my arousal and his cum around my mouth.

"Suck."

I do just that. I take his finger into my mouth and suck on it. My pussy spasms at how hot it is. The taste of us intermingled on my tongue is something all too heady. His nostrils flare, and he rolls onto his back, pulling my body over his. His erection swings between my legs, and I stare down at it in awe, still unable to comprehend its size. I don't remember him being this well-endowed at the creek, but then again, I was just a teenage girl.

"Ride me, baby."

Trapping my bottom lip between my teeth, I nod and lift, pressing his head against my entrance. He lets out a guttural groan when his cum from earlier begins sliding down his cock, falling out of me at this angle. I rest my hands on his chest and slide down his length. My eyes flutter closed, and I moan. Everything feels so full in this position.

It takes my body a few pumps to accommodate his length, but when it does, my hips roll, and I drop my head back, succumbing to a number of sensations and emotions, all so powerful, I feel like I am going to combust at any second.

And all of them have the capacity to destroy me.

Just like this man does.

Chapter Twenty-Three

Endymion

I TAKE A STEP BACK FROM THE ROOM, SURVEYING IT FROM THE DOORWAY. A smile tugs at the corners of my lips as I take in all the girly shit. Luna's going to love it. I can practically hear her now.

"You know, if this was any other time, I'd think you'd fucking lost it, standing here, smiling as you stare into a pink room."

I shoot a glare at Bishop, who's standing beside me. I didn't even hear his approach; that's how focused I was. It's been three weeks since Selene showed up on my doorstep, and I've been all gas and no brakes ever since. We spoke to Luna about the possibility of moving in, and just as I knew she would, she screamed her rejoice, her little face happier than I've ever seen it.

Selene still has her doubts and reservations, which I can understand. Sort of. Everyone seems on board. The only person who looks pensive is Cece, and I think I'm beginning to understand why. Cece has always been there for Selene. They lived together. She was grandma, and sometimes she had to play the role of mom while Selene was at work or school. She shares an unbreakable bond with Luna, and I think, in a way, me coming in and moving my girls in with me, she feels like she's losing something.

"Ready for this, man?" Bishop asks, after a moment of my continued silence.

I nod. "I've never wanted anything more than I want them."

He grins. "You're a lucky son of a bitch. You know that, right? Half the men in this town envy you already. Now they just flat-out hate you." I laugh, but it quickly dies off when I hear a crash from down the hallway. Bishop and I share a look before we pad down the hall to see what all the commotion is.

I had the guys—Bishop, Landon, and Griffin—come over to help Selene and Luna get their things moved in. A few of the crew workers are here, too, trying to speed up the process. I pause in the living room, near the front door, glaring at Landon and Griffin, who are arguing.

"Try not to break anything while you both are bickering, got it?"

"Yeah, whatever, captain. I don't see you lifting shit."

I roll my eyes. I just finished my daughter's entire room. The last thing I want to hear is their complaining. Just as I'm rounding the corner into the kitchen, I hear the pounding of little footsteps before I actually see her. Luna runs through the open front door, and when she sees me, a grin spreads across her little face, and she runs toward me.

"Daddy!" I bend, taking her into my arms. She wraps her little self tightly around me, and I settle her on my hip. "Can I see my room now?"

"You sure can. Where's your mom?"

"Right here," Selene says, stopping in the doorway of the kitchen. She's dressed casually in a pair of pants that hug her shapely legs to perfection and a loose top that has me dying to rip it over her head and take one of her pink nipples into my mouth. As if sensing where my thoughts are headed, heat climbs onto her cheeks, and she averts her gaze, hiding her smile.

"Jesus, you two are like rabbits." Landon huffs, as he passes us to grab a water from the fridge. Luna glances up at me, an adorable frown between her brows.

"Why are you and Mommy rabbits?"

I share a look with Selene, who is fighting her laughter. "Didn't you know, your mommy loves rabbits."

Her little eyes widen, and she looks at her mom as though she can't believe she kept this news from her. "Me too!"

After taking a swig of his water, Landon steps up beside me and pokes Luna in her side, making her giggle.

"What's up, squirt?"

"Hey, Uncle Lan." She's taken to calling the guys uncle, not that I think they mind. Though now, it seems they enjoy the competition aspect of it, the *who is the best uncle?*

"You ready for another game of tag?"

Luna giggles. "Yes! But first, my daddy is going to show me my room."

"Your daddy? What about me?"

"Okay, fine." She sighs. "You can show me." Luna glances up at me, silently asking for my permission. This is the first time she's ever done it. Usually, she goes to Selene for permission, but the fact that she came to me first has warmth flowing through my chest.

"C'mon, squirt. Let's give your mom and dad a chance to kiss in private so that it doesn't gross us out." That draws a laugh out of Selene, and we both watch as Landon walks off with Luna. Once they're out of sight, I close the distance between us, tugging her into my arms. She falls into me, her soft curves at home against my body. She rests her chin on my chest, staring up at me.

"You look beautiful." I tuck the stray chocolate strands behind her ears.

She smiles up at me, and it hits me square in the chest. "So we're really doing this?"

"We are. You having second thoughts?"

Selene shakes her head. "I'm not. You were right. This feels right. Being here with you feels right. I'm just having a hard time leaving my parents there. Especially now that my dad..." She trails off, her eyes glistening with moisture. I tighten my grip around her.

Dipping my head, I press a kiss to her lips, soaking in her taste, trying to kiss her pain away. "It's going to be fine. They're down the street. We'll stop by every day if it makes you feel better."

She gives me a wobbly smile. "It does. Thank you."

As if remembering something, she digs into her purse and pulls out a folder. I glance down at it with a frown when she hands it to me.

"This is yours. Well, not technically, but—whatever. Just open it."

Taking the folder from her, I open it, and my chest squeezes when I see what's inside. It's Luna's birth certificate with my name beneath the father's information. My daughter is no longer just a Drake, but officially a Black.

"When did you do this?"

She nervously tucks stray hairs behind her ears. "Started the process the day after I told you the truth. Your mom helped me with your signature to make it official. You should really pay more attention to the things you sign, you know."

So many things are happening inside me all at once, and I can't seem to pin it down to just one. I pull Selene into my arms and kiss her. I kiss her fiercely with a passion that has fire shooting through my veins.

"Thank you."

"Don't thank me, End. This is what you deserved from the very start."

I give her one last peck on her lips. "Come on. Luna is probably blackmailing Landon and the rest of the guys into buying her more toys."

Selene laughs, nodding her head, because it sounds exactly like something our daughter would do.

Taking her hand in mine, I lead us down the hallway, and we pause outside of the bedroom, watching as Luna prattles on and on about this and that, her excited little gaze flitting around the pink unicorn room. Bishop and Griffin are finishing up putting the final pieces of the dresser together. Landon is sitting on the bed, eyes wide as he listens to my daughter talk like she has an endless supply of breath to spare.

He notices us standing there and raises a brow at me that clearly says, *what the fuck?*

A laugh bursts from my chest, and Luna glances our way. "Mommy, did you see all the stuff Daddy bought me for my new room?"

Selene purses her lips. "Oh, I see it, all right, little miss. Remember what I said about picking up after yourself, though. I see a lot of toys on the floor already that I know your dad didn't take out."

She pouts. "I wasn't the only one. Uncle Landon took out some with me, too."

Landon chokes, shooting her a wide-eyed look. "You told me to!"

"I'm a kid," she deadpans, with the most serious expression on her face.

I bite back my laughter and step into her bedroom, lifting her into my arms. "Don't worry about it. I'll help you clean up."

"Thanks, Daddy." I'm just about to set her down when her next question has me stilling, my brows drawing together in a frown. "What's a whore?"

All the air is suddenly sucked from the room, and I hear Selene's sharp gasp behind me. My gaze drills holes into the guys, but they all raise their hands in surrender, clearly not the ones who let the word slip in front of her.

"What?" I ask dumbly.

"Where did you hear that, baby? It's not a good word."

Luna shrugs, looking at me. "At the party at Nana and Papa's house. That lady with the pretty blond hair said it while I was playing on the playground."

Fury boils in my veins, and I narrow my gaze. "Did she now?"

She nods, shooting a wary glance at Selene. "I think she was talking about Mommy."

I feel Selene step up beside me. She brushes Luna's stray waves back away from her face. I flatten my lips in a grim line, and my nostrils flare as I work to process my anger. Holly has always been a fucking pain in the ass. I should've known she wouldn't know how to speak around a child.

"Do you remember what she said?" Bishop suddenly asks, his tone tinged with anger on our behalf.

"She said to her friend that she hated kids. If it wasn't for that stupid whore who opened her legs, she'd still be with him."

Fire billows in my chest, and I feel red seeping into my vision. I suddenly have the urge to confront Holly. To strike her, something I've never wanted to do to a woman. Who the hell does she think she's talking about?

"She called me a little bitch, too," she says, so casually, as if the word is a compliment. The look on Selene's face is pure rage.

"Baby, why didn't you tell us about this sooner?"

Luna shrugs. "I forgot. But when I saw her at breakfast with Aunt Julia, and then when she made you cry, I remembered."

Selene flusters. "I did not cry."

"You had tears, Mommy."

She sighs and rolls her eyes, obviously knowing that arguing with Luna over that will get her nowhere.

"Endymion, can I speak to you for a second?" Selene asks, with a slight edge to her tone. I drop Luna on the bed beside Landon and walk down the hall into the master bedroom.

She glances around momentarily, taking everything in. She still has to put all her things away, but for the most part, all her stuff is here.

"This is not okay, End. She called our daughter a bitch."

"You're right. Holly was way out of line. She's obviously jealous or crazy. I really don't know. She means nothing to me. First thing tomorrow, I'll set this shit straight."

Selene's lips thin, and she crosses her arms over her chest. "No. I don't want you talking to her. At all."

A grimace steals across my face. "Do you not trust me?"

She sighs, rubbing at her temple. "I trust you. It's *her* I don't trust."

I pull her into my arms, pressing a kiss to her forehead. "Alright, I can respect that. We'll do it together, yeah?"

Some of the tension slowly dissipates from her body. She expels a deep sigh, falling into me. "Thank you. Also, I'd like the record to show that I *really* don't like her."

I can't help the chuckle that bursts from my chest. "Yeah, me either."

The next morning, I roll over, my chest squeezing at the sight before me. Last night, I went to bed wrapped around Selene, and this morning, I wake up to my little girl stretched out between us, fast asleep. I didn't even hear her come in, the little ninja.

As I stare at both of my girls, an unfamiliar warmth swirls through my chest. Luna's little face is innocent with sleep, and Selene looks as beautiful as all hell. My gaze is drawn to the freckles on the bridge of her nose and the dark eyelashes casting shadows across her face. Her pink, plump lips are slightly parted, and I have to fight the urge to kiss her.

Luna starts to stir, the little cupcakes on her pajama dress smiling up at me with various grins. Slowly, her eyes flutter open, and she gives me a sleepy smile.

"Morning, Daddy."

My nostrils flare as a stab of emotion pierces my chest. I've missed a lot in my daughter's life, but this is the first time I've woken up beside her, and Jesus, nothing has ever felt more perfect.

"Morning, baby," I whisper back. She opens her mouth, probably to say good morning to Selene, but I press my finger against my lips to shush her. "C'mon. Let's make your mom breakfast while she sleeps."

Hurtling herself into my arms excitedly, I pad out of the bedroom, shutting the door behind me softly. Setting Luna on the island in the kitchen, I peer down at her.

"What's Mommy's favorite breakfast?"

"Hmm. She likes pancakes. With chocolate chips. And lots of fudge."

I raise a brow in challenge. "You sure that's not *your* favorite?"

She giggles, and it's the most beautiful sound. I poke her in her side gently, earning another round of giggles. "Let's get started on those pancakes then."

I hoist Luna around the kitchen, having her help me make breakfast. She's deep in concentration, her little tongue poking out of the side of her mouth and brows pulled down as she focuses to pour the milk into the mix.

"Do you love Mommy?" she asks out of the blue as I'm flipping a pancake. I decided on chocolate chip for her and blueberry for Selene and me. As I'm flipping the pancake, it splatters, making a mess. I clear my throat, glancing back at my daughter.

Lowering the heat, I cross my arms over my chest. "What makes you ask that?"

She shrugs, sneaking a chocolate chip into her mouth. It's

obvious this isn't the first she's eaten. The chocolate stains at the corner of her mouth give her away. "Because Uncle Landon said you're a blind fool."

"You've been listening in on an awful lot of conversations."

"Old people talk an awful lot," she parrots back, surprising a laugh out of me. "So do you?"

I grin down at my daughter. "How can I not?"

She smiles mischievously. I can just imagine what she's plotting in her head over this news.

When we finish up with breakfast, I let her eat before we plate Selene's food. Luna demands she bring her mom the biggest glass of orange juice, and I let her because I'm a sucker for this little girl, though I'm hoping like hell she doesn't spill it.

As soon as I open the door, I notice Selene is already stirring in bed. She stretches her arms over her head lazily, causing her nightshirt to expose her midsection. Her skin there is creamy and perfect, just calling to me. She blinks the sleep from her eyes, an adorable frown appears on her brow, and she sweeps her hair out of her face when she spots me and then looks down at the tray of food I'm holding.

"What's all this?" she asks, her voice raspy with sleep.

"Breakfast in bed." I set the tray on the bed as she pushes herself upright against the headboard. Her chocolate waves tumble around her shoulders, and Jesus, the way the sun is shining through the bedroom windows, casting a warm glow across her skin, she looks fucking perfect.

Closing the distance between us, I run the pad of my finger along her shoulder, smirking when her breath hitches, and a shudder wracks her body at the soft touch. Leaning in, I press a kiss against her lips, soaking in as much of her as I can before Luna comes in with that juice.

I rest my hands on the top of the headboard, caging her in as I stare down at her. Unable to help myself, I dip my head down, and through the thin T-shirt she's wearing, I find her breast and take her nipple into my mouth, sucking through the material. She lets out a sharp gasp, her hands going straight to my head.

Placing one last lick over the hardened peak, I look down at my handiwork and feel my cock twitch in my pants. I can see her pink nipple peeking through the material of her shirt, just begging for more attention.

When I hear the sound of soft footsteps, I back away, leaving a safe distance between us, relishing in the flush of arousal coating Selene's cheeks. Luna appears through the doorway soon after, footsteps slow and sure, concentration written all over her face as she keeps her gaze trained on the glass of juice she's holding, trying not to spill any.

"Morning, Mommy! We made you your favorite for breakfast."

Selene laughs, staring down at Luna with a softness in her eyes that makes me want to kiss her senseless. The love she has for our daughter is the purest thing I've ever witnessed in my life.

"You guys really did all this for me?"

"Yup! And guess what else?" Luna grins at me and then her mom. "My daddy said he loves you."

Selene's eyes widen.

Those plump lips part, her gaze shooting to mine with questions written all over her face.

I look up at the ceiling, holding back a smile.

So my daughter has a big mouth. That's good to know.

Gripping the bottle of my beer by the neck, I lean against the pillar of Gavin's house on the porch, watching Selene play with Luna. It amazes me how good she is with her. I know it's her daughter, but some people aren't meant to be parents. They don't share a bond with their child like Selene does with Luna. It's the most beautiful and pure-hearted thing I've ever witnessed.

The screen door shuts softly behind me, and when I glance over my shoulder, the corners of my mouth tug up. Gavin settles next to me on the porch, his gaze riveted to his daughter and granddaughter.

"Beautiful pair, aren't they?" I nod my acquiescence. "You're a lucky man, End. Don't take it for granted."

Taking a pull from the bottle, I shoot a glance at him. "I wouldn't dream of it."

That seems to make him happy because he smiles. The bags under his eyes are dark, like he hasn't been sleeping much, and the hollows of his cheeks are starting to make his face look thinner, gaunter. The sight is a punch to the gut.

"How are things going so far? How does Luna like the place?"

I take the seat next to him, setting my empty bottle beside me. "It's been going well. Luna loves it. Swears it's the best bedroom she's ever had, but she somehow still finds her way into our bed every night."

Gavin laughs. "Sounds like her."

"Selene seems to be happy, but I know she's worried. She doesn't like being away from you guys."

Gavin glances at me, a sad smile pulling at his lips. "That doesn't surprise me. She's always quick to worry about everyone else but herself. Even as a kid, she was the same way. More empathy toward everyone else's needs but her own."

I avert my gaze, watching Selene lie in the grass with our daughter as they catch their breath.

"I can see that being true."

Gavin shifts beside me, and when I hear the sound of paper crumpling, my brows dip, and I shift toward him with a questioning glance.

"Give this to her for me, will you?" Gavin says, passing off an envelope and a small box to me. I glance down at it, feeling a pit enter my stomach. It's a plain white envelope on the outside, but on the inside, it's the very thing that has the potential to break Selene. It's going to hurt her; whatever it is he's written in there. I want to say it's too soon. He doesn't need to give this to me yet, but when I look back up at him, I see how tired he is. His agony is only beginning.

I clear the sudden thickness blocking my throat. "Yeah, I can do that. When do you want me to give it to her?"

He watches his daughter, her carefree laugh floating around us. It's scary that just in a few shorts months or weeks, that sound will dim when Gavin loses his battle with this sickness.

"You'll know when to give it to her. You'll know when she needs it most. Hang on to it until then. And just..." He trails off, rubbing at the back of his neck like he's suddenly uncomfortable. This isn't our norm. This isn't what our friendship was like over the years, and it's obvious he's struggling with this new line of friendship and the man who is now in his daughter's life. "Just take care of her. Selene has waited her whole life for a love that sweeps her off her feet. One that rivals the mythology written about goddesses of the cosmos; one that is all hers. Don't deprive her of that, please."

Pressure builds in my nose, and I nod, setting my jaw in a hard line, working to control the sudden bout of emotion burrowing into me.

"I promise."

After we say our goodbyes to Gavin and Cece, we head home, and by the time I pull Luna out of her car seat, she's out cold, her little mouth gaping, fatigue written all over her face. Selene is unusually quiet, even after she gets Luna cleaned up and put in bed.

"Tell me what you're thinking."

She climbs onto the bed in one of my T-shirts. She's taken to wearing them to bed instead of her own pajamas, and I've never seen a more beautiful sight. Her perfect body encased in my clothes that drown her small frame—I fucking live for it. Something that is inherently possessive when it comes to this woman loves it.

Sliding under the sheets, she shifts her body toward mine, tucking her hands beneath her cheek. "Just thinking about my dad. And my mom."

"What about them?"

"I'm worried about my mom. How she's going to handle dealing with this on her own? And my dad…I-I guess I still haven't come to terms with all of this. I can't imagine a world where he isn't here with me."

Reaching out, I sweep the pad of my thumb across the freckles dotting her skin. She's perfect. "I get that. This isn't going to be easy, but I'm here, and I'm not going anywhere."

She smiles while her eyes simultaneously glass over. "You're a bit of a rare find. You know that?"

I smirk. "That's what they tell me."

She laughs under her breath, nudging me in the shoulder. I catch her wrist, splaying open her palm and caressing her cold fingers. "More of that, babe."

"More punches? Gladly."

"More of those carefree smiles, Selene."

Her smile tapers off, and something warm enters her eyes. Scooting closer, she wraps her arms around my neck, drawing her body against mine. I relish in her warmth, the feel of her curves pressing into me, like pieces of a puzzle I never knew I was missing.

"Did you mean what you told Luna this morning?" I nod, searching her gaze, trying to read her innermost thoughts. There's an adorable frown marring her face. It's a hint of disbelief. "How can you be so sure?"

"You've carried my child. You've raised her into this beautiful, sweet little human that I'll forever be thankful for. There's no way I can't love you."

She smiles, but there's a sadness behind it. At times, she's the easiest person to read, her thoughts written on her face. She wears her heart on her sleeve, just like now. For whatever reason, what I said makes her sad, and I can just imagine why.

"I don't just love you because you gave me Luna. Even if she weren't in the picture yet, I'd have no other choice but to love you, Selene. You're the one pure thing in this town. You're the bright light I've been searching for my whole life. I just didn't realize you were right there under my nose all along. I was too blind to see it then, but I'm not now."

Her mouth opens, then closes, like that of a gaping fish, as she tries to string together a sentence. It draws a chuckle out of me. "I know this feels fast, but I know what I want. And I want you. Always."

"I've waited years to hear those words fall from your lips, Endymion Black."

She presses her lips against mine in the sweetest kiss that hits me square in the chest. I roll her body on top of mine, gripping the hem of the shirt and peeling it over her head. Her round tits press against my chest when she leans back down to kiss me again. My tongue tangles with hers. With sure movements, Selene works my briefs down my legs, exposing my cock, and I work my jaw back and forth to refrain from groaning when she strokes me from root to tip. She presses her heated center over my cock, and even through the thin material of her panties, I can feel how wet she is. The damp cloth clings to her drenched pussy.

Gripping her hips with one hand and the other going to her lower back, I sit upright with her. She gasps, hands flying to my shoulders for support. Our eyes lock, and I slide one hand between us, rubbing her clit through her panties, enjoying the way her hips swivel in time to the motion. She traps that bottom lip between her teeth, and I just about lose it.

I slide her panties to the side, and Selene positions herself by holding on to my shoulders and lifting herself up, so we are both sitting. She then wraps her legs around me as I press the head of my cock inside her wet heat. Her nails dig into my shoulder as she lowers herself onto me. We hold our breath as my cock spreads her inch by inch. Holding the globes of her ass tightly, I thrust my hips against her, fucking into her. I drive inside with long, hard strokes that are no longer gentle. My movements are punishing, searing, as if I'm marking myself inside her physically to match what she's already done to me emotionally. We're at eye level like this, and I pull back the slightest bit to get a better look at her. She bites her lip to contain her moans, so she doesn't wake Luna, but it's futile. They're growing louder and heavier each time my cock is completely inside her, pressed to the hilt. Each time I squeeze her ass and pull her onto me, hitting her throbbing, already sensitive clit with the movement, she chokes, and her nails pierce my flesh.

"You're fucking perfect," I groan, as I bury my hand in her hair, tugging on the strands gently to bow her body into me. She lets out a groan that almost has me spilling my load too soon.

"God, Endymion. Don't stop. Please don't stop."

"Never," I whisper into the crook of her neck, grinding my cock inside her. I reach between us and stroke her clit until she's a quivering mess in my arms. When her pussy clamps around my cock, milking me, I make sure to watch her face. Her lips part, and the sexiest expression overcomes her as she rides out her orgasm. It's one I realize I can watch for the rest of my life and never tire of it.

Chapter Twenty-Four

Selene

"WHY CAN'T YOU COME WITH US, MOMMY?" LUNA WHINES, as we get her buckled in the car. I blow out a heavy sigh.

"Because I have to work. You'll have fun with your dad and your cousin at the zoo. You won't even know I'm gone."

She frowns. "Yeah, I will."

I shake my head, biting back my smile. "I don't think so."

"But I will."

I hear Endymion chuckling behind me, and I grin down at my sweet girl. "Be a good girl, okay?"

"Okay, Mommy."

When I close the door, Endymion pulls me into his arms, pressing a hot kiss to my lips that travels all the way down to my toes.

"You don't have to go to work, you know. I can take care of us just fine."

My lips thin, and I shoot him an unpleasant look. "Nuh-uh, mister. We're not doing that. I'm not going to move in with you and suddenly quit everything in my life and let you take care of me. I've been working since college, and I'm fine doing it now."

He sighs, clearly not happy with the decision. "That was different, Selene. You don't need to work there anymore."

"But I do! If I ever want to open my own business again, I'll need to have money to do that. Money I will not take from you, understand me?"

He raises his hands, but I can see he doesn't agree. He's only dropping the subject for now to appease me. "All right. I get it."

"Thank you." I press one last kiss to his lips before I walk toward my car.

He's taking Luna to the zoo today with his parents and his sister. She'll get to play with her cousin, something she's been begging to do for the past two weeks. I'm a little disappointed I'll miss it, but I've been to the zoo with her plenty of times. It's only fair Endymion gets to experience this with her, too.

Things with Freya, his younger sister, and I still aren't the best, but she has warmed up to me a bit more since the barbecue at their parents' house. I mean, I get it. This is her brother, and she'd do anything to protect him. If someone hurt him or, in my case, kept his daughter a secret from him for years, there is no way she wouldn't be upset or hate that person.

At work, I wait tables alongside Julia. It's a Saturday night, so we're a little busier than we are during the week, but it's nothing we can't handle. I've been on my feet for the last three hours, and I'm in need of a break. There's an incessant ache at the soles of my feet that is absolutely killing me.

"How can you look so exhausted, yet look like you're glowing at the same time? I don't get it."

I roll my eyes at Julia as I refill drinks at the fountain machine. "I'm not sure what kind of compliment that's supposed to be."

She's getting the tab ready for one of her tables when she shrugs, shooting me a grin. "Not so much a compliment, but it is a segue into my next question. How hard is he banging you? I mean, you moved in fast. Is Endymion Black as good as they say?" She waggles her brows, and I frown.

"If you haven't already noticed, I don't like hearing how many others in this town think he's 'good,' and excuse me, I moved in with him because I love him, Jules. We have a daughter together, and we're trying to be a normal family."

Julia laughs. "Ah, so he is as good as they say. You lucky bitch. No wonder you're glowing. He's probably banging you into next week." A laugh bursts from my chest because she's not far off. "Moving on from your Greek god, I want to show you something."

Julia pulls out her phone, scrolling through the photos until she lands on one in particular. My brows draw in. "What is this?"

"So, I know this might be a bit premature, but I noticed this space is on the market. It's downtown on Alpine, which means it's right in the middle of everything. It would be a great place for a business, you know, if you were considering starting over here."

Taking the phone from her, I inspect the picture, nibbling on my bottom lip. She's right. The space itself looks great, from the photograph, at least, and if I was considering opening another store, I'd want to do it somewhere with enough traffic to keep the business afloat.

"I don't know, Jules. I feel like there is so much happening right now. What if I'm never in a good place to open Moonchild again?"

With a grin, Julia wraps her arm around me, tugging me into her side. "You're my best friend, Selene. You can do whatever the hell you want as long as you put your mind to it, and I have no doubt that Moonchild will be up and running soon."

Unexpected tears sting the backs of my eyes. "I love you to pieces. You know that, right?"

Her lips twist ruefully. "You better."

Just as she's tucking her phone into her apron, her expression falters at the sound of the bell chiming, indicating we have new customers. I follow the trajectory of her gaze, and my own smile tapers off.

"Don't worry about it. I'll take their table." Julia pats me on the butt, heading toward Holly and a few of her friends. She's always willing to slay my demons for me. Holly's gaze clashes with mine, and I swear I see sparks of hate ignite there. I square my shoulders and look away, focusing back on the task at hand.

Dealing with Endymion's former flames will be the hardest part about staying here in Dunsmuir. I'll never not run into Holly. There's so much I want to say to this woman—hell, I'd like to slap her across the face for calling my daughter a bitch—but I need this job, and I won't let her be the reason I lose it. End and I agreed we'd do that together, and I need to respect that. I make an effort to ignore her while she eats her meal, and Julia makes sure she handles that side of the diner.

A few hours later, after my lunch break, I spot someone sitting in my section, and my stomach twists in uncertainty. Since Julia is on her break, I can't ask her to take this table for me, too, so I suck it up and walk over, pen and pad in hand, summoning the strength.

Thomas glances up, and when he sees me, his eyes flash with anger. The black eye he was sporting not too long ago has healed, though it seems he hasn't forgotten why it was there in the first place, and who gave it to him. He eyes me with such a blatant disdain that I shift awkwardly on my feet.

"What can I get you?"

"Beer and a burger, little moon."

I'm surprised that's all he says, and for one brief second, I think I'm in the clear. I think he might actually listen to End's orders to keep away from me. But I should've known he wouldn't; nothing is ever that easy.

Once his food is ready, I bring it out to him, along with another beer. It's his third draft of the night. But judging by the smell wafting off him, I can't imagine this is his first drink of the day. That is just how Thomas and his friends are. They are partiers.

When I ask if he needs anything else, he leans back in his booth, his lazy eyes half-mast as they drag up and down my body. A tremor wracks my body, but it's not a pleasant one.

"You think you're really something special, don't you?"

My brows jump into my hairline. "Excuse me?"

"You think because you spread your legs for him and had his baby, you've suddenly found the perfect guy?" He laughs, and the sound is sharp and ugly. "I can assure you, you haven't. Do you even know how many women he's fucked in this town?" he goads.

My heart twinges at his words, but I steel myself, not about to let him see his words are getting under my skin. He's telling me things I already know—preying on my deepest fears. I'm nothing special to Endymion. I could be replaced at any moment, and that's such a scary thought. It's crushing to even think about.

"What is it with you women and Endymion Black, huh? You guys lose your fucking minds when you get near the bastard." He slams his fist down on the table, rattling the dishes. I glance around, pink rising to my cheeks when I realize the people dining inside are looking at us with frowns on their faces.

"Please calm down, Thomas. Just enjoy your meal."

"You too good for the likes of me, babe. Is that it? You think you have some golden pussy because Endymion Black is the only man who's been inside of it?" Thomas reaches out, his hand clasping onto my apron, and he tugs. The movement is so unexpected I go tumbling into his side of the table, my hip connecting with the corner. Pain flares, and I wince at the burn.

"What are you doing? Stop it," I hiss, trying to smack his hand off me, but he doesn't let up. His hand slides around the back of my thigh, dragging me closer to him. Panic flares, and I shove against him, but it does nothing. He's incredibly strong for a man who is tipsy. When he reaches higher, almost exposing my backside to everyone, I'm just about to scream when a meaty hand grips onto Thomas's shoulder and shoves him away from me.

Bobby is standing behind me, eyes ablaze with anger. "Get out, Tommy, and don't even think about coming back. I mean it this time."

"Fuck you and this stupid bitch. Oh, and fuck your wife, too, Bobby."

Bobby lets out a growl, and his fist sails into Thomas's face. His head knocks back, blood spilling out of his nose upon impact. A gasp rips from my chest, my hands flying to my mouth in shock. He drags Thomas up from the booth and tosses him out as if the man weighs nothing.

I whirl around when I feel a warm hand on my shoulder. It's Julia. Her eyes are wide, mouth agape in shock. "You okay, babe? Did he hurt you?"

I lie even though my hip is aching. "No, I'm fine. He just scared me is all. He was drunk and saying stupid things."

Her face grows stormy. "I can just imagine what the bastard was saying. I heard Holly and Reina talking earlier. She wants to try to win Endymion back, so she broke things off with him. My guess is he isn't too happy."

I tense. Holly is going to try to win End back? Is she a goddamn insane person? Over my dead body. That woman will not be allowed anywhere near my child if I have anything to say about it. Hell, at this rate, End won't even be able to look at her without wanting to strangle her for the things she said about Luna and me.

Heaving a sigh, I rub at my temples, feeling a headache coming on. "Jesus. I'm ready to go home and sleep. This is too much drama for one day."

Julia scoffs. "Where have you been? Dunsmuir has always been drama. Welcome back." She pats me on the butt before getting back to work. As if it was meant to be, I spot Holly hanging around out front and decide to take matters into my own hands.

I call out to Rita and tell her I'll be taking my break as I make my way outside. At the sound of the bell chiming, Holly turns, her face scrunching in distaste when she sees me.

"Can I help you?" She raises a brow, clearly annoyed by my presence. I'm not exactly chipper to be standing here with her either.

"You called my daughter a bitch, Holly. She's a child, for Christ's sake. Do you not have an ounce of respect for anyone in this town?"

Anger flares in the depths of her eyes. "I did not call your child a bitch. Would you go harass someone else?"

I scoff. "Are you seriously calling my daughter a liar, right now?"

"Well, it would definitely make sense. Like mother, like daughter."

I jerk back. "What the hell is that supposed to mean?"

Fury clouds Holly's expression. "It means you fucked my boyfriend! Lying obviously runs in your family."

I send a menacing glower her way, and my hands curl into fists at my sides. "You know nothing about me or my family."

She laughs, taking a step closer. "Oh, I know enough. I know you're not this sweet, perfect girl this town makes you out to be. You're not the girl Endymion thinks you are."

"And what, you are?" I challenge.

"I'm a whole hell of a lot better than you! The only reason he's with you is because he accidentally got you pregnant. You have to know that."

Pain rips through my chest. I suck in a ragged breath and narrow my eyes. "If you say anything about my daughter again, our next conversation won't be half this civil. I couldn't care less about what you think about me, but you'll keep her name out of your mouth. Oh, and if you really think I'm the source of all your problems, you need to have a look in the mirror and ask yourself why you were never enough for Endymion to begin with."

Her face shutters.

With those harsh parting words, I turn on my heels and head back into the diner.

On the drive home from work, I stop at the empty store lot Julia was telling me about earlier. I don't know why I do it. It's not like I'll be able to have it, but she's right. It is a cute place. I can't even remember what store was here as a kid, but she said the town hasn't been able to sell or lease the spot. It's in downtown Dunsmuir in a prime area. The storefront is brick and rustic, and with a little TLC, it could be something special.

Maybe.

In the far future.

If I ever decide to follow my dreams again.

With a quick glance at the clock, I decide to pull over and park along the street outside of the empty building. Endymion still isn't back home with Luna yet anyway. I spoke to him after I got off work, and he mentioned they were still at his parents' house having dinner. He told me to stop by, but I said I'd meet him at home. I didn't feel like rehashing my day in front of his parents.

Locking my car behind me, I walk up to the building, assessing everything about it. It's too dark out here to see inside. I'll have to stop by during the day, but I still peer in through the windows. It's shadowy and difficult to see what condition the inside is in, but as far as space goes, it's a good fit. A little bigger than the last place I leased in Pasadena.

A part of me wants to say to hell with it and make this happen, but a bigger part of me is afraid. Afraid of failing again. I did this once, and while things were good, it was really good, but it didn't last. Even though this is my dream, something I've always wanted, I don't believe following your dreams is the smartest thing to do anymore. At some point, we have to let them go. Maybe they were dreams for a reason? Always meant to be a distant goal, nothing that would ever come to fruition.

The sound of glass shattering behind me has me whirling around, a gasp catching in my throat. My eyes widen, and my stomach drops when I see who caused the noise. Thomas reeks of alcohol, and when I glance down at the shattered tequila bottle on the ground, I can guess why.

"Well, well, well, funny running into you here, Selene Drake."

I glance around the street, trying to find anyone else out walking around, but it's quiet, deserted, even for being a Saturday night. I swallow thickly, taking a wary step back. My heel collides with the building behind me, and my stomach cramps.

"Thomas, what are you doing here?"

He closes the distance between us, and with each step he takes toward me, I feel the blood roar through my veins, and my heart hammer against my chest, trying to burst through my rib cage.

"I could ask you the same thing, little moon. It's almost like fate put us on the same path tonight, isn't it?"

I shake my head, swallowing the lump blocking my throat. "I should go. Endymion is waiting for—"

End's name was the wrong thing to say. Anger flares in the depths of Thomas's dark brown eyes, and he slams his hand against the glass behind me, caging me in against him. I let out a shriek of fear, stilling against the glass. His breath fans my face. The heat of his body smothers me, making it impossible to breathe. My pulse is pounding so hard, it's making it difficult to think clearly and find a safe way out of this.

"Endymion. Endymion. Endymion. It's always about Endymion, isn't it?" He glares down at me, eyes filled with a turbulent heat, his lips twisted in a snarl. I don't know what happened to Thomas while I was gone, but the handsome football player from my childhood has turned into a drunken mess. The town disgrace.

He leans into me, pressing his nose against my cheek, smelling me. My bottom lip trembles, and bile rises up my throat, fear clawing at my flesh.

"P-please don't hurt me," I whisper.

His eyes flash to mine, and he chuckles. The sound turns my stomach. "Hurt you? Oh, no, little moon. I want to make you feel good. Show you what it's like to be with a real man. Do you know how long I've wanted you? How long I've waited?" In a flash of movement, his hands are on my hips, squeezing in a painful grip. I struggle against him. With adrenaline coursing through my body, I shove at Thomas's chest, trying to get him a safe distance away.

"Thomas, stop it. I don't want this."

He slams me up against the window behind me, banging my head. A burning twinge shoots through my skull. Thomas presses his body flat against mine, and I can feel his erection digging into me. It spurs a sob to rip from my chest. I try to knee him, but he must sense it coming because he smothers me with the weight of his body, his hand digging into my hair and pulling so hard, I feel the strands rip free from my scalp. I cry out in pain at the sting as it burns across my flesh.

Taking advantage of my weakened moment, Thomas kisses me, shoving his tongue in my mouth. I gag at the invasion, shoving at his chest, doing everything I can to get him off me. For someone as drunk as he is, he's strong, so much stronger than I expected he'd be.

"Get off me!" I yell, but it gets muffled beneath his lips.

"What's the matter, sweet little Selene? Scared to get fucked by a real man? Spread those legs for me. I know you can."

He reaches his hand between us, and I panic. Bile threatens to expel. Adrenaline flows through my body, and I strike him, clawing at his face. He lets out a strangled roar, and in the blink of an eye, his hand sails down across my face. The hit is jarring. Pain flares in my cheek, dazing me. I've never been hit before. Especially not by a man.

There's a ringing in my ears that drowns out the sound of everything else around me. When I feel his hand trying to reach up my dress, I snap out of it and dig my nails into his forearms, ripping open his skin.

"You fucking bitch!"

This time his hit is a fist, and the second his knuckles make contact with my face, I feel the skin split. Black dots dance around my vision, dazing me. The throbbing reverberating from my skull is endless. A cry of pain rips from my chest, and I fall onto my side, skidding along the pavement. My elbows scrape against the gravel there. Glass from the shattered bottle embeds itself into my skin. I struggle to push myself upright, hot tears rolling down my cheeks.

"This works out perfectly," Thomas murmurs, as he shoves me back down onto the ground when he sees me struggling to get up. I fight beneath him when I feel him settle on top of me as he works my dress up my body. I'm bucking so forcefully he can't get ahold of me. With a punishing grip in my hair, he shoves my head down onto the sidewalk, applying pressure to keep me pinned down. I still fight. I fight against the throb radiating from my face. I fight against the feel of his heavy body on top of mine. I fight against the visceral fear percolating through my veins. The flesh of my cheek scrapes against the concrete as I try to get away, but it's no use.

When he attempts to dig his hand up my dress, I scream. The sound echoes around us, painfully bouncing down the quiet street. Tears pool beneath me, every part of my body burning as I feel him work to lift the dress to get better access.

"Hey!"

He freezes at the sharp voice, and so do I.

"Hey, what the fuck?!"

Thomas scrambles to his feet. When his heavy weight is no longer crushing me into the pavement, I try to inhale a deep breath, but it gets trapped in my throat. I slam my eyes shut, and a sob rips past my lips when I hear his footsteps pound away as he flees. Shame washes over me. Pain grips my body, and an ache blooms in my chest at what could've happened. What almost happened.

I hear the sound of pounding footsteps in time with my racing heart. A sharp pain shoots through my arm when I try to move, and when I glance up, the side of my face burns. Someone skids to their knees before me, and when my eyes clear on the figure, tears of relief spring to them.

"Jesus Christ," Landon breathes, his face crumpling when he sees me. "You all right, Selene? Tell me where it hurts."

I press my palms into the concrete, trying to push myself upright. In doing so, he gets a good look at my face, and it tells me what I already know. It's more than just a scratch. He lets out a string of curse words. "That son of a bitch."

Landon helps me into a sitting position, taking stock of my injuries as he pulls his phone out of his pocket. I know who he's calling, without even having to ask, and my stomach drops.

It's on the tip of my tongue to beg him not to say anything, but there's no way I can hide this or stay silent about this. I'll be the talk of the town. News will travel back to my parents, and it will worry my dad.

"End, we have a problem." There's a pause as he glances at me. He proceeds to recount what happened in a low tone.

I wince when I hear the roaring sound of Endymion's voice on the other end of the line. *Great.*

My eyes slam shut. The side of my face is burning, and there's a dull, incessant throb at the base of my skull. I can't escape it. A cold chill shoots down my spine, and I flinch when I feel Landon's hand on my shoulder. His hand is gone immediately as if sensing I don't want to be touched after what happened.

"I'm sorry, Landon. I didn't mean—"

His brows pull in, and he looks frustrated. "What are you

apologizing for, Selene? You did nothing wrong here tonight. Nothing."

I nod, swallowing thickly because I don't know what else to say. He takes a few steps away, giving me a little privacy as he calls his dad, who works for the sheriff. I hear his hushed tone, and even though I can't exactly make out what he's saying, I imagine he's relaying what he saw.

In what feels like no time at all, everyone is pulling up, parking near my car on the empty street. My heart stumbles in my chest when I see End. The muscle in his jaw jumps wildly, and his eyes light with a burning rage as he stalks toward me, his gait stiff. Despite all the anger I see written all over his face, I can clearly see the fear and the panic there, too. It crumbles the wall I'd just built around my emotions. I didn't want to fall apart in front of an audience; I wanted to do that in the privacy of our home, but apparently, that isn't going to happen. Dropping to his knees before me, he pulls me into his arms, and I grip onto him, a sob ripping from my chest.

"Shhh. I'm here," he soothes, trying to keep his tone even. Despite that, I still hear it in his voice. The anger. The rage he's barely restraining. He pulls back ever so slightly, gently taking my face in his hands. His expression turns murderous as his moss eyes sweep across my features. His nostrils flare, and he shoots an undecipherable look at Landon.

"What happened?" he demands. I glance over his shoulder, toward the officer that is heading our way.

"Where's Luna?"

"She's with my parents," he says, putting me at ease before turning back to Landon. "Now tell me what the fuck happened before I lose my shit."

"I heard a scream, so I followed the sound. Then I saw—" Landon pauses, his gaze darting to mine. I glance away, feeling entirely too vulnerable. As if sensing that, End tightens his hold around me, and I seek his warmth, falling into him. "He had her pinned to the ground. I didn't see what happened before. He got spooked when he heard me coming and ran off."

End stiffens. I feel him crane his neck to look down at me. I keep my gaze planted on the ground. His touch on my chin is gentle as he lifts my face to look at him. His gaze rakes over my battered cheek. It lingers on the cut that's just above my cheekbone. He presses his lips together in a grim line, shifting his gaze to get a better view of the flesh there that is scraped.

A hot tear rolls down my cheek, and with the gentlest of touches, Endymion catches the salty moisture with his thumb. It almost has me breaking into another round of sobs.

"Everyone all right?" Sheriff Wentworth asks, pausing in front of us. He has Deacon, Landon's father, who is another officer here in Dunsmuir, with him. When I glance up at both men, sympathy passes over their features when they take in the tear tracks and the rest of my distressed state. End takes my hand and squeezes, as if knowing I need all the extra support I can get.

I lick my dry, cracked lips before I retell the events of what happened. I start with the confrontation at Rita's to what happened in front of the building. Sheriff Wentworth sighs. The sound is full of fatigue and disappointment, which makes sense. Thomas is his son, after all. Though he's now more of the black sheep of the family. He finishes taking down my statement, a contrite expression on his face.

"I'm sorry about this, Selene. Thomas has done a lot of dumb stuff, but this one..." He shakes his head, glancing away for a few seconds, deep in thought. My stomach cramps at the sound of his name. I'll never be able to hear his name again, let alone look at him, without thinking about what happened tonight. "This time, he won't be able to run from this. I won't let him."

"Thank you, Sheriff Wentworth and Officer Scott. We appreciate you guys coming out here," End says. He takes charge of the conversation, sensing I don't have it in me to force any more words past my lips. I'm spent. Physically and emotionally drained.

Once we finish giving statements, End helps me into the car. He's treating me like I'm made of glass. It's as if he's afraid I'm going to shatter at any given second, and he might not be far off. I feel disconnected from what happened with Thomas, but at the same time, I feel incredibly vulnerable. It feels like there is ice swimming through my veins. I can't stop feeling his breath on my skin, the sensation of his hands gripping and prodding at my flesh.

After a quick trip to the emergency room (at End's insistence) to make sure I'm okay, Endymion drives us home. I can practically feel him stewing the whole way. Thankfully, he doesn't say anything about what happened tonight. I think he knows I need a moment to collect myself.

"What about Luna?" I ask, the second we step over the threshold into the quiet house. It feels odd, not hearing her soft giggle or her pounding feet as she skids around the corner.

He keeps his hand firmly planted on my lower back as if he's afraid I'll disappear. "She'll be fine at my parents' place for the night. I told them to give me a call if there are any issues."

My heart twinges at the thought of being away from my sweet girl for a whole night, but I nod. In the bedroom, I bypass his king-sized bed, opting for the bathroom instead. My chest caves, and my lungs squeeze painfully when I look at myself in the mirror. A small cut on my cheekbone is slowly scabbing over, a purple bruise forming around it, and the scrapes on the other side of my face look just as bad as they feel. It's just on a small portion of my cheek, but it's there, and I'll have to find a way to explain to Luna what happened. How do I explain to her that someone hurt me without frightening her?

I feel End come up behind me, his warmth emanates around me, enveloping me in a secure blanket. His hands settle on my waist gently.

"Where did he touch you?" In the mirror, his face is blank and impassive, but his tone gives him away. He's barely hanging on by a thread.

Flashes of Thomas's hands on me have bile rising up my throat. My bottom lip trembles, and I squeeze my lids shut.

"Nothing like that happened. But…I think it would've if Landon hadn't come when he did. Thomas was so angry. About you. About me. And Holly. He was drunk—not that that makes it any better. I should've gone straight home after work. I shouldn't have stopped there. I don't know what I was thinking."

"Hey," End admonishes, gently turning me around to face him. "This is not your fault. You understand me?"

"Why do I feel like it is?" I whisper, feeling a fresh wave of tears sting my eyes. The muscle in his jaw strains, and he pulls me into his arms. My hands wrap around his waist, and I dig my fingers into the material of his shirt, never wanting to let go. Endymion is my safe space at this moment. He's the warmth I'm clinging onto in the hopes it'll wipe away all the bad that happened tonight—a clean slate.

"Let's get you cleaned up."

I allow End to help me out of my filthy clothes. He's careful of my wounds, and once I'm standing before him, completely naked, his eyes rake over my flesh, looking for anything he could've missed.

In the shower, his hands are soft and gentle as he cleans me. He doesn't explore or grope; he just takes care of me in a way I didn't know I needed. A way I never thought a man like him would ever be capable of. Under the warm spray of the shower, I tilt my head back, taking him in.

Standing this close, I'm enthralled by the way the rivulets of water roll down the sharp planes of his face. They stream down his thick, gorgeous hair and eyelashes. I watch the droplets glide down along his angular jaw. His hair looks brown when it's soaked like it is right now, the blond and light brown pieces hidden. The strands are stuck to his forehead and neck, and when the water sluices down his soft mouth, I want to reach up and drink it down. Sensing the weight of my stare, he pauses, glancing down at me.

"Thank you."

His hand slides around my hip, and he draws my wet body flush against his. "Don't thank me for this."

He cups my cheek, and with the softest kiss that I feel down to the depths of my soul, he presses his lips against mine. There's nothing heated or crazy about it. It's soft and oh, so perfect. I find myself clutching onto him like he's a lifeline. My lifeline.

We rest our foreheads together, catching our breath. His grip is still secure on me as if he doesn't want to let go. His jaw grinds back and forth as he works through his anger.

"I want to kill him for hurting you."

My heart squeezes. "I'm okay. I promise."

"I'm not," he grits. "The thought of his hands on you…the idea of him hurting you, it fucking kills me."

"I don't want you doing anything, understand me? We're letting the police handle this, End."

His gaze rakes across my flesh, taking in the scars and the cuts. "You're mine, Selene, and that means I'm not going to let anyone hurt you. I *can't* let this slide."

I shake my head, my gut churning with worry. "We have Luna to think about. I can't… She can't lose you, Endymion."

He seems to understand everything I'm not saying. The muscle in his jaw twitches, and it's obvious he's not happy, but he still presses a soft kiss against my lips that steals the breath straight from my lungs.

Chapter Twenty-Five

Selene

I TAKE ONE LAST LOOK IN THE MIRROR, ONLY WINCING SLIGHTLY AT MY reflection. The scab on my face is mostly healed, but that doesn't stop the pitying looks. News of what happened traveled fast, just as I figured it would. Telling my parents was the hardest part of all, mainly because I could see the worry written all over my father's face. He wanted to tear Thomas limb from limb.

He wasn't the only one.

I think the only saving grace was that Endymion was there with me every step of the way, silently promising he'd kill him if he ever stepped foot in this town again. That was the thing about Thomas. This wasn't the first time he'd been in trouble here in Dunsmuir. He'd ran off enough times to hide out until the dust settled. He'd always come back when he thought the town forgot about his previous mistakes; only this time, it wasn't just a small mistake.

"Mommy," Luna groans, trotting into the bathroom. "Daddy wants to know if you're done yet."

Twisting the lid on the lip gloss, I drop down to my haunches, leveling my gaze with my sweet girl. I braided her hair in a fishtail braid on each side, adding little sunflower bows to each end. We're both wearing soft blue sundresses with tiny flower prints. I paired hers with a jean jacket and some cowgirl boots. She looks as cute as a button.

"You look very pretty, Mommy," she says, cupping my cheek.

"Thank you, baby. You look very, very pretty, too. Are you excited?"

Her grin widens. "I am. I've never been to a party like this before."

Guilt stabs me in the chest. We didn't exactly know a lot of people in Pasadena. We didn't have any reason to attend any parties that involved anyone in the city or hang out with friends. It was just birthday parties with the three of us. This is the first time she'll get to experience this town and the yearly events that happen.

I wonder idly if that guilt will ever pass. Part of me thinks it will over time, but the other part, I think it's something I'll have to deal with for the rest of my life. Something I'll have to keep making up to her and her father, day in and day out.

It's the town's yearly Summer Fest. I remember coming here with my parents as a kid and dancing under the stringed lights, eating the food, and hanging out with Julia. I used to look forward to these events until Endymion came along. Then I just spent my time watching him from afar. It's strange to think that now, after so many years, he'll be the one at my side tonight, with our daughter.

"We ready to g—" The sound of Endymion's voice cuts off when he steps into the bedroom, looking our way. A smile lights up his face when he looks at Luna. She does a little twirl for him, making us both laugh. At the sound, his gaze drifts to me, and the smile slowly slides off his face. His eyes alight with heat. The green there is a force to be reckoned with. His gaze has a texture to it, one I can feel roll through my body in waves.

He closes the distance between us, an unreadable expression on his face as he takes me into his arms. That angry swarm of bees is back wreaking havoc inside of me. I can't help but wonder if the feeling will ever go away when I'm near this man. Will I ever look at him and not feel the way I do now? His warm hand tightens around my hip, his fingertips digging into my skin, sending electric zaps straight to my core.

I rest my hand on his firm chest as he stares down at me, the heat in his eyes almost unbearable. His calloused hand cups my cheek, and my heart flutters in my chest.

"You're so fucking beautiful."

"That's a bad word," Luna pipes in.

My smile is instantaneous. Like gasoline on a fire, it starts on one end and spreads to the other. As much as I want to chide him for his language, I can't bring myself to do it. "Thank you," I whisper, trying to keep the heat from settling into my cheeks. It's no use. I should come to terms with the fact that I'll always be that girl who blushes too hard.

Endymion swoops down, taking my mouth in a kiss that evokes deep body quakes. The effect he has on me is visceral. I feel the kiss spread through my body like wildfire. He presses my body against his, and heat engulfs us both.

"Gross." Luna groans, prompting us to pull apart, resting our foreheads against each other. The laugh that tumbles past my lips is the most carefree it's ever been.

Every year Summer Fest in Dunsmuir is held at an old barn that was refurbished years ago. The structure is a historical landmark here, only a few miles away from the famous rail line that was built in the 1880s. Though, most of the town is considered historical. Dunsmuir is a tourist favorite because it is one of the few small towns here in Northern California that has preserved an authentic 1920s and 1930s look and feel.

My heart thumps with nostalgia as I take in the barn I recognize from my childhood. It's a weathered brown color that gives the wood character, letting everyone know just how long it's been here. The front doors are rolled open, and I can clearly spot the wooden tables covered in white tablecloths and the small fairy lights strung across the borders and crisscrossed along the ceiling inside. From my trajectory, I can even spot hay bales, and it takes me back to years ago when I was forced to sit on them and deal with the hay poking me in my thighs.

A surprised smile lights my face as we walk over the threshold. Even the smell in here is the same. It's a mix of delicious food and something woodsy. Hints of nature tickle the back of my nose. I spot my parents seated on one of the hay bales at a table and feel emotion grip my chest. Last night I mentioned to Endymion that I was sad that my parents wouldn't be attending. Dad is only getting sicker, and I knew going out is the last thing he would want. I was still bummed they wouldn't be here. Somehow, I know this is Endymion's doing, getting them to go out. There's no denying how sick my father looks. But the smile on his face as he talks to a few of his friends has tears burning the backs of my eyes.

I tighten my grip around Endymion's hand in a silent thank you. He glances down at me, an emotion in his eyes that has heat crawling across my skin.

"I was wondering if you'd show." I turn at the sound of Julia's voice, and my brows disappear into my hairline when I see who she's with. Griffin has his arm slung around her shoulder, looking all too comfortable.

"What makes you think I wouldn't?" I retort, feigning offense.

She rolls her eyes. "Because I know you like the back of my hand, Selene Drake."

"Oh! There's Valeria. Can I go play with her?" Luna asks us both, vibrating with excitement. Endymion nods, scooping her into his arms, and she giggles.

"C'mon, I'll go with you." End tugs me into his side and presses a warm kiss to my lips that has my stomach fluttering woefully. I watch them go and try to mask my surprise when Griffin presses a kiss to Julia's cheek.

"Catch up with you later, babe."

Once he's out of earshot, I grip onto Julia's arm and squeeze, my eyes narrowing into thin slits. "You gonna make me ask, or you just want to tell me what the hell is going on?"

She sighs. "I gave in, okay? You were right. I do like Griffin a lot more than I let on. He's a manwhore, but Jesus Christ, the things that man can do with his tongue you wouldn't belie—"

I pretend to gag. "Please stop. I don't need the dirty details. I just want to know why you didn't tell me. Is this payback for me not telling you?"

Julia brushes her booted foot through the dirt beneath our feet, stalling. "Don't be ridiculous. It's because I didn't want to ruin it. If I talk about it, it's bound to ruin things, right? I figured if I didn't tell anyone, it would make it hurt less when this all goes to shit."

I frown. "Jules, talking about something good in your life, something that makes you happy, won't make it go to shit. Don't speak your negativity into existence, only the positive."

Julia's lips quirk. "You're a goddamn hippie. You know that?"

I nudge her in the side with my elbow playfully. "Oh, shut it. You love me and my hippie-dippie ways."

"You're not wrong. Now, let's go sit with your parents. Your mother looks like she's bored out of her mind."

She's not wrong. My dad's been talking to a handful of his friends, but my mom is still just sitting there, looking unenthused. I think being in Pasadena changed something in her. I know she misses it there. It's a completely different way of life. One a big city and the other a small town where no secrets are kept.

"Looking a little bored there, Cece," Julia comments.

My mom sighs. "This town hasn't changed one bit. It's all still taking some getting used to."

Out of the corner of my eye, I spot movement, and a grateful smile takes over my face when I see who it is. Endymion and Luna are heading our way, but in tow is his family. They take the empty tables next to my parents' table, and Aurora heads straight for my mother, pulling her into a hug and taking the seat next to her. The two dive into conversation like they've been the best of friends their entire life.

"Well, that was easier than I was expecting," Julia comments. I laugh in agreement because that is not what I anticipated. I thought Julia and me would have to sit next to my mom for the rest of the night and keep her company so she wouldn't lose her mind.

It feels good to watch our families connect and spend time together. It's sad to think we could've been doing this long before now.

"Selene, can we talk for a sec?"

My brows draw in, and I tense at the sound of Freya's voice. I haven't had a conversation between just the two of us in years. Endymion's younger sister seems to go out of her way to avoid me, and ever since the truth came out and she's made her feelings about me known, I've done the same.

Glancing over Freya's shoulder, I share a look with Julia. She just raises her brows, clearly as surprised by this as I am. Plastering a smile on my face, I nod, following in step beside Freya as she puts some distance between our families and us.

"Look, I just wanted a moment to clear the air with you. I had no right to give you the cold shoulder the way I did during the barbecue at my parents' place. I was...angry, on my brother's behalf, but I didn't have all the facts. I didn't know how he felt about you, and I didn't know about that night. At the creek."

My face flames with embarrassment.

"Did End put you up to this?"

A small smile quirks her lips. "He did, and didn't, if that makes sense. He explained everything, and I felt the need to clear the air with you. Despite what has happened, we are family, and I love my niece to absolute pieces. So, thank you for being an incredible mother, and thank you for loving my brother the way you do. He's never quite felt like he belonged here in this town, with anyone, until he met you."

"Thank you, Freya. That means a lot. And for what it's worth, I never wanted to hurt any of you, and I'm so incredibly sorry if I did."

Freya's eyes soften, and she pulls me into a hug. "I know, Selene. We're sisters now, and sisters stand together. Always."

I tighten my arms around her and breathe out a sigh of relief. "Thank you, Freya."

"Don't thank me, just do me a favor and keep my brother off the dance floor tonight? He has two left feet."

That draws a laugh out of me. Freya locks her arm with mine, and we head back to our families. The weight of guilt sitting on my chest has slowly begun to ease. It may take time, but I'm beginning to forgive myself for the past.

Watching Luna laugh with both sets of her grandparents is the highlight of my night. As is the father-daughter dance. One of the many historic traditions here; it happens every year at Summer Fest.

Endymion scoops our little girl into his arms, and she squeals. They head over to the center of the barn, where every other father and daughter are beginning to dance. He sets her on his feet, and there's still a ridiculous height difference. He bends, dancing with her to the music, and my heart just about explodes. So do my ovaries. I watch on, warmth filtering through my chest, happiness capsizing my soul.

"I don't think I've ever seen you smile this hard."

I glance up at the sound of my dad's voice. He's standing beside me, his gaze darting between End and Luna, then back to me. I shrug, opting for the truth.

"I guess I haven't been this happy until now."

He places his hand between us, palm up. "It's been a while since we've danced at this thing. Let's show them how it's done, baby girl."

A mix between a sob and a laugh escapes my lips, and I nod, trying to hold back the sudden bout of tears. It's been a while since we danced at this thing. Years, in fact. Once I got into my teens, after Endymion had moved here, I stopped, afraid it would make me look too much like a child, though he never noticed me enough to care anyway. I didn't realize until now that I may have neglected my father long before we stopped talking. The thought is an icepick to the heart.

I place my hand in his bony one and fight to tamp down the emotions barreling to the surface. If I don't get a cap on this, I'll turn into a blubbering mess in front of everyone, all because I'm dancing with my father.

Soft music plays as my dad takes me into his arms. Lewis Capaldi's throaty voice fills the barn as he sings "Before You Go." With my hands resting on his shoulders, I glance around, taking in the rest of the townsfolk and all the daughters dancing with their fathers. A grin spreads across my face when I spot Luna still dancing with her dad. Her grin is wide and carefree. It's incredibly beautiful.

"I'm proud of you, Selene."

I glance back at my dad and make a face. "I don't know why. I've failed at so many things, Dad. My business is just the tip of that iceberg."

He sighs. "You didn't fail. You did what so many people are too afraid to do. You chased your dreams. So what if it didn't work out over there in Pasadena. Because I think, if it had, you might not have ever come back."

I process his words, knowing there's some truth to them. Now that Luna has Endymion in her life and we're in a good place, I can't imagine not being back here with him. I can't imagine not being here for my father.

"Never thought of it like that," I whisper, my voice quiet.

"I think you were always meant to come back here, Selene. Fate, the cosmos you believe, you were always going to end up here. And that doesn't have to be a bad thing. I just…I want you to know I'm proud. So goddamn proud of the woman you've become. There hasn't been one moment where I've not been proud of you. Maybe I haven't said it enough over the years, but I need you to know that."

A tear slides down my cheek. I hate it when he gets like this. When he starts talking like he's not going to wake up tomorrow, it makes all of this real. It makes the pain of our reality all the more undeniable.

"Thank you, Dad. Maybe one day I'll get to show you what the next venture will be."

His brows raise, a smile lighting his eyes. "So, you are thinking about opening up here."

I blow out a huff, glancing around with a frown. "I want to. But Dunsmuir is small. I don't exactly see an apothecary doing well here. I mean, we do get tourists, but I'm not sure it will be enough to keep it afloat."

His smile grows despite the negativity I'm spewing. After telling Julia not to speak negativity into existence earlier, I sure am acting like a hypocrite. "But you're still thinking about it, that's all that matters."

"I am. It was the whole reason I was out on Alpine…"

His eyes grow stormy at the mention of that night. His gaze sweeps over the slight scars. I've hidden them well with makeup, but it's my father, and he knows they're there.

"You're brave, Selene. The strongest person I know. Don't ever let what happened that night bring you down."

"I won't. It's been hard. I almost expect him to hop out when I least expect it, but I have to have faith, faith that when he does turn up, he'll be put away, and I won't have to worry about him."

The soft strains of music play as I sweep across the floor with my dad. We laugh with each other, and it feels good. I've missed this.

Being this close to him. It makes me want to hold on to him a little tighter, to try to get him to stay here with me just a little while longer. I want him to see Luna go to first grade, then be there when she graduates from high school and so many other pivotal moments in her life—in our lives.

He suddenly grows serious, both of us now people watching while we dance.

"I've been thinking," he starts, and I quirk a brow, waiting for him to elaborate. "I want you to have the house."

My stomach dips painfully, and I shake my head. "No, we're not going to talk about this. Not yet."

He sighs. "We need to. It's inevitable. And I mean it. I want you to have it. I know you have Endymion's place now, but…I want you to choose to do with the house as you please."

My chin quivers with emotion. "But what about Mom?"

He smiles sadly. "We've spoken about this already. She agrees with me. She thinks you should have the place. I think it holds too many memories, good and bad, for her to want to hang on to."

My throat suddenly feels dry and my tongue swollen, not sure what to say. The thought of keeping the house that I grew up in, a house filled with memories, some not always good, but a house that will always hold the memory of my father, is frightening. I'm not sure how that makes me feel, having to carry the weight of that decision on my shoulders. I don't know if I'd ever be able to part with it.

"I love you, Dad," I whisper, pulling him into a hug in the middle of the dance floor. His arms wrap around me, and he hugs me back, his grip just as tight as mine, almost like he hears the same ominous clock ticking that I do.

A sudden round of applause erupts in the barn, signaling the end of the father-daughter dance. "C'mon, let's get some food. I'm starving."

He's lying. The man's appetite has been nonexistent lately, but I go along with it anyway, letting him have this.

My steps falter as I'm walking back toward our families' tables when I glance at the barn entrance and spot Holly and Reina walking through, looking all dolled up.

I know it isn't her fault what happened with Thomas, but my mind immediately drifts to thoughts of him and that night, and a cold shiver travels through my body. My gaze clashes with Holly's, and I don't know what I was expecting to see there in her eyes, but it certainly wasn't anger.

What the hell is she angry with me for?

Shaking it off, I head back to the table with everyone else, and Endymion immediately pulls me into his side, Luna resting in his arms. It seems all that dancing has tired her out.

"You hungry?" he asks, looking down at me. I press a kiss to his lips.

"Yeah, I was already going to head there. I'll grab a plate for you and Luna."

Her little head jerks up at the mention of her name. "Aww. I want to pick my food."

I roll my eyes at her whine, stifling my smile. Hell, she was just on the verge of falling asleep only a few seconds ago. "All right then, let's go pick some food, Luna Bella."

Taking her hand in mine, we walk across the barn and get in line behind the others that are already waiting. We're not standing for long when I hear a giggle behind me, prompting my jaw to clench. I'd know that laugh anywhere. I peek over my shoulder and, of course, it's Reina and Holly. My annoyance is indeed confirmed. She catches my eyes, still looking angry and blatantly bitchy.

I'm not surprised.

I clutch Luna a little tighter to me, thinking about all the things she said in front of her. I've never been much of a violent person, but at this moment, I'd like nothing more than to sock Holly in her pretty face. Obviously, I can't do that in front of my daughter, so I keep my gaze trained ahead of me, doing my best to tune them out.

The line moves along slowly with no issues. That is, until they purposely raise their voices, so I can hear their conversation.

"She was out in the middle of the night. Probably asking for it," Holly confirms under her breath. "I don't feel bad for her. Everyone is acting like she's some kind of victim. She just wants the attention. She always has."

Something inside me snaps at her words. A spark of anger lights within my chest, and I grind my back teeth together. I turn, softly pulling Luna behind me, shielding her.

"I didn't ask for *anything*. Your boyfriend assaulted me. I don't know what your problem is with me, Holly, but get over it. So what, I had a child with Endymion. Stop blaming me for your failed relationship. I feel sorry for you. The fact that you have to belittle me and name call my daughter is just sad. All for what? To make your miserable, boring life seem all that better?"

Holly jerks back as if I've slapped her. Color rises to her cheeks, and she looks like she's going to blow. "You're a stupid cunt, and so is your daughter."

My arm swings out, and I strike her across the face. Resounding gasps from bystanders ring out across the expanse of the barn.

"That's enough." Endymion's sharp voice materializes from thin air. Silence descends around the barn. He steps up beside me, frustration emanating off him in waves, and takes Luna into his protective arms. He's a knight in shining armor at this moment, slaying every dragon out to cause us harm. "Back away now, or you'll regret it."

"You never cared about me, did you?" End's jaw clenches with anger at Holly's accusation. He's so close to losing it. "It was always her, wasn't it?" The way she utters "her" while glaring daggers at me takes me by surprise.

She can't mean me, can she?

Endymion didn't even know I was alive back then.

"You think I didn't notice the way you would look at her? You never looked at me the way you do her. You never fought for my honor or got upset when someone flirted with me."

"That's because I love her. That should be answer enough for you. Now leave."

Holly looks as if she's going to argue, but she tosses the plate down and storms away. I watch her go, a frown marring my face as I try to make sense of what she said. Does she really believe End cared more about me all those years ago than he did her?

What the hell is she smoking?

I jolt at the sensation of End's hand sliding around the nape of my neck. He squeezes me reassuringly, prompting me to glance up at him.

"You okay?" he asks, his intense gaze searching mine.

I smile, though it comes out wobbly. "Yeah, I'm okay. I didn't mean to snap like that," I mumble, glancing around at all the eyes that are now firmly fixed on us.

Great.

His brows dip. "Don't apologize for defending yourself or our daughter, Selene. Holly is and will always be a troublemaker. Angry with the whole world because the attention isn't on her."

I want to ask him about all the other things she said, but as I glance around at the barn filled with people, I realize now may not be the best time.

As if sensing I'm ready to let this go, End presses a kiss against my lips in front of everyone, and I feel my cheeks redden in embarrassment. There are a few whistles and hollers from everyone around us, but all I see is him.

Always him.

From the doorway, I watch as Endymion lies down in that small bed with Luna snuggled on his chest. He's been reading the same princess book for the past hour, and my sweet girl is still cuddled against him, hanging on to his every word. Warmth swirls in my chest, and I rest my hand over my heart.

As if sensing my presence, End glances my way, a smirk twisting his lips. The effect of it hits me straight in my core. After we got back from the barn, we all came home, showered, and got ready for bed. As part of her nightly routine, Luna wanted her daddy to read her a story. It's something I've gladly given him full rein over.

I watch for a bit longer until she falls asleep in his arms. He gently slips out from beneath her, pulling the covers over her. It's such a dichotomy, watching this broad-shouldered man be so gentle with her. It's like he was born to do this.

He meets me at the door, his hands sliding around my waist. His hold is a possessive one, one I find that I adore. Pressing a kiss against my neck, he inhales deeply, and it sends a wave of flutters through me. End guides us into our bedroom, and my core clenches when he locks the door behind him, prowling toward me with a predatory gleam in his eyes.

The way he touches me and holds me is a contradiction to the heat swirling in those green depths. He handles me with such care, cupping my cheek gently here and petting my curves there. His thumb swipes over the skin on my shoulders, and his gaze rakes across my flesh. As I stare up at him, I get the urge to say the words I've been too afraid to let go of.

"I don't know a lot about love, other than what I feel for you." I slide my arms around his neck, drawing our foreheads together. My next words come out thick and unsteady, but directly from my heart. "I love you, Endymion Black. And what is between us? I want it forever."

Something akin to a possessive growl reverberates in his chest.

His hand finds purchase at the back of my head, and he grips there. He leans closer, bringing the scent of the sage soap he uses and something that is purely Endymion. The scent of him is so familiar, it's burned into my memory, so much so, that he feels like home.

His green eyes are wild with lust and a handful of so many other emotions I can't pin down. "Do you know how fucking long I've been waiting to hear you say that?"

My heart is beating like an angry metronome in my chest at his admission. "How long?"

"Since our daughter let it slip all those weeks ago that her father was in love with her mother."

I laugh, just thinking about the memory.

Since the day I spotted him in that damn grocery store, I've felt the words. I just never had the guts to say them aloud until now.

Did he really not know how I felt about him? Judging by the expression on his face, I realize that maybe he's been waiting for me to tell him all this time.

Cupping my face in his calloused hands, End leans down, grazing my lips with his.

"I love you, Selene. I want to give you forever and everything after that. I want years of us building a happy family with Luna. Years of hearing your stories about the moon and why you love it so much. I'd chase the moon and bring it to you if I could. I'd handpick every goddamn star in the sky if it were possible, and I'd do it all for you."

A constellation of fragmented shells and sand floats in his light brown hair as he stares down at me. The way he's looking at me right now is something I've always dreamed of. *He's* something I've always dreamed of.

"You once mentioned that you looked at the stars because it was like staring up at dreams and endless possibilities. You're that star for me, Selene. You're the entire goddamn universe, consuming my orbit. Consuming my every thought."

Emotions clog my throat. "How can you possibly remember that?"

He smiles. "I remember, Selene. I always have."

My lips part. "So what Holly said back at the barn tonight, about you…about me…that was true?"

Those vibrant greens search mine, and he nods. "I've never not noticed you, Selene. How could I?"

Something filters through my chest while an ache simultaneously blooms in my core. "Kiss me," I urge.

Endymion doesn't waste a single second. His mouth swoops down, and he takes my mouth in a kiss that's soul-binding. It's one of those kisses I'll remember for the rest of my life. It's passionate and perfect, erasing all lingering thoughts of Holly and our messed-up past. It's just us. Here and now.

With a need like never before, I strip out of my clothes, and Endymion follows suit. His hands take their time as he explores every inch of my skin. The touch is heaven. It leaves a trail of fire across my flesh in its wake. His mouth is sucking and nipping at me like he's starved. It's as if some part of him can't get enough of me—I know I can't. We fall back onto the bed in a tangle of limbs, and his strong, warm body settles between my legs.

My core throbs and clenches, painfully so, as he takes his cock, rubbing the swollen head against my drenched slit. I'm leaking for him. Every part of my body vibrates with need. Swirling his thumb through my slick core, End drags the moisture up to my clit and swirls it around the sensitive nub. He does it until I'm a writhing mess beneath him. He takes my legs and hikes them up on his shoulders. With slow, teasing motions, he dips the head of his cock in and out of my entrance. The sensation drives me wild—being penetrated but not feeling his full length inside me. The stretch of my lips around his head, but not feeling him against my walls.

When he finally slides his cock all the way into me, I have to bite the edge of the pillow next to my head to keep from waking Luna. Endymion curses as he bottoms out, and I feel like he's gone further than my stomach. Maybe he's touching my soul in this position, chipping away at it, so he can permanently etch himself there. He rotates between lazy, long strokes that curl my toes and short, fast thrusts that make my breasts shake and have my walls clenching around his thick length.

The sound of our slapping flesh fills the room, followed by our grunts and groans of pleasure. It's so loud and incredibly erotic. End shifts, changing the angle of his thrusts, bending over me. I can feel his chest and stomach, all corded and tight, rub against my damp breasts. His stubbled jaw grazes my cheeks as he bends down, fucking into me. Making love to me.

The way his hips grind as he delivers short, deep jabs that I feel in the center of my being drive me wild. I can feel the stirrings of my orgasm build. That warmth swirls in my core, and when he hits that deep spot, everything inside me unravels, and I come around him. Deep contractions squeeze my core, and I gush. I feel my juices slipping out of me, sliding down the trembling curve of my backside.

Endymion doesn't stop, though. His thumb works circles over my clit while he stares down at me with a fire in his eyes that sets my soul alight. Sweat beads on his forehead, and his strong jaw is clenched. He kisses me, taking my mouth sweetly as his hips work savagely. He keeps working my body, pounding into me, his chest heaving wildly over me.

When he breaks the kiss, I open my eyes and look into his intense gaze. It is equal parts love and desperation. It's the way I'd always dreamed someone would look at me—not just someone, but this man. I wanted to be looked at like I was someone's entire world and then some. I wanted to worshipped, loved on a level that was incomprehensible. That's the way Endymion stares down at me.

"Christ, if only you can see how beautiful you are like this, Selene."

"I love you."

My words are his undoing. He grits his jaw, his eyes clenching shut, and he groans, spilling inside me. His hips jerk and twist in a final thrust as I wring him of every last drop. The kiss he presses to my lips is a sealed fate of sorts. It's loaded with promises and tells the story of his love without words.

It sets my heart ablaze for this beautiful man.

Chapter Twenty-Six

Selene

ONE MONTH LATER

AT MY FATHER'S FUNERAL, END HOLDS MY HAND THE ENTIRE TIME, HIS grip tight and secure. He's the backbone Luna and I have needed over the past few days. Hell, the past month has been hard on everyone. Especially my mom. I've tried to be there as much as possible, but it'd been hard watching my father lie in that bed, watching the life slowly drain out of him.

I grip onto Endymion's hand for strength as a sob sputters past my lips, thinking about the last moments I had with my father.

"I'm not ready to say goodbye yet, Daddy," I choke out through my tears. There's a wildfire in my chest. It's reckless and incredibly devastating as it sets my other organs aflame. My dad softly pats his frail, skinny hand over mine, trying to comfort me. He's so weak. It's breaking my heart to see him like this.

I need more time with him.

It's all I've been asking for, just a little more time.

I hate that I let so many years go by when I didn't hug him every day. When I didn't talk to him every day. It's all hitting me now that I took it all for granted. I won't be able to do any of it anymore. I won't hear his warm, throaty laughter. I won't get to listen to his long-drawn-out explanations. I won't get to see his smile that reminds me so much of my own when I look in the mirror.

"So many beautiful things await me, Selene. Just like they do for you. I may not be here to hold your hand through it anymore, but I love you, and I am so damn proud." A tear leaks out of his eye, rolling down his pale cheek, and I crumble. I crawl into bed beside my father, and I rest my head on his bony chest, listening to his heartbeat. Sobs wrack my body, and he rubs my back, telling me in hushed tones everything will be okay. That it's going to be fine. But it won't. Because the first man I've ever truly loved is dying. He's leaving me.

My father passed away the next evening while we were all there. The last week has been trying. And if it wasn't for Endymion, I'm not too proud to say I would've already crumbled. I would've fallen into a mess of culpability.

Luna is heartbroken, just as I knew she would be, but she's still young, not yet able to grasp that her papa won't be coming back because he's in heaven now. She doesn't understand why he had to go. Last night we found her curled up with one of my dad's shirts. It was tucked around one of her stuffed animals like a blanket, and I fell apart. It's soul-crushing, realizing he won't be here to watch her grow up.

Endymion has been the glue holding us together, and I thank God. I thank my father, the cosmos, and my lucky stars that I have him, that I was somehow able to find him again.

"I love you," I whisper, squeezing End's hand in mine. I don't know if I've said it enough over the past few days, but if I haven't, I need him to know. He gently tucks his fingers beneath my chin, lifting my gaze up to meet his. He wipes away my hot tears, his finger tracing the planes of my face as he does it.

"I love you, too. I always have."

I smile through the tears. End was always my sun. I was chasing him. I spent most of my childhood chasing, wishing on every star with his name in mind. I've always loved this man. But what has made me love him even more? The way he loves our daughter. Luna is our brightest star, the only one that matters to us. I thank my lucky stars every single day that End decided to chase me—to chase the moon.

After the funeral, we head back to the house, the house that feels empty without any trace of my father. His warm laugh. The sound of his news playing softly in the background. Endymion's mom offered to help with the food here for everyone after the service. I think everyone knew my mother and me wouldn't be up to it after today. Upon walking into the house, I hear a broken noise leave my mother, and when I glance at her, my eyes still puffy from the funeral, I see tears streaking down her face. I follow the trajectory of her gaze and my chin trembles with emotion.

The table, where my father's coffee mug would usually rest beside the coaster, is now empty. My mom drops to her knees, and I catch her just in time as a sob rips from her chest. I fall to the floor with her, grabbing at her, trying to squeeze and comfort her while wading through my own pain. The new reality that my father and her estranged husband is gone.

"We spent so many years fighting. So much wasted time."

I tuck her head beneath my chin, tightening my grip. "It's going to be okay. I promise."

I repeat the phrase over and over again until I actually believe it.

That night, I head out to the creek, needing a moment to myself to gather my thoughts. Gripped tightly in my hand is the letter and the small box Endymion gave me. It has my name written on the front in my father's handwriting. I've been sitting here, running the pads of my fingers over the letters, tracing each of them. There's this inexplicable tightness in my chest. I want to read the words inside, but then again, I don't. I'm afraid I won't be able to handle them.

Sucking in a lungful of air, I close my eyes and tear through the envelope, pulling out the folded sheet of paper inside. With trembling hands, I open the letter, and a sob catches in my throat when I read the first words.

Darling Selene,

I'm sorry. I'm so sorry I won't be here for as long as I'd like. As fathers, we look forward to the day our daughters grow up and marry, just the same way we despise it. I hate that I won't see how beautiful you'll look on your wedding day. I hate that I won't be there to hold my next grandchild. I hate that I won't get to watch our little Luna grow up into a beautiful young woman, just like her mother.

A lot of life is simply about luck, and I was lucky enough to have it in spades when your mother agreed to marry me. I held on to that luck over the years, because it gave me a beautiful daughter who became the light of my life, then it gave me a granddaughter who owned half of my heart, alongside her mother. That luck of mine has run out. I wish I had the words to make you feel better. I wish so many things were different, but they are not.

I often dreamed about your wedding day and imagined filling up with tears as I walked you down the aisle. The only comfort is knowing the man I'm positive you'll end up with is a good man. If there was ever anyone I'd agree to give my daughter away to, it's Endymion. I know it's easy to hold on to the hurt of the past, but I can say with utmost uncertainty that I've never seen a man look at a woman the way he looks at you. Like you and Luna are his whole entire world. That's what every father wants for his daughter, someone worthy of her love.

Remember to laugh while I'm gone, and don't forget to smile through the pain. The way you light up a room, Selene, is one of the most beautiful things about you. You never laugh at 50%; you always laugh at 100%. It takes over your whole body and is highly infectious. I hope you never lose that. And I hope Luna won't either.

When Luna is old enough to understand, I hope she'll know how much I loved her and how much I cherished each moment we spent together. Remind her to be strong in the face of every challenge. Never let anyone put her down or crush her spirit because she is the beauty we find in life. She is the happiness you and End get to keep for yourselves. Tell her to keep speaking her mind, to keep believing she's capable of anything. There is nothing in this world she can't do.

Despite the many mistakes in my life, I need you to know you're the single best thing I've had in my life, Selene. I know growing up in the house with your mother and me wasn't always easy, and that's something I'll have to face every single day. It was never you, Selene. Nothing was ever your fault. It was ours. Having you as my daughter has been the greatest accomplishment of my life. Thank you for teaching me about love and happiness more than any other person.

You are the moon, Selene. You're the bright light in the darkness. You're the beauty in the night, and don't you ever forget it.

Enjoy life. Live it fully and happily with no regrets.

And never forget, I'll always be here. In the midst of the waterfalls, the ripples in the creek, the chill of the cool breeze, in the stars scattered across the sky—I'm always here.

I love you forever, sweet girl.

Dad xx

After the tears have soaked my face and neck, I fold the letter and hold it against my chest. My heart feels heavy, each beat a slow-drawn-out metronome. There is a perpetual quiver in my chin, a continuous twinge in my heart that I don't think will ever go away now that my father is gone.

With quaking hands, I open the small box next. A broken sob tears from my chest once I see what's inside. Just like the one he bought me when I was a child rests another moon necklace, only this time, the back is inscribed.

I'll meet you at the moon,

Daddy

I clutch the necklace to my chest and I cry.

The sobs are gut wrenching, wracking through my body in powerful waves.

I glance up at the moon with a heavy weight on my chest and tears glimmering in my eyes. It doesn't matter how many times I blink or wipe them away; they're always there.

The stars seem brighter tonight against the dark canvas of the sky, and it's like my father demanded they shine a little brighter for all of us tonight, almost as if he knew I would be out here, reading his letter, thinking of him. I tighten my sweater around my shoulders, warding off the cold chill that's traveling through my body. A stitch of pain burns through my chest at the thought of him and the breeze. The air is brisk tonight. It chafes against my cheeks, and it settles into my bones. If I close my eyes and think about it hard enough, I swear I can almost feel him—my father. He's in the air. In the sounds of nature.

Lying back, I soak in the feeling. I bathe in the moon's glow, ignoring the tears sliding down my temples and into my hair. I don't startle when I hear footsteps wading through the thick grass. When I glance to the side, a small grin lights my face when I spot End. He looks handsome, so incredibly handsome. He's still dressed in his slacks and button-down shirt from earlier. His light brown hair is in disarray at the top of his head, and I find myself wanting to run my fingers through it. There's a blanket tucked under his arm, and it sends my heart into a tailspin. This man…he is almost too perfect.

He drops down next to me, laying the blanket over my body, his forearms resting on his knees, his gaze glued to mine.

"You okay?"

"Yeah," I whisper. "I think I am. Where's Luna?"

"She's with your mom. I think she needed the distraction. My mom is there, too, in case Cece doesn't want to be alone."

Tightness cramps my chest. "I'm worried about her."

He sighs. "She's strong. It might take some time, but your mother is strong, Selene. She's just like you."

I smile sadly, cupping his cheek in my hand. I relish in the feel of his stubble beneath the pads of my fingers. Even though I'm not yet ready to discuss the letter, I am ready to discuss something else. Laying us both back, he pulls me into his arms as we stare up at the night sky.

"I've made a decision."

"Let's hear it."

This is what I love most about him, his willingness to listen to whatever it is that I'm going to say. It doesn't matter when or where we are, he's always there as my sounding board, my protector, and my lover.

I suck in a sharp breath, not sure how he'll react. "I want to open the apothecary. Here. Who knows, it might fail. It might not, but I want to try. I want to try for my dad. When I was younger, I always talked about setting intentions and following my dreams. It was the faith I lived by, but after losing everything, I wanted to give up. I don't know when I gave up on my dreams. I don't know when I stopped reaching for the stars, End, but I want to try again. I don't want to be afraid of failure. I want to live with no regrets."

End squeezes my hand. "It won't fail. I promise you. And your faith, your willingness to reach for the stars never truly left you, Selene. It just got buried for a little while there. But you've found it again, and that's all that matters." A hot tear trickles down my cheek. "Your faith in the cosmos, in following your dreams? It helped me follow mine."

My brows crease together in a frown. "It did?"

End nods. "You once told me that I could do anything I wanted. You told me to reach for the stars. And I did. I started the company with the guys, and since then, I've never looked back, not even once."

My heart pounds in my chest at his admission. "How do you remember that?"

End leans in, cupping my face with a gentleness that is so at odds with everything else about him. "Isn't it obvious by now, Selene? I remember every conversation we've ever shared. I tried to pretend I never noticed you back then because it felt wrong. You were this beautiful, sweet girl, and I was me. You were always too good for me, even now. I remember everything; not even one drunken night was able to erase my memory. We belong to the cosmos, babe. Me and you? We were always meant to be."

There's a riot of emotion inside me. It's spreading through my chest like dry ice. "I didn't think it was possible to love you any more than I already do."

His mouth inches up into a warm smile that stokes the fire in my chest. "I find that I love you more and more every day, babe."

I press my lips against his, relishing in the current that rolls through my body at the contact. I love this man with every fiber of my being.

Pulling me into his side, we lie on the grass, covered in the blanket, and stare at the moon, glimmering against the sea of stars. "I used to sit out here so many nights when I was sad or when I felt alone. Now that I'm sitting out here, I feel a little bit closer to him, a little bit closer to my dreams, and I can't explain why."

"Because he's with you everywhere. Always."

We lie in silence for a long beat. I relish in the feel of his warm body beneath mine. The staccato of his strong heartbeat is a song I never knew I needed to help soothe me. His hand glides up and down my back in rhythmic motions.

"Did I ever tell you what made me fall in love with the moon?" I feel him shaking his head. "My dad. He was the one who introduced me to Greek mythology. That thick book I carried around when I was younger? It was from my dad. I became obsessed, fixated on the goddess who shared the same name as me. I think deep down, he knew how hard it was for me to listen to their constant fighting, so he tried to give me something his words wouldn't heal. He tried to give me fairy tales—stories of love that have spanned centuries.

"I think I fell in love with her because, as the goddess of the moon, she personified life's constant changes. In the myths, as the Titan goddess, she would drive her chariot with the moon across the sky at night. She was considered this all-seeing eye of the night because the moon would always be visible in the black sky, and no one could run from it. That light? For a long time, it felt like that was all I had to look forward to. Until you rolled into town. By then, I was already obsessed with the moon. I had read every piece of information on Selene and every legend regarding her. And when I heard your name for the first time…" I pause, emotion clogging my throat. "I felt like it was meant to be. I was Selene, and you were Endymion, the shepherd mortal whose love was always destined to fail."

His chest vibrates beneath my ear. "And what about now?"

"Now…now I don't feel like I'm living out that tale of mythology anymore. We're writing our own story. Our own legend with frayed pages, missing chapters, and everything else between, and you know what? I wouldn't change it for the world because I love you, Endymion Black. Just as the sun loves the moon, and the stars love the night."

My stomach cramps uncomfortably as I stand outside the building. I haven't been back here since that night. As I glance around, flashes of memories slam into me, and I flinch as I think about them. I thought it would be worse to stand here, remembering what happened with Thomas, but the tight restricting sensation gripping my throat slowly leaves when I feel Endymion wrap his arm around my middle, tucking my back into his front. We stand a few feet back from the building, staring at the space. The lease sign is still posted there in the window.

"Tell me what you're thinking."

"I'm thinking of that night," I tell him truthfully. His grip on me tightens. "But I'm also thinking that I can't run from everything in my life. I'm done running, End. I want to make the best memories here. Let go of the bad and focus on the good. And this place? It's perfect."

"You really want to do this?" There's a note of skepticism in his tone, and I know it's because he's worried about me. My father just passed away, and I'm already diving headfirst into a huge decision.

After our talk last night at the creek, I woke up this morning wanting to check out the space again. I feel a renewed sense of hope, and though I am still wading through the sadness and battling my emotions, I want to do this for my dad. For me. For that young girl who promised she'd always chase her dreams, no matter what.

"I do want to do this. Do you think it's a bad idea?"

He shakes his head, his warm, calloused hand stroking the back of my neck. "No, I think this is amazing. I think you're amazing."

A smile spreads across my face. I crane my head back, pressing a kiss against his lips. Turning back around toward the building, I hold on to this sensation, that warmth billowing in my chest as I dig my phone out of my purse and dial the number. The first thing I need to get is a quote, but I've come to a decision, and I want to stick to it. Even if I can't end up having this place, I won't stop searching for the perfect fit.

After I leave a message inquiring about the space, End tugs on my hand. "Come on, let's get ready."

My brows jump into my hairline. "Get ready for what exactly?"

He smirks down at me, his eyes dancing with mirth and heat. "I'm taking you out on a date."

"A date?" I grin, glitter bursting and billowing in my chest. "Little late for that, don't you think?"

"It's never too late," he leans in, whispering against my lips.

Back at home, I do as End instructs and get ready for our date. I have no clue where we're going, nothing to go on at all. He just mentioned that I should bring a light jacket. That's it.

"I have a secret, Mommy, but I'm not supposed to tell you," Luna mentions, as I'm swiping the wand of mascara against my lashes.

My lips twist wryly. "Oh, really? So we're keeping secrets now, Luna Bella?"

She heaves a deep, tired sigh, as if she didn't realize keeping a secret would be this difficult. "Daddy made me promise." She pouts. A laugh catches in my throat, and I screw on the cap, and turn, dropping to my haunches in front of her.

"You don't have to ruin the secret, okay? But you do have to tell me how I look." Pushing to my feet, I do a little twirl for her, waiting to hear her thoughts. She cocks her head to the side, her little eyes assessing everything about my outfit. I decided to go with a pair of jeans and a long-sleeved dusky pink knit sweater that hangs off the shoulder. The fall season has brought in a cold front, and I figured I'd play it safe with this. It's perfect for something indoors, and with a light jacket, it'll be just enough for anything outdoors.

"You look like a princess, but with jeans."

A laugh tumbles out, and I scoop my daughter into my arms, squeezing her tiny body to me. "I may look like a princess, but you *are* the princess."

"I know that, Mommy," she tells me so matter-of-factly that I have to stifle my laughter. What the hell am I going to do with this girl?

With my hand secured in Luna's, we pause in the living room where Endymion is waiting. I breathe a sigh of relief when I see his outfit of choice. Dark washed jeans, black boots, and a blue flannel draped over a black thermal Henley. He looks incredibly handsome with the way the light strands of his hair hang over his forehead. I can feel his penetrating gaze roaming up and down my body. I rest my hand over my stomach protectively, trying to quell the sudden bout of nerves.

"Is this okay?" I ask, referring to my outfit.

The pale green of his eyes deepens. "You're perfect."

I feel heat rise to my cheeks, and it makes me smile. "So are you."

A smirk steals over his features, and I feel the effects of it in my chest. "Can I go with you guys, Daddy?"

Endymion crosses the room and pulls Luna into his arms. "Remember what we talked about? We can't give Mommy her surprise if we don't do everything according to plan."

She pouts. "I don't like surprises, and I don't like plans."

His brows shoot up. "Oh, really?"

"Fine. I do, but this surprise isn't fun."

He rolls his eyes playfully. "It will be. I promise."

After we both say goodbye to Luna, leaving her with Endymion's sister and her little cousin, he drives us through town. Every time he turns down a certain street, I think I know where we're going, but then, when he keeps going, I realize I'm wrong. Part of me thinks he's just driving in random circles now to throw me off. It isn't until he takes the route toward Mr. Jackson's property that my heart skips a few beats.

Old man Jackson owns the hardware store back in town and this property. He's always been a quiet man who mostly keeps to himself. It's been said he owns a lot of property in Dunsmuir that dates back to past generations. One of the properties is this two-story cabin he built for his wife years ago. It's beautiful, with a wraparound balcony up top that gives you a sprawling view of the waterfall below. Hell, when you stand outside, you can hear the echo, feel the mist, and smell the freshness in the air. It's heaven.

"Mr. Jackson's place?" I ask, as End takes my hand in his, leading the way up the steps to the log cabin.

I don't know how he's managed to get Mr. Jackson to agree to let us come inside here. The inside is beautifully decorated and refurbished. It's woodsy and male, with hints of color thrown in here and there that surely belong to his wife.

When End leads the way up the staircase, and we reach the top floor balcony, I jerk to a halt, taking it all in. There are little lights hanging from the back French doors to the columns of the balcony and a table with white linen and sunflowers in the center. There are two place settings in front of two chairs that face the waterfall my father used to take me to see as a child.

"How did you manage this?"

End shrugs, his gaze glued to mine. It's almost like he doesn't want to look away. I know that feeling all too well. "I asked Mr. Jackson for a favor."

My eyes sweep across everything, from the table setting to the beautiful waterfall in the background. "This is beautiful, End."

"I wanted to give you something beautiful. You deserve it."

My heart thumps steadily in my chest, and my stomach dips wildly. Closing the distance between us, I cup his cheek, running my fingers over his stubble. "You've already done that. You've given me Luna. You've given me love."

Heat flashes in his eyes, and then he's kissing me. His kiss is hot and anything but chaste. I feel it tugging deep in my loins and taking my breath away.

When he pulls away, he swipes his thumb across my lower lip and jerks his head toward the table. "If we don't sit now, I'll end up fucking you and ruining this."

I laugh as he helps me lower myself into the chair. He takes the seat across from me, and my eyes are drawn to the sunflowers. They are the perfect touch. They're like having Luna here with us. They tug at all the emotional strings inside me. Sitting at a white table with linen and china on top, he lifts the domes covering our food, and I grin. Our meal isn't anything special, but the fact that he put this much effort into this speaks volumes. It's steak and potatoes with a side of asparagus. I find it's the best meal I've ever had, and it's because he made it for me.

I'm unable to keep my eyes off the waterfall. The way the warm orange, pink, and purple hues from the sunset glint off the water is almost magical, like a sea of sparkling stars, a kaleidoscope of colors.

My stomach turns when End pours me a glass of wine. For the past few days, I've been feeling off. At first, I chalked it up to sadness, the after-effects of dealing with my father's death, but this morning, I wondered if it could be something different. I'm still not sure how to broach the subject with End. He's mentioned he wants more kids, but now? So soon? Especially after dealing with such a tragedy. I'm not sure if that's the case anymore.

I took one of those home tests earlier. Julia wasn't ashamed to walk into the pharmacy and throw a handful onto the counter, saying they were all for her. Mrs. Weithers, the woman who's worked behind the counter for years, just shook her head at her as though she wasn't even surprised.

Back at home, while End was out with Luna doing all this, I presume, I took the tests. All four of them were positive. It explains everything. The emotions. The queasy sensation in my stomach.

We are going to have another baby.

I fork around my food on my plate, and End's brow crinkles. A sheepish look passes over his features.

"It's shit, isn't it?" His gaze darts down to the food, a knowing gleam in his eyes. My own widen, and I shake my head frantically.

"No, God, no! It's not that at all. I've actually been meaning to tell you..." It's on the tip of my tongue to say it, but instead, I tell him my other news, figuring I'll start there first. "I got a call back earlier, regarding the space downtown. It's..." I clear my throat, a sudden sadness building in my chest. "They already have a buyer. They're drawing up the paperwork already."

End's brows pull in, and he searches my gaze. "You really wanted that place, didn't you?"

I suck in a breath. "At first, I didn't, but now…now I do. I'll just have to look somewhere else."

"You'll find something." He seems certain of this. It eases the tightness in my chest and draws a smile out of me. I play with the words on my tongue, the words that will let him know he's going to be a father again, but before I can spit them out, he cuts through my train of thought.

"Want to go down for a better view?"

"There's a better view than this?" I ask, my eyes growing wide. "I feel like I can see everything from up here." He laughs. The sound is husky, and it hits me right in the core.

"You'll see." End takes my hand in his and leads me down the staircase. He's not wrong. As soon as we step out of Mr. Jackson's back doors, my breath catches in my throat. The view was spectacular up there, but here? It's otherworldly.

Endymion leads the way down the hill near the waterfall. I think this is the closest I've ever been. I knew Mr. Jackson and his wife had an incredible view of the waterfall, but it's even better than I realized. Splashes of water mist my face. We're close enough to touch the body of water. Close enough that I feel like I'm somehow closer to heaven.

Out of habit, I reach for the chain around my neck, rubbing my fingers over the moon resting there lovingly.

I can feel his gaze on me. It sends heat swarming through my body from head to toe. "You look beautiful."

A smile tugs at the corners of my mouth. "You flatter me."

I hear End shift behind me, and when I glance over my shoulder, my heart jumps into my throat, my pulse pounding erratically.

Warm tingles erupt in my belly, the force of the sensation takes my breath away. There behind me is Endymion, down on one knee. I turn to face him with my heart lodged in my throat.

"I've made a lot of mistakes in my life, Selene. The biggest being the fact that I almost let you slip through my fingers. I never knew what true happiness was until you came back into my life. You're a light I never want to part with. Your beauty is breathtaking, but your heart, it's fucking gold, babe. It's where I want to live forever. You've given me a beautiful daughter I'll love until my dying breath, just like I will you.

"I want to give you the world, Selene. I want to stand by your side and help make your dreams come true. I want to give you all the kids you could ever dream of having, because I'm an asshole like that, and I imagine you pregnant is one of the great wonders of the world. So, marry me, Selene. Spend your life with me and let me show you every day how much I love you and just how much you mean to me."

A gasp tears past my lips when he cracks open the velvet box he's been holding to reveal a ring. It's a white gold emerald cut, but the band it's attached to is what has my heart melting for this man. The white gold band has small crescent moons filled with diamonds that wrap around. It's absolutely stunning.

I don't know when it happened, but I feel the tears streaming down my cheeks. I press my hand over my sternum, feeling my heart pounding like a steel drum in my chest. Everything about this moment is so right. So perfect. There will never be anyone like this man. No one who owns my heart the way he does.

A wide grin splits across my face, and I nod vigorously, as if the tears rolling down my cheeks aren't answer enough. "Yes. Yes, a thousand times yes!"

End rises to his feet and crushes me in his arms, taking my lips in a rough kiss that I feel all the way down to the marrow of my bones. He's no longer just under my skin. He's a part of me now. He's the blood in my veins, the breath in my lungs, and the muscles that keep my heart pumping. He's my everything.

Once he slides the ring onto my finger, I stare down at it and then back up at him. I slide my hand around the back of his neck, relishing in his warm skin.

He's perfect.

And mine.

"Those babies you were talking about? We might be getting them sooner than later."

He chuckles but then pauses, his eyes widening as he processes my words. "Wait, are you saying…?"

A fresh wave of tears coats my eyes, and I nod my head. "I'm pregnant."

Endymion laughs, and the sound is so carefree, so filled with joy, that my heart bursts. He lifts me into his arms and kisses me. It's filled with heat and love—filled with everything I've searched my entire life for.

As we walk back to the cabin, I glance up at the sky as the moon slowly makes its appearance against the setting sun. The crescent shape in the sky draws a smile out of me.

When you wish hard enough, even the most unrealistic dreams come true.

Chapter Twenty-Seven

Selene

FOUR MONTHS LATER

"WHAT IS GOING ON?" I ASK BENEATH THE BLINDFOLD THAT IS covering my eyes. The grip around my hand tightens in reassurance, keeping me moving. I can tell we're on a street. I've heard enough cars pass by to know that much. I can hear snickering and the sound of someone whispering. There's a slight crunch whenever I walk, the telltale sign I'm walking through snow or sludge.

"Just a little bit farther, then you can take it off."

"Is it dark under there, Mommy?" I hear Luna ask from somewhere beside me, her little hand gripping my free one.

"Very. Want to tell me what's happening?" I try to squeeze the truth out of her, but my daughter laughs as if I should know better.

"I can't do that, silly. It'll ruin your surprise."

I huff out a breath.

Once we jerk to a halt, I wait for the blindfold to be removed. And once it's gone, my eyes water at the sight before me. There, just as I envisioned it, is a sign that reads *Moonchild Apothecary*. The black steel industrial letters stand out against the rustic white brick. My bottom lip trembles, and I whirl around, searching for End, surprise and emotion written all over my face.

"How is this possible? Someone bought it already."

End shrugs a conspiratorial grin on his face. "I made an offer they couldn't refuse a while back. Been working on it ever since."

"But you've been helping me search for new places. How is this even possible?"

He smirks, clearly proud of himself. "All to throw you off."

"This is the important job you've been finishing with the guys?" My voice trembles slightly, my throat thick with emotion.

He nods, his greens searching mine. "Want to see the inside?"

I laugh, but it comes out as more of a sob. "Please."

End opens the front doors for us, and the second I step over the threshold and the lights flick on, I see all of my friends and family yelling out *surprise*. I lose my battle with my tears. There's a sweet ache that's blooming in my chest.

"I asked your mom for help. We looked over the layout of your last shop, went over what worked and what didn't. Julia and Beth-Ann helped us find vendors. Bishop, Landon, and Griffin helped with the flooring and electric. The rest of the guys from the crew helped out, too."

Slowly, I turn, walking around the space and taking it all in. With black rustic fixtures and white brick inside, the apothecary is chic and all clean lines. It looks upscale and inviting. The pops of color come from the vases of various plants in white marble pots and sunflowers in others. Everything is here. A section of crystals. Other sections of incense, soaps, candles, body oils, you name it.

Everything is perfect.

I rest my hand over the slight bump in my stomach and meet End's gaze. He's been watching me like a hawk, waiting to hear what I think. There aren't words for how incredibly amazing and thoughtful this all is.

"This is...beyond perfect. I don't even know what else to say. Thank you somehow doesn't seem like it's enough."

Tears swim in my eyes, and I watch as he crosses the distance between us, his gait sure and confident, then pulls me into his arms. He tucks stray hairs behind my ears and caresses my cheekbone. "You don't need to thank me. You've given me so much. This is my way of giving back to you. This place is yours, Selene. Your dream. Live it the way you want to. Just never stop reaching for those stars, baby, and I'll never stop chasing the moon."

Endymion

Bishop sighs. "She's already pregnant, man. Looking at her like that isn't going to suddenly fill her up with another."

I chuckle, cracking a smile. "My wife is hot. What can I say?"

Bishop grunts. "You're not wrong."

I shoot him a glare. Even as she bears my child, wears my ring, and has taken my last name as hers, I'm still possessive of this woman. I'm positive I always will be.

My gaze has been glued to Selene ever since I watched that blindfold come undone. I've soaked in every second of her reaction to seeing this place. We've been working on this for months. Since the night I asked her to marry me, as a matter of fact. We had plans for a big wedding after this little guy is here, but about two months after popping the question, she suggested eloping, and who the hell am I to say no to this woman? I'd take her in any form I could get her.

We got married at the small Catholic church her parents got married in with only our close friends and family in attendance. The rest of Dunsmuir threw us a small reception at the barn. Julia and the guys took care of the decorations for the party and watching my wife's reaction when she walked into the barn lit up with stars and lights strung from every corner was one of the most beautiful sights I've ever witnessed.

She was a vision. With her long, dark brown hair hanging down her back in a loose braid, it was a stark contrast to her creamy skin and white dress. Julia and Dalia added baby's breath throughout the braid, and it was the cherry on top. She looked perfect. Like a goddamn angel. With her pale skin and dark hair, decked out in her all-white dress, she looked like the moon. Her dress was perfect. The way it clung to her curves, the satin material was like liquid pearl against her porcelain skin.

That was hands down the greatest moment of my life, saying *I do* to this woman in front of our daughter. Watching the smile spread across Luna's face was something I'll never forget. I'll love them for the rest of my life. That was my vow. I want to give them the world and then some.

With another five months to go until she's due to give birth, Selene's baby bump is still relatively small. It doesn't keep me from feeling that possessive warmth filter through my chest when she rests her hand there, though. She's been following Julia and her mom around the store as both of them finish walking her through the list of inventory and all the new additions. She's fucking beautiful.

She's always been gorgeous, but Jesus, now that she's pregnant? She's a goddamn vision. She is quite literally glowing. And I don't think she's ever been more beautiful than she is right now. She's in her element. Happiness just wafts off her as she takes everything in.

"I'm happy for you, man," Landon says, clapping me on the back. His gaze is on Selene, too. It tightens my stomach. "Still can't believe you managed to get her to marry your dumbass after all these years."

I shoot him a glare, and he laughs, purposely trying to tick me off. The bastard is just like Bishop. They know how to get a rise out of me.

"How's Beth-Ann?" I shoot back. It works, if the scowl on his face is any indication.

There's a sudden tugging on my jacket, and I glance down. "Daddy, can we get ice cream?"

I stifle my laughter. It's the dead of winter with snow sludge decorating the streets, and my daughter wants ice cream? Christ.

"As soon as we're done here." She smiles victoriously and skips off, standing at Selene's side. My wife looks down at our daughter with a soft smile on her face. The impact of it hits me square in the chest.

I can't wait to watch her stomach grow bigger until she's begging me to help her walk. I can't wait to experience all the things I missed out on the first time with this new baby. I want to watch Luna take on the role of big sister. I want it all.

"You've never looked happier, son," my dad says, clapping me on the shoulder. Our eyes are glued to Selene. She's dressed in jeans and a knit black top with a jacket to ward off the cold weather. The outfit, in particular, isn't anything special, but on her? She looks fucking beautiful. She's deep in conversation with my mother and her mother, a slight flush on her cheeks and a wide grin on her face.

"I've never been this happy," I admit.

"Selene is lucky to have you."

I shake my head, unable to look away from her. Waves tumble down her back. The chocolate strands pop out against the white jacket she's wearing. The snow has come early this year, bringing the cold front with it. Luna screamed at the first sight of it. She was ecstatic that she lived where it snowed. The wonder of it all hasn't faded for her yet, but I imagine it will soon enough.

The love I have for my girls is fierce. It billows in my chest, a live wire surging through my body. I can't imagine what life would be like without either of them. Without Selene and our little moon.

"I'm the lucky one. I always have been."

And I mean every damn word.

Epilogue

Selene

TEN YEARS LATER

"YOU SURE YOU HAVE EVERYTHING HANDLED? YOU DON'T NEED my help?" I ask down the line. I can practically envision Julia's eye roll.

"Everything is fine. Jesus, woman. I can handle this. You've just given birth. Why don't you lie down and breastfeed or something."

My eyes narrow. "Don't tempt me. As you've said, I just had a baby."

"What number is this now anyway? Eighteen?" she teases, and I fight my smile. She knows damn well how many kids I have. Hell, she's the godmother to most of them.

"You're such an ass. She's number four."

Julia whistles. "End really took the term barefoot and pregnant to heart, didn't he?"

I laugh because she isn't wrong. The man has no qualms about coming inside me. Not that he should, as he's my husband, but you'd at least think after four kids he'd want to slow down.

He doesn't.

"You're horrible. You know that?"

"That's why you love me," she singsongs. "Oh, I gotta go. We have customers."

"Okay, I'll be in later to check on things once End gets back from work. He took Gavin with him, so I'm sure they'll be back sometime soon. You know how that kid is. He's the biggest complainer. A lot like you, actually."

Julia huffs, "Har, har, har. Goodbye, Selene. Kiss my sweet little baby Flora for me."

"I will."

Moonchild has been incredibly successful here in Dunsmuir. I took a risk bringing this baby to life in Pasadena, then again here, but it's performed so much better than my wildest dreams. Tomorrow officially marks ten years that we've been open, and I still can't wrap my head around it. It's my dream come true, and I get to live it every single day.

After hanging up with Julia, I check on Flora, our youngest. My sweet little girl is still fast asleep in her crib. So far, she's been our calmest child, and for that, I'm all too thankful. There's not a lot of downtime these days.

I have Luna, who is now a sixteen-year-old and sassy as all hell, Gavin, a nine-year-old who seems to roughhouse with his six-year-old little brother, Zander, any chance he gets, and finally, our sweet Flora who is eight weeks old. On most nights, our house is filled with bickering children or their vivacious laughter, but I wouldn't change it for the world, and I know Endymion wouldn't either.

It hasn't been easy, raising a family while running Moonchild, but my mom and Julia are incredible at helping pick up the slack when I need it. After much consideration, my mom decided to stay in Dunsmuir. I think, despite the heavy memories of the past, she couldn't bear the thought of being away from her grandchildren. With my father's house officially in my name, I told my mom she could stay there as long as she needed. It was also in part because I couldn't stomach the thought of letting the property go. It had Gavin Drake written all over it. It was the last piece of my father that I truly had.

Endymion and the guys still own the construction company, though now, they've broadened their customer base. They don't just limit themselves to work in the surrounding areas anymore. They've since expanded to all of northern California. End is great when it comes to traveling. If he feels like the job is too far, he makes arrangements for the guys and handles his blueprints from home.

He's all about family first, and when you see him with our kids, it shows. Endymion is an incredible father, and dare I say, an even better husband. He's the very best thing that's ever happened to me.

I'm in the kitchen cleaning up the mess from lunch when I glance out the window, spotting Luna and her friends. They're in the backyard, and a smile tugs at the corners of my lips when I spot the sunflowers. One summer End took it upon himself to plant over three dozen sunflowers in the backyard, all in varying sizes. Luna just about cried when she saw what her dad had done for her, and me? Well, I did cry, like a baby.

I pause what I'm doing when I notice the look on my sweet girl's face. Luna has always been the spitting image of her father, but she's a lot like me in so many ways. My heart squeezes at the expression on her face. It's one I know well.

I follow the trajectory of her gaze, and my stomach dips.

Oh, no.

Aiden Saint.

He must sense Luna's gaze because he glances at her, his brows furrowing when she looks away. He does the same, going back to pretending she isn't there, but I notice the way he watches her when no one else is looking. The way his jaw tightens with frustration when someone else sits and talks to her. It's a trip back to my youth.

Grabbing a handful of water bottles out of the fridge, I head outside. At the sound of the porch door opening, everyone looks my way.

"If you guys get thirsty, here are some waters." I leave them on the porch next to Luna, who looks like she'd rather be anywhere else than here.

As I'm walking away, I hear the comment made by one of the boys, and my heart squeezes for my daughter.

"Jesus Christ, Luna. Your mom is hot as hell." It's my niece Valeria's boyfriend. Her boyfriend is best friends with Aiden, the one boy my daughter can't seem to keep her eyes off. The same boy who can't keep his eyes off her, too. "She's hot, ain't she, Saint?" Val's boyfriend directs the question to Aiden. I hear his deep reply.

"Yeah."

Back in the kitchen, I press a hand to my sternum, rubbing away the sudden ache there as I take in the pain that's written all over Luna's face. His comment hurt her, for obvious reasons. I make a note to have a discussion with her later about how idiotic young boys can be.

I drift back to the pain I felt whenever I'd see End with Holly. Even though she's no longer an issue in our lives anymore, I still can't help but sympathize with that young heartbroken girl who felt like she never quite compared. After hearing about our engagement and my pregnancy, Holly finally backed off, and it was a relief. Not because I worried End would fall for her ever again, but because we didn't have the looming black cloud of her presence hovering above us.

For a while, I constantly worried about Thomas, wondering if he'd ever come back to hurt me, but thanks to Landon and his father, I didn't have to worry about Tommy anymore. They purposely kept it hush-hush, but Deacon, Landon's father, found him hiding out a few counties over about eight months after the incident. It was a weight taken off my shoulders, one I hadn't realized I was carrying around until I knew he was gone.

Endymion's truck pulls into the driveway not long after and

out hops my little man, Zander, and End. They bypass Luna and her friends, stopping to give Valeria a hug. It doesn't escape my notice the way End watches the boys through narrowed slits. Even though Valeria is his sister's problem, I don't think he enjoys the fact that our house has become somewhat of a hangout for the older kids. I'm not sure how I feel about it either. Luna is only a freshman, while Valeria and her boyfriend and Aiden are seniors.

I turn at the sound of the front door closing, and I smile when I spot my boys. Zander presses a kiss to my cheek before he heads off to his room, and when End walks into the kitchen, he pulls me into his arms and kisses me deeply. His hand cups my ass, and he squeezes, making me moan against his lips.

When we pull away, his gaze seeks out the window, and he frowns. I don't even need to ask why.

"Is it necessary for them all to hang out? Whatever happened to girls sticking with girls?"

"They're all friends. Stop it."

He glares. "They're too young for boyfriends."

"You mean to tell me you didn't have a girlfriend at fifteen, sixteen, or seventeen?" I quirk a brow.

"I did, and that's the problem. I know exactly what is going through those boys' heads, and I don't fucking like it."

I laugh at the seriousness in his tone. He really doesn't like the idea of our daughter dating. Ever. He's in for a rude awakening if what I suspect between Aiden and Luna to be true.

Wrapping my arms around his neck, I press my body flush against his and toy with the back of his hair. He smells like hard work and everything I love about Endymion. The stubble on his jaw is growing thick. He hasn't shaved for the past three days, and I find I like it. Especially when it chafes between my thighs.

"Baby, Luna is smart. Give her some credit."

"It's not her I'm worried about," he grumbles. His thumb

strokes my cheek, and I find myself falling into him, seeking his warmth. The anger is slowly seeping from his gaze as he stares down at me. "I missed you today."

I smile. "Me too." Pushing onto the tips of my toes, I press my lips to his in a kiss that has heat stoking through my body. My tits suddenly feel heavy, and as if he can sense I'm growing horny, End's grip around me tightens, and he groans into my mouth.

"And this is why I have so many siblings," Luna deadpans.

I laugh against End's lips, and he smirks when we pull away. "What can I help you with, Luna Bella?"

"Can I go with Val to the movies?" she asks, gaze darting back and forth between her father and me. It's then I notice the audience behind her. My cheeks heat at being caught lip-locking the way we were in front of her friends.

"It's up to your dad."

Luna shifts her gaze to End, giving him her puppy dog eyes. "Please, Dad. I'll be home right after. I promise."

He sighs, raking a hand through his unruly hair. His gaze falls on the boys behind her, and his lips thin. "All right."

"I'll meet you guys outside. I'm gonna change really quick."

Crossing my arms over my chest, I shoot Endymion a playful smirk. "You're such a sucker for her puppy dog eyes."

Somehow, his lips thin even more. "Fucking Christ, I know. Ten years and you'd think I'd at least learn how to say no."

I toss my head back and laugh. "Oh, baby. If only it were that easy."

When Luna steps back out from her bedroom, dressed in an off-the-shoulder sundress, I feel Endymion stiffen beside me. "A little dressed up for the movies," he comments, an edge to his tone.

Luna frowns, looking down at her outfit. "It's a sundress and a pair of Vans, Dad. Nothing too special."

"A dress equates to boys with wandering eyes."

Luna rolls her eyes. "Believe me, Dad. They're both too busy salivating over how hot Mom is."

Okay, so she's still definitely angry over that comment. Duly noted.

When Luna's gone, Endymion turns to me, questions in his eyes. I relay the conversation I overheard earlier, telling him about the comments they made. He laughs. "The fact that someone in high school calling my wife a MILF can still make me possessive tells me I'm fucking insane."

I roll my eyes. "I never said they called me a MILF. And, I could've told you that, babe."

He swats my ass playfully, leaving me while he goes to shower the day off.

Endymion

True to her word, Luna came home right after the movie was over. Though, I expected her to be in a much better mood than she was. She was quiet and kept her eyes downcast throughout dinner. As much as I wanted to ask her why, I figured calling her out in front of her brothers wasn't the best way to do it.

My boots wade through the long grass until I spot her slumped form in the distance, sitting by the creek. When Selene showed her this place years ago, she was drawn to it. Now, it's one of the places she goes when she wants to talk to Gavin in private. Apparently, she doesn't feel anything when she sits at his grave, but when she sits here? She says she can feel him.

After dinner, she asked if she could go to the creek for a while. It was on the tip of my tongue to say no, but when Selene set her hand on top of my arm and nodded, I changed my mind. After I helped her clean up, she suggested I check on Luna to see what was wrong.

At the sound of my footsteps, Luna turns, and my heart slams to a screeching halt when I see the tears glimmering in her eyes. There's this inexplicable tightness in my chest when I take a seat next to her, careful not to crowd her.

"Everything okay, Luna?"

She nods. "Just came out here to talk to Grandpa and listen to the water."

"You miss him, don't you, babe?"

Luna sniffles, staring out at the creek. "I do."

"It's hard. I know your mom misses him a lot, too. But that's okay, means his memory is still alive."

She smiles at me through her tears, and it still feels like a physical punch to the chest. She's grown up so much in the past few years, and now she's looking more and more like her mother every day. She's looking more like a woman and less like my little girl. We're silent for a long beat, staring out at the rippling water.

"When was the first time you really noticed Mom?" she asks suddenly, her brows pulled together as if she's deep in thought.

I grin at the memory. "The night I moved here and saw her at the Grab-N-Go."

Her frown deepens. "I thought you went years not noticing her?"

"No, I noticed her. It was hard not to. Your mother isn't someone who can be overlooked, no matter how much she believes she can. She's a lot like you, actually."

"You think so?"

"I know so. You remind me so much of your mom. Scares the shit out of me."

She begins fidgeting next to me, so I brace myself, knowing

what's coming next. "There's this guy." My hands curl into fists at my sides. "I really like him, but the thing is…I know I shouldn't."

I slam my eyes shut.

Jesus fuck. I know it's that damn Saint kid. I'd bet my left nut the little fucker is nothing like a saint.

I clear my throat, trying to play it cool. "All right…"

"Sometimes I think he likes me, but other times, it's like he doesn't even know I exist. I just…I don't know. I feel like I'm wasting my time waiting around for him to notice me."

I chuckle darkly. "Well, seeing as you're only sixteen and not allowed to date till you're thirty, I'd say this is all a moot point, right?"

Luna glares at me, nudging me on the arm. "Dad! I'm being serious."

"Fine. I'm sorry. You're still my baby girl, that's all. I didn't think I'd have to talk about boys with you for another ten years."

She rolls her eyes and laughs. Her smile is so much like Selene's. It's a wonder I haven't strangled any high school boys just yet. Luna leans into me, resting her head on my shoulder and hugging me. "I'll always be your little girl, Dad. No matter what. Even when I'm thirty, and I have like eighty kids."

Fuck. My eyes grow misty.

I hug my sweet little girl back. "Good. And make it fifty, yeah? Thirty is still too young." I press a kiss to her head and give her the only advice I can. "And listen, Luna, any kid out there would be lucky to have you. If he doesn't realize that, he doesn't deserve you."

I hear a soft sniffle. "I love you, Dad."

"I love you, too, baby."

Back at home, I wrangle the little ones into bed and stop inside Flora's room. Selene is already in there, rocking Flora in the chair. Her gaze flits up to mine, that soft smile on her face.

"Hey, babe," she whispers. "How'd it go?"

"Other than the fact that the world is ending because my baby girl likes boys? Well enough."

She laughs, then her face sobers a bit. "You look tired."

I am. I've been working overtime with the guys. We had an influx of contracts this past month, plus a project I have us all working on the side. I shrug my shoulder, brushing it off as I walk into the room. I look down at my sweet little girl sleeping in her mother's arms and press a kiss to her head.

"Let's go to bed."

"I thought you'd never ask."

Back in the bedroom, I lock the door behind me and begin stripping off my wife's clothes. She's just as beautiful now as she was the first moment I met her. She still has that ethereal glow. She still has the same beautiful heart and soul that made me fall in love with her.

"I love you, Endymion," she whispers, just as I slide my cock inside her. My love for this woman knows no bounds. It's all-consuming, a soul-filled bond I can't imagine sharing with anyone else. Our love is otherworldly.

"I love you, too, Selene. Always."

Our love is otherworldly. It always has been.

We belong to the cosmos, forever me and my moon goddess.

THE END.

Acknowledgements

I'm sure most of you know this, but writing can be an incredibly intimidating job. It doesn't get easier with each book. If anything, it only gets harder. And that was the case with Chasing the Moon for me. It was tough—I cried a lot, felt way too much, and second guessed myself. It was simply a passion project, a compilation of everything that is near and dear to my heart, all rolled into one, and I wasn't sure how you, the readers, would take to that. I try to separate myself from most books I write, and this is the first time I've deviated from that unspoken rule. So, if you hate it, you hate me. (Totally kidding.)

I think this is the first book that I've truly written for myself out of pure enjoyment. If it isn't obvious, I've always been obsessed with Greek Mythology and the moon. I have about four tattoos (and counting) simply dedicated to my love for the moon, and with this story, these characters, I really wanted to bring that to life. My love for the spiritual things. My love for the universe and the blanket of stars. And most of all, my love for the moon, and it's many incredible phases.

There are so many people I want to thank for helping shape this story into what it is, without them, my tribe, I would be lost.

To my editing team, who is always there for me every step of the way. Paige Smith, your attention to detail is unmatched, and your encouragement means the world to me. Jenny Sims, my stories would be trash without you. Thank you for making time for me when I pop an email in your inbox at least once a month. My hope is that you'll never tire of me. Rebecca Barney, you're fantastically intelligent and the sweetest human I've ever met. Thank you for taking care of my stories and putting up with my stupidity.

Special thanks to my beta readers, Chelé Walker, Ratula Roy, Sonal Dutt, Aundi Marie, Sarah Plocher, Serena McDonald, Melissa Sagastume. You are the realest of the real. Thank you for telling me when my stories suck dick.

To my cover designer, Naj. You put up with my countless emails, so many of my rambles that make absolutely no sense at all, and you do it all with so much professionalism and grace. Thank you for making this cover so goddamn beautiful. It is the embodiment of Selene and Endymion. Regina Wamba, as always, your photography skills are INSANE! To my amazing formatter Stacey, you make the inside of all my books flawless. Never leave me, okay? Ever.

To my Selenites, my ARC Squad, and my Baddies, you're all so amazing. Thank you for every shared post, and for your constant excitement. You put a smile on my face every single day. I wouldn't be able to do any of this without you, so thank you!

To the countless bloggers who push my books so freaking hard! You make this writing gig worthwhile. I want you all to know that I appreciate every single one of you. I see you. You're loved. So incredibly respected. Always.

To my family and friends, thank you for your constant stream of support. It feels good to have you all rooting for me.

Finally, to my readers, thank you for taking the time and reading this book. I know these are hard times, and I appreciate the fact that you spend your hard-earned coins on my simple words. You make this small girl's dream come true every time you decide to pick up one of my books. Thank you for taking a chance on me. I'm forever grateful.

Please consider leaving a brief, honest review.

With so much love,
Selena (S.M.) Soto xoxo

Let's keep in touch!

Make sure you stay in the loop with me for any updates on new releases, sales, free books, and behind-the-scenes peeks of upcoming projects, here:

Join my reader group: facebook.com/groups/smsbaddies

Sign up to my newsletter: /bit.ly/2U8Sl5S

Follow me on Instagram—@authorsmsoto

Like my author page: facebook.com/romanceauthorsmsoto

About the Author

S.M. Soto was born and raised in Northern California where she currently resides with her son. Her love for reading began when she was a young girl and has only continued to grow into adulthood. S.M. lives for reading books in the romance genre and writing novels with relatable characters. She refers to herself as a bit of a romance junkie. S.M. loves to connect with readers and eat copious of donuts that will surely lead to her demise.

Follow links:

Instagram.com/authorsmsoto

Twitter.com/AuthorSMsoto

Facebook.com/romanceauthorsmsoto

Stay tuned for brand new releases from S.M. Soto!

The Seasons of Callan Reed
An Enemies-to-Lovers Office Romance

Coming December 2020

Add to your TBR on Goodreads: https://bit.ly/3cSgJ1w
Preorder here: books2read.com/u/4jWoOX

CPSIA information can be obtained
at www.ICGtesting.com
Printed in the USA
BVRC091813110321
602213BV00007B/23
* 9 7 8 1 0 8 7 9 1 5 2 5 8 *

9 781087 915258